CADIAN HONOUR

More tales of the Astra Militarum from Black Library

CADIA STANDS
A novel by Justin D Hill

HONOURBOUND
A novel by Rachel Harrison

STEEL DAEMON
A novella by Ian St. Martin

SHIELD OF THE EMPEROR
An omnibus edition of the novels *Fifteen Hours* by Mitchel Scanlon,
Death World by Steve Lyons and *Rebel Winter* by Steve Parker

SHADOWSWORD
A novel by Guy Haley

BANEBLADE
A novel by Guy Haley

YARRICK
An omnibus edition of the novels *Imperial Creed, The Pyres of Armageddon,*
the novella *Chains of Golgotha* and several short stories
by David Annandale

THE MACHARIAN CRUSADE
An omnibus edition of the novels *Angels of Fire, Fist of Demetrius* and
Fall of Macharius by William King

• GAUNT'S GHOSTS •
By Dan Abnett

THE FOUNDING
An omnibus edition containing books 1–3:
First and Only, Ghostmaker and *Necropolis*

THE SAINT
An omnibus edition containing books 4–7:
Honour Guard, The Guns of Tanith, Straight Silver and *Sabbat Martyr*

THE LOST
An omnibus edition containing books 8–11:
Traitor General, His Last Command, The Armour of Contempt
and *Only in Death*

THE VICTORY

Book 12: BLOOD PACT
Book 13: SALVATION'S REACH
Book 14: THE WARMASTER
Book 15: ANARCH

CADIAN HONOUR

JUSTIN D HILL

BLACK LIBRARY

A BLACK LIBRARY PUBLICATION

First published in 2019.
This edition published in Great Britain in 2019 by
Black Library,
Games Workshop Ltd.,
Willow Road,
Nottingham, NG7 2WS, UK.

10 9 8 7 6 5 4 3 2 1

Produced by Games Workshop in Nottingham.
Cover illustration by Darren Tan.

A CIP record for this book is available from the British Library.

ISBN 13: 978-1-78193-983-3

See Black Library on the internet at

blacklibrary.com

Find out more about Games Workshop
and the world of Warhammer 40,000 at

games-workshop.com

Printed and bound by CPI Group (UK) Ltd, Croydon, CR0 4YY

*For Beth and Alex. Just read the Emperor's Tarot,
and it's looking good.*

It is the 41st millennium. For more than a hundred centuries the Emperor has sat immobile on the Golden Throne of Earth. He is the Master of Mankind by the will of the gods, and master of a million worlds by the might of His inexhaustible armies. He is a rotting carcass writhing invisibly with power from the Dark Age of Technology. He is the Carrion Lord of the Imperium for whom a thousand souls are sacrificed every day, so that He may never truly die.

Yet even in His deathless state, the Emperor continues His eternal vigilance. Mighty battlefleets cross the daemon-infested miasma of the warp, the only route between distant stars, their way lit by the Astronomican, the psychic manifestation of the Emperor's will. Vast armies give battle in His name on uncounted worlds. Greatest amongst His soldiers are the Adeptus Astartes, the Space Marines, bioengineered super-warriors. Their comrades in arms are legion: the Astra Militarum and countless planetary defence forces, the ever-vigilant Inquisition and the tech-priests of the Adeptus Mechanicus to name only a few. But for all their multitudes, they are barely enough to hold off the ever-present threat from aliens, heretics, mutants – and worse.

To be a man in such times is to be one amongst untold billions. It is to live in the cruellest and most bloody regime imaginable. These are the tales of those times. Forget the power of technology and science, for so much has been forgotten, never to be re-learned. Forget the promise of progress and understanding, for in the grim dark future there is only war. There is no peace amongst the stars, only an eternity of carnage and slaughter, and the laughter of thirsting gods.

PROLOGUE

The Ramilies-class star fort *Imperial Heart* was a weapon built on the scale of a planetary moon, a behemoth of plasteel and ceramite. Six months earlier, wheezing tugs had dragged it from its ancient orbit about Holy Terra and pushed it through the hectic space-lanes, past the gantry locks, scaffold-rigs and ore-barges of Mars, and out to Mandeville point 4HA. The transition had cost the lives of two Navigators. The remaining five had worked without pause or respite as the transparent blue eggshell of the Geller field crackled and strained. One Navigator led while the others kept watch for treacherous warp reefs and sinkholes that could suck the *Imperial Heart* and its complement of top brass, regiments and ancillary support staff down into madness.

The warp had been exultant, like a sea whipped up to a tumult of waves. Brave men went mad. Infected units were purged. Some had nothing but faith to hold on to for the months of travel.

When the *Imperial Heart* was ready for re-entry, the immaterium bulged and strained and finally tore open with a scream of psychic despair. The Will of the Emperor held true. The star fort dropped back into real space with a gout of unholy light. Bulkheads burst open, circulation pipes blew scalding steam, and quadrants vented their atmospheres out as the sudden imposition of the laws of gravity sent shock waves through the vast craft.

Once systems had been suitably stabilised, the plasma generators were powered to maximum and arc-lights within the *Imperial Heart*'s central basilica crackled to life. If any expected a fanfare they were disappointed. There was no welcome. No joy.

The *Imperial Heart*'s galvanic beacons illuminated a massacre.

Clouds of Imperial battleships and cruisers hung dead in the void, their frozen guts draped about the broken wrecks in sparkling clouds. As they moved forward, the crews of the long-scopes could make individual details out. Amidst the spiral clouds of oxygen ice were trails of plasma slime, water-casks, monumental square cases of slowly revolving unexploded munitions, and the corpses of thousands of dead crewmen, some with arms and legs outstretched, others cupped in foetal sleep, all of them glittering with reflected light.

The stillness was chilling.

It was a wall of death that they had to pass through.

Colossal blocks of ice and stone, which for thousands of years had hung in balance, tumbled into the outer void, or began to fall towards the sun. The *Imperial Heart*'s own complement of tugboats gently nudged the larger wrecks from her path, while the smaller ones were tipped from their millennia-long orbits by the gravitational pull of the star fort, and started a deadly spin towards the inner system.

As the procession moved deeper into the system, the planet to which the *Imperial Heart* had been sent began to appear on the projector screens of the long-distance auguries. The Imperium had returned to the world of El'Phanor.

Once a lynchpin in the warp routes between Terra and the Cadian Gate in the years after the Horus Heresy, El'Phanor had been a bastion world, the lodestone to the Cadian System. The planet had stood defiant, proud and impregnable to all but the mightiest of warhosts under the mastery of the fierce kromarchs, who re-engineered their planet to be a flat and featureless killing zone, marked only by trenches, rockcrete bastions and the ventilation stacks of underground barrack-cities. They had shrugged off assaults that would have crippled systems, and sent Chaos armies tumbling back in retreat – until the mightiest of warhosts *had* come.

The traitors of Abaddon, known to the Imperium as the Black Legion.

It was the Black Legion that had set about crippling El'Phanor with brutal efficiency. Warships had shorn the bastion-world of her orbiting defence networks and monitors, as the eagle strips the claws from the crab. Each time a defence bastion revealed itself, teleporting Terminators mounted instantaneous retribution. Within a week there was nothing the defenders could do except watch as the last of the stars went dark.

The Black Legion's fleet surrounded the planet like a shell of hate. Veteran warmasters personally led the assault onto the planet's retrofitted landscape of obstacles, rockcrete redoubts and trenches. At their fore went Abaddon, who impaled the Governor of Surface Defences through the heart, and set his forces in siege about the unbreakable walls of

Theodos. It had taken him a fortnight to break through the outer defences, and then they were inside, battering at the Grand Citadel of Kromarch Parateckon. But none would force an entry until Abaddon himself broke its plasteel gates, and led the charge through the outer barbican, where the salvos of disciplined las-fire were like strobing starbursts.

The fortress had a garrison of two million veteran warriors. They were like children before the hatred of the Black Legion. Abaddon and his retainers murdered their way through the citadel. Parateckon's twelve sons were slain defending their father, and when he too died, the population of El'Phanor was slaughtered and the planet was systematically stripped of life, ecosystem and atmosphere. This was the planet to which the *Imperial Heart* had been sent, like a bride to a dead man's wedding.

As the *Imperial Heart* approached to within hailing distance, the bridge crew sent out the requisite signals and protocols. It was a matter of form. None were answered. The planet was as cold as a morgue-slab. The debris cloud of dead ships and defence platforms was as impenetrable as a thicket of iron thorns. The planet was white with the bones of a hundred million defenders.

The *Imperial Heart* fell into orbit above the planet and started spinning a web of defence platforms, construction rigs, Mechanicus derricks and sheerlegs. The Ramilies was the centre of ten thousand overlapping contiguous space flights, all working towards a single aim.

Explorator brigs, slow-moving shallops and surface barges landed on the barren world. Preachers in rotary-jointed extreme environment suits cleansed it of the taint of Chaos, cast down heretic icons, reared the bodies of Imperial saints and made the planet spiritually pure. Archaeo-surveyors and their gangs of servitor excavators scoured the surface for ancient technology and when all was ready, tug-monitors and push-boats dragged the clenched fists of comets out of their orbits.

The dirty celestial snowballs impacted upon the dry world, dumping water and steam, ammonia and methane onto the surface. As the swirling debris settled, plasteel seedpods released clouds of algae spores and specially selected bacteria down into the planet's nascent atmosphere.

For a moment nothing happened.

Monitor screens were watched closely. The flat line of lifelessness began to tremble, then spike. It was like a shot to the arm of a long-dead corpse.

El'Phanor choked and spluttered. It took less than a minute before the planet took a new breath.

A pulse had returned.

Like a wounded soldier determined to fight on, El'Phanor was returning to the battlefront.

PART ONE

'And lo! He had a bronze helmet and wore a coat
of bronze.
  On his legs he wore bronze greaves, and a bronze
javelin was slung on his back.
  His spear shaft was made of iron, and its blade
weighed six pounds.'

– Book of Samael

ONE

From the ceiling of the Macharius dining room, situated in Upper D Quadrant of the *Imperial Heart*, long chains of gilt-framed portraits hung down the walls. They were the faces of Astra Militarum generals with starched uniforms, gold braid and rows of ribboned medals, all meticulously reproduced with oil and brush. Many were cracked with age, or stained a deep yellow by centuries of after-dinner smoke. Cadian generals filled one entire wall, a fact that galled the Praetorian general, Ser Reginald Monstella de Barka.

He brooded as the table conversation focused on the upcoming crusade.

'Who should lead?' a voice queried from the end of the table.

'The Cadians,' a blunt Catachan voice stated. 'This was their territory once. Theirs to reclaim.'

There were murmurs of agreement in a dozen accents. Mordian. Aquarian. Saturnine.

Ser Reginald could bear it no longer. He slammed his hand down a little too hard. 'No, the Cadians should *not* lead,' he pronounced. 'They are not up to it. Not now. Not since the debacle of the Cadian Gate. The Mordians are as good as any Cadian outfit. Any one of your armies. Or, indeed, my own Praetorians!'

The other generals, old even by Astra Militarum standards, turned to his end of the table in surprise.

Ser Reginald felt emboldened. He gesticulated expansively. 'We've given the Cadians everything they wanted since anyone can remember. The best arms. The best supplies. The toughest assignments. But look! The prison-warders were caught napping. Their failure has set the whole Imperium in doubt!

'Where are the Cadians now? See, none of them are here. They daren't show their faces!'

As he spoke, an ornately carved and decorated antique dining chair scraped back across the polished walnut. There were a few shocked gasps as the man stood and showed himself. He had the same pale complexion as many of the portraits hanging on the wall, the same drab uniform, and the badge of the Cadian Gate, in black on a field of white. He fixed the Praetorian with pale, violet eyes. 'If I may say so, general, you don't know what you are talking about.'

Lord General Reginald de Barka's cheeks coloured, but he ostentatiously swilled the last of the claret about his mouth. 'You should address me properly. I am a *lord general*. And I know exactly what I am talking about.'

A frock-coated attendant saw the danger and came forward with the bottle of amasec. The Cadian put up a hand. 'No, thank you.' His jaw was tense, his cheeks flushed red. 'You may be a lord general,' the Cadian said, 'but that does not stop you being a damned fool.'

The silence deepened. Even the servo-waiters stopped in the half-open doorways and stared at each other in slack-jawed confusion, boats of cream and red sorbet held in their unthinking hands.

The Cadian spoke louder this time. 'I demand that you withdraw your words.'

Ser Reginald paused for a moment, and then slid his own chair back and stood to his full height of six foot five. 'Tell me your name, sir.'

'Bendikt.'

'Well, General Bendikt. You cannot demand anything from me. Those days are over. The Cadians are a dying breed. Failure hangs around your necks. Your defeat is like a brand burned into a criminal's cheek. As for your behaviour this evening, I shall expect a formal apology from you and your commander.'

Bendikt crossed the space between them in two strides. 'Here's my apology!' he hissed.

His fist caught the lord general under the chin. There was a sharp crack of hind teeth being slammed together, a low grunt of pain and then Bendikt was on the bigger man, hands reaching for his throat.

It took two of the younger generals to haul him back. At last they held his arms out to either side, and he stood dishevelled, breathless, furious as a pit-slave.

Ser Reginald pushed himself to his feet.

He dabbed his lip. There was blood.

A Saturnine Dragoon general stepped forward. There were splatters of blood and wine on his white frock coat. His face was severe. 'Make peace, men. This will not do. Not at all. We are military officers. We all serve the God-Emperor. Shake hands and we shall all forget this happened.'

'I would rather die,' General Bendikt spat.

Ser Reginald put his hand to the worn pommel of his duelling sabre. 'That can be arranged,' he said.

TWO

'Don't record this,' Lord Militant Warmund said to his scribe as he entered Bendikt's private chambers. They were on the mid-levels of C Quadrant, and Warmund was chief Cadian on board the *Imperial Heart*.

He was a slab of a man. Solid, ruthless, deeply loyal to everything that his home world had once been. Behind him trailed an entourage of attendants, savants, scribes and a pair of hovering servo-skulls. The sudden bustle within his private quarters shocked Bendikt.

'Bendikt,' Warmund said as he strode inside. 'I had to take a lighter from A Quadrant and it's still taken me an hour and a half to get here. You've caused me a lot of trouble.'

Bendikt leapt to his feet. 'Sorry, sir.' He saluted smartly.

Warmund waved him back to his seat. 'I said don't record this,' he repeated, and the bald-headed savant nodded. His metal claw lifted the stylus from the parchment roll. There was nothing organic about the movement.

Warmund's voice had been enhanced for battlefield audibility, but he kept it to a low rumble now, like the purr of a giant feline. It made the wood-panelled walls tremble. 'Bendikt. I've been told that you struck Lord General Reginald Monstella de Barka with your fist. Is that true?'

Bendikt paled. He cleared his throat. His voice betrayed him. 'Yes, sir.'

'Good man!' Warmund's face broke into a huge grin. 'We're all glad you hit that pompous prat. He's been challenging our leadership since day one!' He seized Bendikt's hand and there was power within his handshake that Bendikt had not felt before. Warmund's hand had been augmented, he realised, and as its grip closed on his own, grinding bone and gristle together painfully, he felt the unspoken threat.

Warmund let go and paced up and down, hands behind his back, head thrust forward on a thick, bull neck. He had a brisk, businesslike manner that was familiar, even though he and Bendikt had never met before. It must be, Bendikt surmised, a Cadian trait. 'We've all been celebrating your punch, General Bendikt, but I'm not beating about the bush here. You'll have to go to that damned Praetorian fool and apologise.'

Bendikt nodded. He understood.

Warmund went on. 'You don't have to do it publicly. I can arrange a private venue. It doesn't even have to be particularly profuse. Sorry *if*, all that, you know…'

Bendikt tried to speak, but Warmund kept talking.

'We've allied with the Saturnine Dragoons and together we're petitioning people with influence. Navigator House Benetek are with us. They tell me that this is going to be the next front line. The new Cadian Gate! El'Phanor is on the shortest route from the Cicatrix Maledictum towards

Holy Terra, apparently. It's going right to the top. The High Lords of Terra.'

Bendikt coughed to clear his throat. 'I'm afraid I cannot do that, sir.'

'Do what?'

'Apologise. In all good conscience.'

Warmund stared at him for a moment. 'I don't care about your damned conscience. The position of the Cadians has become precarious. Vultures are circling and they wear the two-headed aquila of the Imperium of Man. De Barka might be the most pompous but he is not alone. There are a number of other lord militants and lord generals who think *they* deserve command. Our representatives are fighting round the clock to make sure Cadian generals retain control of this front. This is the chance we need, to repair the loss of Cadia. A chance to regain our glory!'

Warmund went on at length. At the end Bendikt nodded. 'Yes, sir, I understand, but I'm afraid I cannot do as you wish.'

Warmund stopped pacing and fixed an augmented eye on him. 'Can't or won't?' There was threat in Warmund's voice now and the water glass on Bendikt's bedside cabinet rattled. 'I don't care about your pride, Bendikt. I'm *ordering* you to apologise.'

Bendikt's voice seemed quiet in comparison. 'I am very sorry, sir. I cannot.'

'Bendikt–'

Bendikt cut him off. 'Sorry, sir. If you would excuse me, but someone has to make a stand. It's not just the ownership of this front that is at stake here. It is the honour and pride of every Cadian who still draws breath.'

Warmund started to laugh. 'Bendikt. Be serious. You're a soldier, not a preacher.'

'I'm a Cadian,' Bendikt said. 'And, with respect, this is beneath you.'

Warmund turned his whole body towards Bendikt and his voice was low and deep and made the whole room rattle. 'What do you mean, exactly?'

Bendikt felt the vibration in his gut. 'Cadians have nothing to be ashamed of. We held the Cadian Gate since time... for as long as anyone can remember.'

'Yes. But the Cadian Gate fell.'

'Not through any fault of the Cadians.'

Warmund waved a hand in a dismissive gesture. 'Don't be an idealist. We've lost whole sectors of Imperial space. Let's face facts. Maybe de Barka has a point.'

Bendikt felt his blood rising. 'Lord militant, were you on Cadia?'

'No. You know I wasn't.'

'Well then. With all due respect, sir, you cannot say the Cadians failed. De Barka is wrong. You are also wrong. I was there. I know. We were *winning*. Creed was winning.'

Creed was a word that everyone used once. Now his name was passing into memory. But it gave Bendikt strength.

Warmund laughed caustically. 'If you were winning, how did we lose?'

Bendikt could barely control himself. 'The Imperial Navy let us down. The Imperium let us down. Throne be damned! Every Cadian who was not there let us down. Lord Militant Warmund, if you were not there, then *you* let us down!'

Bendikt found that he was shouting into Warmund's face.

There was a dangerous look in Warmund's eye as he stepped forward. Bendikt swallowed, but he did not back down. He was done with manners. He was a soldier, and a fighter, and he fought his corner.

'How dare you accuse me, Bendikt. If anyone failed, it was you and Creed and all the other defenders. Cadia fell on *your* watch, not mine!'

Warmund was shouting too now. The vibrations were sickening and the bedside lumen cracked. Bendikt had to swallow back his nausea as he returned the lord militant's stare. He remembered Ursarkar Creed's words about the dreadful old waxworks who ran the Cadian forces, how hidebound they were, how their warfronts were on Holy Terra, in the infernal politicking of the Administratum.

He started to speak but Warmund put up his hand. 'I am fighting the war for the survival of our regiments. That is why you must go and apologise. *Today.*'

Bendikt took in a deep breath and paused for a long moment. 'I am afraid I cannot, sir.'

All the charm had fallen from Warmund. He bristled. 'I am giving you an order, Bendikt.'

Bendikt looked to see if there was a commissar in the room. There was. Warmund had planned this all along. Bendikt had been cornered. He took a deep breath. This was now a matter of life and death.

Bendikt spoke deliberately. 'I understand that, sir. But still, I cannot allow the name of the Cadians to be impugned in this way.'

'That was a command.'

From the corner of his eye Bendikt could see the commissar put his hand to his bolt pistol. Bendikt nodded. 'I know that. If it means me dying, then that is what I shall do.'

He watched as the bolt pistol slid from its black leather holster, then looked away.

The commissar stepped forward. Bendikt drew in a long breath. The barrel of the bolt pistol was cold against his skin.

Warmund watched his face almost eagerly.

'Do it,' Bendikt hissed, and quoted an ancient song. 'Weep for those whose faith is weak. I rejoice, for my faith is bottomless.'

He heard the click as the firing pin was brought back. Bendikt closed his eyes. There was a long silence. Lord Militant Warmund paused and turned to the savant. 'What is General Bendikt's old unit?'

His savant answered without a moment's pause. 'Cadian 101st, tank regiment.'

'And where are they serving?'

'The Gallows Cluster.'

'Bendikt. Consider yourself under house arrest. I shall leave you now in the guard of my men. You have three hours to apologise to Lord General Reginald.'

'Or what?'

'Or you will be sent to the penal colonies and your name shall be struck off the Imperial monuments. Your regiment will be disbanded. Their colours will be consigned to the regimental shrine on Ophelia IV, and the companies will be broken up to fill the ranks of other, more reliable regiments. The name, the proud legacy, the existence of the Cadian 101st shall be no more. The whole regiment shall die with you.'

There was a twitch under Bendikt's left eye. It pulled once, twice, three times. He felt his throat tightening. He felt tears welling up and by sheer force of will he drove them back. He dared not blink. He could not show weakness.

From somewhere he felt stillness within him. He closed his eyes and drew in a deep breath. 'I will apologise,' he said at last, 'when de Barka does likewise.'

'That'll never happen.'

'Then I leave the fate of the 101st in your hands, sir. There is only one way to resolve this honourably. We leave it for the Emperor to decide who is right.'

'Don't think I'm making empty threats, Bendikt.'

Bendikt opened his eyes. 'Unfortunately, I don't.'

The lord militant sighed. He had tried threat and bluster, and neither of them had worked. Now he tried a different tack. 'He'll kill you, you know.'

'That is not certain.'

'Have you seen him fight?'

'No, sir.'

'Well, that's one thing Praetorians *are* good at. And de Barka is the best duellist on this quadrant.'

Bendikt nodded. He was strangely calm. 'The Emperor will decide.'

Bendikt stood at the door as the lord militant and his staff filed out.

Warmund's handshake was brief. 'You're a stubborn fool, Bendikt. It'll be a shame to lose you.'

Bendikt nodded and said nothing. He did not trust his voice not to betray him.

Warmund gave a curt nod. 'Goodbye then, General Bendikt. I do not think we shall meet again.'

Bendikt nodded and shut the door, closed his eyes, and tried to swallow back the grief.

But nothing could stem his pain and humiliation.

He was Cadian. The Holy Emperor had entrusted his people with a sacred duty: to defend the Imperium against the enemies of mankind. To do this they had been given the best weapons, the best training, forge worlds devoted to furnishing their every need.

And they had all failed.

THREE

The time and location for the duel was set by their go-betweens.

Dawn. Firing range Alpha-2, on the second sub-level of D Quadrant. 'It's a quiet spot,' Bendikt's adjutant, Mere, said. 'On an unused deck of the *Imperial Heart*. I'm assured no one will disturb you.'

'When?'

'Tomorrow morning.'

Bendikt nodded and took the news with calm detachment. Duelling was officially banned by Administratum protocol, but it had an archaic status among many martial cultures within the myriad regiments of the Astra Militarum, and there were simple precedents to follow. No armour, no lasweapons, no interference from other men, no champions, no psychic tricks. Just a straight duel, blade to blade.

It would be left to them. No one would intervene or stop this fight. Just Reginald, Bendikt and their appointed seconds.

May the Emperor aid the righteous.

At 0300 hours the next morning the lights came on in Bendikt's chambers. He'd closed his eyes, but sleep had not come. He spent the night thinking back over his life. A child, a cadet, and then the long period of active service, a time he thought of as being both terrible and jubilant.

He could hear Mere in the antechamber starting to prepare, and pushed himself up. He had not got used to the size of the Ramilies star fort. It was like being on a planet. Each quadrant had a separate day, so that as one quadrant went to sleep, the next one was waking up. The only sounds were the distant, low hum of the plasma generator, the moan of the superstructure being pulled at by the planet's gravitational field, the echo of other quadrants still at midday, and the resonant clunks of cruisers docking alongside the Ramilies.

Bendikt was buttoning up his shirt when Mere entered. 'I'm sorry to involve you in this.'

'I'm honoured,' Mere said. His involvement in this duel would be a stain on his otherwise untarnished record.

'You don't have to come.'

'I wouldn't be anywhere else. Honestly.'

Mere stood silently watching as Bendikt finished buttoning up his dress-jacket of Cadian drab, the embossed brass buttons each individually polished to a parade-ground brightness. Bendikt laughed bitterly. In a pistol fight or a match of military acumen the Praetorian would be a dead man. But the weapons of the duel ring were blades, and

Bendikt was shorter, smaller and facing a man whose planet and class meant that duelling was the chief sport.

Mere watched his commander closely. He didn't fancy Bendikt's chances and, fate being the bitch she was, he knew these would be the last moments he saw his commanding officer alive – so he drank him in, as a man will drink water before going out into the desert. Mere thought back through their days on Cadia; the long sojourn on Observation Post 9983; the time that Creed came to visit them; the wonder of the Salvation Sanctuaries, buried under the Cadian land-scape; and finally, the long-awaited counter-attack and the dreadful moment when Cadia started to break apart...

'My sword,' Bendikt said and Mere handed over the sword belt. Bendikt wrapped it about his waist, pulling the buckle tight. His blade was a heavy chopping broadsword, perfect for cutting through heretic flak armour or helmets, but quite unsuited to delicate duelling.

Mere knew how the fight would end. He checked his chronometer. It was nearly 0400 and they still had a long distance between them and the site of the duel.

'Are you ready, sir?'

Bendikt nodded.

'Then we'd better go.'

The guards outside Bendikt's quarters were fellow Cadians.

The officer was a thin man with a scarred lip. He stepped in front of Bendikt. 'May I shake your hand, sir? We all heard what the bastard said.'

Afterwards the officer saluted. 'Good luck, sir.'

'Thank you,' Bendikt said, and then Mere tugged at his sleeve.

'He's here,' he said.

Bendikt turned. A neutral officer from the Saturnine Dragoons was standing in dress uniform at the end of the corridor. The man saluted. 'The lift is waiting, sir.'

Bendikt shook each of the guards' hands and then followed Mere to the lift.

The doors slid into place. Bendikt could feel the cool air welling up from below. Then the lift began the long descent.

It took them down through deck after deck. From their smell you could tell what each was used for. The human stink of barrack blocks; the dry, papery scent of administrative silos; the counter-septic of medical wards; the dusty and stale air of uninhabited decks – kitchens, messes, storage chambers, levels that had been put into quarantine in ages past, and never unlocked; and finally the fyceline stink of the magazines, which were dark, silent, deserted. The temperature rose at first, as they approached the plasma reactors, and then dropped as the minutes dragged on and they descended into the bowels of D Quadrant.

The hum of the gravitation drives grew louder. At last the lift slowed, coming to a stop as the floor aligned with its hazard warning stripes.

The dragoon had not spoken, but now he took out a piece of parchment and checked the location. 'This is it,' he said, and unlatched the doors and pushed them open.

When they were all outside he slid the grille-door closed again. 'You call the lift with this chain,' the dragoon said. He spoke to Mere, not Bendikt. 'It takes some time.'

Mere nodded. 'We'll remember that.'

The dragoon's cheeks coloured. He looked briefly to Bendikt, then nodded. 'This way.'

The dragoon turned left and led them through a broad,

silent corridor. He kept up a brisk pace and the two Cadians hurried behind.

Lumen strips flickered to life then extinguished again
as they passed by. There were shoulder-height bundles of
cabling strung like ship-rope along the wall, brass pipes with
white labels, wheezing ductworks, and beneath the floor
the deep hum of local generators. At one point Mere realised that his hands were sweating. He wiped them on his
trousers and tried to concentrate. The grav-plates had not
been tuned for a long time: in some places they were running strong, and every step was a strange effort, like wading
through water, while by the end of the corridor they were
under-performing, and Mere felt himself float for a moment
between each footfall.

Going down the steps, Bendikt and Mere had to put their
hands up to stop their heads from catching on the ceiling.
In the darkness they could feel spaces opening up to either
side. Cool breezes came from some, while others blasted hot
air at them, tinged with the distinct ozone stink from coolant
heat-overflow ducts. They passed what smelled like a sewage
recycling facility. The greasy smell of gun stores. A doorway
with 'No Entry' tape crisscrossing the entrance way, the hazard warning stripes still gleaming despite the years of dust.

At last they reached a long, empty, sand-floored firing
chamber. Old pressboard targets were stacked against the
wall. They were lost in the shadows, but Mere could make
out the typical Munitorum-issue figures of men and the more
common xenos races: greenskins, eldar, genestealers.

The galaxy was stocked with terrifying enemies, but humanity's chief danger came not from the hostile universe or from
xenos races, but from within itself.

Bendikt had spent most of his military life shooting

heretics. They came in standard human form. Nothing strange or alien about their shape, usually. It was their minds that were gone.

The Saturnine Dragoon paused at a pair of double doors that stood open. 'This is as far as I go.'

Mere peered through the doorway. 'So, this is it?'

'It is. At the far end of this hall. The floor is marked with a skull.'

'Cheery,' Mere said. The dragoon did not smile. He briefly shook both Cadians' hands, saluted and turned, his booted feet ringing out on the metal flooring as he made his way back to the inhabited regions.

Once he had gone, Mere stepped through the doorway and looked around. The hall was silent, empty, overwhelmingly vast. It made them both feel diminished. There were doors at the far, dimly lit end.

They stepped further inside. There was a long, thoughtful pause.

'This is just like Observation Post 9983,' Mere said.

Bendikt nodded. His memories of that place were of being trapped and impotent. It was not a good omen.

It was a short walk until they reached the designated firing range. Like everything on this ship it was vast in scale, and stretched away with low lumens flickering in time with the plasma reactors.

No one else was here.

'Are you sure this is it?' Bendikt said.

'Yes, sir,' Mere said. 'Look.'

Bendikt saw a chalk saltire underneath the crude image of a skull. He drew in a deep breath. The door was unlocked. The handle clean. He pushed it open.

Again, they felt the open space ahead of them. The air was a little warmer, and above the low drone of grav-plates, there was the tenor note of the maintenance systems.

They walked inside.

'Well, when I was a Whiteshield, I never thought I'd end up like this,' Bendikt said, 'but then I never thought I'd make general either. Thanks to Creed, of course.'

Mere looked at him. He was obviously trying to remain cheerful and light, despite the occasion. 'He was a good man.'

'He was, wasn't he?' Bendikt paused and drew in a long breath. 'Feels odd talking about him in the past tense.'

'Yes,' Mere said. He gave a strained smile. 'Cadia stands!'

It was the slogan that Creed had used throughout the hundred days of fighting on Cadia. Once it had brought hope, but now it seemed almost mocking.

Bendikt turned away. 'It's ironic when you think about it.'

'What?'

'This is *exactly* what we are deciding here,' Bendikt said. 'Does Cadia still stand, or not?'

Mere caught his gaze. He nodded.

There was a long pause. Bendikt checked his chronometer. 'Are you sure this is the right place?'

'Sorry, sir. Yes. I arranged for us to come down ten minutes before Ser Reginald. I thought that you might like to have a look around. I thought you'd like that.'

'Good thinking,' Bendikt said. Mere was right. It was one of his tics as a commander – to not just rely on reports and other men's opinions, but to get down on the ground. To see and smell and taste the place himself.

Bendikt turned his back and paced forward, looking about an empty room. The duelling circle had been marked out in chalk halfway up the range. It was fifteen paces in diameter. Standard form.

'A good killing zone,' Bendikt said. The grav-plates felt like they were a little off on one side of the duelling circle. Bendikt could feel himself being pulled down on that side. He felt out the area. It followed the line of rivets in the metal flooring. He consigned the fact to memory. It might be useful, he thought.

You never knew.

He puffed out his cheeks. It couldn't be long now. He really ought to start focusing. He was here, he reminded himself, to fight for the honour of every Cadian. They were a rapidly dying breed. Which made his task even more important, because ten, twenty, fifty years from now, there might be no Cadians left.

No one to show what a fine body of soldiers they had once been.

The weight of ages fell on his shoulders. He braced himself for it. If this was his moment to be judged, he would not be found lacking.

Suddenly, from the other side of the firing chamber, a door opened, and after a moment's pause, two figures entered. They were no bigger than Bendikt's thumb, so distant that the clip-clip of their smart leather boots came a second or so after he saw it.

'They're here,' Mere said.

Bendikt nodded.

Yes, he thought as he took in a long breath, they were.

FOUR

The Praetorians came in their full dress uniform: spiked topi, red velvet jacket, striped trousers and pristine white puttees. Ser Reginald was taller than Bendikt remembered, and he took in the long arms, broad shoulders and smooth, confident gait with a sinking feeling.

This was going to end badly, he thought, and felt warmth rising up to his collar.

Mere was watching him.

'I know what you're thinking,' Bendikt said.

Mere looked uncomfortable. 'You could still apologise.'

Bendikt took in a deep breath to calm himself. 'I think death would be a better epitaph than dishonour.'

Mere nodded. 'I'll go and greet them.'

Ser Reginald's second was dressed like his commander.

The man had a red-lens augmetic monocle, a double-barrelled hotshot laspistol in a worked leather holster, long waxed mustachios, and cheeks so closely shaved the skin was still raw.

'Adjutant Mere,' Mere said, and put out a hand. The handshake was brief and perfunctory.

'Lieutenant Hezekia Monstella de Barka,' the other man said.

The other man clearly read Mere's expression.

'Yes. I am the sister-son of Ser Reginald.'

Mere nodded. In normal situations this would have been a conversational opening, but Mere had no interest in prolonging the exchange. They went through the formalities briefly. There was an efficient briskness to their conversation. At last Lieutenant Hezekia said, 'The appointed time is five minutes hence. But as we're all here shall we start in three?'

The duellists nodded their approval. The adjutants checked their chronometers. 'Agreed,' Mere said.

The two seconds shook hands once more and turned back to their men.

Ser Reginald was already warming up. Mere watched him for a moment. He had a fencing rapier with a cup hilt, and a long reach. His booted feet moved quickly for such a big man.

There was a cruel beauty to the way he covered the ground. The Praetorian looked both lean and clinical. Mere had to drag his gaze away.

Bendikt looked almost clumsy in comparison as he drew his broadsword, unbuckled his sword belt and threw it and the sheath away behind him. He rolled his shoulders and made a few quick sweeps of his blade to loosen his wrist.

He stepped back and forth, practising his moves. Mere was too tense to watch. He kept his eyes on his chronometer. With twenty clicks to go he warned, 'Almost time.'

Bendikt nodded and drew himself up.

A few seconds later the chime rang out. It was a single, high *ping*. Bendikt turned smartly to his second, saluted for the duel to start.

As Bendikt strode forward towards the chalk circle Mere whispered to himself, almost as if the words were a prayer, 'Cadia stands!'

To Bendikt, he said, 'Kill the bastard!'

FIVE

Bendikt put up a respectable resistance, but as the duel went on it was clear that the Praetorian was playing with him.

Bendikt started stiffly, but his breaths grew more and more ragged, his footwork more clumsy. He jumped aside as the Praetorian's blade whistled past where his face had been, but as he fell backwards the next blow slashed across his left arm.

The Cadian let out a snarl of pain and frustration as the razor-sharp blade opened up his dress coat and cut a deep score in his flesh.

The next minute was painful to watch. Bendikt was bleeding from a dozen wounds. His left arm was cradled, the floor was slick with his blood and his face was disfigured with pain.

Just kill him and be done, Mere thought, but the Praetorian was intent on inflicting as much humiliation as possible before the coup de grace.

At last there was a low grunt as the Praetorian's blade

sheared through Bendikt's wrist. Hand and sword fell with a clatter to the metal floor. Bendikt's stump swung pathetically before the Cadian understood that he had lost both hand and weapon, then the sabre stabbed him in the upper thigh, and he fell forward, like a penitent on his knees, clutching what was left of his arm, his life blood pumping out onto the floor.

Mere felt sick. Just end it, he thought.

Bendikt clutched the stump as his blood pumped out. The Praetorian stood over him, fresh, untouched, merciless. He lifted his duelling blade and pointed it towards Bendikt. 'If you apologise, I will spare you.'

Bendikt's face was pale. He was going to bleed out. Mere took half a step forward, before Bendikt answered. He spat at the Praetorian. 'Never.'

The Praetorian's sabre flicked casually, cutting a nasty gash across his cheek.

'Beg, Cadian dog!'

Bendikt spat the word out, despite the bloody foam that filled his mouth. 'Never!'

Three more blows landed. Bendikt cast about and caught his broadsword with his left hand and held it up in a weak defence.

'You are beaten,' de Barka announced. 'The Holy Emperor has shown my case to be fair and just. The Cadians are disgraced, unworthy. You are a dying breed, and the sooner we are rid of the stench of failure, the better for us all.'

Mere made the sign of the aquila. De Barka prepared to dispatch his crippled enemy with his trademark blow: the stab to the heart.

But as the Praetorian stepped forward, Bendikt twisted to the side, and with a cry of effort and pain he threw himself upwards.

It was an ugly blow, but it did the job. The point of his blade caught the Praetorian in the gut and the aristocrat fell backwards, innards slipping out.

Bendikt pushed himself to his feet. His visage was gore. Blood ran from his mouth and cheek but he spoke proudly and well as he readied his backhand blow. 'Ser Reginald de Barka. The Holy Emperor has shown my case to be fair and just. You are a dying breed, and the sooner we are rid of the stench of failure, the better for us all.'

The broadsword flashed out, and both bodies fell to the ground.

PART TWO

'*My servants, the righteous shall inherit each earth.*'
– Psalm of Guidance

ONE

Minka was as good as dead when they found her in the foot-hills of Markgraaf Hive, arms raised above her head, a warm corpse, waiting to be pulled out from the earth.

Each night since then her dreams had taken her back there: cold and shivering in the tox-pool.

Each night she felt warm hands pulling her free from the embrace of the dirt. And each night she woke with a start, and found herself sitting bolt upright in her cot, eyes wide open, cold sweat running from her armpits, and her heart flapping like a trapped bird in the cage of her ribs.

She swung her legs over the bunk and landed softly on the warm metal of the barrack-hall flooring. The war for Marquis had been a damned hell, fought in some of the most appalling conditions the Cadians had ever seen. This world was a toxic cesspit infested with vermin and sump-maggots that could take a man's head off with one bite. They had spent weeks underground, being sniped at, ambushed, raided by enemy combat teams and suffering from lack of sleep or rest. Within days, smart, fit, young units had been reduced to starving, filthy, terrified groups of survivors. Now these survivors called themselves the Hell's Last. However, to the officials of the Munitorum, they were the Cadian 101st.

The thousand survivors of the once-proud 101st now slept on three-tiered bunks at the stern-end of Barrack Hall IX aboard the Lunar-class cruiser *Kossak Blade*.

Acres of empty bunks stretched away along the barrack hall. The unmade beds were testament to the terrible losses their forces had suffered.

Minka's fingers traced the ends of each bunk as she made her way through the tightly packed room towards the entrance. Her mouth was dry. Her heart was urgent. In that month in the underhive, Minka had become accustomed to the many types of darkness. She knew its shades and contours, could sense threat long before it struck. She sensed danger now as she passed by the cots on her way to the main gates, where a complement of sentries stood at attention in a pool of crackling galvanic light.

Now, tonight, the sergeant on duty was Valdez. She knew him by name, but he challenged her as she padded barefoot out of the shadows.

'Who walks tonight?' Valdez demanded.

She was dressed in loose cotton leggings and a camo top. 'Minka Lesk,' she said.

'Can't sleep?'

'No,' Minka said. 'I felt something. Something strange.'

Valdez looked pale. He frowned. 'We re-entered real space. Half an hour ago.'

Minka cocked her head as if listening. The throbbing pulse

of warp pressure on the ship had gone, replaced by the low rumble of plasma drives, the creak of structural beams readjusting to gravity, and the low moan of metal as their transport altered course. 'Did we arrive?'

Valdez nodded. 'We're planet-bound as we speak. Potence, capital world of the Gallows Cluster.'

'And it's not the front line, is it?'

'I hope not,' Valdez said, and laughed briefly. 'If it is then half the sector has fallen since last communications.' He nodded towards a box of parchment that stood by the side of the sentry post. The red wax seals were still warm. 'It's all in there. All the news from the galaxy.'

Minka nodded. Through ways that were not clear to her, the planet of Cadia had held the Eye of Terror contained, and its fall had torn a great rift across the Imperium of Man. Those tsunami aftershocks were still rippling through the warp, leaving them blind and deaf whilst in transit, unable to communicate and unable to receive communications. Now, with their return to real space, astropathic links had been re-established, and this was the backlog of Imperial dispatches and orders. Minka said nothing, but the news was like a balm. Perhaps that was it, she thought, and forced a smile.

But the truth was she needed a break. Just enough downtime to get her head straight. A moment to draw breath. A chance to evade the nightmares that haunted her at night.

Valdez tossed a file to her. It was a bundle of information posters, still warm from the screen-printing rolls. Valdez had slid one of them out from the middle. He held it towards her. The type was smudged.

The title of the poster read 'Reinforcements'.

'Looks like we're going to make friends.'

Minka scanned the notice. 'So we're not being disbanded?' She tried to take it from him, but Valdez held it back.

'Not yet. They're still working their way down to us.'

At the breakfast canteen there was only the usual: fried slab and reconstituted egg. But there was a buzz in the queue and among the seated soldiers. They'd all noticed that the plasma drives were operational again. They were all looking forward to going planetside.

'Heard the news?' Trooper Prassan said as Minka queued.

Minka was staring off into the distance as Prassan addressed her. He had to repeat himself before she heard him. He was her age, approximately. Had been on Cadia too when the end came. She didn't ask him about it. Didn't want to know.

'We're landing?'

'No,' he said. 'Not that.'

'So then, what?'

'We're being brought back to strength.'

'Yeah. I heard.'

'Know who?' He didn't wait for her to answer. 'Three regiments – the Black Dragons, the Cadian 966th Rifles and the 2000th Redskulls.'

The names meant nothing to her. 'Know anything about them?'

He shook his head.

'Were they *there*?'

'Cadia? No. They were on the Eastern Fringe,' Prassan said. 'There's no record of which warzone the Redskulls had been involved in. Since their recall, the Black Dragons and the Rifles have been engaged on the northern edge of the Cicatrix Maledictum.'

She reached the front of the queue, where strips of lumens kept the food warm. 'Lucky them,' she said.

'Not really.'

She laughed as she filled her bowl. Yeah, she couldn't think of anything worse than being stuck on a ship for months or years.

Prassan followed her as she moved to a table, and sat down opposite.

They were quiet as they shovelled in their food. After a pause, Prassan spoke. 'How are you doing?'

'Good,' she said. 'You?'

'Oh,' he said, 'not bad. I just meant, after Marquis. You know.'

'What?'

'You know. Bale-sickness?'

'Oh that. I'm fine.' She quoted Medic Banting. '*Nothing a series of injections can't put right.*' Even in her own ears she sounded too breezy. He caught the forced jollity in her voice.

'Yeah? I hope so.'

She looked down and chased the last scraps of egg with her spoon, then shoved them into her mouth, and stood, lifting her bowl. 'I'd better go. We're disembarking this time tomorrow.'

'Right,' Prassan said, and he half stood.

'No, don't get up. You eat. I'm fine. Honest.'

He looked at his slab. It didn't seem so appetising now. 'Are you sure?'

'Of course I'm sure.'

He paused. 'Well, if you need a hand with anything?'

She was defiant as she returned his stare. She had a horrible feeling that he was coming on to her. 'Like what?'

'Oh,' he said. 'I don't know.'

TWO

When Minka tried to piece the fragments of memory back together, they were like shards of different pots: they did not fit. From her whole platoon only she and Grogar had made it out alive, through a hell of sump-pipes and sewage vats. When the evacuation teams did their final sweep they had been practically done for, their boots worn through, their insignia almost unreadable.

They'd both been shaking so hard they could barely gut a heretic. They'd spent a month in recovery afterwards, pumped full of stimms, enduring fevers, lurid dreams and night sweats. Confessor Keremm had come over to them and offered them the Emperor's Blessing. Minka had tried to push him off, but she couldn't make herself understood, and she was too weak to stop him.

'Toxic shock,' Banting, the grey-haired medicae, said, sniffing as he flipped through her file and speaking across the bed to his orderly. 'Typical for soldiers who have spent too long in the underhive.'

Banting flipped through more sheets and turned to go. This was all run-of-the-mill for him. 'Nothing a few injections won't cure.'

If Minka had been standing she would have struck the damned fool, but she could barely lift an arm.

As they started to walk away, from somewhere she had found the strength to speak. She was a fighter, Throne-take them. She was one of Hell's Last.

'Ten minutes was too long in that frekking hole,' she'd croaked, and the medicae had looked up and forced a brief smile as he hung her notes back onto the end of her cot.

'I'm sure,' he said.

The next morning Minka reported back to the medicae.

As she came out she passed Grogar. She caught his eye and gave a brief nod.

She could barely look at him for more than a second, and she guessed the feeling was mutual. Survivor's guilt, or something like that. They'd been through that hell together. She'd die for him if need be, but until then she didn't want to see or hear anything about him.

It was Banting on duty. He had her lie down on a bench, and took her pulse, blood pressure and shone a light into her eyes.

'Any continued symptoms?'

'No.'

Banting held a clipboard and took a stylus from behind his ear. He made a few marks on her form. 'No dreams, tremors, nothing?'

'Sleep like a baby,' she said.

'And are you saying your prayers?'

'Every night,' she said.

'Good.'

He signed the form and handed it over to her.

'You are released back to active service.'

She took the paper and saluted him. 'Thank you, sir.'

The *Kossak Blade*'s day cycle was out of sync with the planet.

On the day it docked in orbit, the systems switched to planetary time and the lumens flickered on three hours later than normal.

Those three hours were torment. Minka had lain with her eyes wide open, sweat beading on her forehead, willing the darkness to recede.

At last she could bear it no longer. She ran to the latrines and slammed the lights on. She locked herself in the low, plasteel cubicle, and sat on the toilet lid and put her head in her hands, trying to force the sweats back. She wanted to scream. She wanted to be sick. She wanted to get off this damned transport.

The regimental office was amongst the string of cabins that ran along the portside of the barrack hall.

Minka was there ready when it opened. Colour Sergeant Daal's hair had been freshly buzz cut. The grey spikes were as neat and regular as a palace lawn.

She immediately felt under-polished. Daal had that effect on most people. He was as punctilious as anyone she'd ever met as he stared up from the desk where he sat, his jaw clenched tight.

'Ready for active duty,' she announced and threw the slip of paper from the medicae down.

Daal briefly picked the chit up between thumb and forefinger. He looked at it and nodded. 'All packed?'

'Yes, sir.'

'Good. Then go get a mop and start cleaning. It's filthy
out there.'

She turned to go, but he called her back and she turned
to see his hand out.

It took a moment for her to get over her surprise, but then
she took his hand and returned the shake. Firm and hard.

He did not smile. Daal never smiled. But he held her with
his cold blue gaze and said, 'Welcome back, Lesk.'

She paused. 'Is it true... That we're going to be on fur-
lough for a while?'

His expression did not change. 'Potence is at peace. So yes.
We'll all be getting a break.'

'Thank you, sir. I'm glad, sir. And I'm very pleased to be
back on active service.'

Minka and the team with her were still cleaning as the plasma
drives powered down to a low hum. Daal arrived just before
handover to make sure all was shipshape.

He took off his peaked cap, and there was still not a hair
out of place as he stood with his hands clasped behind his
back, and creases down the front of his combat trousers that
were as sharp as a honed blade.

There was nothing soft about the man. War had beaten
any gentleness out of him.

He stuck his chin out as he walked, taking his hands out
from behind his back only to shine the lumen under beds
or into dark corners. 'Not bad,' he said, running a finger
along the top of a bunk and checking for dirt. He peered
under bunks, inspected the metal walls for graffiti and even

turned the mattresses over. 'Not bad at all,' he said at last, and Minka and her team let their shoulders relax a little. 'Well done,' he said, and then Brandt, captain of Fifth Platoon, strode towards them.

'The blue-suits are on their way down,' he announced.

Daal turned to the lift head and drew himself up full-square as a party of six Naval ratings in dark blue flak suits, with pump-action shotguns holstered at their hips, appeared. The inspection officer who led them was a short, dark man, with laspistol, hatchet and clipboard. He took off his helmet and met Daal's stiff formality with a pleasant smile, his steel-capped teeth gleaming pale, and a weary air of officialdom. 'All done?' he said.

'Yes, all present and correct,' Daal replied, arms clasped behind his back, feet slightly splayed to the side and shoulders set ramrod straight.

'Mind if I check?'

Daal seemed to stiffen at the suggestion, but he nodded and stepped backwards. 'After you.'

There was an air of menace as Daal and the Naval officer strode together along the banks of bunks, the Naval officer ticking boxes on his form. Minka tried to get a glimpse of them, but he was moving too quickly, and the light was poor.

'Damaged bunk,' he said and pointed to the offending article.

Daal nodded briefly, but his cheeks coloured. At the end the officer handed Daal the form. 'If you can sign here, please.'

Minka watched as the colour sergeant printed his name at the bottom of the form, then handed it back.

'All good planetside?' he said.

'Yes. We're already through standard protocols.'

'When are we disembarking?'

'As soon as the militia are off-ship.'

'Who?'

'You haven't heard?'

'No.'

The rating shook his head. 'A crusade's been launched. Officially they're called the Order of the Sons of the Emperor. But they call themselves the Brotherhood. We've been asked to get them off first. Special request from the cardinal.'

Daal said nothing, but he did not need to. Everyone was standing and staring. The silence was palpable.

But, we always go first, Minka thought. We're *Cadians*.

The Cadians kept themselves busy. But the mood among the 101st's hangar was tarnished.

Daal set them to cleaning the hangar-bay. Minka was part of the squad being sent around to check that nothing of worth or that belonged to the regiment was being left behind.

'Just make sure,' Daal told them.

'Sure,' she told him a few minutes later. The barrack was spotless.

'Good,' he said, and looked about for something else for them to do. His Cadian pride had been hurt.

After six hours the klaxon rang.

'That's us,' Daal said. He turned to them. Just the barest flicker of pleasure on his lips. 'Right. Let's get off this damned tub.'

At the aft end of the hangar, the regiment's heavy materiel was being loaded onto wide pallets by power lifter sentinels. Cadian support staff manned the chicken-legged machines as they picked up wooden crates of dry rations, medicae supplies, rolls of ammunition, wooden crates of ordnance and large cases with spare parts for the regiment's armoured platoons and transports, ready to be loaded onto the heavy lighters.

Daal seemed to be everywhere, issuing orders with his usual air of tired irritation. 'Right. Now, grab your packs and get up to hangar bay nine. HQ has decided that we're going down combat-style.'

'I thought this planet was peaceful,' Prassan called out.

'So it is,' Daal told them. 'Got to keep up appearances, you know. Something about impressing the local dignitaries.'

'Nothing about this Brotherhood lot going down before us?'

Daal's eyes narrowed dangerously. 'Move along, trooper,' he stated flatly.

An hour later the Cadian 101st approached the open air-lock doors of hangar bay 48. Minka was about ten rows from the front. As she stepped over the threshold she had a rush of vertigo at the scale of the space before her. The ceiling yawned upwards, with endless lines of lumens stretching above her like a highway, and for two miles were parked more drop-ships than she could count.

She swallowed the spit from her mouth and tried to calm herself.

A memory. The first time she'd ever seen one of these immense craft was as a girl on Cadia. There had been ten of them, flying in formation high above in the pale blue winter sky with long white contrails stretching behind them. From the ground their long bodies and short wings had looked sleek and beautiful, like migrating geese.

But another memory contended. The lander that evacuated

her from Marquis. Lying foetal in the corner, in a pool of her own vomit, a medicae crouching over her as her organs began to shut down.

'Alright?' Breve said. He wore the Cadian-drab coveralls of a tank crew and his pips identified him as a driver. He was the kind of trooper who always seemed to miss what was going on about him.

Minka could barely speak. It took all her will to force the words out. 'I'm fine.'

'Yeah?'

She nodded.

The drop-ships were ungainly and stubby, like seabirds on land, with oversized beaks of armoured ceramite. Beneath them was all the armour that the Hell's Last had left; they looked well supplied. Files of Chimeras and tanks were reversing up the front ramp onto the lower deck as marshalling officers shouted and whistled to be heard over the roar of engines.

They were still a hundred yards from the ramp of their drop-ship when they fell under the shadow of its wings. Its fuselage would have filled a cathedral planetside.

Breve sniffed. 'So what's this world called?'

The sweat on her forehead was cold. 'Potence.'

'Any hive cities we should know about?'

'None,' she said.

'Thank the Throne.' Breve sniffed. 'So why are we taking combat landers down?'

Minka closed her eyes. She felt a wave of nausea rising up her gullet. 'HQ's nose is put out so we're making a show of Cadian prowess.'

'Oh good. Thought we were going back into the hellfire.'

He was starting to irritate her. 'Why are you so fussy? Tank crews didn't go into Markgraaf.'

'No,' he said. 'But we stuck around to pull you out.'

The nausea made her gag. She had to turn away and close her eyes. Breve hadn't noticed. He kept on talking. 'You were a mess, I can tell you.'

Minka blinked her eyes open. The thought of leaving the safety of the *Kossak Blade* made her stomach churn. She looked at the driver, but she couldn't tell if he was talking about pulling the rest of the regiment out, or Minka in particular. 'Me?'

'All of you. You alright?'

'Yeah,' Minka said.

'You look pale.'

The nausea was coming back again. 'We've been in the warp,' she said. 'It doesn't do much for your complexion.'

'No, really. You look green. Sure you're alright?'

'Sure. I got doctor's clearance.'

'You don't look it.'

An officer at the front of the line shouted an order, and Minka's column started jogging, two abreast, towards the first lander. All drop-ships were much of a muchness, despite different patterns and forge worlds. They had one task in life – to deliver a payload of troops and armour to the deadliest part of the battlefield in as short a time as possible. And then, Throne willing, get the hell out of there.

The one they were running towards had a long hangar body with cockpit, defensive weapon points, short stubby wings and a rear assault ramp. Squadron marking 'A-987' was spray-painted in giant letters along the fuselage. The white lettering was chipped down to the blue-and-black leopard camo pattern.

It was Daal who was in charge. As they filed past he shouted, 'Bayonets fixed!'

The Cadians responded immediately, Minka included. Her hands shook uncontrollably. She slid the blade onto the end of her gun. This was a peaceful landing.

She reminded herself: there are *no* enemy forces on Potence.

As she took her place in the lander's assault chambers, Minka was getting cold sweats again. She was not going to do the Whiteshield thing and vomit. She willed her breakfast to stay down as the troopers of the 101st crested the ramp and took seats, their packs in rows along the floor.

There were rotating ceiling vanes set at regular intervals. The one above her revolved slowly, and each time it blew on her she could feel the sweat on her forehead cool. She looked about to see who was sitting around her. There was that pair of blond twins from A Company, a load of troopers she knew by sight and a handful from G Company. All that were left, pretty much, after Markgraaf.

On the decks below she could hear the last checks being run and the final tanks being lashed down.

A whistle blew and the ramp began to retract. The dropship's engines fired up. The roar became deafening and the whole craft began to shake.

Minka closed her eyes. She felt the shudder as the lander took off, then the yawing drop in her stomach as they fell into space. It was always the same.

The temperature dropped. She could see her breath steam before her face. The condensation on the inside panels began to freeze and then rime white with ice, and the rows of seated Cadians swayed from side to side like forests of seaweed caught in underwater currents.

When they hit the upper atmosphere the craft rattled dangerously and the ice went within a minute. The temperature rose to that of a sauna, and then stabilised as the drop-ship began the long parabolic descent to the landing field.

Her pack lay between her legs. She clung to it. Everything she owned was in there – her uniform, weapons, a few lucky mementos and a piece of rock that she had brought with her from Kasr Myrak.

It wasn't much. It was pitifully little, to be honest. But she liked it like that. When she was gone this would be all that was left of her.

That, and a long string of dead heretics.

THREE

Breve was driving the Chimera down the assault ramp. Sat inside the cramped space, Minka still felt sick. At least the sweats had gone. Prassan sat opposite looking sympathetic. She could have punched him.

She looked away and gritted her teeth. Sergeant Dido was next to her, a short, hard woman, all muscle and attitude and sharp elbows. She was the kind of soldier who exuded calm. Minka was glad of her presence.

'Smells good,' Dido said.

It was true. The air of Potence here didn't have any taste. Not the stale and oily flavour of recycled ship-air, nor the chewy smog-grime of Marquis.

Minka breathed deep.

It tasted *clean*.

It was like breathing the air of the Cadian uplands.

She half stood and threw one side of the roof hatch open.

Dido reached up and opened the other. She stuck her head up and whistled.

The others shoved each other for a view. Minka waited her turn. When the others had stood down, she pulled herself up and sucked in another breath. Marquis had been a polluted hell of a world, with ash wastes and a poisonous brown atmosphere. The air was so thick with pollutants you could almost chew it. But now, as she stuck her head out of the top hatch, she had a glimpse of blue sky and high, thin clouds, and far off on the horizon, a row of snow-capped peaks.

'What's this planet called again?' Dido asked.

'Potence,' Minka said. The name had a new ring to it now that she saw the place.

The starport was set in the middle of a vast, level plain. Irrigation sprinklers were revolving round their central pivot. The circular fields were an intense green against the dry, brown scrubland, contrasting with low, white farming habs set among shady groves. In the far distance the plains rose abruptly to foothills, dark with pine forests, then high rock cliffs and the bright gleam of snow.

'That's the Supramonte,' Prassan told them.

'Is there nothing you don't know?'

He blushed. 'Didn't any of you read the standard planetary reports?'

'No,' Dido said. 'That's what frekkers like you are for.'

To the other side of the plain was a sprawling tent city, and beyond it was a single rocky outcrop. Tumbling down the sides of the rock to meet the high walls encircling the base was a white stone settlement with roofs of heavy terracotta tiles. Squatting over the town like a castle of old, was a vast walled fortress, and within it, at the summit of the acropolis stood a great, gold-topped building. The beauty was profound. Nothing, she thought, could be more unlike the hive wastes of Marquis.

Prassan clearly had been reading the reports. He joined her in the open hatchway. 'This is the throne world of the Gallows Cluster. Single major habitation. Home of the Richstar family.'

Minka presumed he was confused. 'But the Richstars were on Marquis.'

'Richstars run the whole cluster. All of them are descended from the original settler. Can't remember his name.'

'That's one hell of a family,' Minka said.

'Been running it since Compliance.'

'What's Compliance?'

Prassan frowned as he looked at the faces of the troopers opposite him. They all knew the word, but it was old history. 'Being part of the Imperium, I guess.'

'So what's this place called?'

'It's called the Evercity,' Prassan said.

'Why's that?' Minka asked.

'Don't know,' he shrugged. 'Maybe it's because it will last forever.'

'I hope so,' Minka said.

There was a long, long silence. No one needed to speak. As they drew closer they could see up the steep tiers of houses, and at the top, the gold-roofed cathedral. Prassan pushed forward. He had to see.

'Early Imperium,' he said.

Early Imperium meant about as much to Minka as 'Compliance'.

'It looks like a fortress. Do the Richstars live there?'

'I don't know,' Prassan said.

'Well, thank Throne for that,' Dido said. 'Keep much more stuff in your head and they'll make you a savant.'

Prassan pulled a face which told Dido where to go, but the clean air and the sunlight after so long in the recycled and artificial environment of the *Kossak Blade* was like a shot of stimms.

The Evercity grew only more beautiful. As they approached they could make out the stucco facades, lattice balconies, statues and gargoyles of carved limestone, and the golden domed roofs of the city's many chapels. Even the city walls were a thing of beauty: rockcrete surface inlaid with alternating bands of black and white marble, and loopholes with mosaic borders.

Minka stood as they approached the city gates. Her hair whipped across her face.

'Careful,' Prassan said, and tried to tug her back down, but Minka refused to sit. She scanned the battlements. There was no danger, she was sure. No snipers. Nothing that could take this view away from her.

The rockcrete road surface was smooth and unbroken. The lead vehicles were already passing into the darkness of the gateway.

Minka felt weightless as their transport crossed from the smooth road to the cobblestones of the bridge, and over the dry moat.

Dido shut the top hatch. The troopers stood to peer through the vision slots as they wound up through narrow streets. Minka had brief and disjointed glimpses of ornate pedestals, the feet of marble statues and carved friezes along the panels of the bridge railings, dressed stone arches, tall, whitewashed habs and the faces of people with colour in their cheeks. An excited silence filled the space until the convoy slammed to a halt.

'What's up?' Dido demanded.

There was a pause. She punched the cabin door.

A voice sounded through the vox-relay. It was Breve. His voice was taut. *'Sorry, guys. Something weird,'* he said.

Minka became suddenly very calm. Her skin prickled. She could feel her heartbeat starting to quicken. Her palms were hot. She was starting to sweat again.

Dido stood. Her head was out of the top hatch. 'We should keep moving!' Dido said to Breve, but then the sergeant saw something through the vision slot. Minka didn't know what it was, but she saw Dido's body stiffen, and her voice assumed command.

'Safeties off!' she ordered.

The Cadians moved as one. The ramp slammed down. The troopers' response was almost instantaneous. Their boots clattered on the ramp as they piled out of the back of the Chimera.

The sudden sunlight was blinding. Minka had a brief impression of a busy street, tall buildings, deep shadows that she could not penetrate. She threw herself into cover, overturning a table, tin mugs of recaf spilling over the wall. She took up a firing position.

In the street there was an old man with a stick. A woman with a black shawl, shouting up at a balcony. A gang of boys, mouths open in horror. The man with the stick pointed down the road, to where a procession of black-clad girls was shuffling towards them. They had dark boots and coats and hair cropped short. They were holding hands with each other in a confused knotwork of limbs, but the lead girls had their palms held out before them, as if feeling their way.

Minka raised her carbine. She could not see any weapons. She looked to Dido. The sergeant was moving forward.

A fat man with a short towel thrown over his shoulder rushed out of a doorway. 'Away!' he shouted at the girls. He waved the cloth at them. 'Back!'

The girls lifted their hands up and shuffled towards him. Their fingers were open and grasping.

'Away!' the man shouted, but he backed away from them, tripping back into a round table.

One of the girls' hands caught the lip of the table. Her fingers moved like a spider. They found the edge of a customer's plate and closed around a piece of bread, grabbing it and shoving it into her mouth.

'They can't see!' Dido shouted.

Minka understood. They were blind and hungry, and they moved through the town like a many-tentacled sea creature edging sightlessly across the sea floor.

The man struck one of them. The girl started crying, a high keening sound. A dark-haired woman suddenly appeared at the other end of the street.

'Back!' the lady shouted. 'Back!'

Dido lifted her hand. She opened her mouth to speak. Dido's lips moved, but Minka could not hear anything as an explosion ripped through the building opposite. In an instant the air was full of dust and debris and Minka felt a great pressure on her chest, and then she was lying on her back. All about was silence. The sky above her was white. The silence was absolute – dull, mute, deafening.

Minka shoved herself back to her feet. There was grit in her eyes, a white dust-fog filling the canyon of hab-blocks. She was in shock, she knew.

The world was white. Ghosts were stumbling towards her, their hair and faces all bleached of colour. The only people pushing forward were the Cadians. The street before them was filled with rubble. Her feet caught on blocks of brick and stucco.

It took a moment before she understood.

A hab-block had collapsed. The building had fallen into the street. Rubble heaped up on top of the carelessly strewn bodies of women and children and men. The crowd, which had been so scared and angry moments before, stood in utter shock, like statues, clothes, faces and hands all white with dust.

Then suddenly, like a switch being thrown, the noise returned and everyone was screaming. A young boy stumbled towards Minka. His mouth was open, as if he were about to cry, but no sound came. 'Here!' Minka shouted, but he could not hear her. She grabbed him and dragged him down into the cover of the doorway. He was as white as the rest of them.

'What happened?' she shouted. Her hearing was still dulled. She had to half lip-read. He was stiff in her arms. She repeated the question, but he looked about bewildered, mouth open as if to scream.

'Bomb-deaf,' a voice said. It was Dido, pushing past. 'Fyce-line,' she said.

Dido was suddenly next to her. She was shouting. 'If we had not stopped…'

Minka nodded. If they had not stopped then the Cadian convoy would have been struck by that explosion.

Minka nodded. There was blood on her hand. It wasn't hers; it was the boy's. She turned him over, looking for a wound, but all she saw was dust. For a moment no one moved or spoke, and then, all at once, the boy started to vomit blood.

FOUR

The enforcers turned up about ten minutes later, as the Cadians pulled the lead Chimeras from the rubble. One of the tanks had suffered a serious breach. They'd pulled the crew out, alive or dead, and brought the medic forward.

Banting had come at a jog. 'I'm here,' he said, self-importantly dismissing the ministrations of the troopers.

There were three he had to stabilise. After a minute he declared, 'They're out of danger. Step back and let me work.'

At that moment an open-top compact with black roll bars and double-width tyres arrived from a side road.

It screeched to a halt, and a pair of black-uniformed officers climbed out. They wore body armour and goggles. One was smoking a lho-stick. They had sidearms holstered at their hips, and the enforcer that remained in the car had a single-barrelled shotgun in his lap.

'Who are you?' one of them demanded.

Dido stepped forward. 'Sergeant Dido, Cadian 101st.'

'Identification,' the officer said. He put out a leather-gloved hand.

Dido paused, and then tapped her shoulder where the 101st badge was sewn onto her uniform. 'There,' she said.

The officer gave her a long, hard look. His uniform named him as Enforcer Palek.

He took in the number of Cadians and decided it was not worth making a fuss. 'What happened here?'

'There was an explosion,' Dido said.

Palek took off his goggles and sniffed. He pushed past the Cadians and casually picked through the rubble. 'Alright. Back to normal.'

He started back towards the compact.

'That's it?' Dido demanded.

'What do you want me to do?'

'There was a bomb. Aimed at us.'

The enforcer laughed and dropped the stub of his lho-stick into the dirt. 'That wasn't a bomb. That was a thermal overload. Happens in this district. The off-worlders move in and they tap into the promethium pipes. The vapour builds up, and then, boom!'

'Can't you smell fyceline?'

'No,' the enforcer said. 'I smell promethium.'

He turned to go, and Dido grabbed his shoulder and spun him back round.

'You're leaving?'

'Yes.'

'That's it? What about these people?' Dido pointed to the wounded civilians.

The enforcer reached under his body armour and pulled a fresh lho-stick from his inside breast pocket, turned on his heel and climbed into the front seat. 'I shall include them in my prayers.'

'You can't just leave them.'

'No?' he said, and winked, before pulling away with a roar.

It was two hours' journey up through the city, the convoy going slowly through the ancient, narrow streets. Inside the Chimera the mood had fallen. They were dusty and tired, their fingers raw from picking through rubble.

'What the hell happened down there?' Prassan said, as the Cadian convoy finally began to lift up from the city to the naked base of the high, rocky acropolis, where narrow switchbacks had been blasted from the earth. On a low shoulder of the high rock stood the palace complex and on the summit, at the end of a long, steep staircase, there was a circuit of heavy rockcrete walls, from within which the golden domes of the cathedral rose.

The convoy of Chimeras, halftracks, Leman Russes and ancillary support vehicles were strung out in single file. They were halfway up the west side of the rock when the lead vehicles paused.

Dido pulled the vox-comm from the Chimera's wall. 'Breve. What's up?'

'Enforcers. I think they're checking paperwork. Cathedral is out of bounds, apparently.'

'That's not very charitable. I mean, we've got souls that need saving.'

Breve laughed. *'Speak for yourself. No. We're going to the Intake Barracks. It's past the palace complex. We're just checking directions.'*

Dido closed the link. Everyone had heard the conversation. They were all tense, on edge.

'Can't be that complicated,' Minka said. 'I mean, there can only be two ways to go. Either to the cathedral or to the palace.'

'You'd think so,' Dido said.

After a few minutes the convoy started forwards once more.

'Almost there,' Breve voxed.

No one spoke. Minka couldn't get the image of the black-dressed girls, shuffling forward, or the boy's screaming mouth from her mind. She looked at her hands. She'd rubbed the dirt from them, but around the sides of her palms and under her nails there were half-moons of blood and dirt.

Dido passed her water bottle about. Minka took a swig as the Chimera came to a halt again.

'We're there, apparently,' Breve reported. *'Now just checking formalities.'*

Through the firing slot Minka had a brief view of local defence troops – named Calibineer – in smart night-blue greatcoats, then a glimpse of a servo-skull humming over the ground, trailing wires.

In a moment they were through a check post with a heavy metal gate. The Chimera's tracks rattled over the flagstones. They passed through a broad barrack yard, and then plunged down. The mountain rose up on one side, while the other was pure air.

The Chimera stopped. *'We're here,'* Breve voxed back. *'Intake Barracks.'*

The ramp locks disengaged and they stumbled out into a square courtyard that abutted the cliff wall.

Wounded Cadians were being carried on stretchers towards the medical block. Banting was holding a drip in one hand, while local medical orderlies in stiff black uniforms were hurrying from the doors. Banting shouted orders with his usual brisk manner. Minka took that as a good sign. If any of the wounded's lives were in danger, Banting would be cursing fluently by now.

The convoy was filing into the barrack yard, each vehicle emptying before swinging around to the south, where a wide gateway, marked out with hazard stripes, led to the reinforced storage areas and the magazine. Squat military buildings made up each of the sides. They were topped by a low firing step and parapet, while to the south, where the sheer white cliffs rose up, cave chambers had been excavated into the white granite.

Minka drew in a deep breath. She wanted to get a look at Potence. She dumped her pack against the barrack walls and followed the other Cadians up onto the roof parapets. To stand there it felt as though you were floating in the air.

The Intake Barracks sat halfway up the rock. The palace complex stood on a low heap of rocks below them, while the cathedral was at the top of the acropolis. The barrack outcrop had been made level with rockcrete buttresses and platforms, and a square compound built on the overhang. There were steel generatorium chimneys sticking out of the stonework, with four void shield pylons at each corner, where what had to be Hydra gun emplacements were hidden under camouflaged tarpaulins.

The heat of the day had faded. It was late afternoon and the light was golden over the city, which lay beneath them on the lower slopes as they fell towards the flat plains. From this height it was like looking down at an antique map, with every garden, every cupola, every tenement, dome and piazza statue painted in exquisite detail. But the Cadians felt weariness, not elation, and a strong desire for water to wash the dust away.

'That's the Basilika,' a voice said. It was Prassan. He was looking up to where a low rockcrete wall skirted the upper slopes of the acropolis, and over it, like an ancient castle, were the distinctive domes of an Ecclesiarchy cathedral. It dominated the Evercity like a prize bull, with heavy buttresses and narrow windows like loopholes set within the massive stonework.

'It's seat to the cardinal of the Gallows Cluster. Shame we're not allowed up there. It's a wonder of early settlement architecture apparently,' he said.

Minka gave him a look. He sounded like a military briefing. She'd had her fill of that crap.

Prassan prattled on about the planet and the family who governed it, but Minka had stopped listening. She was looking at his face. His jaw was boyish still, with patchy stubble, and a red mark where his chin strap had fretted against the skin. She was tired, and irritable. He went on and on. At last she couldn't take any more of his bleating.

'Listen, Prassan,' she said at last. 'All I know is that since the Great Calamity, this backwater is now a front-line system, and that we have to hold the enemy back here or the way to Holy Terra lies open. That's what I care about now.'

Prassan's mouth hung open for a moment, but then he stopped and shut it. 'I'm sorry. I thought it was fascinating.'

'It's not. And just for the record. I'm not interested. In you, I mean. Just thought I should spell that out. The whole couple thing. I've been there, done that.'

Prassan's eyes opened up for a moment, then colour rose from his neck to his cheeks.

'Right,' he said. 'I was just…'

She felt bad then. 'Listen, looking after myself keeps me busy enough.'

He looked down at his boots for a moment, then took in a deep breath, and forced a smile. 'It's alright,' he said.

Minka felt terrible as she descended the broad stone steps back to the drill yard, grabbed her pack and found the female barrack hall. As she passed under the parapet she could hear Prassan's fellows laughing. She puffed out her cheeks and let all the tension go. She didn't enjoy that, and she could probably have been gentler about it. But it was best getting it over with.

Someone fell in step with her.

She stopped. 'Listen–' she started, about to put Prassan straight, but it was Dido.

'How you doing?' she said.

'Not good,' Minka said.

'You did your best.'

'I did.'

'We all die, at some point.'

'We do,' Minka said. The boy she had picked up in the street had died. She didn't have words. She stopped and looked up to the thin, blue sky. Her voice was less tense now. 'My brother was that old.'

Dido sniffed. She was staring out into the distance too. It was like they were trying to look back, into the past. 'He's gone?'

Minka shrugged. 'I think so. Well, last time I saw him was the day the war started.'

Dido didn't ask which war. They all knew which war she was talking about. The one for Cadia.

Their homeland.

The war that they had lost.

Minka looked at her hands. The edges were still stained

grey and brown with dust and dried human blood. 'That explosion was no accident,' she said. 'No matter what that idiot enforcer said. Someone was aiming for us.'

Dido and Minka stared at each other. Minka could still feel the weight of the boy in her arms. Could see his mouth open to scream. The blood drip-dripping onto the dust-covered paving slabs. 'Keep breathing,' she'd told the boy, as her fingers found the wound and plugged it closed. But she'd not known if he could hear her, and within a few moments his body had gone limp.

She closed her eyes for a moment and put that death, like so many others, behind her. She was a Guardsman. No point dwelling on loss. It was a fact of life, like breakfast and evening-eat.

Dido put an arm about Minka's shoulder. 'I'm sorry,' she said. 'Come, let's get inside.'

Minka nodded. It couldn't be helped.

Dying was a tradition in the Guard.

They found their quarters, and slung their packs onto the beds they wanted. Then it was back out as the final cargo 8s arrived with all the regimental gear, and the M Company whistle blew the 'All hands'.

Within five minutes they were all standing at ease in platoons along the southern wall, in the shade of the acropolis.

Daal came out and gave the orders, and each platoon sergeant took their assigned cargo 8s. Prassan took one of the sentinel lifters. It bore Calibineer markings, now chipped and rusted, with only the Richstar emblem visible, and the number 47. It took him a moment to get the battery to wake, and when it did start up, the left leg dragged. He carried the pallets from the open back of the cargo 8 and limped through the open magazine doors, and put each load down on the ground before them.

'Looks like you've been drinking,' Dido taunted as she used her knife to cut through the cargo netting, then the troopers lined up to pull the crates off and the quartermaster's officials checked all the supplies in. There were spare battery packs, rations, sights, body armour, boots, dust goggles, smoke grenades.

'You drive it, then,' Prassan cursed as he struggled with the controls.

They spent an hour unloading crates. When Prassan got the last crate down, it took him three attempts to get the lifter in through the doorway, and he parked it by the entrance.

'Not used to the exercise?' he said to Dido as she wiped the sweat from her forehead onto her arm.

'Not as fresh as you, that's for sure.'

Minka had her sleeves rolled up and sweat had stuck her shirt to the small of her back as she handed the last case to the quartermaster's storemen.

The regimental quartermaster sergeant was Rufin. He was a tall, thin man with a drawn face, and a long, crooked nose. He peered down from his great height, checking the inventory off against a sheaf of papers that he held with his clipboard.

He scratched away, ticking items off, then looked up and seemed to notice Minka.

'Lesk, heard the news?'

'No,' she said. 'What?'

Rufin tapped the pencil against his nose. 'It's just been put up on the regimental noticeboard. They're handing out stripes.'

Minka stood up, stretching her back out. She wasn't sure why she was being told all this.

Rufin checked another box as it slid onto the stores' counter. 'Saw your name.'

'Frekk you...' she started, but it wasn't the way to address an officer. 'Sir. Are you joking?'

'No joke,' he said. He turned to take in the piles of crates. 'Look at all this. When would I find time to joke?'

Dido stretched as she stepped out of the magazine doors. The heavy armoured portals had been rolled back into the recessed niches. Their interlocking teeth stood out a foot from the wall. The evening air was clean and cool. It tasted fresh.

She stood and breathed it in deep.

When Minka appeared she had an odd look on her face.

'What is it?' Dido said.

Minka frowned. 'Rufin doesn't joke, does he?'

'When he does it's painful.'

'Well, he just said I've got stripes. It's on the regimental notice board. I've made sergeant.'

'About time too.'

'I don't believe it.'

'Well, let's go see.'

They crossed the drill square to the north side of the block where a small crowd had gathered. Dido pulled her by the elbow and pushed through to the front. 'Look!' she said.

There it was. Plain as print. Arminka Lesk. Sergeant, Sixth Squad, Fourth Platoon. M Company.

Beneath each sergeant's name were the names of their troopers. Minka looked down through hers. Most of the names were from the new recruits – Black Dragons, the 966th Rifles and the 2000th Redskulls.

'Have the new lot arrived yet?' Minka asked.

One of the men standing behind her overheard and interrupted. It was Hesk, the vox-officer. He tilted his head to the west, where Shock Troopers were milling around a row of parked halftracks. 'They're over there.'

There was something ominous about Hesk's manner, but Dido wasn't one to be put off.

'Come,' she said.

They crossed the courtyard to the command office, where the regimental banner of the Cadian 101st hung, a black cross on a red field, stitched with the emblem of the Cadian Gate and a solemn-looking skull.

They approached the barrack entrance and saw the new intake stood, or slouched, or sat along the wall-base, their packs at their feet, and their helmets pulled down low over their faces. Minka didn't like the look of them.

Minka's feet felt heavy and they stopped twenty yards off. 'They *can't* be Cadians,' she said. 'Look at them!'

Dido didn't answer, but the two of them stared at the new recruits with horror.

The new troopers were all dressed in Cadian drab but there were dark patches on their uniform where badges had been ripped away, and they looked like a rabble from the local guard. But as they turned to go, one of the troopers looked up and took the lho-stub from between his stained teeth. He spoke in a distinctive Tyrok accent. 'Oh, we're frekking Cadians alright.'

'What's wrong with you?' Minka said.

'You're our last chance,' the speaker said.

'Throne,' Minka said, and turned to go.

'Oh, don't go so quick, pretty girl. We've been in lockdown for too long. Here! We can offer you a few credits, if we all chip in.'

The whole bunch of recruits started to laugh and Dido spun round. 'Say that again and I'll rip your tongue out!' she spat.

The man pushed himself up from the floor as his comrades cheered him. 'Oh, I wasn't talking to you. I was talking to the *pretty* one.'

Minka shoved Dido aside and marched forward. The man's name-badge read Arktur. There was an unnatural sweetness on his breath that was not just grinweed. 'Right, I'm here. Try it on.'

She shoved him and he shoved back. He was bigger than her, but she was quicker and angrier and her fury gave her strength. In a moment she had him up against the wall, her hands about his throat and he was choking for breath.

'Get a grip on yourself,' she spat. 'You're a frekking Cadian.'

'Right, and that makes me the joke of the Imperium,' the man gasped.

She kneed him in the groin and let him drop to the floor, groaning.

'You have just struck an officer!' he cursed, and waved a hand at her. There were dark shapes on his jacket sleeve, where previous badges had been removed. 'That is a capital offence within Penal Regulation A-248.'

'Frekk you!' she said, and kicked him in the balls.

FIVE

It was not just the Brotherhood and the Cadians who had made the crossing from Marquis aboard the *Kossak Blade*. Hidden in the ballast decks in the miles-long superstructure were thousands of souls who had, over the course of the last six months, been driven like a bow wave before the forces of heresy, and stowed away by unscrupulous sub-lieutenants and mid-deck ensigns. Hivers, traders, nobility and their bastards had all bought passage from warzone to planet with whatever they could sell or steal, and the crews of the *Kossak Blade* had grown rich, selling berths within the bowels of their ship.

One of those was a young man named Carkal Struff.

He paid a prince's ransom for the journey, and when he'd been ferried aboard among the promethium scuttles and cargo-tugs, he'd assumed that he had reached safety.

And he'd learnt that assumptions were as frail as wind-blown smoke.

* * *

Six months earlier Carkal Struff had been an artist's apprentice, mixing paints in the studio of his master, the portrait artist Gustav Rinkkenti, on the hive world of Guardia Rex. He had thought himself set for a good life. Everyone had told him that he was on the ladder to fame and wealth. His guardian, Agatha, had declared it on the day his apprenticeship started. She had patted his shoulders and said, 'It's a fine appointment. Especially for the son of a still master. An especially lucky chance for an orphan.'

Yes, Carkal had thought sardonically. I'm lucky, *for an orphan.*

Carkal's father, while he had lived, had been the sole male representative of a branch of mid-hive traders with links to all the main settlements of Guardia Rex. Their particular hive, Reshon, had prospered since the last member of the ruling house had died childless, and an oligarchy of chief trading families had assumed control. The whole hive seemed energised as light-shafts were cleaned and repaired, and mid-hivers saw sunlight for the first time, and production in the lower factoria had risen precipitously.

All this was of passing concern to Carkal. He had been a child when the oligarch had taken over, but it had brought wealth to his family's business, which was to filter toxins from the water sump and sell sterile water back upwards.

But there were inherent dangers with such trade. While sterile water was one product of the purification process, the other was concentrated toxins that caused itching skin rashes and malignant growths among the work-gangs. And the more the factoria boomed, the more filth there was to deal with.

Cancers had eaten away at his mother when he was a boy. His only memories of her were as a thin husk of a woman, propped up in bed, wheezing through a bloodstained cloth.

Carkal had stood by her bedside, stiff with emotion. Everyone about him spoke in whispers, and at some point he had realised that his mother was going to die.

It was an odd time. Death was beyond his understanding then. But he was probably no more than six or seven, and Agatha, their housekeeper, had held him to her ample bosom, which felt comforting and safe in a way his parents never had.

He couldn't remember his mother dying, but he remembered her coffin, before it was sold. Only up-hivers could afford the luxury of a true burial. Hive cities were vast termite mounds of humanity, and like termites, which cannibalised their dead, human cadavers were sold to be boiled down and recycled. In his mother's case, no doubt, she was rendered into constituent parts that fed into the underhive economy. That had not struck him as odd. He had been a termite, then, like all the others.

Carkal didn't remember his father that clearly. He'd managed to be both distant and indulgent, and had followed his wife into the rendering pits when Carkal was twelve. Carkal remembered the journey to the under-gate with the coffin, where a party of underhivers were waiting, all of them dressed in long, black coats and black, broad-brimmed hats, their pinching fingers clad in fingerless leather gloves.

'Greetings up-'iver,' the gang chief had said, putting his hand to his hat. He was a short, thin man, with a thin nose and long fingers.

He'd taken the coffin and assessed the body, then weighed it, and counted out the credits.

He had six fingers, Carkal remembered very clearly, and a goatee, and sagging skin that showed the red under his eyeballs.

'Good luck to you, up-'iver,' he'd said, and put his hand to his hat. 'We'll be seeing you as well, some day, no doubt. Not me, I'm sure. I'll be boiled down to soup by then as well.'

He cackled at his own joke, which Carkal didn't understand at first.

'What does he mean he'll see me one day?' he asked Agatha, and she pursed her lips and did not answer at first.

'Well,' she said. 'I suppose he means we all end up as underhivers, one way or another.'

Carkal had not ended up in the underhive. That, at least, seemed a small victory.

His share in the recycling business was taken by the remaining uncles, and when his father's debts were settled in full, it transpired that his father had never been much good with money.

Investments in a new trading fleet had failed, and Hive Reshon's booming economy had provided ample opportunity for scammers. It soon became clear that there was no way Carkal could remain in his family home. His mother's ceremonial clothes and his father's jewellery were sold off, and the next day bailiffs arrived with their shock-rods and autoguns, and Carkal was ejected from the hundred square feet of reactor-side apartment that he'd called his home.

Luckily for him, Agatha had connections with a skyside portrait painter named Rinkkenti, who had a seventyfifth-layer studio, and earnt a good living painting the illegitimate offspring of the Richstars, minor mistresses and their myriad pets.

'They'll teach you,' she'd assured him, and she had not lied.

As a young man of education and standing, Carkal had taken up a position between the painter's family and the servants. He'd been well educated, by the standards of the time, and could recite the philosophy of Trezn and the poetry of Delada. His learning amused Rinkkenti, and when Carkal's duties were finished his master had started teaching him simple draftsmanship with a carbon stick.

Rinkkenti had long moustaches and an aquila tattoo beneath one narrowed eye. 'Maybe you can be a painter too,' Rinkkenti had mused, and nodded to himself. 'Keep working hard, my lad.'

'I will, master. I promise!'

And Rinkkenti had nodded and smiled. 'Good, my lad. Good.'

Carkal *had* worked hard, and showed such promise that he'd graduated within two years to be a grinder of paints.

'It's an honoured position,' Rinkkenti had told him, and Carkal had learnt to take precious stones and mix them with oil and rare xantha gum from as far away as the sector capital on Regis Prime. He'd even been allowed to sit in on the portrait of a woman named Ezmerelda Flowers, who spoke with a crisp up-hive accent, and wore a high-ruff and a shawl of gold leaf, carried by a matched pair of silver-plated servo-skulls.

Carkal had never seen someone who'd been through rejuvenat before. There was something almost inhuman about the stretched skin, full lips and taut smile, and Carkal had sat, hunched over the desk, grinding golden flecks into albumen, bewitched by the sight of her. He wondered how many mid-hive lifetimes the madam had enjoyed. She had to be a hundred or more. Maybe two hundred.

'She's three hundred years old,' the painter's daughter, Elope, had told him that night, as they sat in the cupboard under the family's own water-tank, a rare luxury fed by spire-gutters, and dreamt of what they would do when they grew old enough to leave the generously named 'sky-side', and perhaps go up a hive-level.

'How many levels up shall we go?' Elope mused.

Carkal puffed out his cheeks. He couldn't really imagine. 'Three,' he said. It seemed like an impossible number and she snuggled into his arm as if he had promised to take her to the very peak of the hive, a mile above their heads.

Three levels higher, he thought. What wonders would be hidden up there?

Elope was a pretty little thing, with black hair, nut-brown skin and dark eyes. Carkal had promised to paint her when he grew up. 'You'd make such a beautiful picture,' he had told her, and she'd lowered her face and looked at him from under her thick locks.

'Do you think so?'

'Yes,' he said. 'Very much so. Much more than Madam Ezmerelda.'

Elope laughed and in that moment Carkal had thought of his own mother, and how she had died young.

'It isn't right,' he said. 'This world we live in.'

'No?' she said.

'No,' he told her. 'I mean. We should marry.'

She blanched at that word, and there was a nervous tremor in her voice when she hushed him up.

'Well, I don't know how we can wait for me to graduate,' he said. 'My mother died when she was only twenty-seven. If we wait till then, we could both be dead.'

Carkal had started flirting with low-hive radicals at around the same time as the forces of the Scourged arrived on his home world.

The Scourged were *heretics* and had taken the hive of Annenn after a three-month siege. Their warlord was named Drakul-zar. Carkal had no idea what he looked like, but imagined a dark shadow, with roaring flames about him, and glittering red eyes. He was fearless, unstoppable, insatiably hungry.

No one seemed surprised that Drakul-zar's warriors had taken Annenn.

Annenn was a hive that had been in terminal decline ever since its ore deposits had become too deep to mine. The ruling branches of its ruling house had been feuding for generations, and last anyone had heard, the two main branches were holed up in their respective towers, while the central hive had fallen into ruin. It was the kind of settlement that would fall to heretics.

But the arrival of the Scourged had given the other hive rulers a moment to put aside their trade rivalry and tariff monopolies and act in concert. In this, they had showed ineptitude on a gross scale. Within weeks Hive Afos had fallen, and it was followed in quick succession by the thriving hives of Leadburg and Ararat.

No one could understand how a small number of heretics could penetrate defences so quickly. 'Heretic' had barely ever been mentioned in polite, mid-hive conversation. If it was ever spoken it was in a horrified whisper, behind closed doors. But now, many started to look for ways of escaping from the planet before their own hive fell under the relentless progress of the Scourged.

Carkal's idealism told him that he should stand and fight, but he had put that aside when the Rinkkenti household had used their connections with the Richstar family to get passage to the planet's central-hive-cum-starport, Stellata.

They travelled at night, as most hivers did when exposed to the outside world.

When the thick brown smog cleared briefly, the sight of the sky terrified them all.

Carkal hung on to his sanity as tightly as he held on to the frock coats of Master Rinkkenti. They moved from trading post to mine-dome, and then from planet to planet, as the Scourged swept all before them.

But with each transit the cost became more and more expensive, and at the shrine world of Ignatz not even Rink-kenti's connections with the Richstars could help them.

'Sorry, Carkal,' Rinkkenti had said on the steps of the God-Emperor's shrine in Ignatz's Spiral City. 'But I cannot afford to bring you this time. I have only enough credits left for my wife and daughters.'

'What will happen to me?' Carkal asked and the old painter patted him on the head.

'I don't know. But you're a bright lad,' he said. 'You'll work something out.'

Carkal had gone that night to say goodbye to Elope. She had been crying, and Carkal flattered himself that her tears were because of him.

'I've come to say goodbye,' he said, and she stared at him, sniffed and nodded. But she gave him nothing. Not a smile, or a token or even a kind word.

'You'd better go now,' Elope's mother said, her hands on his shoulders as she showed him to the lodging door. He'd always found her a rather stiff woman, but as he left she gave him a pouch of coins and food for a week, and sent him out into Spiral City with the words, 'May the Emperor protect you,' before closing the door.

The Emperor had protected. Carkal found himself almost thriving in Spiral City, and through a combination of education, charm and a fast tongue he ended up falling in with a grain merchant who was stockpiling food. Having stolen what credits he needed, Carkal blagged or bought himself passage from Rampo to Quence, from Ardsley to Brey's Watch, staying ever ahead of the tide of heresy.

But Carkal realised that he could not afford to keep jumping just one step ahead of the enemy. He had to leap-frog deep into Imperial territory. Gossip in the Spice Mazaar said that the Imperial Navy was picketing the inner worlds, drawing a line past which the Scourged could not pass.

'Well, they haven't stopped the heretics yet,' he heard one man say to another.

His companion nodded. 'If I was to go anywhere, I'd go to Potence. The Richstars won't let their ancestral home fall.'

Potence.

That name had lodged in Carkal's memory and come to symbolise safety, rest, a place beyond danger. And it was to Potence that he set his sights.

He managed to stow away with a lighter that was taking Munitorum families onto a defence monitor named the *Belle Époque*. They transited to the promethium rigs above Telken's Rest, and then they switched to a vast fuel transport – the largest craft Carkal had ever seen – for the hop to the trading world of Malori. There they docked at Orbital City, where the defences had been hastily reinforced by a pair of Dauntless-class cruisers in the faded colours of Battlefleet Cadia. Carkal had a brief view of them, their sleek shapes silhouetted against the light of the nearest sun. As he was transferred onto a troop carrier it all appeared in order, but someone, somewhere, had taken an excessive cut, and by the time the stowaways were transferred to the *Kossak Blade*, they had no credit or connections to bribe the lower deck hands. They argued and shouted, but they had no choice. Ship law was harsh. It was void-venting or compliance.

The whole complement of refugees became allies as they were herded down into the subterranean darkness of the ballast decks – mile-long chambers, each one filled with putrid bilge water and toxic coolants that dripped from the vast brass pipes above their heads.

At first the lower deck hands shared their food with them. But the refugees were too numerous, too hungry, and after they beat one of the deck hands for bringing too little, the hatch doors remained shut. Without adequate food or water, friendships and alliances broke down.

It was man against man, family against individual.

Only the cruellest would survive.

Carkal realised early on that no one was coming for them.

Some of the stowaways had brought supplies of rice, or flour, or slab with them. They hid it as best they could, gathered in clandestine groups for hurried repast in secluded corners. Secrecy was their chief safeguard, and also their chief vulnerability.

To be alone with food made you a target.

Carkal's first victim was a young man named Owwan. He was roughly Carkal's own age, with a nervous voice and wide blue eyes, and claimed to be a silk merchant from Stanbol. Carkal had spoken to him many times before their transfer to the *Kossak Blade*. They'd even played regicide together.

But that was before, and this was now.

Carkal had lain on a narrow shelf, and waited for Owwan to make the usual trip back from the water tap.

Owwan had splashed his way under the frigid coolant pipes, moving surreptitiously, like a thief, then there was a pause, and in the darkness Carkal heard the unmistakeable wet sound of eating. Of food being bitten and chewed and swallowed.

Carkal had been so hungry then that his first reaction was that Owwan had betrayed him.

In his fury his fingers had tightened over the end of a rusted iron bar that he kept as a weapon against other predators.

Owwan was eating, Carkal raged. Without sharing.

In his madness he leant forward and peered down. Owwan was hunched over a leather bag that he held to his mouth.

The sound of a bar hitting a human head had surprised Carkal. It was a dull, muffled thud, followed by a splash as the other lad hit the water.

And then it was done.

It was that easy.

Carkal slid down, ankle-deep in bilge water. Owwan's muscles twitched, but he did not rise, and soon he lay altogether still.

Carkal found the bag of rations floating a few feet away. The hard-baked ship biscuit was sodden, but he did not care. It was food.

He swallowed it all but his stomach growled for more, and there was no more to give it. He needed more.

That night, Carkal's guts rebelled against the food that he had murdered for, as if a hand were wringing them out.

When Owwan's body was found there had been an outcry. Carkal had joined in with the others. He had wept and silently sworn that he would not kill again. But after two more days of hunger his stomach spoke louder than his guilt.

Next time he was less cautious.

'Give me that food!' he had hissed as he came upon a short, balding man, hidden in a dark corner of the bilge tanks. The man's name was Frust, or something like that. Carkal couldn't remember exactly. Frust had been a dragoman operating out of Orbital City who had cashed in his silk futures at the right moment.

A man who had got lucky, like Carkal himself. Until his luck ran out, of course, when Carkal decided to kill him.

'I'll make it quick,' Carkal had promised, but Frust had turned to run, splashing through the water, and Carkal had rushed after him. It had been a desperate pursuit, under pipes, over sumps, along a tunnel that forced Carkal to bend double, Frust shouting all the time for help.

The chase ended when Frust tripped.

There was a noisy splash and Carkal was on him before he could stand.

'Please!' Frust had gasped, his voice echoing along the endless pipes. But no aid came.

'Shut up!' Carkal had hissed. The bar had broken Frust's arm as he tried to protect his head. The arm-bone broke in three places and the man's hand flopped uselessly.

Carkal didn't finish it immediately. He was angry and frightened and his fear made him lash out. Blood gouted from Frust's mouth as Carkal ate the dragoman's food.

Frust's mouth bubbled red as he tried to speak.

'Shut up!' Carkal said again, as he crouched by Frust's head.

Frust's eyes were closed. The word was faint.

'Did you say "Mother"?' Carkal demanded.

The word came again.

It made Carkal angry. 'We all want our mothers,' Carkal had told him, licking the crumbs from his fingers. But he felt guilty now, and took Frust's head and forced it under the water.

A few bubbles rose. Carkal did not want to know what words were being said beneath the water. He could not bear this thing that he had become, and he held Frust's head down until the bubbles stopped, and then cursed all mothers.

Especially his own for dying so young.

Carkal became a ghost.

A haunter.

A hunter.

He became less human and more animal, and in the weeks that followed there were many others that Carkal killed. The weak, the old, the unlucky.

Afterwards the guilt pains wracked him. He was not proud. But there was no other way. He had to survive until the ship arrived at Potence, and then they would open the bilge gates and let them out, and he would be safe. Maybe he could go back to grinding paints, and even painting for himself. He entertained himself by imagining Elope. How chance would throw them together again. How she would have fallen on hard times that he could save her from. That it would all turn out alright in the end.

The fantasy ending was powerful and compulsive. Carkal believed in it as devoutly as a religion. Something better would come.

The days – if there were such things in the madness of the warp – merged into each other. But at some point in the journey he heard the whine of the Geller drive powering down, and then the dull roar of the engines as the plasma drives woke. Understanding washed through him like warmth after a long winter.

He heard the gurgle of coolant in the pipes above.

Heat returned, and the bilge decks began to steam, and the air became a stinking sauna of noxious gas. The water pipes had long since run dry, and gangs now ran the water-licks, so he was forced to suck condensation off the walls until his tongue was stained with rust and oil.

After a period of darkness that might have been days or weeks, there were new sounds from above. The thuds and clangs of lifts operating across the ship. He grew giddy then.

He pictured Elope, and swore on her soul that he would not kill again for food. He held on to her image as day by day the sounds of activity came deeper into the belly of the ship. At last the sound was of many footsteps descending a metal staircase above his head. He put his hand to the low ceiling. He could feel the vibrations. There were people on the deck just above where he stood. He could feel their footfalls, could hear the muffled banter as they tried the bilge hatches.

The human within him began to return. He started to speak again, and when ship ratings brought abhumans down to pry the heat-distorted hatches open, Carkal could feel the heavy thud of their feet, could hear the moans and dull thunder of their hobnailed boots. He shouted up, 'I'm here! I'm here!'

His voice sounded thin as it echoed through the long chambers. It rang back to him from left and right. 'Let me out!' he shouted, and the words came back as if from a hundred voices, and he started weeping and screaming.

When the light came it was like a stiletto blade to his eyes.

He howled with pain and put up his hands as if to ward off a blow.

Tears flooded down his face as he fell back.

'I'm here,' he croaked, and then he felt a hand on his.

'Up you come,' a voice said, and hands reached down and pulled him up from the darkness.

SIX

At Intake Barracks, Minka was still getting used to the idea of her promotion.

'So what happens next?' Minka asked Dido.

'You have to report to regimental offices. Sparker will want to talk to you. Give you a little pep talk. Make sure you're the right material for command and all.'

The regimental offices were still being set up at the north side of the barrack square. Major Kastelek strode inside with a trail of adjutants and officials hurrying behind him. In his wake there was the usual assortment of injured Guardsmen, sentry details and uncertain troopers holding forms that needed filling in and marking with appropriate stamps.

Minka mounted the steps. Two grunts from A Company were standing at attention. She saluted them and passed inside, put her shoulders back as she caught sight of Colonel Baytov. He was a broad block of a man, with a strong jaw and the look of a man who was content to send his forces into a meat grinder if it would bring a speedy victory. But he was liked as well because he didn't waste lives unnecessarily.

At this moment he was striding down the corridor to his office. His presence only added to the atmosphere of nervous bustle. His voice echoed off the walls. It conveyed a sense of stress and growing irritation.

'We're the first Imperial presence on Potence...' he was arguing. 'So we're directing the defence of the entire system at the same time as we're reorganising the entire regiment. Did anyone think this through?'

If anyone answered, Minka didn't hear it.

But then she heard Baytov's voice again. 'Well. Thank Throne for that!'

Minka found it hard to feel much relief at Baytov's exclamation.

In times of war, populations looked to the Cadians to bring backbone and discipline. Just their presence helped settle the nerves of unsteady governors and local auxiliaries. But if the 101st were spearheading the defence of the whole warzone then that meant a stack of extra administrative detail to wade through: intelligence reports, surveys of local loyalties, faction analysis, strength of defence networks, abilities of local commanders and troops. Three years ago the 101st had managed such crises well. But now... having been decimated in repeated campaigns, it would be a tall order, even for Cadians.

She suddenly realised why she had been promoted. A voice in her head said it was not because of her skill or ability. It was because everyone else was dead, and they'd finally started reaching down to the bottom of the pit.

She gritted her teeth and tried to dismiss this fear, but it clung to her. She tried to find her company office. No one knew where it was. Hectic confusion reigned. The 101st was being brought back to full fighting strength with the scraps of four regiments. Clerks and administrative staff were trying to find desk space, while the top brass were starting to dig through precarious stacks of brown card-files. Almost everyone of rank had just been promoted or delegated dead men's duties. Newly promoted captains and lieutenants met their military secretaries, and tried to get a grip on their new administrative responsibilities.

At last she found M Company's desk. It was at the far end of the corridor behind the ornate brass samovar, which had a yellowed paper note slung about the tap that read 'Awaiting repair'.

The desk was a camp table with thin legs and a battered wooden surface. Sitting behind it was Sergeant Tyson. He was talking to Putben. Minka had come across Putben in the medicae wards. He'd broken his arm on Marquis, and it was still in a sling. He'd been made sergeant as well. Clearly, he was not pleased with the appointment. He had stooped shoulders, stripped unit badges and a day's stubble.

They exchanged words as Minka took her place behind Putben, and she heard Tyson's response. 'Listen. We're *all* dealing with shit up to our necks. You're nothing special. Now get in there and see Colonel Sparker.'

Sergeant Tyson was a short, muscled man with a shaved head and strong, jutting chin, his meaty fists held together on a leather-topped desk. His violet eyes had cold, clear centres, with shocking dark rims and long lashes. Minka stepped forward and saluted. He had a hard look in his eye as he reached for a file at the side of the desk.

'So you've heard,' he said, with no warmth in his voice, leafing through for the sheet he wanted.

At last he pulled it out and gave it to her. A list of names and a brown paper bag with 101st insignia badges. 'These are your troopers. Get them to stitch these on. Today. We've been sent some real dregs. See what you can do with them. The commissars are edgy. I don't want any of M Company to be shot. Understand?' Tyson gave Minka a short, hard look. His pale eyes were chilling. She understood perfectly. Tyson nodded towards the platoon office.

'As soon as Putben is done, get in there.'

Putben's face was even redder when he came out. 'Frekking mess this is,' he muttered as Minka stepped forward, knocked smartly and waited for the call.

When she stepped inside, Colonel Sparker was sitting at his desk, looking in a drawer. He had a frustrated expression on his face, as if he had just lost something. 'Come in!' he waved, and stood up. 'You're…?'

'Arminka Lesk, sir. I've just been transferred to M Company.'

He shook her hand, a perfunctory gesture, and waved her to sit down. 'Please,' he said. 'So. As you know, we're returning the regiment to full strength. Officers are from the 101st. Troops are largely from restructured units. We've troopers from three regiments. I think you have eleven troopers in your squad. No, twelve.' He held up a piece of paper to read through the list.

'That's not normal, sir.'

He sighed. '*Nothing* is normal at the moment, Lesk.'

She nodded. 'I've met some of the new lot already.'

He read her face. 'Hmm. Yes. Luckily we've got time to get them into shape. That's what I want you to do. I need them ready when the Emperor calls. You were on Cadia, weren't you?'

Minka's face flushed, despite herself. 'Yes, sir.' There was a pause. 'Everyone here seems pretty panicked. How long do we have until the forces of heresy are here? I mean, we were told that this was a peaceful place.'

'Yes.' He took in a deep breath. 'Unfortunately we have less time than we were led to believe. Much less. While we were in transit the forces of the heretics have made unprecedented advances. Nothing immediate to worry about, of course. The Imperial Navy have a squadron of cruisers that have thrown a picket across the Dellax Gap and the battleship *Admiral Pesaquid* is leading a squadron from Battlefleet Terra to reinforce them.'

'Battlefleet Terra. Is that normal?'

'As I said. *Nothing* is normal.' He paused. 'Think of it as a sign of the strategic importance that is now being placed on the Gallows Cluster. In a month or so, there will be hundreds of regiments arriving. What we have to do is to make sure things are organised before they get here, so they can hit the ground running. What you have to do is to make sure you get your squad battle-fit. Understood?'

'Yes, sir.'

'Good.' He half stood and put out his hand to shake and spoke in a faintly jocular tone. 'Well done. Take command and remind them what it means to be Cadian.'

Minka saluted and left. She walked back to the barracks and took out the paper, looking at the names of her new squad. Corporal Arktur; Troopers Belus, Dreno, Emersan, Jaromir, Jason, Lasmonn, Donson, Rustem, Silas, Thaddeus and Viktor.

She checked their backgrounds. Two had come from the Black Dragons, six from the 966th Rifles and three from the Redskulls. Viktor was the only other trooper from the 101st. He'd come from First Platoon. He seemed solid enough.

She folded the paper and slipped it back into her breast pocket.

At that moment they were just names on a list, but already she felt protective of them. She found herself suddenly full of opinions about the kind of squad she wanted to lead. They should be the toughest. The smartest. The fittest. She paused and took a deep breath. They should be the fiercest frekkers in the segmentum this side of the Cicatrix Maledictum.

There was a brief ceremony that evening at 2100 hours.

Minka was in a line of ten newly appointed officers in the pool of light outside the HQ entrance. They stood at ease before the flag staff, where the 101st banner hung in the still, warm air.

The bells of the cathedral started to ring, and Sergeant Tyson had to raise his voice to be heard. They snapped to attention as Colonel Sparker stepped out. He moved down the line. Minka ground her teeth together as he stopped before her. Tyson stood at the colonel's side as he pinned the three stripes onto her left arm. She felt the emotion rise within her, and bit the inside of her cheek, returned the colonel's salute.

As Colonel Sparker moved along to the last of the promoted officers, Minka looked down at the three embroidered chevrons and felt a dreadful responsibility. It was as if the Emperor Himself were standing behind her. Judging her. Finding her lacking.

At the end Confessor Keremm arrived to give them all the Emperor's benediction.

Keremm was a short, bearded man, with wide-set, intense brown eyes. He had been born on Tolukan, chief hive of Macharius, and his arms were covered in tattoos that chronicled his rise from indentured labourer to his final position as armsman, first class, on board the Vengeance-class cruiser *Vigilanti Eternas*, of Battlefleet Cadia. But he had never satisfactorily explained how he'd gone from armsman to confessor.

He moved along the line with raised fingers and a quick, mumbled prayer. After a few muttered words in High Gothic, he said, 'So. You got stripes, Sergeant Lesk.'

Minka nodded.

'You don't seem pleased.'

'I am,' she said.

'But?'

'Well. I got the new lot.'

'And that's bad?'

'Some of them are. Haven't you seen them?'

'No. Not yet. They've been in political training all day.'

'With the bats?' 'Bats' was the name that the Cadians gave the members of the Commissariat. It was the commissars' role to enforce devotion to the Emperor and iron discipline. 'Were any of them shot?'

'Not that I heard of.'

'Shame. I met a frekker yesterday on grinweed.'

The confessor pulled a face. 'Oh dear. I have them tomorrow for basic scripture.'

'The Emperor is my shield and my sword and my bayonet. All that stuff?'

'Yes.' He nodded to himself, and said, 'Well, good luck!'

Next morning there was a general kit inspection. The regiment paraded in company order. M Company were due to parade at midday. Minka found her troopers after breakfast. She shook the hands of each of them, and said 'Welcome to the 101st' and gave them their badges. 'I want these on by parade. Understood?'

Each of them had nodded. A few seemed pleased, but most of them had an air of apathy that she found challenging.

She'd scanned through their service records.

Thaddeus, Silas, Donson, Rustem, Dreno and Belus were all from the Rifles. The first four seemed solid enough. Rustem was the only other woman. She must once have had the kind of physique that would have been described as boyish, before the years of service. Now she was a sandy-haired whip of a woman stitched together with scars. She had a veteran badge on her chest and greying hair.

Dreno and Belus were from the last two drafts that had got off Cadia. Minka took an almost instantaneous dislike to them. She'd seen their like before. They didn't like having a woman in charge, and from their manner she could tell that they were hyenas. They'd nip at her heels, wait until she was down, then go for her throat.

The two blond fighters were Jaromir and Jason. They were both from the Black Dragons. They had fresh drake tattoos on their arms, the symbol of their old regiment picked out with simple barrack-yard artistry. Jaromir was a magnificent-looking man, tall and broad as a power-lifter. His medical assessment was borderline. In better years he'd have retired to the reserves. He'd taken a bolt shell to the head five years back. 'Has squint and reduced verbal ability. Serviceable,' the medicae's report had said. Minka promised herself that she'd keep him alive. Jason seemed eager, at least.

Viktor Blahk was the only one of her squad from the 101st. He was a thin, quiet man still carrying a shrapnel wound from Marquis. She'd expected him to be upset about not being made sergeant but as they lined up he had sought her out and shaken her hand. It was a firm, friendly shake. 'Congratulations.'

'Thanks.'

'Better you than me. I'm honoured to be serving under you.'

She thought he was making a joke at first, but his face seemed sincere and she smiled and thanked him.

'Well, thanks,' she said. 'I appreciate that.'

The rest were Redskulls. They lingered at the rear. Lasmonn and Emersan. She shook their hands, and then the last man stepped forward – Arktur. He greeted her with a limp and unfriendly smile. His face seemed familiar. She looked at him for a moment, trying to think why, and then realisation hit her like a splash of water.

Her corporal was the frekker from the day before.

He'd shaved and washed, but it was *him*.

'How are your balls?' she said. 'Still think you're the joke of the Imperium?'

'Yes.'

'I'm going to change your mind.'

'Going to kick me again?'

'Yes,' she said. 'If I have to.'

He did not shake her hand. There was mockery in his salute as he turned and followed the others back to their barracks.

By the time Minka got back to her dormitory, the M Company whistle was blowing. She cursed as she shoved a blanket and rain cape into her pack, flipped the lid closed and ran out into the drill yard.

She wasn't the last, she saw with relief. So much had changed that everyone was a little confused. At least her squad had arrived on time. She ran her eye over them. Twelve troopers with their kit.

She went along the line quickly. There was too much to sort out and too little time.

The order came for them to stand at attention. 'Look smart,' she ordered and hurried to her position at the end of the line.

They weren't well turned out, she knew, though they'd made something of an effort.

Tyson gave them a brief going over. He was pretty gentle on the new lot. She could see him and Medicae Banting exchanging looks as they moved through Second Squad. Thankfully Minka's squad were not the worst. Arktur was there, and only Dreno got a dressing down for dirt on his boots, while Jaromir was not holding his weapon properly.

'Sorry, sir. Not used to the carbine,' he apologised. 'I came from an infantry regiment. We had lasrifles.'

Tyson helped him get the grip right and then nodded and moved along. He gave Viktor's jacket a dusting down. Troopers of the 101st were held to a higher standard.

Minka tensed as he moved on to her. She braced her shoulders back until her shoulder blades were almost touching. The stripe-badge on her arm was still stiff. His scrutiny ran over her, feet first.

'All good, sergeant?' he asked at the end.

Minka gave a brief answer. 'Yes, sir.'

'Keep their standards up,' he said.

She nodded.

At that moment there was a dull rumble. In an instant the Cadians stiffened like a pack of hunting dogs that had caught a whiff of prey. Minka remained at attention, shoulders back, face forward.

Tyson turned and looked to the guards on the parapet. There was a plume of white smoke rising into the clear blue sky above the Evercity. Another bomb, Minka thought.

'Someone find out what the hell happened there,' Tyson ordered, then turned to the company and gave the order to fall out.

'You will not believe who's in my squad,' Minka said.

Dido didn't bother trying to guess.

'That frekker from yesterday,' said Minka.

'The one you kicked?'

'Yes.'

'Speak to Tyson. Get him transferred. Throne. I'll take him.'

Minka paused. 'I can't. I mean, what will people think if I pull strings? I'll sort him out. Get him straight.'

Dido made a face. There was a long pause. 'So, what do you think?'

'About what?'

'That explosion today. Did you hear what Tyson said?'

'Yeah. Promethium fumes?'

They threw their packs onto their beds, taking off their uniforms.

Dido hung her jacket up at the end of her bed. One side of her mouth was lifted in a kind of smile. 'That's what the enforcers said yesterday.'

Minka paused. She didn't want to be the source of unfounded rumours, but Dido was a fellow sergeant, and, knowing the Astra Militarum, it would soon be common knowledge. She lowered her voice. 'Listen. Sparker told me that the Scourged are advancing faster than expected. Much faster. The Navy are picketing the Dellax Gap.'

'Well. Remember what happened last time we relied on the Navy.' She was talking about the Battle for Cadia. Dido pulled her combat jacket from the three-drawered chest at the side of their bunk and pulled it on. 'No wonder there's such a panic on. Better get your squad into shape. Looks to me like the Scourged might be here already.'

'On Potence?'

'Well, either that or there's a hell of a promethium problem on this planet.'

SEVEN

The ration hall was accessed through a double staircase in the south-western corner of the barracks. Brass chimneys vented a mix of hot air and the scent of whatever slop the chefs were serving up.

Minka paused at the noticeboard by the doorway.

Her squad were up for patrols that afternoon. She went around the long trestle tables, making sure her troopers knew.

'Parade in half an hour,' she told them all.

'We've just paraded,' Arktur said.

She wanted to punch him, but smiled pleasantly. 'Yes. But this time it's in combat gear.'

She should have done this earlier, Minka realised. But she'd only just been made sergeant, and she was learning. Better now than never, she told herself. Stamp her authority on them all. So when the dozen troopers assembled she cleared her throat and started the speech that she had been practising in her head.

'I've met you all individually, but now we're all together I want to do this formally. For those of you who don't know, my name is Arminka Lesk. Veteran of Cadia. Trooper of the 101st for three years. This is my first command and I'm proud to be leading you. I tell you here and now that I expect the best from myself. And I expect the best from my squad. I don't care what has happened before – I know what fine fighters you can all be. I want you to be the first into battle, the last to fall back. I want the dead to pile up before our lines. I want the enemy to single us out for destruction, and when the artillery bombardment begins, we will have already moved forward, to engage them in combat. I want your bayonets red with the blood of heretics!'

She had meant for the speech to be rousing, but the response from the squad was muted.

She went through their combat gear. Jaromir was still struggling with the carbine. Rustem's bayonet was soiled around the handle and Belus had his webbing too loose. Arktur was a mess. She stood before him and looked at him in disgust.

She didn't know where to start.

'Jonas Arktur. You are a corporal in the Cadian Shock Troopers. Look at you. Have some respect for yourself!'

'I know all about respect.'

'Then look like it! We're going out on patrol today. We are the head of this squad. You and me. We've got to be working together.'

'Right,' he said. His tone was not conciliatory.

She had said all she could without losing her cool. She moved on, but she barely saw the rest of the squad.

At the end she stood back and counted down from ten before she made her announcement. 'We're due to go out on patrol at seventeen hundred hours. After yesterday, and this morning's explosions, I think we can expect trouble. I want all eyes out for anything unusual. Full combat gear. Spare powercells. Reassemble sixteen hundred hours. That is all.'

They saluted and fell out.

The squad reappeared for patrol on time and with the right kit. Minka inspected the Chimera with Breve. She didn't know much about the vehicles, and she could tell that Breve was waiting to see if she knew the tricks and shortcuts that drivers used.

'Listen,' she said. 'I don't know anything about Chimeras, except that they take me to the battle and keep me and my squad from getting killed. If you were a sergeant then what would you look out for?'

Breve showed her briefly what to look for. 'This is where the unctions are poured. Overfill it and the seals will burst. Simple error.'

She was more confident with the weapon mountings. 'Make sure they're oiled and armed. You got any of the new lot as crew?'

'The gunner. Jinkan.'

'What's he like?'

'Seems solid.'

'Great. So listen. My orders are to get out to the tent city. Impose some order and assess if it's the kind of place that could be harbouring heretics. Can you take us there?'

Breve laughed. 'Of course. Hard to miss it.'

When her squad were ready they piled in. Minka swung in last, and helped lock the rear ramp back into place.

The Chimera rocked them back and forth as they wound down the narrow acropolis highways towards the upper level of the Evercity.

Minka tried to make conversation but each effort ended in an awkward silence. Rustem had her eyes closed, her lips moving in a prayer. Thaddeus held his bayonet up to inspect the cutting edge. It was newly oiled and whetted. He wiped an excess of oil away on his sleeve and then returned it to its sheath. Jason had a bandolier of grenades over his shoulder, and was checking the launcher's magazine feed. Jaromir was staring straight ahead. There was a twitch in the corner of his eye that he did not seem to notice. It kept tugging at the scars at the side of his eye. She had to look away.

Last of all she looked at Arktur. He had his eyes closed, and mouth open. He looked as though he were about to start snoring. 'Arktur!' she snapped. 'Stay alert.'

Her corporal's eyes blinked opened. He put a finger to his head in a desultory salute and Minka's cheeks coloured.

From the corner of her eye she saw Dreno and Belus exchange a smirk.

Frekkers, she thought and looked instinctively towards Viktor. His gaze was forward, at his carbine, which was freshly cleaned and polished. He felt her looking at him, and glanced across the armoured interior. He said nothing, made no gesture, but she knew he was with her.

She puffed out her cheeks. They were entering the upper circuits of the Evercity. She was tense. She took in a deep breath. Her shoulders ached.

They wound down through the city streets for an hour. She got brief views of the steps to once-grand houses, the moulded facades now faded with sunlight, chipped by passing vehicles, or worn away by the repeated touches of many hands. She saw an old woman shelling beans into a galvanised zinc bowl, three children sitting with their chins in their cupped hands, staring as the Chimera passed by, and another woman and her child, sitting by the side of the street with their felt caps on the floor before them, begging.

Nothing happened. No bombs. Nothing. Just general military tedium, one of those repeated patterns of life, worn so deep they were a rut. At last the Chimera ended up in the broad flat thoroughfares of the Manufactorum Quarter. Beggars squatted on each corner, the air was brown with promethium fumes, and through the razor wire they could see gangs of indentured labourers in faded blue overalls hurrying back to their dormitory wings.

'Leaving town,' Breve voxed.

They reached the end of the city. Through the thick glass of the targeting periscopes she saw a dry moat strewn with old paper and a few pieces of broken furniture, with dirty brown effluent puddles in the bottom. There was the buzz of flies, and the stench of rot and decay.

'Heading towards tent city.'

Arktur closed his eyes again. She kept her eye on him, just in case he fell asleep. She felt Dreno and Belus watching her. After twenty minutes, Breve voxed again. *'Tent city coming up on the left.'*

'Great,' Minka said.

Dust rose as the Chimera accelerated across the flats.

'Right. Something's up. Roadblock.'

She flipped the vox-bead on. 'Who is it?'

'Not sure. But they're armed and they've driven a cargo 8 across the track.'

'Get ready,' she ordered.

There was a taut air of alertness as the Chimera started to slow. Her troopers picked up their carbines, engaged powercells, flipped the safeties off. Minka went through the same routines, checking her webbing, frag grenades, powercells, bayonet.

'*Stopping in ten seconds,*' Breve warned.

The Cadians were up and standing, weapons ready.

At that moment Minka remembered Tyson's instructions to her. 'Get out to the tent city. Impose some order on this planet.' At this point she realised she had no idea what exactly he had meant and how she was going to do this. All she had was one Chimera and a Cadian squad against hundreds of thousands, perhaps a million, refugees.

EIGHT

The light slowly strobed Carkal's face as the hydraulic elevator ascended from the bowels of the *Kossak Blade*. The whine of the hydraulics was deafening.

The refugees from the eastern reaches of the Gallows Cluster all pressed close, but none of the other stowaways would stand next to Carkal. It was as if they knew what he had done down there. Knew what he was.

They passed disused storage chambers, the reinforced munitions galleries, then up through the habitable decks where indentured crews laboured in darkness. They had brief glimpses of abhuman stokers, lit by the glow of their furnaces, and then they were into the civilised promenades where order and protocol ruled.

As the light increased, Carkal looked at his rotten clothes and leather boots. If his victims' blood stained them, then those marks were lost among the oil and filth. He rubbed at his face and months' worth of beard, matted and thick with lice and filth. He had fled his home to save himself, but now he saw that his old self had died as truly as if he had stayed on Guardia Rex.

But it was not a loss so much as a transformation. Before he had been a lapdog. Now he was a jackal.

The lift elevator platform slowed suddenly and came to a gradual halt, stopping a half-inch above the metal plates of the deck. As the doors slid back, Carkal found himself at the front. His eyes lifted from the hazard warning stripes, and he saw a line of Navy ratings staring at him, their boarding shields ready.

An officer stepped forward. He wore full combat gear – body armour, steel-reinforced boots and closed helmet with ornate cheek guards, and the black visor pulled down to his stubbled chin. In one hand he carried an assault shotgun, and in the other the restraining leash of a pair of cyber-mastiffs.

The mastiffs had bald patches where their skulls had been reinforced with ceramic plates. Tubes wormed their way into the flesh of their necks, pumping like snakes with combat stimms. They dragged the officer a foot forward, mouths lowered and open in a terrifying snarl.

'Exit is that way,' the officer shouted above the din, pointing along the broad, low metal corridor. 'Proceed with haste!'

A woman screamed as the cyber-mastiffs strained against their leashes, pulling the officer further across the metal deck plates. Their breath was a noxious combination of cheap lubricants, combat stimms and rotten meat.

The crowd began to push Carkal forward.

He cursed. The mastiffs' breath was hot in his face. He felt spittle fly from the gnashing jaws and gagged as he pushed back against the irresistible muscle of the crowd.

Bodies were thrust into the wall of boarding shields and

there was the electric crackle of a shock maul striking flesh, and a shrill scream as the victim's muscles went into paralysis. A shotgun fired. The screams were all about him now. Another firearm was unloaded. Carkal felt a sting on his cheek.

He was being pressed dangerously close to the animals. He slid sideways, and shoved the man who had been shoving him. The man tripped and fell, and the mastiffs were on him in an instant.

Carkal felt no remorse as he heard the man's cries. He pushed past the picket lines, and had a brief glimpse backwards as the man disappeared into the interweaving knot of cyber-mastiffs.

Carkal fled forward, along a wide corridor, low lumen globes flickering above his head. They ran for about a hundred yards, then there were screams as they met another line of Navy ratings, shotguns ready, more cyber-mastiffs snarling and snapping their huge jaws shut.

'Move towards the lighter!' a loudhailer voice commanded. The instructions rang out from every flat surface: the walls, the low ceiling, the metal-grilled floor. The crowd pushed him forward. Before him was a planetary lander with its loading ramp open. Yellow lumens flashed. More orders were being shouted. He saw more walls of boarding shields, the blank visored faces of the Navy ratings.

Another shotgun fired. The retort echoed through the cold hangar. The refugees panicked. Carkal pushed; he shoved. The crowd was pressing all about him. He felt the floor lift beneath his feet, and looked down to see the worn hazard stripes of the loading ramp. Armed ratings herded them like sheep onto the landing craft. More and more were crammed inside. Carkal kept shuffling. There were men, women, children. All of them were pale and terrified. Families clung on to each other.

Carkal found his place among other single young men. He felt his whole body shake with relief. He was still alive. His new home was only hours away. The wave of emotions overwhelmed him and he started to sob like a baby.

'Move forward!' The loudhailer orders kept coming. 'Move forward.'

Carkal felt himself being carried forward into a breathless crush. More and more refugees shoved aboard. Families, gangs, impromptu groups. Carkal felt the breath squeezed from his lungs. The press began to hurt. People started to shout and scream. Carkal used his fists and knees to make enough space about him, enough room to draw breath, and then finally the loading ramp was shut.

The darkness returned, but the sounds were different now. There was weeping and prayer and the low moan of people slipping to the ground and being slowly crushed to death as they experienced the tumult of planetary descent.

The descent took nearly an hour. When at last the craft landed, a nervous murmur rose from the thousands inside. They had made it to the ancient capital of the Gallows Cluster. The seat of the Richstars. In Potence, at least, they would be safe. Some wept. Some shouted their thanks to the Holy Emperor, or Saint Ignatzio.

Carkal closed his eyes and thought of food and warmth, of washing and of making a new start. He was safe, he told himself. That knowledge warmed him like bathwater. He was beyond the reach of the heretics who had torn his home from him.

The lander settled with a roar of thrusters and then there

was a long pause as locks were disengaged, and the ramp's hydraulics powered up.

As the bay doors opened he caught his first sight of this new planet. The sunlight was blinding at first. The taste of clean, fresh air restoring. He breathed it deep, and stumbled forward. The crush reversed. There were shouts and cries as some were trampled underfoot. Carkal would not fall. Not now. Not so close to his destination.

His eyes watered as he blinked in the daylight. At last he could make out white clouds, stark against the violet sky, and a damp scent of good earth; and from far off came the insistent rattle of gunfire.

The outside never ceased to amaze him. All the vagaries of nature. Wind. Light. Vegetation. Horizons. Only up-hivers could afford air so pure. For a moment he felt like a rich man as he filled his lungs again and again, and then he stood on the top of the ramp and looked out and saw a dry planet, and a white city on a high rock with golden domes at its rocky summit. Before him he saw women, children, fathers, each family clutching what meagre possessions they had managed to salvage from their home worlds. On the ship their numbers had been their protection. Now he saw that numbers would be their downfall.

He looked at them almost with pity. He was young, strong, capable. Times like this gave a young man opportunity.

Then the gunfire started again, much closer this time, and a woman before him screamed.

NINE

Minka was taut as a bowstring as they approached the tent city.

Breve's voice gave her the basic breakdown of the gangers at the roadblock. *'There's twelve of them. Seven to the left. The rest to the right.'*

As soon as the Chimera stopped, Minka commanded, 'Out!'

She went first. Number one rule of command.

There were two gangers with intricate blue tattoos covering their faces. They had red cloths wrapped about their necks and they wore old Guard-issue flak jackets. Their cheeks bulged with grinweed. One of them cradled a grenade launcher under his arm. He grinned at her. His teeth were stained dark brown. He put a finger to his temple in a salute that oozed menace.

The other was short and fat. Half of his head was shaven, while the other half was hidden behind a mop of green hair. He wore a bandolier of powercells about his neck and a broad machete at his waist.

Minka trained her carbine on him. 'Who are you?'

He did not have a pleasant smile. 'I am the Kartell,' he said. 'We are the guardians of the tent city. Who are *you*?'

'Remove your checkpoint. I am Sergeant Lesk of the 101st Cadian regiment of the Astra Militarum, of the Holy Emperor of Mankind. We proceed in His name.'

'And if I say no?'

'Then we will brush you aside.'

More gangers were crowding around. Their leader put out a hand and rubbed thumb and forefinger together. 'I say to you what I say to the enforcers. We charge for entry.'

She lifted her carbine and aimed it at his head. 'Weapons down!'

One by one the gangers dropped their guns. All except the commander.

'I'll count to three…' Minka shouted.

The ganger raised his hands to his chest in a gesture of calm. 'Let me call the boss.'

He turned and walked into the tent. There was a vox-unit behind the table. Minka cursed. She'd just let him dictate the pace of events.

She turned. Her squad had the gangers covered. Even Breve had swung the turret round. The heavy flamer hissed as it ignited. She trained her gun back onto the gang leader.

'Move slowly or I shoot,' she said.

The fat ganger put one hand to the vox-unit. He lifted the receiver. Minka's hands were sweating. The seconds ticked past – not many, but they went too slowly. Minka kept her carbine's sights on the ganger's left temple. She could remain like this for hours, if need be.

The man in the tent put the vox-unit down. She looked to him briefly as he turned towards them.

'Right,' he said, his voice rising in volume. 'The boss wants guarantees.'

'Tell him…' Minka started but at that moment someone fired. There was the flash of a las-bolt in the corner of her eye. It hit the gang leader in the thigh. He let out a snarl of pain and grabbed his pistol.

In an instant the scene erupted as gangers dived for their guns. Minka fired a double-tap into the leader, throwing him into the back of the tent. The Cadians started cutting them down. A flamer went off. A Cadian screamed. The cargo 8's heavy stubber rattled as it fired.

Minka threw herself forward as hard rounds slammed into the space where she had been. Thaddeus went down to a salvo from an autopistol. Silas cursed as he dropped his gun, wounded in the arm and shoulder.

She shouted orders, but there was no order to be imposed. This was up-close and deadly. Only training and discipline could keep them alive. She fired with clinical speed, knocking out three gangers as they charged. The first dropped his axe, the next two howled as las-bolts burned through their unprotected guts.

'Sarge!' Viktor shouted, and pointed.

Another three were scrambling to get a missile launcher loaded and primed. She hit each of them in a deadly salvo. One shot to kill and another to make sure.

As she crouched, two more gangers appeared. One carried belts of ammo over his shoulders while the other one was a pin-headed slab of muscle who lugged a rotary cannon. She started to aim, but realised she was too late.

He lowered the barrel and fired, and in an instant the air

was full of ricocheting hard rounds and swirling clouds of dust.

She threw herself behind a sand-filled barrel, and felt the thing shudder with successive impacts.

Someone cursed.

'Three troopers down!' one of her squad shouted.

Minka's first command was in danger of turning into a massacre. She didn't know how many of her squad were left alive. She rolled to the side.

A ganger leapt onto her back. She bent and threw him over her shoulder, put her boot on his throat and stamped down hard enough to crush his windpipe.

'Breve!' she shouted, not knowing if he was still alive. 'What the frekk are you doing?'

At that moment the Chimera's heavy flamer roared to life. A stream of burning promethium singed her face as it passed overhead. The gangers' command tent went up with a whoosh. There were figures within the inferno, thrashing out their last.

The cannon opened up once more. It hit the Chimera with the ringing of a thousand discordant bells.

'Someone's got to get him,' she hissed, and realised that that someone had to be her.

She crawled forward and got a glimpse through the dust. The two gangers were advancing as they fired. She aimed but the moment had gone already. She cursed silently, and waited as another salvo sprayed over her head.

'Halftrack approaching,' Viktor shouted. 'More hostiles.'

She looked east. A vehicle was speeding up from the south, its red flag stiff in the wind of its own passing.

'I'm going to take out this frekker. As soon as I do, everyone back inside. Breve! Cover us!'

There was another furious salvo. At this rate they would have to change ammo belts.

There was a brief pause, and Minka changed position, crawling along the side of the burning tent.

A body fell in front of her. A ganger, his skin burned away, showing a rictus of weeping muscle and teeth. She flinched, and then suddenly the two gangers toting the cannon were in front of her. They were trying to get around the flank as well.

The lead ganger swung the ponderous weapon round. Wisps of smoke were curling from the barrels. There was no time to aim. She fired as she rolled into the burning tent, and then the ground about her exploded.

The ganger truck arrived, travelling at high speed. It had an autocannon jury-rigged onto the back. It started firing wildly towards Viktor and the others.

'Let's get the hell out of here,' Breve shouted.

The Cadians scrambled back towards the Chimera. Jaromir appeared confused. He was looking at his gun, as if trying to work out how to fire the thing.

Viktor pushed him forward. 'Get him inside!' he told Jason.

The two Black Dragons ducked through the hatch. Jason covered Viktor as he dragged Thaddeus back into their transport. The 966th Rifles trooper had been burned along his right side. Silas had taken a hard round to the forearm.

'Where's Lesk?' Viktor demanded.

No one knew.

Viktor looked out. The air was thick with smoke and gunfire. 'Minka!' he shouted.

Breve was already closing the back ramp as he slammed the Chimera into reverse.

'Where's Lesk?' Viktor shouted up at him.

Breve didn't hear. He was shouting to the forward gunner to take out the gun-truck. The heavy bolter spat fist-sized bolts towards the enemy. As their internal propellants ignited, the heavy-calibre shells roared forward, black trails of smoke weaving one over the other.

The salvo lasted only moments, but as the smoke cleared, the wreckage of the gun-truck came into view.

'Lesk!' Breve shouted. The Chimera rattled as hard rounds slammed on its outside. More gun-trucks were speeding from north and south. 'It's like a frekking convention,' he cursed. 'Listen, we have to get out of here.'

'Just wait, damn it.' Viktor ducked out and kept low.

As he ran towards the barricades, a figure caught his leg.

A ganger playing dead. Viktor fell and twisted and kicked out with his other foot, but the other man had him fast and he cursed.

A shadow fell over him and there was the unmistakeable silhouette of a spikey gang hairstyle.

He was done for and scrabbled for his knife, but somehow it had come loose in the struggle.

'Move aside, Viktor.'

He blinked up in surprise as a las-bolt flared for a moment, and the ganger holding his feet let go.

It was Minka. There was ash and dirt and splatters of blood on her face and scorch marks on her jacket, but it was her alright. She had the gang leader thrown over her shoulder.

'Come on, Viktor. Get up and help me with this grunt.'

'Yes, Lesk!' he said, then corrected himself. 'I mean, sergeant.'

They dragged the unconscious man up the ramp. He fell heavily against the reinforced plasteel floor as it closed behind them.

The heavy bolter roared, hard rounds rattled against the Chimera's flanks, but Minka heard nothing. She wanted to salvage something from this fiasco.

She tore the ganger's top open, yanked her medi-pack off her belt and stuffed the wounds full of gauze.

'Stop him bleeding out,' she ordered Viktor. 'Then tie his hands.' She stood up.

'Right. Who the frekk fired without my permission?' she demanded.

No one answered but all of them knew.

Minka turned to Arktur. She was trembling with fury and adrenaline as she grabbed him by his collar and dragged him forward. 'Do that again and I will execute you myself, understand?'

TEN

Carkal pushed through the crowds along the avenues of white tents. His first hours had been an extreme of elation, as his release and escape sank in, followed by the chill depths of fear as he learnt from wayside preachers and the rumour mill that contact with Orbital City had been lost a week earlier.

Although no official announcement had been made, the view on the street was that the warp route way station had fallen to the Scourged.

'That's impossible,' Carkal told them. 'I was there a month before. The Navy was there. I saw them. They had two cruisers.' But no one listened to him.

'Nothing has stopped them so far. Why do you think that will change? No one cares about us.'

'The Emperor sees and He knows and He cares,' Carkal declared, but then he fell silent as the implication of his words struck him. If the Emperor was all-seeing, then He knew about the murders Carkal had committed. He had seen the depths Carkal had sunk to.

His immediate instinct was to try to flee once more, but where was there to flee to? How could he get back onto a transport?

It was impossible.

'How long until they get here, then?' he asked.

The man shrugged. 'Who knows? They could be here in days. Or a week.'

The prospect was chilling, and he turned away, back to the crowded streets of the tent city, which no longer appeared comforting. It looked bleak and desperate.

Carkal felt trapped, duped, deserted. Wherever he fled, Drakulzar, the heretic warlord followed. There was a doomsday atmosphere within the camp. Everywhere Carkal looked he saw fear, hunger, despair. Preachers sermonised against a hundred kinds of heresy. There were crude icons that were the object of adoration of chanting crowds; processions of penitents with needle-filled balls, stabbing their chests till the blood ran freely; trails of naked repentants, arms lashed to stakes holding their arms out to either side, simple black hoods tied over their heads; and behind, a gaggle of shaven-headed women, handing out cheap printed cloth badges. And at each intersection gangers stood watching from the back of their gun-trucks and halftracks.

The rumours were of religious images that spoke prophecies, or that sweated blood. Anxious, ecstatic crowds gathered in anticipation of religious manifestations, praying in expectation of the end of their world. There were rings of feverish women dancing ritual steps to drive sickness away, rumours of sacred icons weeping or speaking to the True. There was a feeling of nervous exhaustion. And through it all Carkal wandered.

He knew no one, understood nothing. He was shoved, cursed at, threatened and tempted. And he was fearful as he watched three gangers drag a young man out into middle of the crossroads. He was Carkal's age. Someone like him.

Carkal watched in horror as the gangers tripped the boy up, let him crawl a small distance before stepping on his leg.

'This sump-scum is a thief,' the chief ganger called out, patting his club into his open palm. He put his foot into the small of the boy's back. 'I declare thee guilty, sump-scum. And here is the punishment of the God-Emperor of Mankind.'

The club rose and fell, and then it was done. Carkal's mouth went dry. He had killed, just like that, but not in daylight, and before a crowd.

'So die all thieves!' the ganger shouted, and somehow Carkal felt the gangers' eyes on him, and he turned and hurried away.

There were sanitary posts between each gang's territory. Medicae volunteers stopped everyone from passing on.

Carkal queued. He was almost grateful for the human interaction, the rough hands of the medical orderly who shoved Carkal's head down and puffed white counterseptic powder over his head and shoulders.

'Open your top,' the man said. 'Lift your arms.'

Carkal obeyed and was pushed through the barricades.

A woman was standing with a bucket in her hands. 'Credits for food,' she said, and handed him a food-chit.

Carkal wanted to say thank you, but the people behind him pushed him on.

He tried to go back, but wardens waved their electro-goads at him. 'Move along. No more credits for you.'

Carkal did as he was told. He tried at another intersection, but the counterseptic powder marked him out, and this time he got a crack on his back with a long cane.

The chit said that it entitled Carkal to a meal. He was not sure what to do with it, and shopkeepers waved him on. 'Not here,' they said.

Finally Carkal saw another man handing over the credit chit for a jug of grog.

The stall was named 'House of Matteo'. It was a down-at-heel kind of place. There was an 'L' shaped counter in the corner, and a thin, weary-looking man, with a short, dark beard and stained apron ready for orders. A plain board showed what was on the menu. There were two choices on offer. Slab or slop.

Carkal clutched his food-chit and stepped forward. Another man sat behind the awning with his chin on one fist, staring out into the street. There was an autogun under the counter. Carkal could see the butt – standard Munitorum issue sprayed white with a serial number.

'I have this,' Carkal said, holding up his credits.

'Slab or slop,' Matteo told him without looking up.

'How much is the brew?'

'Six credits.'

The serving for slop looked bigger, so Carkal took slop, and a cup of brew. As the thin man started to fill a cardboard box, Carkal handed over the chit and six more credits, then quickly counted out how much he had left.

At this rate he'd be out by week's end.

'Where you from?' Carkal said.

'Here,' the man said, as he took the money and handed the bowl over.

'I mean before.'

'Before. Who cares.'

'I'm an off-worlder too,' Carkal said.

'You and every other frekker in this hellhole. Listen. I get paid to give out victuals. Conversation costs extra.'

Carkal took his bowl and cup.

He started inside. The man with the gun stepped in front of him. 'Eating inside is another credit.'

Carkal saw the dark barrel of the gun aimed at him. He felt his cheeks colour and took a step back. 'Never mind,' he stammered.

Carkal squatted in the filthy street.

The slop was warm at least but the brew was sour. He shovelled it down, and felt it coating his stomach. The man next to him wore a Golden Throne badge. He slurped his mash broth and scraped his bowl clean. He had a long face with buck teeth, and scraggly grey hair.

'How long you been here?' the stranger said.

'Landed yesterday,' Carkal said.

'Where did you come from?'

'Guardia Rex. I came via Ignatz and then Bray's Watch,' Carkal said.

The man sniffed and looked at him. He'd not heard of them. 'Richstars where you came from?'

Carkal nodded.

'Frekkers,' the other man said. 'All of them. Look at that.' He turned and nodded up to the Evercity. It was small with distance, but the white masonry looked beautiful in the light of the setting sun. 'Won't let us in. Not even to pray.'

The man went on and on, but Carkal wasn't interested. He wanted to be up there, in the Evercity, where families with credits would request the rarefied services of a painter. The other man moved on to religion, which Carkal found even less interesting.

'And the Richstars are Templars,' the man said, as if Carkal should know what this meant.

'What are Templars?'

'Heretics,' the man said.

Carkal had read the posters. Heretics were crazed monsters. Rabid animals in human form. They hated life and order and they hated art. The word chilled Carkal. 'You mean like the Scourged?'

'No. But heretics all the same.'

Carkal thought of the Richstars he had seen as a boy. None of them seemed to fit this description of a heretic. He scraped his bowl clean, and returned it to Matteo for the deposit. The man with the gun handed the credit back begrudgingly.

Carkal slipped it into his purse. He felt better now with a full belly. He stood and wondered which way to go as a procession of black-robed men marched up the road towards him. Before them went a band of penitents. One came towards Carkal. She was old and bent, but her eyes were kind, her grey stubble was patchy, and the skin of her scalp flaky and sore.

'The Emperor loves you,' she said, and she embraced him.

It was such a brief and sudden moment of human kindness and warmth that he did not resist as she pressed him into her sagging chest. He closed his eyes for a moment, and it was like being with Agatha once more. The long-lost sense of being loved and cared for, and safe. 'The Emperor loves you,' she said. 'Admit your sins and be chastised, and then you will be reborn.' She held his arms and looked at him face to face. 'Have you sinned, my child?'

He didn't know if he was being accused and stammered a brief answer. 'I... I... I...' but did not know where to start.

'When you are ready, come and find us. Here,' she said and pinned a yellow cloth to his chest, which showed the Palace of the Emperor on Holy Terra, with a rising sun behind it. 'A crusade has been announced. Join the Brotherhood and repent your sins.'

Carkal remembered the sound of the first man he'd killed on the *Kossak Blade* – the dull thud of steel bar shattering his skull, the splash as he fell, face down, into the water. 'I repent!' he said, but the words were formulaic, and she was already letting go and moving onwards, embracing the next in the crowd, telling him, 'The Emperor loves you.'

It was an hour later that he stopped outside a slop-bar and put his hand in his pocket, only to discover that his credits were gone. He checked everywhere, but they were empty. All of them. The only person he could think of was that woman. The penitent!

He turned back, desperately retracing his footsteps, shoving his way desperately through the crowds that divided him from the procession. 'Have you seen the Brotherhood?' he asked, and people pointed him north, south, east and west. He heard one procession – the slap of whips on bare flesh, the clang of cowbells, and the smell of censers burning – and grabbed a grey-haired shaven-headed lady. But this one had a lazy eye, and the next was too tall, too thin.

He was mad with fury. He had been tricked and betrayed. He grabbed another penitent and a man shouted. 'Off!' he said, and shoved Carkal away. 'You are the enemy of the Holy! Repent!'

Carkal was struggling to get up as fists and kicks rained down on him. He cradled his head in his arms, trying to keep the blows off, and at last the Brotherhood passed on. Carkal pushed himself up as the crowd closed behind the crusaders, and he was alone once more.

ELEVEN

As soon as Minka's squad got back to barracks the ganger was carried off to the medicae unit.

Chief Commissar Shand came out of the regimental office. He saw the stretchers and paused, then walked towards her.

She pretended she hadn't seen him, and started speaking to Breve, but Shand's voice called out, 'Sergeant! Come here.'

She turned. Shand was a tall, thin man with a quiet and chilling manner. His augmetic eye gleamed red, and the rest of his face was taut with scar tissue. 'There was fighting?'

Minka stammered for a moment, trying to organise her thoughts. 'Well…' she started. 'We went to the tent city. The place is run by gangs. I was discussing entry with their leader when…'

'How did the new intake perform?'

'Well, sir, we left twenty of them dead, and captured the leader. I brought him back for questioning.'

'Did you lead your squad into unnecessary danger?'

'No, sir! A gun was discharged.'

Commissar Shand loomed over her. 'Whose gun? Sergeant, the discipline of the regiment is my concern. Remember, it is your duty to deal with insubordination in your ranks. Any failings you cannot deal with should be brought to me. It is a capital offence for an officer to hide things from a commissar.'

While her discipline was previously dealt with by officers, now she was an officer herself her performance came under the direct jurisdiction of the Commissariat. Shand's gaze seemed to suck the information out of her. She had to cover for Arktur. 'Well, Corporal Arktur's gun had a malfunction...' she stammered. 'He thought we were in danger.'

'Corporal!' Shand called out. His voice was clear and compelling. Arktur was heading back to the barrack block. 'I want to speak with you.'

Everyone turned then.

Arktur stopped. He seemed small as Shand's authority reeled him in like a hooked fish.

'Corporal. You tell me. What happened on the patrol this afternoon?'

Arktur's eyes met Minka's. 'My gun misfired,' he said. 'I was not used to a carbine.'

But his demeanour was odd enough to raise Shand's suspicions.

'Stand straight!' he commanded and Arktur snapped to attention.

Minka tried to give a warning, but there was something odd about Arktur's movements. They were slow, and sloppy, and Shand had clearly noticed it.

'I'm bringing you into custody, Corporal Arktur.'

'What for, sir?' Arktur blurted, but Shand did not reply as he led him away.

Within minutes, black-clad commissars were striding towards the barrack rooms. The sudden flurry of Commissariat activity was ominous.

Jaromir turned to Minka. 'Did you report him?'

'No! I said nothing.' But Minka knew that she had screwed this up. 'I said nothing. Listen. I've got to go to the medicae unit, but afterwards I'll go speak to the bats on Arktur's behalf. The rest of you, get a good rest. Drill, tomorrow morning. Zero-five-hundred hours. Understand?'

They nodded. She let them walk away. She was exhausted and started for the barracks.

Someone stepped up behind her.

'So, it went badly?'

It was Prassan.

'Yeah,' she said.

'I'm sorry.'

Her defences were back up again in an instant. 'I've seen worse,' she said.

During Minka's rehabilitation she had spent more time than she liked with Medicae Banting. He'd made it clear, many times, how little he cared for military incompetence. There was no sympathy for Minka in this, just a dislike of the way that poor commanders cost him time and effort.

He gave Minka a withering look as she stepped inside his room. 'Sergeant Lesk. I have been hearing about your little adventure.'

He had already cleaned out Silas' wound, covered it with pink counterseptic powder and bandaged it.

'How is it?' Minka asked.

'It's too tight,' Silas said, flexing his hand.

'It'll stretch,' Banting told him.

Silas took a lho-stick and lit it one-handed. Banting gave him a look.

'Outside with that,' he said.

Banting moved on.

A medical aide was working to stabilise Thaddeus. The young man was lying in bed, shivering violently. Minka and her squad had done their best in the back of the Chimera, but now his jacket had been cut away to reveal skin red and charred. Where the blisters had been rubbed away, the raw, red flesh showed through, and clear fluids oozed down his back.

Banting inspected the burn and called for an extra shot of soporific.

'Don't think you can go now. As you're responsible for these men, you can wash your hands and come and help.'

He gave her the gauze to hold as he covered Thaddeus' wounds. She stood and watched as his burn was cleaned and then dressed with gauze. Thaddeus closed his eyes as the soporifics kicked in. His lips were moving. Minka didn't want to know what he was saying.

It took nearly an hour to finish.

Banting went to clean his hands. The nurse threw Thaddeus' ruined jacket into a sack labelled 'Incineration'.

The soporifics were wearing off.

'Anything I can bring you?'

Thaddeus shook his head.

'Sure?'

He nodded.

Minka was a little stuck for words. She noticed the ward

ceiling was decorated with baroque images of the Emperor. 'Well, this is a grand place to lie sick.'

Thaddeus half laughed, half winced as he gently lowered himself down on his side. 'Yes, sarge. At least I'll have something to look at.'

She helped him get comfortable, then said, 'You'll be here for a while, I think. Sure there's nothing you need?'

He paused, taking this in. 'Well. Something to read.'

She slapped her pockets. She didn't have anything, except her Primer. It was one of the few things that she had saved from Cadia.

'Lose this and you will be shot,' their trainers had told them when they were ten years old. As Whiteshields they'd taken the whole Primer business seriously. It was a ritual joke played on all new conscripts. Now she weighed it in her hand and handed it over to him.

'Lose this and you'll be shot,' she said. He half laughed again. 'It'll keep you going until I get something. Until then you can buff up on Principles and Regulations.'

'Thanks,' Thaddeus said.

As she left, Banting called her over. 'So, I hear you brought a ganger back and I have to go and patch him up.'

'Sorry.'

'Don't apologise. Putting holes into people is what you're trained to do.'

'I do my best.'

'Indeed. Well, doesn't seem like today was a very good start. Are you sure you're up to this?'

'Yes,' she said.

'Really?'

'Yes.'

Banting's manner was clear. She had frekked up. 'From

what I heard you were lucky. It could have been much worse.'

'It could always be worse,' Minka said.

When she came out of the medicae ward, Commissar Cadet Knoll was waiting for her. He waved a form at her. 'Sergeant. Commissar Shand has found a large quantity of obscura in Corporal Arktur's possession. Were you aware of this?'

'No,' she answered quickly.

'You are sure?'

'Yes,' she said. 'I mean, I suspected grinweed.'

Knoll marked the form and she scribbled her signature on it. 'If you, or anyone else is complicit...' Knoll warned, leaving the second half of the sentence unspoken. She could tell from his manner that he was excited about the find, excited because Arktur would be shot. No doubt Knoll wanted to shoot someone himself.

'I understand,' Minka said.

By the time she got to the mess, dinner had already been served.

Minka grabbed one of the plates that had been left for stragglers. They were filled with scrapings and leftover slab.

When she was done she went to her quarters and looked for Dido, but her bunk was empty, and instead there was only a pair of troopers bent over a map of Potence.

The afternoon shadows were lengthening.

Minka wanted a bit of quiet. She went out into the barrack yard. There were worn steps leading up to the firing parapet. It was almost cold enough for a jacket. There were fine views out over the southern expanse of the Evercity.

She paused and took in a deep breath.

The golden light reminded her of better times. Her mind

lingered as she stood, elbows on the battlement, looking down from the high barrack quarters. The sun set quickly here. She stayed until the bright colours were funnelling from the sky, then let her fingers brush along the parapet as she strolled towards the east side.

A figure stood there, hands braced on the lip of the rockcrete buttress. It was Shand. He appeared suddenly, as if he had been seeking her out.

'Sergeant,' he said, and she knew she could not avoid him.

She saluted and walked forward. The sound of gunfire rose from the Evercity. She felt she had to say something. 'It doesn't seem very peaceful down there.'

'Nowhere is peaceful,' he said.

There was something painful about the expression on his lean face. It was cold and hard and distant. His scarred knuckles were white. The tension within him alarmed her. Then, quite suddenly, he turned and looked down on her. 'You know we found obscura in Arktur's belongings?'

'Yes, sir.'

'And you know the penalty?'

'Yes, sir.' She didn't need to ask. Arktur would be shot.

'No. I mean the penalty for not reporting relevant material to a commissar?'

'Yes, sir. I didn't know anything about it, I swear.'

'No?'

Her cheeks coloured purple. 'No, sir. I mean I knew he was lax, they all seem lax, this new lot. I thought a bit of discipline would sort him out. If I had any suspicions of obscura I would have brought it to your attention immediately.'

Shand paused. 'You were on Marquis,' he said. It was not a question; it was a statement.

'Yes, sir.'

'I have been going through your reports, Lesk. On Marquis you were a trooper in D Company.'

She became stiff. 'Yes, sir. We went in with the first wave. In Hellbores.'

'D Company suffered...' he paused and picked a Guard euphemism, '...heavy casualties.'

'Yes, sir. Only two of us made it out. Myself and Grogar.'

'Only two out of a hundred and thirty-seven troopers.'

Minka spoke carefully. 'That is right, sir.'

Shand drew in a deep breath, as if quelling the pain, then said, 'That is lucky, don't you think?'

She spoke defensively. 'What, sir?'

'You tell me.' He turned his baleful red eye on her.

He'd been fighting and shooting troopers so long that his whole body exuded menace. She couldn't look him in the face.

'In your report, you mentioned finding a chapel in the ruins of the city.'

'Did I?'

'Yes,' he said. His tone was definite. 'You did. Describe it.'

Minka felt sweat on her brow. 'It's not very clear, to be honest, sir. The medicae said I had toxic shock.'

'Describe it to me.'

Minka stiffened. She described it as far as she could remember. At the end she looked up at him. He had turned away and was staring out into the darkening sky. A flight of three fighters was making a sweep across the city. They looked like Thunderbolts from here, and in the distance a lander was making its ungainly descent to the starport. It looked too big and fat and slow to fly.

He nodded to himself. 'And you say you saw a heretic.'

'There were many heretics.'

'You know what I mean.'

She swallowed. 'Yes,' she said at last. She knew what he meant. She coughed to clear her throat.

'Do you know what they call themselves?'

She shook her head. She didn't want to know.

'They call themselves the Eaters of Worlds.'

Minka said nothing.

'They are the enemy that we have to face. To break. To eradicate from the galaxy. The Holy Emperor gives us the strength we need to purge the unclean.'

She felt sick. 'Yes, sir.'

He turned to her again. 'Are you strong enough to break them?'

'I...,' she stammered. For a moment she was back in the underhive while the heretic Space Marines came at her. Eight feet of rage. Half a ton of hatred. Each of the band of Guardsmen she was with had thrown themselves at it, and each had been cut down. 'Nothing stopped it.'

'How did you survive, then?'

'I cannot say. I don't remember.'

'Don't, or won't?'

She rallied now. 'Confessor Keremm examined me at length. It was not pleasant. But I have been passed fit for duty, not only physically but also spiritually.'

She looked from his human eye to his augmetic one, and back again. He did not look like he believed her.

'We do not flee from the enemy, Sergeant Lesk. That makes them stronger. We die defying them and their creed. That is our duty as Guardsmen and women. With our deaths we make ourselves martyrs. In death we conquer. That is the motto of the 101st. Do you know what that means?'

She nodded, but she could not look him in the face any

longer. Her voice was thin. 'Yes, sir. I know that, sir. I live by that standard.'

She stood next to him for a moment, looking out over the city as the lumens came on, and lit the major arteries.

The mess bell rang. It was ten minutes until lights out. At that moment there was the distinctive sound of a shot, ringing out across the barrack square.

'Ah,' Shand said. 'I think Arktur has gone to make his peace with the Emperor. Be careful, Sergeant Lesk, that you do not follow him.'

TWELVE

That first night on Potence, Carkal found a pile of rubbish in a quiet area of the tent city to sleep on. He looked out towards the distant lights of the Evercity. I must get out of this hell, he told himself. He tried to rest, but night in the Tent City was haunted by angry shouts and screams, and then the deathly silence that came after gunfire.

He got up before the sun rose, mouth filled with saliva, and his stomach echoing and empty. He could smell freshly baking bread. It took him half an hour, following his nose, to find the place. Only the desperate and the homeless were up at this time.

The bakery truck stood alone within an empty pair of blocks, where no tents had been raised and the ground was strewn with weeds and shrubs. The rear carriage of the truck had been converted to bread ovens. Under the discoloured linen awning figures worked, sliding trays of bread out of proving chambers into ovens, and then out into a short marquee of red, white and blue striped plastic cloth, where people were eating.

The scent was so strong he could almost chew upon it. He was about to walk across the open space when he heard the sound of knives being sharpened. He moved closer. Through the open flap of an awning he saw labourers mixing sacks of ground beans and flour, kneading and cutting dough, a few men standing over large vats. There were enormous heaps of dough waiting to be cut and shaped. And there, on shelves, were long white loaves, dusted with flour. Carkal moved closer.

Another vehicle had pulled up, and he hunkered down as labourers filled it with baskets of freshly baked crusty bread, piled up on the open back.

Carkal could barely believe his luck. He waited until the labourers had gone. The drivers were exchanging stories. Carkal hurried into the shadow of the truck. He could hear a voice talking on the other side of the vehicle, and looking under the chassis he saw two booted feet, standing, turning and then walking away.

He heard the name 'Zarpal' and 'orders'. Zarpal seemed important from the way they spoke his name. But the smell of bread was overwhelming. Desperation gave him confidence. Just one loaf. Two, maybe.

The metal was slippery and hard to get a handle on. He pushed and pulled and got his head over the side, looking down onto crates of loaves. He grabbed one. And another. And another.

The bread was still warm. He tore off a bite. The breaking crust let out aromas he had almost forgotten about in his long months on board the ship. In a rush of memories it brought back his life as a mixer of paints. In terror and elation, he shoved the three loaves down his front, grabbed a fourth and then dropped to the ground, and started to run back the way he had come, but in his haste he tripped and fell flat on his face, one hand still holding the loaf up to save it from the dirt.

He cursed and looked back to see what had caught his foot. The ugly face of a thick, bald, heavyset man, with steel teeth and a nose that had been broken more times than a china pot, looked down on him. He had a leopard tattoo leaping up his neck. Carkal started to apologise, but the man moved forward and stepped on his hand. Carkal cried out.

When the man spoke his voice was a deep rumble, like a landslide. 'You thieving little turd. I'll tear your eyes out if I find you in my territory again,' the man said. 'Do you understand?'

Carkal took the opportunity to speak. 'Sorry, sir. I only arrived yesterday. I'm a painter.' Carkal spoke quickly. 'I painted the Richstars. I can serve you.'

'Richstars,' the man growled. 'Don't speak to me of Richstars.'

He reached down and took Carkal's face in one hand. The strength in that grip had to be genhanced. The man dragged Carkal to his feet and lifted him from the floor.

'What is your name?' the steel-toothed man said.

'Carkal,' he said.

'Well, Carkal, we're sick of your kind skulking about, stealing. Thieving. Robbing. Do you understand?'

'Master Zarpal sent me,' Carkal said, confidently.

The name seemed to work like a charm. The man put him down and dusted his front down. 'Oh, I am sorry. Master Zarpal. You should have said.'

'Yes. No matter. I understand what it is like. Everyone starving.'

'Exactly,' the man said, nodding towards the starport. 'All they do is bring more thieves. Every day. And who is policing them? No one. They leave it to us. We have to look after ourselves in this world.'

'I know,' Carkal said, desperate to get away. 'Zarpal sends his compliments.'

'Does he now?' the bruiser said. 'To me?'

'What's your name?'

'Hamma,' the brute said.

'Yes. You.'

Hamma smiled, steel teeth glimmering with reflected lumens. 'That's mighty kind of him.'

Carkal brushed off the dirt from his clothes and turned to go. He could not believe his luck.

'Wait,' Hamma said, and Carkal turned.

He had a brief glimpse of the man's ugly face, before the headbutt hit him square in the face. Then all was pain.

Hamma bent down to him and picked him up as if he were a rag doll.

'Now, Carkal. Tell me how it was that Zarpal spoke to you when only yesterday I cut him open from neck to navel. Has he come back from the dead?'

THIRTEEN

The ganger that Minka had brought back from the tent city refused to speak until it was made clear that he had little choice.

The information he gave was added to files compiled by the Cadian intelligence officers. All these were taken up to Colonel Baytov.

Colour Sergeant Daal had then been summoned by Major Kastelek.

'It's a damned mess,' the major said, tossing the file down on the table.

'Yes.' Daal said. 'Sorry, sir. It was my fault. I thought it would be straightforward. I didn't realise that the enforcers have given up on the place. From what I heard, Lesk did well, I think, not to lose her entire squad. She's young, but tough.'

Major Kastelek did not seem convinced. 'Baytov is not going to be impressed.'

Daal knew that.

Kastelek went on. 'So. What next?'

'We go in hard. Street gangs understand one thing. We'll have to drum it into their heads that we're here and we're not going to let gangs tear that place apart.'

'Right. Let Fourth Platoon take this. Give them everything they need. I suggest they take tanks and blow... what do they call themselves?... the *Kartell* halfway to hell. Then I'll make a full report to Baytov.'

Daal smiled. 'Yes, sir.'

An hour later three squadrons of Leman Russ tanks accompanied Fourth Platoon in a convoy of five Chimeras.

There was no debate this time as they approached the Kartell territory. As soon as the gangers saw the armour they tried to pull back, but as they leapt into their improvised gun-rigs, the lead Leman Russ fired.

The range was over eight hundred yards. A long shot with the tank moving at full speed.

The high explosive shell hit the nearest truck squarely. The impact tore the vehicle apart, throwing bodies into the air like dolls, and a salvo followed, pounding the enemy checkpoint.

The shrapnel ripped through flesh and steel, but the shock waves killed many more, and the survivors fled in panic, leaving the burning wrecks of their transports.

The wrecks were still burning as the Cadian convoy rammed them to the side.

They pounded any gangers they could find and burned their bases, and when they were fired upon they responded with extreme force.

After three hours they returned to base, leaving a square mile of tent city burning.

Tyson had led his platoon. He was in a foul mood as he strode into the colonel's office. Sparker was sitting with his feet up, smoking a lho-stub, a sheaf of parchment reports open on his lap, half read.

He put his feet down and sat up as Tyson entered.

'Right,' he said. 'Tell me.'

Tyson pulled a chair up opposite and sat down. Colonel Sparker handed a lho-stub across the desk. Tyson put it between his teeth as he leant forward to light it.

Tyson took a puff, then exhaled a thin cone of blue smoke. 'Well, we cleared the Kartell out. But gangers are running the whole place. Hive-gangers, mostly. They're fighting over territory.'

'Any sign of the enforcers?'

'None. They've given up entirely. Gangers have taken over everything. They're selling food donations. And they've clearly got their hands on an arms shipment. The Kartell had heavy weaponry. Goliaths. A couple of halftracks.'

'Are they loyal?'

'Throne knows. But no signs of heresy.'

Sparker nodded. 'But the desperate turn to desperate means. Think we can bring them over to our side?'

'Are *we* that desperate?'

Sparker nodded. 'Apparently, yes. Orbital City fell ten days ago. Looks like the Navy frekked up again.'

'Any sign of the Calibineer?'

'Not a whiff, or at least not yet,' Sparker said. 'They're running scared, I think. Or digging in. At this rate the Scourged could be here within weeks. Days, even. We might need the gangs fighting on our side.'

Tyson said nothing.

Sparker sighed. 'And there's this.' He pushed a card file

towards Tyson. It was marked with the Commissariat's stamp. The red letters read 'Executed'.

'Corporal Arktur. Lesk's squad. He's been shot.'

Tyson puffed out his cheek. He took the file and opened it. He'd not seen an executed stamp for a long time.

'The commissars found enough obscura to get half the regiment dazed.'

'Frekk,' Tyson said.

Sparker nodded. 'And in my company! I've had Commissar Shand in here for two hours. He's taken this all very personally. If anyone steps out of line...'

Tyson nodded. 'Can we have the executions registered to the Redskulls?'

Sparker pursed his lips. 'I'll try. Officially they're ours, of course. But...'

'But the 101st have not had a man shot for three years. I'll be damned if this new lot are going to bring us all down.'

Sparker said nothing. He looked as if he felt the same, but he couldn't say so. 'I'll talk to Shand. We'll need to get Lesk another corporal.'

'Viktor?'

'No. Make it one of the new lot. For company cohesion and all.'

'I'll look into it.'

Colonel Sparker nodded and took a long drag of his lhostub. He picked up one of the reports in his lap. 'System command is clearly running scared. Apparently Potence can't fall. This place has huge symbolic significance for the whole sector. Something to do with the local saint. He's the founder of the local dynasty. They've sent us an Imperial general to take command of the defence.'

'Great. Another Richstar?'

Sparker smiled. 'No, actually. He's Cadian, apparently.'

Tyson laughed. 'Then there is hope after all.'

Sparker quoted an old saying that was taught to Cadians in their third year of scholam. 'Don't trust in hope...' he started.

Tyson put up his hand. 'I know. Hope is the first step on the road to disappointment.'

FOURTEEN

Across Potence, the Calibineer were finally taking up defensive positions, while a general mobilisation of reservists was set in motion. At the same time a general evacuation of the outlying steadings, ore-quarries and intakes had been ordered, to happen within the week, leaving only skeleton crews to keep the operations running.

Meanwhile, the defence of the Evercity began in earnest. Reservists used dozer-blades fitted to the fronts of cargo 8s to build tank emplacements and earthen redoubts against possible attack. The walls of the Evercity were fortified with razor wire and sandbags, while the approaches to the main gates were surrounded by fields of rusting steel tank traps.

The Cadians spent the next morning digging trenches around the acropolis.

The Ecclesiarchy authorities had insisted that they did not enter the cathedral itself, but they fashioned defensive positions on the main approaches to the acropolis, heavy weapon platforms overlooking the steep roads, and tanks and artillery used their dozer-blades to pile up earth to offer them protection from below. Where the rocky terrain did not allow for tank scrapes, the Cadians laboured in work-gangs, rolling water barrels into place, or laying sandbags along low walls.

The news of Arktur's execution cast a shadow over them all. A few blamed Arktur. Some blamed the bats. Most blamed Minka. Disapproval hung about her like a bad smell. Even Sergeant Daal bumped into her as she was filling sandbags.

Daal took the back of her head in his hand and pulled her face close to his. 'Lesk! Why didn't you tell me? If anyone frekks up then you come and see me, understand? We sort it out within the regiment. Understand?'

She felt stupid. It felt like the hundredth time she had given the same excuse. 'Yes, sir. But I didn't know.'

He squeezed her neck and shook her. 'First execution in three years, for frekk's sake!'

'I reported what happened at the tent city. That was all. A few days' penal. If he hadn't got obscura on him...'

Daal was not interested. 'Hush! Do you know what happens when one commissar gets a scalp? Do you know what all the others start thinking? I'll tell you what. They start thinking, "Where's mine?" Have you seen the look in Knoll's eyes? He's itching to shoot someone. They start to get competitive. "How many frekkers have you shot this week?" That's what they start thinking. The bats tell themselves that they've been too soft on us and they want to make sure they're doing their job.'

Minka was sick of having the finger of blame pointed at her. 'You mean the next person who gets shot is my fault?'

Daal's temper was up. 'Yes,' he snapped. 'That's *exactly* what I'm saying.'

When they got back to barracks, an information bulletin had been posted. It confirmed what everyone knew – contact with Orbital City had been lost. On top of that the Scourged were now within a short warp jump from Potence, a planet-wide evacuation of smaller habitations was taking place and the Navy picket was being pulled back to the way station of Namarra.

Captain Firwuud happened to be standing there. He had been a sergeant a week ago, and was now struggling with the command of Second Platoon. The others turned to him. 'When do you think the Scourged will be here?'

'When? I think it's really still *if*. But seeing how quickly they've made it from Brey's Watch, I'd say they could be here within the week.'

The atmosphere changed noticeably at that. Some stared up at the noticeboard, others moved off in silence.

Minka made herself scarce. Dido found her sitting cross-legged on her bunk, her carbine disassembled on the blanket before her.

'Hey,' Dido said.

Minka did not look up.

'Hey,' Dido repeated, louder this time.

Minka dropped the weight of the pull-through down the barrel and pulled the cotton bung up. 'I screwed up,' she said.

Dido tilted her head in a non-committal gesture. 'Well, yeah. But it wasn't your fault.'

'He let off his gun. He almost got us all killed. I didn't know he was dealing obscura. But thank Throne the bats found it. He deserved to be shot. Now everyone is giving me that *look*.'

'What look?'

'The "You've let me down" look.'

Dido forced a smile. 'Have you spoken to the squad?'

'No.' Minka paused, the barrel and butt of her carbine in her hands. Her body language said it all.

Dido pulled an encouraging face. 'They'll understand. They know what happened.' She didn't sound confident. There was a faint click as Minka twisted the barrel of her carbine back into place. She lifted it to her eye and checked it. 'I wish I was just a trooper still. Taking orders. Doing my job. Shand is on my case. He started asking about Marquis. How Grogar and I survived.'

'How did you survive?'

'I don't know,' Minka answered. For a moment there were tears in her eyes. 'I have dreams. But all I know is that they dragged us out of the slime. The rest is a mess.'

Dido didn't speak for a long moment, but at last she said, 'Well. The Emperor's called you.'

'Do you think He has?'

'Of course. Otherwise you wouldn't have made it.'

'Do you think it works like that?'

'What do you mean?'

'I mean, do you think the Emperor cares about what one of us does? We're just troopers. There are millions of us. Billions. Do you really think He cares what we do, or how we fight, or how we die?'

'Of course He cares,' Dido said. 'We're Cadians.'

'Yes. But really. Do you think He cares about *you*, Dido Frevren? Is He watching *you*?'

Dido pulled a face. 'I don't know.' She paused. 'I've never thought about it like that.'

'You haven't?'

Dido shook her head. There was a long silence as Minka kept fitting the bits together. 'I think about it all the time,' she said at last.

'And do you have an answer?'

Minka shook her head. 'No,' she said. 'I mean, I *hope* He watches us. I tell myself He's watching us. When I'm terrified I remember His sacrifices. His pain. And His great gift to us all. And I imagine He is standing behind me, and sometimes that makes me strong.' She was about to go on, but stopped. This felt taboo. The kind of thing one should not say aloud. Minka drew in a deep breath. 'But sometimes I have black thoughts where I *don't* think He's watching us. I don't think He cares. Then all this seems pointless.'

Dido lowered her voice. 'That's how heretics talk.'

Minka stopped. Dido was right. She should not allow herself to even think such a thing. She took in a deep breath and nodded. 'I know. I'm sorry. I'll say my prayers.'

'Good. Don't speak like that, Minka.' There was a long pause. Dido forced a smile and she spoke breezily now, as if she were about to leave. 'Heard about Orbital City?'

Minka nodded. No time for thinking when battle was near.

Dido kept up her banter. 'You should get your squad bonding. You know, as we used to do as Whiteshields. Everyone out, full packs, six miles, thirty-eight minutes. Everyone succeeds or they do it all again.'

It was almost silly to be going back to Whiteshield training, but Dido seemed sure.

'I'm doing it. Binds everyone together.'

'It sounds too simple.'

'Command is simple. You lead from the front and answer every question with a definitive answer. Doesn't matter whether you're right or wrong. Let the regimental historians bother about that. Just make a decision. And remember, the new lot are Cadians too. Whatever has frekked with them had to be bad.'

'Worse than Markgraaf?'

'Had to be.'

'Somehow I don't believe it.' Minka let out a breath. 'But I'll give it a go.'

'Good,' Dido said. 'And that other crap. About the Emperor. Go see Keremm, if you must. But don't talk like that again.'

Minka threw on her jacket and strode through the barrack halls to personally issue the orders. She found her troopers in small groups, playing cards, or lying on their bunks. 'Full kit run, tomorrow, zero-five-hundred hours.'

Some grunted, some groaned, and some appeared not to hear her at all.

She had no time for this. 'Hear me?'

'Yes,' they said.

As she turned to go a figure stepped out in front of her. She tried to go past him, but he stepped in front of her again. She was about to shove past when he spoke. 'My name is Laptev. I'm your new corporal.'

She sized him up. From his scars it was clear that he'd taken a couple of hard rounds in the Emperor's name. But now his hands were thrust deep into his pockets and his jacket was unbuttoned, his belt loosely buckled about his waist. He was the kind of fighter whose smile looked threatening. The kind of thug you didn't want to cross.

'Laptev. Good. Welcome.' She put out a hand, but he did not shake it. Minka kept her hand out. He made no movement.

'I'm your corporal, not your buddy,' he said.

'Right,' she said, and took her hand back. 'Full kit run, tomorrow, zero-five-hundred hours.'

It took a long time for Minka to calm down enough to sleep.

She did not say her prayers, but did press-ups till sweat ran down her face and her shoulders burned and she couldn't lift her face from the floor. The workout helped. She lay on her bed and stared up at the ceiling and calmed her breathing.

At some point she must have fallen asleep, a restless sleep, punctuated by dreams.

In one dream she was thirteen again. A campfire was burning against the night. She was on the Caducades Islands and a sea breeze was whipping at the low flames. Her face and boots were warm. The rest of her was cold, and about her came the sound of wind whistling through the low heather on the moor top.

In another she was a child again, in the hab-zone of Kasr Myrak, walking with her brother to the bread shop, getting a pound of the dense, black tuckwheat loaf. 'Want it cutting?' the baker said. He was a veteran. Had one arm, but managed to get the loaf into the slicing machine, and fed it through into the brown paper bag. 'Here.' She gave him the ration tab, and he dropped it into his bucket.

Walking back with her brother.

Her brother.

In dreams he felt so real. So alive. She could turn and talk to him and he would respond and speak like a living person.

'I'll carry it,' her dream-self said, and he handed her the bag, and she could feel the rough paper in her hand.

What was his name? she thought, and tried to turn to him to ask, but she could not. She was eight or nine, and she was walking home with her brother, carrying the bread ration for that day.

It was a good place to pause, and remember. But her dream-mind lingered too long and the wolves of memory caught her. As she turned to her brother she was no longer in the dark street of Kasr Myrak but underground and the ceiling was drip-lime stalactites. She was knee-deep in slime-pools. She knew she had stayed too long in the past, and tried to wake, but the wolves had her tight and would not let go. She could hear *him*, like the roar of a giant, the flash of red, and in the strobe-lighting of a las-bolt fusillade. Eight feet of power-armoured terror. She ducked and had a brief image of an axe head, chain-teeth whirling, and her legs were like jelly for a moment, and there was gore in her nose. In her screaming mouth. Not just blood, but thick gobs of human hair and flesh, the grit of bone shards and flak armour.

Minka bolted upright.

It was void-black about her. Her hands instinctively whipped her carbine round to fire, but the giant had gone. Her hands were empty. There was sweat on her forehead and down her back.

Her brother.

She focused on that moment to calm her thundering heart.

His name was Tarly. She had promised her mother she would look after him. She had done her best. He would be sixteen now. A Whiteshield. Maybe he was still alive somewhere. Maybe the Emperor *did* care.

She took in a deep breath. She needed to clear her head. Needed to think. She was a sergeant and the Emperor was watching her, and by the Throne, tomorrow morning she was going to get her squad into order.

* * *

Next morning Minka had a cold shower. She dressed and spit polished her boots. At 0455 hours she was standing on the parade ground with the healthy members of her squad lined up before her.

She was tired. Everyone was here, except the new man, Laptev.

'Anyone seen him?' she snapped.

Jaromir stepped forward. The big man stared down at her. He spoke slowly. 'He said he had better stuff to do.'

Minka made the big man repeat it.

'Is that so?'

'Yes,' Jaromir said. His eye started twitching again. She found it hard to look at him. 'I told him but that is what he said.'

Minka felt the eyes of all her squad on her. She felt Dreno and Belus waiting for her to screw up and bristled. 'Viktor! Order Corporal Laptev here. Now!'

She could feel them all thinking, 'Or what? You'll get the bats on him…?'

Viktor saluted and turned, his boots loud on the stone slabs of the parade ground. Her mind's eye followed him through the doorway of the barracks, and down the wide stone flags of the screw-stair, down to the sleeping bays that opened up on either side.

Then Laptev appeared.

'Corporal. I gave you instructions that the squad were to assemble at zero-five-hundred hours for drill.'

Laptev looked at the squad. 'And they're here.'

'But you were not.'

'You wanted me to come too?'

Minka heard Dreno and Belus snigger. Minka's hands were trembling. She'd lost Arktur already, and now this squad were making her look – and feel – like a rookie. She put her hands behind her back so no one would see, and clenched them into fists.

She didn't blink as she said, 'I assumed that was clear.'

'No,' he said. 'It wasn't.'

Minka had read his reports by now. He'd been in service for six years. He'd had a number of early commendations for bravery. Promotion. Specialised in hand-to-hand combat. He'd even made sergeant at some point, though it wasn't clear why he'd been demoted. From his report she'd expected a type common among the Cadians. Fierce, dependable, prone to drink when off-duty. Hot-headed enough to resolve arguments with his fists. She had not expected such hostility.

'I served with Arktur for six years,' Laptev said suddenly. 'He dragged me out of no-man's-land once. I owed him.'

'Listen. I'm really sorry about what happened,' she said. 'If he hadn't been dealing obscura…'

'Officers like you don't live long,' Laptev said.

'Are you threatening me?'

His gaze narrowed. 'No. I'm telling you the truth.'

FIFTEEN

The sun rose early on Potence. At 0600 hours it broke the southern horizon and started to burn down from the clear blue sky.

Rodin and Streck, from Janka's squad, were sitting outside their barrack, cleaning the squad's guns. They had oily rags in their hands, the disarticulated pieces of Kantrael carbines in their laps. Grogar came out, stripped down to his waist. His chest was tattooed with the Cadian Gate and the regimental numbers '101st'. He paused and looked up to where the sun was throwing shadows along the walls of the cathedral as Minka's squad finished their morning run.

Their red, sweat-dripping faces said it all, their boots scraping on the iron panels of the drill ground with a ragged patter like undisciplined gunfire. Like the local militia, or Whiteshields.

Poor frekkers out for a run in this heat. Minka gave him a look as though she felt herself being judged.

'In time!' she ordered, and the troopers made an effort as Minka led them across the metalled drill ground, their footfalls coming in step.

Grogar watched as Minka got to the water butt and stopped. One by one her squad stopped about her, sucking in great breaths.

Throne, they looked beat.

She checked her chronometer. 'Good job!' she called out. Grogar thought she ought to say more, but she was new to leadership. Effective leaders had the knack of saying something pithy, or funny, or inspiring. Always picking the right instrument and striking the right note.

Two of the new lot threw their packs to the floor. Sweat sparkled as it dripped from the ends of their noses. Their shirts were plastered to their backs. Their armpits were dark. They pulled the helmet straps off and threw their heads back, using their cupped hands to catch water from the ornate bronze water fountain. Another wiped his forehead with his forearm, used his helmet to catch water, put it to his mouth like a bowl, and let the water drain down either side of his face.

He made way for Minka, but she gestured for him to take more.

After a long pause she called, 'Fall out! Rifle drill at ten hundred hours.'

They nodded. No one said anything. They were exhausted.

As they went inside, Minka was left standing by the water spout. The sunlight was starting to glare now. It was going to get hot. She filled her water bottle and emptied it in long, desperate mouthfuls, then filled it once more.

Grogar was still watching her. He'd dismantled his squad's

carbines ready for cleaning. He laid each one out in pieces and reached for the next. His fingers knew the twists and clicks like other men knew how to tie a lace.

'Good run?' he said.

'Not bad.'

'How do the stripes feel?'

'How are yours?'

He looked at his own arm. 'One stripe is easy. Two is five times the trouble. Three... don't even talk to me.'

'So I'm learning.' She ran her hand over her scalp. The stubble was still sharp. 'They're not in a good shape.'

'No,' he agreed. There was a pause. 'I heard about your corporal.'

'I didn't snitch on him,' Minka said. 'When Shand spoke to him it was clear that something was up.'

Grogar said nothing. 'I hear you got Laptev as his replacement.'

'Yes.'

Grogar gave a finished lasgun a brief look and set it against the stack, resting against the wall. 'I'm in the same barrack as him. He's a nasty frekker. Be careful.'

'Yes. I've noticed. Normally I'd have him up on insubordination. He's difficult.'

'First rule of command – don't give an order that can be refused.'

'Thanks, Grogar,' she said. 'I screwed up there.'

Grogar put another carbine down. 'Well, you could throw the rulebook at him.'

'After Arktur?' Minka laughed humourlessly. 'No. I've got to sort this out myself.'

'Want me to talk to him?'

'You mean two to hold his arms and two to work him over? No. Thanks. I'll deal with it.'

'Sure?' he said, putting another lasrifle into the pile.

'Sure,' she said. He gave her a look. 'It'll be fine,' she said, more to convince herself. 'Honest.'

News came that morning that a troop transport, the *Righteous Endeavour*, had just arrived in orbit above the planet. Feared lost, the craft's arrival was welcomed with cheers, and it was given priority access to orbital facilities and planet-side landing zones.

By noon the first of the troops were disembarking.

Dido was part of the honour guard of Cadians sent to welcome the new regiment, but when she came back to barracks, queasy from the long climb up the acropolis, she didn't seem impressed.

'Apparently it's a medicae evacuation craft. Not a troop transport at all. Just a load of sick and dying, and one frekking Mountain Infantry unit. They're skirmishers, not line infantry. A mere two thousand at most. No armour to speak of.'

In his office, Colonel Sparker had just heard the same news and was absorbing it with his mid-morning recaf.

The taste made him stop for a moment. 'Tyson. Who is on recaf duty this morning?'

Tyson lifted his eyebrows in a non-committal expression. 'Do you like it, sir?'

'It's magnificent.'

Tyson stepped forward to inspect the cup. 'Recaf seller appeared at the barrack gates this morning. With his own wagon. We let him in, and I thought we'd let you have some. I tried it first, of course, to make sure it was good.'

Sparker took another sip. It was thick and dark as treacle

and had a kick like a bull grox. 'Well. Invite him back. It's the best recaf I think I've ever had!'

Tyson looked pained. 'You mean you don't like the usual brew.'

'Your recaf is very good, sergeant. But this man must excel at one thing. If we put a lasgun in his hand and asked him to fight, I fear he would fall very short of your standard.'

Tyson nodded. Point taken.

Sparker lifted the cup to let the last few drops drain onto his tongue. 'Very fine. Right. How many defending the planet now?'

'Six thousand Cadians, twenty-thousand Calibineer, of unknown quality, and these mountain troops. This is their home turf. They're raised in the Supramonte.'

'What the hell is that?'

'It's a plateau to the west of the Evercity. Nothing there of note, except for the astropathic tower. And foresters, I guess.'

'Any reports on their quality?'

'No, sir.'

'And any idea of the strength of the Scourged?'

'No idea. Estimates reckon anything between a hundred thousand and millions. I'd say millions. They'd need that many to take as many planets as they have in such a short space of time.'

Colonel Sparker paused. The odds were not good, even for Cadians. 'Maybe we could talk to the gangers,' he said. 'There might be another five thousand fighters. Grant them a pardon. Give them regular pay. It's been done before.'

'Yes, sir.'

As Tyson and Sparker sat in their office, the recaf seller – a thin, balding man, with dark hair and a slight hunch – was doing brisk business at the barrack gateway.

Even Chief Commissar Shand came out to see what the matter was.

'Has anyone tested the recaf?' he demanded. 'This man could poison half the regiment in one day.'

Prassan had a paper mug in one hand. 'No, sir. But it is very fine. Here.'

Shand took the recaf and smelt it. He took a sip. And then another.

'That is very good. I'll take this, if you don't mind, and have it examined.'

'Yes, sir,' Prassan said, and then watched crestfallen as the commissar walked away with it, taking another sip.

'Looks like you've been done,' Dido told him.

As Shand walked to the Commissariat office, a burial company were carrying a black body bag out of the door on a stretcher. It was Arktur's corpse.

'Where are you taking that?' he demanded.

'Colonel Sparker said to throw it over the parapet.'

Shand nodded his approval. Men like Arktur were traitors to the memory of Cadia, and traitors did not deserve burial.

He was about to go inside when bells started to ring below them in the Evercity. Shand paused and listened as first one, then more and more, began to chime, and then there was a low *boom!* from above as the great bell in the cathedral rang out.

He was about to go to find out what had happened when he spotted Grogar, taking a bundle of carbines back to the armoury. He hesitated for a moment, then called out. 'Grogar! When you've taken those back, come and see me please.'

Grogar saluted, and Shand took another sip of the recaf

then stepped inside and handed it to Knoll. 'What's that damned ringing for?' the commissar said.

'I'm trying to find out myself.'

'Good. Let me know as soon as you find out. Oh, and Knoll. Get this tested.'

'What is it?'

Chief Commissar Shand's face remained inexpressive as he said, 'It's the best recaf I think I've ever tasted.'

SIXTEEN

The gangers dumped what was left of Carkal in an open sewer, bleeding, groaning, one eye swollen shut. He could still taste the bread in his mouth, but he knew he was going to die. Knew he was done for.

He tried to move, but his body hurt too much, and he lay there as the sun rose and beat down on him. But not even its warm touch could help him now.

As he lay there he heard a strange sound, faint on the wind, but then growing in strength and confidence. It was a thousand bells ringing out from the chapels of the Evercity.

It was a joyous and exuberant melody. He had an urge to stand and walk towards it, but he could not stand, could not walk, would probably never walk again.

But the bells woke the people of the tent city. About him he heard voices lifted in prayer, and a few blocks away he heard the sound of women ululating and clapping their hands.

Carkal started to pray as Agatha had once taught him. To

say his creed, that he believed in the Holy Emperor of Mankind, who sits upon the Golden Throne and sends His light out to all humanity.

He was too weak to do more than whisper, but as he lay there, lips moving faintly, he felt the shadow of someone stopping above him.

He kept praying and guessed that this would be the ending. But no blow fell. No knife. No gunshot.

A figure knelt next to him and a man's voice spoke, 'You are praying. What is your name, my son?'

Carkal tried to speak, but his mouth was too swollen.

The stranger lifted Carkal's head and cradled it in his arms. It was a man, but he was gentle. 'Do you hear the bells? The sign has been given.'

'What sign?' Carkal wanted to say, but his voice failed him.

'Look at you, my son. You are poor and weak but you are dear to the Emperor of Mankind. Do you believe that?'

Carkal tried to speak, but he coughed and there was blood in his mouth. He spat it out as he tried to blink his eyes open, but dried blood had scabbed them closed. They had beaten him too hard. Only a weak nod showed his affirmation.

Finally, he blinked one eye open, and saw a thin, bearded mendicant with the four-pointed Richstar star sewn onto the fabric of his brown woollen overcoat. Carkal could not tell if he had died already. He tried to speak but his mouth was broken and his lips were thick and he couldn't form the words properly.

'The sign has been given. The sun has gone dark. It means that the Feast of Saint Ignatzio is almost upon us.'

Carkal nodded. He knew about Saint Ignatzio from his childhood education. He was the man who brought humanity to the Gallows Cluster, and drove out the xenos. But he had never heard of a feast day or bells, or anything else that was going on.

The figure smoothed a hand over his eyes. Carkal kept them closed. It was easier than struggling. 'Hush. You live, my child,' the voice said. 'Hush. We will make you strong as well. Will you join us?'

The words were soothing but somehow the hands were hard. Carkal struggled to sit up. He fell, but the kneeling figure caught him.

'Are you heretics?' Carkal said. He thought the suffering that his sins would bring would kill him. 'I cannot join the Scourged.'

The man laughed. 'No. We are not the Archenemy. We are the Brotherhood. The armed might of the Emperor of Mankind. We are faithful. If you believe, you will be strong. Do you believe?'

Carkal couldn't speak.

'The Emperor loves you. Can you feel His love?'

Carkal coughed once more. He felt pain but he wanted to be loved.

'The Emperor loves you, my son. Can you feel His love, like a fire through your veins?'

Carkal winced as pain stabbed through his ribs. He was dying. He felt his heartbeat flutter, and then the man put hands on him and after a moment Carkal felt a warmth in his gut that spread to his arms and legs, and the tremor in his heartbeat settled.

'Can you feel *that*?' the man said.

Carkal said nothing for a long time as the love of the Emperor spread through his body. At last he said, 'Yes. I can. I feel it.'

'Good. Concentrate on His strength and He will save you.'

Carkal coughed again as the man helped him sit up. He felt dizzy and thought he might black out, but the man held him tight.

'I feel it,' Carkal said. 'The Emperor loves me.'

'Good,' the man said. He placed his palms on Carkal's chest and pressed down. The pressure was so great Carkal could not breathe. He tried to push the hands away, but the man was too strong, the compression too great.

Carkal struggled for a moment, but the crush grew stronger, and then he coughed, and this time there was no pain, just that sense of warmth, spreading from his torso to his limbs. He sucked in a deep breath that went through him like an electric shock. His eyes snapped open. There were tears in them that he blinked away. He felt strength and life return.

The face that looked down into his was old and lined, with an aquila tattooed under one eye, along with the ordinal '86th'. His eyes were intent. 'Breathe deep,' he said. 'There!'

The man's eyes bored into Carkal. 'There. Good. Are you tired of being weak? Do you want to be strong?'

'Yes, I do,' Carkal said as the man helped him stand. 'Who are you?'

The man said, 'I am The Bringer of News. Are you ready to hear the Word?'

PART THREE

'The Emperor will destroy those who hate Him.
His anger shall be a blazing fire.'

— Song of Vandire

ONE

Tremors ran through the Dauntless-class cruiser *Admiral Sistina* as it began to slow to orbiting speed above Potence. An escort of snub-nosed defence monitors checked her security codes. Once she was cleared for docking, colossal anchor chains unwound from port and aft, and she slowed as these tugged against the high-orbit moorings.

The change in speed woke General Bendikt. He found himself lying in his marble-lined quarterdeck apartments, trying to shrug off a sleep so deep it had left him feeling confused and disorientated.

The oak-panelled cabin was unfamiliar at first, but there was his dress jacket hanging on its stand, with sword and a VonNeidder bolt pistol belt slung over the corner of his bed.

He stood. A little shaky.

He tried to scratch his nose, but there was something wrong. His hand was no longer there. He looked down,

183

and saw the bandaged stump of his right arm and then it all came back to him.

Not just the fight, of course, but the whole reason it had happened. The fall of Cadia – the most heavily defended quarter of the Imperium, left broken and shattered.

The duel was as nothing. But the memory of his home world hit him like a well-aimed punch. Bendikt put his hand out to steady himself, and clenched his teeth together so hard he could feel them grating, swayed for a moment, and let a low, strangled moan of pain escape his lips.

He put his stump to the wall and sobs tore themselves out of him.

This was how he had woken almost every day since the Great Calamity. The worst thing was that Bendikt knew to the core of his soul that everything that damned fool de Barka had said was true. The Cadians had been given a sacred trust, and they had failed.

The docking alarms were sounding when Mere knocked.

'Come in,' Bendikt called, and Mere brought the breakfast tray inside and set it on the table.

Bendikt drew himself up. He had dressed himself and had neatly folded and pinned his right-hand sleeve in place. 'Any word from the shipmaster?' he asked.

'Yes. Not good, I'm afraid. Since our re-entry into normal space, we've had a lot of status updates. Some of them are still being deciphered. Apparently contact has been lost with the planet of Kypra.'

'Kypra!' Bendikt said. He pulled a space chart towards him. Kypra lay a month's warp travel from the front line. The foe had sidestepped the hasty picket at Namarra, and their position now put them within a short warp jump from Potence.

The audacity of the move was admirable. It was chilling. The speed of the assaults spoke of vast and disciplined forces at the disposal of the leader of the Scourged, Drakul-zar.

'Our foe has made a mockery of the Imperial defence,' Bendikt said. 'He must have a warp capable fleet as well. He's split the system in half, and once he has Potence he'll be able to make a move towards Holy Terra!'

Mere nodded. The Scourged had cut the Gallows Cluster in half in a matter of mere months.

'That bastard Warmund must have known. He's sent me here to die,' Bendikt said. 'He sent me here to fail.'

'So prove him wrong. When we get onto the planet you can assess the situation. You've got the 101st with you, remember.'

Bendikt nodded, though to be honest he now feared being reunited with his old regiment.

'I hope they have aged better than me,' Bendikt said. The time since Cadia's fall had broken him. He had lost his pride, his reputation, his sobriety and now his hand.

'Have faith,' Mere said.

Bendikt nodded. He had had faith once, but now... Mere gave him a warning look. There were some things that should not be said aloud.

'I will pray for you,' Mere said.

They sat to eat.

Mere had cut the ship-slab into small pieces, and Bendikt used his left arm to fork his food into his mouth. From classified reports the 101st had been through the wringer since Cadia. The fight for the hive world of Marquis had been one of the bloodiest fights that the sector had seen. It was one of those hopeless battles that Bendikt had seen many times: a gaping hole in a battlefront into which bodies were thrown by the million. Fine regiments, some of the best warriors of the Imperium, had been sacrificed to stem a flood that could not be held back. And its loss had set in motion the terrifying advances of the Scourged.

Mere poured a mug of recaf for the general.

Bendikt rubbed his temples as he waited for the brew to cool. He took a sip. It was thin and sour, and tasted of recycled water. 'Very good,' he said, breezily.

As they went through the most urgent classified reports, Bendikt realised that he was being a little brusque.

Mere said nothing, which made it worse.

'I'm sorry, Mere,' he said at last. 'To be honest I'm a little nervous. There'll be a plaque somewhere, a statue, and a son will say to his mother, "What was Cadia? Who were the Shock Troopers?" And the mother will not know. We're a dying force. A dying tradition. Someday, the Cadian Shock Troopers will be just a memory.'

Mere's face said it all. 'Forgive me, sir. But that is frankly impossible.'

Bendikt ran his hand through his hair. As a general of the Cadian Shock Troopers, he was privy to the coded communiqués of the Munitorum. 'I'm afraid it is very possible. In fact, it will happen. I've seen the numbers. We're losing Cadians at an alarming rate. And there's no one to fill their places. With attrition rates this high there'll be no Cadians left in ten years. Where would new Cadians come from?'

Mere didn't answer at first. At last he spoke. 'If we are gone, does the Imperium stand any chance?'

Bendikt laughed. 'You speak like a true Cadian. How can the Imperium survive without us!'

'And the answer?'

Bendikt remembered the last days of Cadia. How he had prayed. Fervently. Passionately. He tried to speak, but his voice gave way. He had to draw in a deep breath and try to master his emotion. 'I used to be certain about things. But now, the impossible keeps happening, and all my certainties have gone. I'm adrift, like a ship that wanders through the void without purpose or direction. I don't know much these days. All I have is the pride that our fathers and mothers gave us. Pride in being a Cadian. And if we are a dying race, then we should go down in style, so that the chroniclers remember us well.'

Anchor chains were still unravelling as vector thrusters lit along the three-mile-long hull of the *Admiral Sistina*, servitor pilots slowing its forward momentum to match that of the planet's rotation.

It took nearly two hours before the ship had settled safely into the equatorial docking bay above Potence, and when they were in position, the distinctive clunk of mag-locks vibrated through the craft, and then a stillness settled within the ship's superstructure that could only mean that its engines had been turned off.

Disembarkation would begin any moment now.

There was a knock on Bendikt's door. A Navy rating put his head around the door. He was dressed in the blue velvet jacket and white breeches typical of the Richstar personnel, his blue bonnet piped with gilt and a four-pointed star emblazoned on his chest.

He had a thick Gothic accent that Bendikt still had difficulty understanding. He had to ask the man to repeat himself before the message was clear.

'From the shipmaster, sir. Main landers not departing until tomorrow morning, but his private skiff will be leaving in one hour sidereal. It is taking members of the Richstars down.'

'I didn't know there were Richstars aboard.'

'They requested privacy, sir. Some of them are distraught. I believe a number of them have lost their planets.'

'Well, I should have been informed. There's much I would like to know about the Scourged. These people have first-hand experience.'

'I will pass that message along. Meanwhile, the shipmaster wants to know if you would like a place reserved. As a mark of honour, he said, sir.'

'Thank you,' Bendikt said, rather brusquely. 'Yes. I would.'

Mere and Bendikt were the first to arrive at the small bridge deck hangar, just one hour after docking, as the automated day-night systems switched from light to the dull illumination of ship-night. The shipmaster's pinnace had been freshly painted in deep-space indigo. The scent of recycled air and paint hung in the air, but no one else was here yet. A pair of fuelling servitors sat inactive against a far wall, mouths hanging dumbly open.

'What is wrong with these Richstars?'

'Maybe they're overwhelmed. Losing their planets and all.'

'It happens to all of us,' Bendikt said, even though it wasn't true.

'Well. We travel light,' Mere said.

Bendikt nodded. Apart from a pistol and a power sword, and a well-thumbed copy of *The Campaigns of Macharius*, he did not have many possessions. Those few he did have Mere carried in a matched pair of beaten leather travel chests that now sat on the metal grate of the open hangar.

He looked at them. They held the sum of his life's possessions. Not much, he thought.

* * *

An hour dragged by.

Bendikt cursed as he paced up and down. The ship crew had proved themselves to be generally tardy in all things, something that Bendikt found himself unable to come to terms with. He arrived early for all events, and stood about with the staff, who looked both appalled and uneasy with this punctual guest.

But at last there was activity, as the fuel servitors came to life and the cold air echoed with the shouted reports of approaching crewmen, and the low hum of the void-lock as it was readied for opening.

'We were supposed to leave an hour ago,' Bendikt said to the pinnace's chief purser, who wore a long silk gown, belted at the waist with a velvet cummerbund.

'Apologies, sir general. There was an unavoidable delay,' he said. 'Gerent Bianca was sick. It took her a long time to finish her breakfast.'

'And so we all wait?'

'Well, she is the most senior member of the Richstar family aboard. It is only good manners to respect her repast.'

Bendikt cursed to himself. He had seen enough of the galaxy to know that it was the ponderous weight of the Administratum that held the Imperium back, not its soldiers. But worse than that, it was the corrupt aristocracy like the Richstars that fermented unrest and heresy.

The pinnace's crew climbed inside the craft. Servitor insets were coaxed to life and lights flickered on inside the cabin. But there was still no sign of the Richstars.

'What is wrong with these people?' Bendikt cursed, but then a bell rang, and the pinnace lights came on. The slumped piloting servitors sat up with a jolt as their power cables were plugged into data-docks.

A few minutes later the pilots appeared. There were three of them, each one dressed in leather jacket and fur-lined cap. The chief pilot was an ugly-looking man with a round gut and raw wire plugs set into the side of his shaved skull. He sniffed as he climbed up and started throwing switches.

The engines started, and at that moment, the first of the Richstars appeared.

He was a thin, bearded man, hair white with age and hanging down to his shoulders. He wore a gown of red sequins that exaggerated the paleness of his skin. One arm was augmetic and rested on a bladed, metal cane. About him came an entourage of death world bodyguards with buck-skin war-shirts, embroidered with their greatest conquests, blue-feather headdresses hanging halfway down their backs, and power glaives resting on their shoulders. They stopped twenty feet away and eyed the Cadians.

The next Richstar had a pair of identical life-wards dressed in muscled bronze breastplates and ostrich-feather shakos, silk pennants hanging from the end of their power lances. The third had two lean women in non-reflective bodysuits with matching blue-tattooed faces, white hair, tanned skin and the look of death cultists in their yellow cat-eyes. The fourth had short, stocky wards with fur hats, trident axes and broad sabres. They guarded a child with high-collared gold ruff and carefully coiffured white hair. She sat on a grav-throne that swayed gently at the far end of the room, three servo-skulls trailing in the air above her head.

The last was accompanied by a pair of genhanced bodyguards with muscle-slabbed physiques and bronze helmets with horsehair plumes. Their visors glowed red with augmetics, and behind them came a lady in a bodice of black glass, the silk ruff giving her neck a stunted look.

'The Lady Bianca,' her life-wards announced. She was cousin to the Patridzo, the head of the Richstar family and resident of the Evercity, himself. At a distance she appeared no older than sixteen, with plump cheeks and full, red lips, but as she came closer it was clear that she'd been through so many rejuvenat cycles it was hard to locate her age with any degree of accuracy. Her face had a waxy look, the skin too taut for any wrinkles.

Age was in the eyes, Bendikt usually found, but these had been modified too: the irises were neon-yellow with vertical black pupils, like those of a snake.

All the Richstars bowed as she approached, and Lady Bianca ran her eyes over them with an air of weary indifference. She had the balanced, poised, dangerous air of a trained killer. Lastly she turned her gaze upon the Cadians. It paused briefly on Mere and then passed on, and Bendikt's cheeks coloured.

'You are General Bendikt,' she said.

Bendikt saluted.

'I am glad you are here,' she said. 'We put our trust in you and your troops.'

'We live to serve. We die to protect.'

The Richstar companies made their way onto the pinnace.

Bendikt and Mere went last. By the time the ramp was cleared, the void alarms were sounding, and strobing yellow light played across their faces.

But just as the ramp began to rise, two more figures strode out onto the hangar deck. The first was dressed in a plain brown smock and short trews that left his hairy shins and feet bare. A confessor followed behind him, bearing an oversized, leather-bound folio lashed onto his back with tarnished silver chains.

As the hydraulics whined shut, the appearance of these passengers brought a tense, reverential air to the cabin. The barefoot man moved along the lines, giving his hand to the Richstars to kiss. Even Lady Bianca bowed as they approached, and she took the man's hand and pressed it to her forehead.

As the ramp closed with a dull clunk, the newcomer singled Bendikt out and strode towards him. 'General Bendikt,' he said. His voice was clear and strong and confident.

Bendikt was not sure if he should bow or kiss his hand, but the man put out a hand to shake.

Bendikt lifted his stump in apology, and the other man smiled and took his left hand with his own.

His grip was cold and strong. He had a fierce intensity about him. He smiled.

'Welcome to Potence,' he said. 'My name is Shaliah Starborn. I am the Bringer of News.'

TWO

Laptev did not show up for gun-drills that afternoon.

'Shall I get him?' Jaromir said.

'No. I'll go,' Minka said, but at that moment an alarm rang out and Kranus, the drillmaster, dismissed the previous squad.

'I'm done with you. Get off my firing range now!'

Kranus was a mouth on legs – mean, angry, with two volume settings: loud and louder.

He thrust out his chin and roared, 'Hurry up, sergeant! I don't have time for dawdling.'

Minka cursed. 'Right,' she said. 'Into positions!'

'Come on, troopers. Hit the dirt. My grandmother moves faster than you lot. And she's dead!'

As they took their places, Minka was so angry that she could barely hold her rifle straight.

Kranus marched back and forth behind them, hitting his thigh with his swagger stick.

'In the distance you will notice stationary targets. That piece of paper wants to kill you. He wants to tear out your eyes and cut symbols into your flesh. Shoot that frekker. Put las-bolts through his brain.'

The troopers fired as Kranus insulted them.

'Moving targets!' he shouted, and there was a low *clunk* as the targets started to jolt back and forth.

Minka's shots were wild. When the drill was over Kranus looked at her targets with disgust. 'Two misses. That's a fail. Name?'

'Arminka Lesk.'

'Rank.'

'Sergeant. Fourth Platoon. M Company.'

'How the hell did you get stripes when you can't shoot straight?'

Minka said nothing.

'You got to move your lips when you speak to me, Sergeant Lesk. I'm not psychic.'

'Sorry, sir. I will sign myself up for extra practice,' Minka said sullenly.

'Good. If you're not hitting, you're not killing.'

'Oh, don't worry. I'll kill,' Minka said.

'Well. Miss my targets again and I'll report you. Who is your commanding officer?'

'Colonel Sparker.'

Kranus filled in the requisite details. 'Now. Where are the missing troopers?'

'Thaddeus and Silas are at the medicae unit.' She pulled the medicae forms from her breast pocket.

The drillmaster sniffed as he filled out the forms. 'I have twelve in your squad.'

He went through the names. When he got to Arktur, Minka

had to tell him what had happened. Kranus crossed Arktur's name out and made a *tsch!* noise between his teeth, as
if Arktur's death were there to frustrate him. 'Has he been
replaced?'

There was a pause before Minka said, 'Yes, sir.'

'Who with?'

'Corporal Laptev.'

Kranus' temper was wearing thin. 'And where is he?'

'He has the shits.'

'So?'

'Bad shits.' She met his gaze and dared him to disbelieve
her.

'I don't like you, Lesk,' he shouted. 'And I don't like your
corporal. I don't care if he shits on my range as long as he
can shoot heretics. Understand?'

'Yes, sir.'

The next squad were queuing for their turn. They were
impatient. Kranus had a tight schedule. He cursed and
handed her the sheet. 'Come on, troopers. Hit the dirt! My
grandmother moves faster than you lot. And she's dead!'

Minka kicked the barrack door open.

'Where the hell is Laptev?' she demanded.

No one seemed to know. His bunkmate, a thin, blond man
with an aquila tattoo on his cheek, shrugged. 'Not seen him.'

She went to the canteen, the drill yard where troopers
were playing padball, and then to the mess where there were
three tables of men playing dice or cards, under heavy blue
clouds of lho-smoke. She scanned the faces. None of them
were Laptev.

She slammed the latrine door open, banged on the cubicle doors, marched through the shower block.

'Give me five, and I'll be right with you,' one of the men said.

'You wouldn't last seconds,' she told him.

The others laughed as she slammed through the exit, and stood in the corridor, looking one way and then the other. She was almost giving up when she saw him coming out of the bath house. His trousers were wet. He was stripped to the waist, his towel thrown over his shoulders, his block soap in a Munitorum-issue net bag in his hand.

He was six foot two, built like a rockcrete wall, and she remembered he was a specialist in hand-to-hand combat. But she couldn't hit him without warning him. 'Laptev!' she roared. He spun round and tried to duck. Her punch caught him on the side of the face. He rolled, hands reaching for her as she stepped to the side, kicked the back of his knee and half elbowed, half shoulder-barged him backwards.

The blow threw him off balance, even as his hand caught her arm and dragged her towards him. His breath was sour. He caught her with a body blow, his knuckles bruising her ribs. He hit her again and she ducked twice to protect her head and stepped in close.

He hissed, 'I'm not taking orders from you!'

And she spat back, 'Yes, you are.'

They came together, grappling as they got the weight of each other. He was stronger than her and within moments he had his forearm under her chin, one fist clamped in the other as he pulled his grip tight.

'I'll break your neck if you try that again,' Laptev said. He tightened his throat-lock to make his point.

He was good, but Minka was better. She struggled and he tensed, and then she went limp.

He relaxed his grip and she threw herself forwards, hooked

her leg about his knee and twisted his hand down onto the forearm. The big man went down like a sack of meal-flour. The thud took the wind out of him and he lay for a moment, blinking in surprise.

Minka kicked him in the side. He doubled up. 'If anyone is breaking necks, Laptev, it's me. Understand?'

He lay on his back for a moment, then rolled to the side and pushed himself up onto his elbow.

'Going to send me to the bats?'

'Not unless I have to.'

He stood and dusted himself down. She had her fists ready, but she'd made her point.

'I'm your sergeant and you'll obey my orders. You'll go to the firing range when I tell you, or I will show you what hand-to-hand combat is *really* like.'

That evening at mess Minka's ribs hurt.

Prassan winked at her and she cursed him and sat alone, and she was happy no one tried to come and speak to her.

Only when she slid her tray into the washing-up box did Tyson fall in next to her. 'What happened to your face?'

'Nothing,' she told him.

He did not let her get away. 'Redskulls?'

'No,' she said.

'Which one?'

'No one.'

Tyson had always struck Minka as a big, stupid man with a big mouth good for shouting out orders. But now he put a hand on her shoulder. 'Listen. I heard you kicked Laptev's backside.'

'No.'

'They've been through a tough time.'

'Haven't we all?'

Tyson patted her shoulder. 'Yes. But he has a good record.'

'Are you blaming me for Arktur's death? *I* didn't feed him obscura!'

Tyson saw that he had annoyed her. He tried to appear conciliatory. 'Just do your best. We don't want anyone else being shot.'

'I hear you,' she said. She was angry, and rather than speak to Tyson further she turned and stalked off.

THREE

When they landed at the starport, the Patridzo's own lighter was waiting for his relatives, while a military Salamander waited for General Bendikt.

The Richstars hurried aboard. There had been a time, long gone, when the Patridzo of the Gallows Cluster had lived in the palace on the top of the acropolis in the Basilika. Now the Richstar dynasty was housed a little way down the high rock on a jutting headland that thrust straight out about four hundred yards from the summit, and two hundred yards below the Intake Barracks, in a complex known as the Kalvert.

It was to this dwelling that Lady Bianca and the other, lesser, Richstars were taken.

From above, the Kalvert complex seemed a modest affair. There was a high wall of red brick, providing privacy rather than defence, and then the long, tiled roofs of the palace's wings and contemplatorium, with a neatly clipped garden and the dark green of ancient, crooked pines.

Bianca's father had brought her here for the Feast of St Ignatzio two hundred years earlier, and she had the vague memory of following two steps behind him, winding through ancient tunnels and baroque chambers that housed garde-robes, oratories, icehouses, solars, butteries and cabinets of ancient curiosities.

She mused on this as the craft hovered over the palace com-pound, and then descended on its vector thrusters.

Lady Bianca was first out. The lighter had settled in the Lower Terrace, a high-walled garden with low knotworks of carefully manicured evergreens and carefully tended flower beds arranged in steps up to the perscreen wall of the con-templatorium. She breathed deep, and looked up to the pale, rocky limestone crags that rose up behind the palace, and had a brief impression of the size of the cathedral at its summit.

She did not have long to enjoy the view. A man was hur-rying down to greet them all. She noted that it was not the Patridzo himself, but his equerry, Shanttal.

'Lady Bianca,' he said, bowing excessively low. 'We are honoured.'

'Not so honoured that the Patridzo will walk down to greet us personally. Is he working?'

'Yes, my lady. It has been a matter of great concern that so many of the pieces that he created with his own hands have fallen into the hands of the enemy.'

'Sacrilege.'

'Indeed, your highness.' Shanttal started to say more but then Shaliah Starborn appeared, padding down the ramp on bare feet. 'My lord Starborn,' Shanttal said, kneeling. 'Wel-come. You are expected, and as you requested, everything is made ready.'

'What is going on?' Lady Bianca demanded.

'It is the Feast of St Ignatzio. The augurs have declared it imminent,' Shanttal answered. He gave a thin smile. 'Come. Follow me. We are expecting great things to be portended. The promised days are coming. The Richstars have been chosen, and today a huge honour will be bestowed upon us all.'

'Here,' Shanttal said, and showed the Richstars to the Room of the Virtues, deep in the rock.

Lady Bianca walked into a bright and airy space. Shanttal read her expression.

'The room is lit by a relay of mirrors and pipes that bring daylight down into this subterranean level. The Patridzo used to paint here, but he has become more earnest now and devotes himself exclusively to iconography. He has found his private chapel more suitable for that particular kind of work.'

They nodded attentively and admired the frescoes as Shanttal bowed and slipped out of a side door. 'I will see if the Patridzo is ready to see you now.'

The Patridzo was the honorary title given to the senior member of the Richstar dynasty. The current Patridzo was named Urdalig Richstar, the fourth to bear that name, and eighty-third direct descendant of Lord Marshal Ignatzio Solar. He lived a quiet, almost hermit-like life, in meditative silence under the glassaic windows of his private chapel, set deep within the lower levels of his palace.

Today he was working earnestly on a miniature icon for a chapel on Gallen V. His Emperor had dark hair, full battle-plate, skin of gold leaf and eyes of radiant crystal. He had the finest brush of red sable with which he laid down the glue for the gold leaf, which trembled in each breath of air.

The backdrop was how the Patridzo imaged Holy Terra had once been, when the Emperor trod its fields. It was green and verdant, with fountains of clear and refreshing water.

The chime rang from above, telling him his guests had arrived. He moved quicker now, pressing the gold leaf into place. He wanted to finish the left cheek before he was stopped. There were so many interruptions these days. Too many interruptions. Too much news in general, and all of it bad.

He bent over his icons as he felt the rumble of ancient doors opening above him. They were locked with ancient bio-screening that would only let members of the Richstar line through.

He knew the sound of each door as it fell shut, and recognised the clip of expensive boots on the tiled floors. He knew how long he had left before he was disturbed, and let out an exasperated sigh and started washing his brush, straightening the bristles in his pursed lips. He held it up for a moment to check the point, and then set it on the stand and drew in a deep breath and stood.

Life had taught him many things, some useful, others not. But one truth he held on to was that whenever one had a job to do, there was never enough time.

When all was ready Lady Bianca and the others were led down a narrow corridor to the side doors of the chapel.

Two of the Patridzo's life-wards stood at the end of the corridor. One of them was a four-armed warrior who answered to the title of Meroë. The other was a Carthae warrior named Wyryn, whose platinum hair was plaited close to her head. She moved with a beguiling litheness, typical of those who had studied *Ewl Wyra Scryri*. They both stepped back politely, but the mass of Meroë's gene-crafted physique forced Lady Bianca to squeeze past, and up the three steps.

The domed chapel was modest in size, but that was where the modesty ended. The rest of it was an indulgent cacophony of religious statuary, paintings and richly illuminated devotional texts.

At her feet was a swirling mosaic of black and white marble, porphyry insets, and intricately carved marble pedestals. The walls were awash with a cycle of murals depicting the Struggles of the Emperor and the Life of St Ignatzio, and sculptures of the ancient scions of the family, whose busts stood on low pedestals of silver filigree. The ceilings seemed to soar above the head of the viewer, with images of the sky, and space, and Saint Ignatzio's ancient battle cruiser, the *Arnolfiad*, on its conquest of the system. Gold leaf baroque cornices mimicked the architecture of a building, with the long spines of roof supports carved into the rock, and bosses carved with the likenesses of Imperial preachers, their eyes wide, their mouths closed, their helmet visors pushed back, the ends of their lasrifles poking up by their faces. There were chapel tombs and frescoes, catafalques, inset altars, confessionaries and a dozen examples of the Patridzo's finest icons, hanging mute on the walls. All the devotional energies of six thousand years were concentrated into one private and reverential place.

The impact of the beauty and history stunned the Patridzo's guests. Even Lady Bianca paused and found her gaze lifted to the exquisite ceilings. Her cousin's recent intense work had been in response to the fall of Cadia.

The Patridzo had taken off his apron, but he still looked underdressed for the occasion in silk slippers, belted robe and a floppy tasselled cap.

'Greetings,' he said, welcoming each of them. 'Here we are gathered in the light of the Golden Throne. It is upon our shoulders that the burden of decision-making falls. I welcome you in this hour of travail that has come upon us. It cannot be a coincidence that the skeins of fate have brought you all here just two days before the Feast of St Ignatzio.'

'It is not chance. I have seen portentous things in the tarot,' Shaliah said. 'Great events are about to unfold here on Potence, where our forefather Saint Ignatzio first brought humanity to these stars. And by his grace, you will decide whether this is the time for which we have all waited.'

There were murmurs of assent. But the air within the room was breathless, tense.

Shaliah spoke again. 'Yes. We have a momentous decision to make. We have clung on to our ancient faith for centuries while the Ecclesiarchy mounted purges and pogroms and punished any who held to the old ways. Many of our forebears suffered greatly. One way. One road. One path that leads to salvation. I think we should take our dilemma to the Saint.'

'Surely not.' The Patridzo's face showed alarm, but Shaliah looked about for support.

'What greater need could we have?'

'But to disturb his rest…'

'If we do not act now, then all that he built will be lost to the Ruinous Powers.'

The Patridzo paled visibly, but he was not a man with a strong enough will to resist them all. He looked pathetic as he turned to Lady Bianca. 'Lesser cousin. I do not advise this course of action. It is extreme…'

She put up a hand and cut him off. 'Will the Saint speak?'

'We shall have to consult him to see.'

Bianca's yellow eyes widened. 'To see the Saint. That would be a rare honour!'

FOUR

A staircase led down, beneath the altar.

They followed Shaliah, who stopped before a tall, ornate plasteel door, set with bass-relief panels.

Lady Bianca stepped forward to examine the panels. 'These show the Twelve Cleansings.'

Each one depicted one of the twelve xenos races that Ignatzio Richstar had wiped out in order to make the sector safe for humanity. In the middle of the door was an ornate bio-lock.

'It is coded to Richstar blood only,' Shaliah announced. He ostentatiously slid a finger into an indent on the middle right-hand panel. There was a faint, almost inaudible click as a needle entered his fingertip, extracted a pearl of blood and confirmed his identity with a whirl of bio-mechanical cogs.

The door did not open, but slid back into recessed tracks in the wall, and as it did so, lumen-globes flickered to life, illuminating another long, broad staircase.

Faint music began to play. It was the sound of a choir chanting ancient hymns.

Shaliah held out a hand. 'Tread carefully, brothers and sisters, to the hall where our forefather himself is laid.'

The black marble staircase led them down so steeply that some had to hold on to the metal railing to steady their descent. Behind them the lights flickered off, while ahead of them more lights blinked, which gave the odd impression of being on an endless staircase.

After a minute or so the walls to either side were no longer dressed but raw stone, still marked by the swirling pattern of the adamantium mole that had burrowed the tunnel. The air grew chill. There was a musty smell. Then, suddenly, the steps ended, and they found themselves in a simple rough-hewn chamber.

Two tunnels branched off to either side, lit by low candles set along the floor at fifty-yard intervals.

'Welcome to the Place of Death.'

'Where does that tunnel lead?' Lady Bianca said, indicating the other passage.

'To the cathedral,' the Patridzo explained. 'The Kalvert was once named the Sepulchre. It was Ignatzio's mausoleum until our seat moved from the cathedral.'

Lady Bianca shook her head. 'I had always wondered why the cardinal had such a large palace, when your own, forgive me, Patridzo, is so much smaller.'

'Blame it on the vagaries of history.'

'Are we ready?' Shaliah asked.

They all nodded.

'Then let us enter.' He spoke in a hushed voice because this was sacred ground. 'We are now entering the catacombs where the Richstars are buried. And at the end is Ignatzio's mausoleum.'

* * *

They walked through a tunnel lined with niches cut out of the rock.

The air was thick with the dry scent of ages and Lady Bianca had the brief impression of mouldering remains, desiccated bodies, limbs and torsos held together by a thin layer of peeling brown skin.

When they reached the end, they stood in awed silence. The double door ahead was plain and ancient, and opened at a push.

Shaliah led them through to another corridor. The scent of long-dead bodies grew intense, like a rarefied spice, and to either side they could feel the cool, empty spaces as they passed the earliest catacombs, where the very first members of the Richstar family were laid to rest.

The flickering candles only served to throw the darkness of the niches into impenetrable blackness, but over each there were names carved into the stone. Lady Bianca let her fingers brush the engraved letters – Cristoforo the Black, Giuntal the Pious, Bertinal the Elder, Diedi the Conqueror.

'I can hardly believe,' she said to Shaliah, 'that we shall get to see Ignatzio himself.'

'It fills me with joy,' Shaliah said.

The last fifty yards were dark. The tunnel had been damaged in some ancient fire, and never properly restored. The crypts here were empty, the names lost, and the ornate plaster that decorated their surfaces had long since mouldered away. Bare stone showed the herringbone chisel marks of the servitor-masons who had carved the tunnels out of the bedrock. There were a few niches where candles had once stood, and the tunnel bowed gently towards the middle, where millennia of footsteps had worn the floor away.

Finally a doorway of heavy grey plasteel stood before them,

with traces of gold leaf still visible in the fire-discoloured filigree surface. Shaliah stepped forward and pressed his own palm flat against the key-panel. His open hand fitted the impression in the stone. There was no blood this time. No whirl of cogs and gears, just the single, high chime of a hidden bell, and then the panel doors slid open.

Lady Bianca pushed ahead of the others and was right behind the Patridzo.

The smell of decay was absent inside, in its place the air of ages, and a faint hint of sandalwood and amber incense.

'Come with grace.' Shaliah spoke the words with a formality and dignity that spoke of some ancient ritual or mass. 'And remember the many who have trodden this path, and not strayed, despite the years of darkness that press on either side. Despite the faithless and the impure. Despite the imposition of a false faith upon us all.'

Lady Bianca answered with the others, in the required fashion. 'We shall not forget. We shall not stray. We await the return of the light.'

Shaliah closed his eyes, his lips moving in a silent prayer, then he nodded and beckoned them all inside.

Lady Bianca was immediately struck by the sense of space. The room was vast and airy and, almost diminutive in the centre, held in a bubble of shimmering golden stasis, was the body of their ancestor Lord Marshal Ignatzio Solar.

She stepped forward and looked up and about herself at the vast dome that stretched above her head. She saw gold and silver, and the faint gleam of precious stones. In the centre of the chapel stood a round oculus, and from it fell a soft, yellow light that illuminated the smooth marble of the floor, which was set with a symbol of forked lightning and the leopard badge of Ignatzio Richstar.

The private chapel of the Richstars was a wonder of early artwork. A painting of the Imperial Palace showed a gleaming gold-roofed fortress of white and red stone, and in the middle there were texts that would have the whole assembly tried on Ophelia for heresy. Set at regular points around the circular walls were servitor-niches whose occupants had long since died, and whose function had been forgotten. But none of this was of any interest to the visitors.

The family gathered and looked down in stunned silence.

Here was the body, not just of their forebear, but also of a saint, founder, hero and figure of legend. A man who bestrode a powerful moment, when the Imperium of Man colonised the deserted tracts of the galaxy. A man who had been alive in the Age of the God-Emperor.

The stasis field flickered with curling blue corposant.

Ignatzio Richstar looked as though he might be asleep, except for the stillness of his repose. There was no beat of blood in his veins, no lift of his chest as he inhaled, no mist of exhalation about his mouth. He was still, frozen, held in a moment of time that stretched back ten thousand years to the great days of exploration and settlement.

Ignatzio Richstar had the long, lean, chiselled-cheek face of a man much weathered by life and by circumstance. This was a face that had seen worlds put to fire and blade.

The Gallows Cluster had been rich in native flora and fauna when humans arrived. Some had been beautiful. Some sentient. Many deadly. All had been destroyed. This was a man that had looked into the maws of xenos races and consigned their evolutionary journey to extinction, their gene-pool to oblivion.

All this could be seen in the rugged jawline, the crow-foot creases in the corner of his eyes, the stern set of his brow.

Lady Bianca had hoped to see some family resemblance, but there was almost none, except for an authoritarian air that reminded her of her father.

Ignatzio's ornate armour was decorated with a pattern of golden roses and thorns. An enclosed helmet was tucked under one arm, and his legs were sheathed in greaves and thigh plates. His hands were gloved and joined in quiet repose, while a high collar of ceramite lay open.

Sparks and threads of light gently crazed the bubble of the stasis field as its blue glow up-lit the faces of those who bent towards their forebear.

'To think, that face gazed upon the sublime visage of the Holy Emperor Himself.' It was Shaliah who spoke. There were tears in the chaplain's eyes. They fell unhindered as the magnitude of the moment sank in. That face had beheld the Emperor as a divine being, living, moving, speaking. 'Those eyes,' Shaliah said, 'looked into the eyes of the Emperor Himself, if any could hold the gaze of such a divine being. And, no doubt, the Emperor had spoken to him.'

A tear fell from Shaliah's cheek. It hit the stasis field with a brief fizz of golden energy.

'Careful!' the Patridzo warned.

Shaliah nodded, and drew in a deep breath. 'Yes. We are here for a reason. Come. Gather round. We are here to witness.'

They gathered in a circle. Shaliah stood between the Patridzo and Lady Bianca, and opened the silken pouch that hung about his neck. From it he took a pack of antique embossed cards.

'The Starborns have always come here, to the shrine of Saint Ignatzio, to understand the many threads of the future. Here in this sacred space I shall read the will of the Emperor.'

He took the sacred wafers and broke the pack in three places, and then laid the cards out before him on the pedestal. Starting at the left he turned each card.

The first was the Emperor's Throne.

The next was the Eye of Horus, inverted.

Shaliah trembled as his hands moved.

The third was the Lost Child.

Shaliah made the sign of the aquila as he put all three piles together, signifying the Emperor Reborn, and he took the last card.

It showed the God-Emperor.

Shaliah closed his eyes, and pressed his hands together in prayer. The others looked from him to the cards, and back again. Each of them felt a chill run down their back. At last Shaliah lifted his cards and wrapped the pack back in their sacred cloth.

'Brothers and sisters. For our church to succeed, the Imperium as it is must fall.' He looked about from face to face. 'The cards confirm it. This is the hour that we have all prayed for, the moment that our family has devoted itself to. The meaning is plain. The heretics who despoil Holy Terra will be overthrown by the Despoiler. This is our chance to save the Imperium of Man. This is the moment that the Saviour Emperor shall be reborn, and the Imperium of Man restored to its ancient glory!'

Lady Bianca looked from one member of the group to another. 'You can see that in the cards?'

'I can.'

'Then what exactly are you suggesting?'

'That we kill the heretics upon our planet, and raise the flag of redemption before it is too late.'

'And who are these heretics?'

'The cardinal. The forces of the Imperium. Any who stand against us.'

'You are joking, surely?'

'No, I am not,' Shaliah said. 'Did you ever think that the restoration of the True Church would be bloodless?'

'No, but I have dabbled in the Tarot and I did not see what you saw.'

The Patridzo stepped forward. 'Lady Bianca. We must have faith in Shaliah. He is the head of the temple.'

Lady Bianca looked at them all. 'You are frightening me. You are risking everything on this... this desperate gamble. I've heard mystics talk of the End of Days since I was born. Forgive an old lady from mentioning her age, but I am now three hundred and sixty-three years old, and I've seen many of your type in my time. Every defeat is a portent, a punishment for our sins and our lack of faith. You will risk everything on those few cards?'

She looked for support, but it was the Patridzo who spoke. 'I believe. Ever since the Cadian Gate fell we have known that the End of Days is upon us. Either we rise up, or we fall with the corrupt imposters. The Imperium is weak. It is a paper tiger, baring its fangs. A little prod and it will fall over.'

'And then what?'

'We march on Terra and liberate it from the heretics who pollute its paths.'

'I came here for guidance as to how I could take my planet back,' Lady Bianca said. 'Who will fight the heretics if not the Imperium?'

Shaliah smiled tolerantly. 'I have an army of the faithful who will throw the Scourged back to the hell they crawled from.'

'Where is this army?'

'I believe that they have just disembarked onto the planet. The orphans of a hundred worlds. Just waiting for the word.'

She laughed now. 'Oh. I see. You have an army of flotsam and cowards. Underhive scum. Is that the metal from which you forge your army?'

'They are holy warriors for a holy cause. The steel within them is faith. Their weapons are belief. Their armour is certitude.'

Lady Bianca shook her head. 'I cannot believe we have to stand here and listen to this!'

'Lady Bianca,' Shaliah sighed. 'You saw the Tarot. This is the moment that has been foretold to us. When ten thousand years are over, the Despoiler shall be set free. He will take peace from the galaxy. He makes brother kill brother. To him is given a mighty sword.'

'Words,' Bianca spat dismissively. 'The ramblings of a man long dead.'

'Prophecy!' Shaliah stated. 'The guide to our salvation. Don't you see. Mankind must act. It must throw off this despotic and corrupt church, and return to the old, true ways of St Vandire, the Blessed and the Pure.'

Lady Bianca took a step forward. 'Patridzo. This is madness. We cannot not allow this.'

The Patridzo looked out of his depth as he clutched his silk tasselled cap in his paint-stained hands. He looked from Bianca to Shaliah before saying, 'What can I do?'

'Oppose it!' Lady Bianca declared. She looked for support but none of them stepped forward. She cursed. 'He sees what he wants in the cards. If none of you are man enough, then it is up to me to stop this!' A hidden blade appeared suddenly in her hand. She moved with surprising speed for a lady of her age, the blade slamming into Shaliah's gut.

Shaliah looked down at the place where the blade had struck.

The blade had cut through the brown cloth of his smock. 'Lady Bianca. I am disappointed with you. You have chosen failure over victory, stasis over regrowth.'

'I have chosen sanity,' she said, and drove the knife deep into his flesh.

There were gasps, but Shaliah did not move. 'My armour is faith. Do not fear, brothers and sisters. I am not hurt. The Emperor protects those who have faith.'

He stepped back as the others removed the weapon from Lady Bianca's hand and opened his smock to show his unmarked flesh.

'How did you do that?' Bianca demanded. 'What infernal device are you wearing?'

Shaliah shook his head sadly. 'The Emperor protects, and He also punishes those who are weak. I am afraid that you shall have to stay here, my lady, in guarded isolation. We cannot allow you to interfere with the coming liberation.'

FIVE

Bendikt took the Salamander from the starport. He arrived at the Kalvert three hours after Lady Bianca and the other Richstars. It was noon and despite the heat, an honour guard of local Calibineer in full dress uniform of red-and-blue breeches had assembled.

Bendikt took them in with a glance. They looked too smart to make good soldiers. Their captain shouted an order as he dismounted. Bendikt briefly caught the man's eye as he returned the salute. They had clearly heard the news of the fall of Kypra. They looked nervous.

Bendikt made the sign of the aquila with his remaining hand as he dismounted to the broad marble steps. A tall, thin man was waiting for him at the top of the stairs. 'General Bendikt. Welcome to Potence. I am Shanttal, equerry to Patridzo Urdalig Richstar. We are glad to see the face of one who has such a record of service to the Holy Throne. Our forces are brave, but they need leadership.'

Bendikt looked impatient as the man finished his speech. 'Where is the Patridzo?'

His equerry put in quickly, 'Sir, I am sorry but the Patridzo is in conference. We are expecting the declaration of the great feast day.'

'Which feast?'

'The Feast of St Ignatzio,' Shanttal explained. 'It is the most important religious observance on the planet. Well, in the whole system.'

Bendikt didn't understand the importance or the fuss. 'I think I read something about it. Well, as long as it does not interfere with the military preparations.'

Shanttal's face was pained. '*Nothing* happens during the festival. The whole planet shuts down.'

Bendikt was listening now. 'When exactly is this festival happening?'

Shanttal hesitated. 'The exact moment... I cannot say yet. It depends on the brightness of the local star. The augurs are expected to declare it any moment.'

'I am sure you are aware of the proximity of the forces of heresy,' Bendikt said.

Shanttal nodded. His lips remained tight. Bendikt wondered how much the equerry did, in fact, know.

'So listen to me. I need the full compliance of the Patridzo and his forces.'

Shanttal was clearly concerned about something. 'Lord general, the Patridzo has many rituals to fulfil. He is the Saint's direct descendant.'

'I don't care who he is. I care about the defence of this system.' As if to underline his point the sound of autogun fire rose in the air, far off. Moments later a distant siren sounded.

'Of course,' the equerry said quickly. 'I do not know how

familiar you are with our local history, General Bendikt. The Richstars have upheld their sacred duty to the Emperor Himself throughout all these millennia. They hold the Emperor more sacred than any other in the Imperium. I can assure you that the people hold the Richstars just as dearly to their hearts.'

'Listen. I will come back when the Patridzo is available.'

Shanttal took Bendikt's good hand. 'No. Please. I insist. The Patridzo is keen to meet you. As soon as he is ready he will see you. Come, I will do my best to be entertaining.'

Shanttal stepped back as Bendikt and Mere exchanged glances. Bendikt sighed. This was the last thing he wanted, but Mere pulled a face.

'Let's keep the local sweet,' he said. 'Meet him, greet him and then we can move on.'

Bendikt turned to the equerry. 'How long will the Patridzo be?'

'No more than an hour.'

'Right,' Bendikt said. 'You have an hour.'

Shanttal led the two Cadians from one ornate room to another, and showed them a succession of murals that depicted key moments in the history of the Gallows Cluster.

First was the Granting of the Imperial Warrant, which showed a rather romantic Golden Throne, and a strangely lifelike Emperor, bearded and wizened with cares and age but distinctly alive, handing a prominent figure, who, Bendikt guessed, had to be Ignatzio Richstar, his Imperial warrant.

Next were a series of trials that Ignatzio faced in bringing this area to pacification.

To his surprise, Bendikt found his interest being piqued.

'What are these?' Bendikt asked of a mural that showed what appeared to be giant worms.

'Zuayg,' Shanttal said. 'They were the dominant species of the Gallows Cluster.'

'Never heard of them.'

'They no longer exist. No living specimens, anyway. They were wiped out by Ignatzio in his third crusade. They were a form of predatory worm. I learnt only a little about them when I was younger. The hatchlings were no longer than a man. They had a thick layer of fat, apparently. There's a tale from my home world that speaks of how the first settlers were forced to eat them to survive. I can't imagine they were very delicious.'

'You are not from this planet then?'

'No. You cannot tell from my accent?'

'No,' Bendikt said.

'Ah. It is very distinctive to us. I come from Gilgamesh Nine. It is where the best equerries are trained.'

Bendikt was unconcerned with the finer details of equerries. He looked back at the mural.

'If you are interested, general, on Potence we have one of the few remaining examples of the species in existence. It has been held in stasis for the last five thousand years. It is in the Patridzo's private collection. In the contemplatorium. I can petition him on your behalf, if you would like to see it.'

'Thank you,' Bendikt said. 'Maybe later.' He checked his chronometer. 'I must insist that I see the Patridzo.'

'He will be ready soon. Meanwhile, let me show you the Building of the Holy Cathedral.'

Bendikt's patience was wearing dangerously thin. 'Listen, I'm here to organise the defence of this planet. Not to admire its art!'

Shanttal seemed almost hurt by this outburst. 'But if you don't know the history and culture of this system I fear that you will not be as successful as you might be–'

'Sir. With all due respect, I am not a cultured man. Nor do I want to be. I am a soldier. I know about war, which is complicated enough as it is. It involves understanding the potential of soldiers, emplacements, fields of fire, trajectories, supplies and terrain, and most importantly, knowing when you are going to be lucky. This is what I am an expert in. This is what I am here to do. I am charged with rallying the defence of this system, which has, until this moment, been woefully inadequate. I want to meet the Patridzo and then I want to meet my fellow Cadians, because the future of the system depends on them. Do I make myself understood?'

The equerry trembled. 'I understand you clearly.'

Bendikt felt immediately better. He could afford to be conciliatory. 'Now. If you will forgive my bluntness, if the Patridzo cannot see me now, I want three things. Firstly, I want to be taken to the Cadian 101st. Secondly, I want all the local commanders to be brought to me within the hour. And thirdly, tell the Patridzo to come and see me at his earliest convenience.'

Half an hour later, a Salamander was waved through the gates of the Intake Barracks. General Bendikt leapt down from the running plate and marched straight towards the wing where the banner of the 101st hung. The flag was limp in the midday heat and the glare of the sun made him squint as he strode towards the open gateway.

Colonel Baytov was the current commander of the 101st. He and Bendikt had fought together for years. The colonel strode forward to greet the general.

Baytov pointed towards Bendikt's folded sleeve.

'What happened to the arm?'

'I'll tell you some time. But now we have work to do,' Bendikt said, walking towards the entrance. He paused briefly to acknowledge men he remembered. He knew their names and the battles they had fought in. Daal. Sparker. Even Rivald was there. Each old comrade slowed him down, and when he reached the steps up to his office he stopped and paused.

Emotion tightened his throat. He nodded. 'It's damned fine to see you all again.'

Ten minutes later Baytov and Bendikt were standing in the command bunker, going through the latest astropathic transmissions.

The compound post was set in the rock of the acropolis. It had the cool, damp atmosphere of all underground rooms. The similarity to Observation Post 9983 made Bendikt feel a little uneasy. On the table before him lay a chart of the Gallows Cluster. On one side lay the inner-spiral darkness, on the other the home worlds of the Segmentum Solar.

Red markers showed which planets had fallen to the Scourged. He leant forward, almost forgetting that his right hand was missing, and steadying himself on his left. 'It doesn't make sense,' he said.

Baytov paused and looked across. He hadn't thought about whether it made sense or not. He had just been trying to work out how to defend the place. 'Why not?'

'Well. Look. The system should be easily defended. It has its own troops, long ties between the ruling family and their home worlds. How have the heretics managed to drive so deep into the system, and so quickly?'

Baytov shook his head. 'Superior forces?'

'What do we know of the Scourged?'

Baytov pulled a data-slate out, and scrolled through it. 'This is highly classified but their core is thought to come from an Imperial Guard regiment named the Seced 13th. Heavy infantry regiment stationed on Belisar. They slaughtered their commanding officers and rebelled two months before the planet fell. They were thought to have been wiped out before the fall of Cadia.'

'How many were in the Seced 13th?'

'Ten thousand.'

'You cannot tell me that this whole system has fallen to just ten thousand renegade Guardsmen!'

'No. But they seem particularly adept at winning over local forces. On Marquis most of the fighting was against cultists.'

'So there's an elite core with a horde of cultists?'

'Yes, sir.'

'Any of ours?' He meant Cadians. It was a question spoken so quietly that only Baytov could hear it. The other man gave an almost imperceptible nod and Bendikt felt sick at the thought.

There was a long pause.

It was Bendikt who broke the silence. 'So who is Drakulzar?'

'He's rumoured to have once been an Imperial colonel from the Seced troops. Drakul is an honorific among them. With the "zar" suffix it translates as something like "Little Father". No pict-images exist of his actual features.'

Bendikt had nothing to say to that. The name implied affection. A charismatic commander who could bring many disparate forces together with great speed.

Bendikt slammed his hand onto the table. 'What I want to know is how the Throne are they taking world after world?'

Baytov hazarded a number of guesses. 'Speed. Terror. Corruption.'

'On Marquis you say you were fighting cultists?'

'Yes, sir. Reports imply an elite assault on the governor's palace. Decapitation strike. Once it had fallen, the defences appear to have quickly crumbled.'

Bendikt took it all in. 'So, our enemies have an experienced core and an able and charismatic commander. They must also have a fleet. Look at the speed of their assault. Any Navy ships missing?'

Baytov shook his head.

'If we can learn anything from this I'd expect an elite assault on the Evercity aimed at killing the Patridzo. Make sure he's well protected. Is there anywhere else we can garrison?'

Baytov shook his head. 'The Sisters of the Ebon Chalice have a daughter house on the cathedral peak. They have made it clear that they will not accept Guard regiments on the summit.'

Bendikt rolled his eyes. 'And the Evercity is a warren.'

'Yes, sir. I think that might act in our favour. I have identified key thoroughfares to the acropolis if the city should be attacked. None of them will allow a direct assault. With local support we can bog any attackers down for, well, months.'

'Good,' Bendikt said. 'And if the enemy enter the city we should have at least a few days' warning.' He drew out the chart that showed Potence. The acropolis was marked with an aquila, and about it wound the streets of the Evercity, and then the industrial and agricultural districts, and the pale blocks of the starport.

'The tent city stretches from here to here.'

Bendikt nodded. 'Who is guarding the starport?'

224

'Calibineer. The 66th Barolan Mechanised. They are in charge of all critical infrastructure.'

'Are they solid?'

'They're under-strength. But from their service reports they appear reliable.'

Bendikt nodded. 'Look here.' He pointed at the star maps. 'There are three Guard divisions on their way to the planet of Argent's Shrine. And all the enemy have to do is take Domus and the salient is lost. Who was in charge of Imperial defences?'

'The Patridzo, ultimately.'

Bendikt swore. 'We must assume that we have less time than we think. Have all troops put on standby.' He paced back and forth, moved counters, assessed various military strengths and opportunities. At last he had it in place. 'Right. Get these orders recorded. What is the name of the astropathic facility?'

Mere had no idea. He turned to Baytov. 'Nullem Apek. It's a hundred miles away. In the Supramonte, the mountains.'

'Will this festival interfere with it?'

'It shouldn't.'

'Why the hell is it all the way out there?'

'The Evercity is the worst place for astropathic communication, apparently. I was told that the density of shrines and holy places gives off too much psychic pollution. All the pilgrims going into religious ecstasy. The psychic relay is far enough away not to be interfered with.'

Bendikt issued a series of orders to be conveyed to the various commanders in the local systems. He sounded increasingly bullish as he went on, pointing to the neighbouring system. 'We're going to hold the enemy and then we're going to counter-attack at Blackrock. The flanks of the Scourged will be wide open.'

Mere stood over the scribe, making sure the orders were

recorded properly. The dockets were double-checked. At last he said, 'Do you think it will work?'

'We shall see. At the moment I just want to convey a sense of purpose to my commanders. All I see is confusion and ill-judged offensives. What is important now is to steady nerves and to let my commanders know that someone is giving orders. Once we've stopped their advance we can work out how to throw them back.'

At last Bendikt seemed to have exhausted himself. 'Have those sent, urgently.'

The orders were taken under guard. Bendikt noticed belatedly the cup of recaf that had been sitting by the map. It was cold but he took a sip nonetheless and looked surprised. 'Well at least the recaf is good.'

'I have a number of communications,' Mere said.

'The Patridzo sends his apologies for his absence. Canoness Maddelena compliments you on your appointment... standard formal greetings. Cardinal Archbishop Xereum welcomes your appointment and the arrival of the 101st. He would like to conduct a mass on our behalf after the festival. Blessing of the weapons and all that.'

'Good. Stall him. Last thing I need is a bloody bishop wasting my time. If he insists on coming any earlier, see if he can anoint the tanks. That'll amuse the troops.'

'Yes, sir.'

Bendikt took them in. 'Right. Let's get moving before this festival starts.'

The command staff were exhausted. They had been locked up for hours in the cramped bunker. Bendikt led them back up the steps.

When he got to the top the fresh air struck him. He walked out, and looked about.

The sun was setting.

'Why are all the bells ringing?'

Mere had just been handed a note. 'Sir. It appears that the festival of Saint Ignatzio has been declared. We have two days to get everything in order.'

SIX

The peculiarities of the Feast of Saint Ignatzio had all been explained to Cardinal Archbishop Xereum when he had arrived, a few years earlier, from the shrine world of Grater Treen and was invested as pontiff to the Gallows Cluster.

It was his ordinand, Tobias Vettor, who had introduced him to the local customs. Vettor was a thin cleric, with hooked nose and bright blue eyes, sitting in an alcove outside the cardinal's bedchamber. 'The feast comes around every eleven years,' Vettor had explained, 'when the solar cycle of the local star, named the Leopard Star, throws up a series of dark spots that move towards the centre and lead to a significant dimming of its light.'

'So there is no set date.'

'No,' Vettor told him. 'It is the movement of these spots towards the sun's equatorial regions that signifies the conjunction, a solar event that commemorated the great victory of Ignatzio over the xenos races of Potence. It is not until the sunspots begin to conjoin that the feast day can be predicted with any certainty. While eleven years is the usual recurrence, feast days have been known to come as quickly as every seven years, or as far apart as sixteen.'

Cardinal Xereum's palace was set within the ordered gardens of the cathedral, at the summit of the acropolis of the Evercity. He had few luxuries in his life, but one of them was the collection of ornithopters that he kept on the roof of his palace.

The Basilika was far bigger than any cardinal of Xereum's modest desires could need. It tumbled down the upper slopes of the acropolis, giving the appearance of a building slowly slipping from the summit. The lower courses were overgrown with vegetation, the rooms they contained having seen better days. Their iron-barred windows and gateways were boarded up and abandoned to mice and lizards. The generatoria that had once powered their ice chambers had run cold, their intake vents now sealed up with bricks and mortar. And within the vast basements were stone-lined cisterns, storerooms of giant amphora, chapels, mess-rooms and void generators that had been long since sealed and left to moulder.

The cardinal and his personal household lived in the upper central chambers, which had been kept clean and neat, although the many murals were starting to show their age, and suffer from the carelessness of staff who brushed past, or ran the food trolleys a little too fast from the kitchens.

The cardinal had many plans for the Basilika. All this unused space should not go to waste. He would establish an orphanage for the children of Potence, a langar for pilgrims, meeting rooms, prayer halls. All these plans moved about his head, and he would start on them just as soon as the authorities could establish peace within the Gallows Cluster.

Cardinal Xereum wanted to improve the world, and he recalled a conversation from only this morning with Vettor, who had told him of a family who had been found dead at the gates of the Evercity.

'They starved to death,' Vettor had said.

'Why did they not let them in?'

'It is the orders of the Patridzo,' Vettor said. 'With the feast day due to be announced any day soon...'

'Ah, yes, the feast of Saint Ignatzio. So we sit and wait for the augurs to make up their minds, and meanwhile the people suffer.'

'The Patridzo does send them food.'

'But what use is that if it does not reach the hungry?'

The augurs had been watching the Leopard Star for nearly two months, each of them eager to be the one who saw the signs that declared that the feast day of Saint Ignatzio had come. A feast day was due, of course, but it was not until the distinctive spots began to coalesce that they put the cathedral staff on warning.

That morning, at dawn, the augurs saw and affirmed the readings, and when all three of them were in agreement, they came as a deputation to the cardinal's bedchamber, their hands clutched in nervous excitement.

The cardinal had taken the tidings with stoic calm. He listened, said a prayer of thanks and let the augurs make an announcement to the Evercity. He wondered how long it would take for the news to disseminate, and had recaf brought, and his morning posset of egg and milk and sweet wine.

When the bells began to ring he was sitting propped up in his four-poster bed. He listened for a while as they called out over the city.

When he was ready he shouted for his ordinand. 'Vettor!'

Vettor stepped through the doorway and bowed. 'Yes, your holiness?'

'Help me down,' Xereum said, and threw back the sheets, sticking his pale, hairy feet out of the bed.

Vettor hurried forward, picking up the cardinal's slippers, pressing them onto each foot before they touched the cold floor. 'Here, your holiness,' he said, and took the cardinal's hand and helped him down.

The music of bells rang over the whole city. 'So, the augurs have made the proclamation.'

'You do not sound happy, your holiness.'

'No? I am. I know how much the feast means to the people here. I hope they get the portents they desire.' He paused. 'I suppose it is that I still do not feel as though the people have taken me to their hearts.'

'That moment will come,' Ordinand Vettor assured him. 'The people here are not so used to strangers. Until the Great Calamity, we were just a small scatter of dots between the two arms of the galaxy. The Gallows Cluster was on the way to nowhere. We were left to our own customs. We always appointed our own cardinals and ecclesiarchs. You are the first cardinal from outside for nearly a thousand years.'

Vettor spoke clear Gothic, without any local accent. The cardinal forced a smile. 'Sometimes I forget you were born here. Would you prefer a cardinal from among your own?'

Vettor laughed. 'You think I want your job?'

'It has crossed my mind.'

Vettor laughed once more. 'No, your holiness. It's all yours, I promise. I could not do it as well as you.'

'I do my best,' the cardinal said with a sigh.

'You are a rare thing in this galaxy. You are a good man,' Vettor told him.

The cardinal stopped. 'Thank you,' he said. 'You are not the first person to say that to me.'

Vettor held his gaze. 'It is true.'

Cardinal Xereum was nicknamed 'the Owl' by the cloistered community of the cathedral.

He was a small and bent man, with short-cropped hair, a small hard mouth and wide surprised eyes that did indeed give him an owlish appearance. This morning, after prayers, he entered the library at the top of the palace, and the tech-parts of the servo-scribe whirred gently as it went from sleep to active mode.

Vettor's eyes followed the cardinal as he strode to the leaded window and looked down on the cathedral gardens, where the shape of the aquila was marked out with neatly trimmed yew hedges.

'I found the lists from the last ceremony,' Vettor announced with pride, and unwound the rolls of vellum onto Xereum's parchment table, using a velvet pouch filled with sand to weigh the two ends of the roll down. He started to dictate to the servo-scribe in the corner of the room. The quill-hand scratched away on individual dockets for each of the prepa-rations that had to be fulfilled. There were Ecclesiarchy robes to be brought out of storage, tons of incense to be carried up from the cathedral storerooms, holy books to be retrieved from the stasis chambers, shoes to be bought, and deputa-tions to receive from all the religious and civil bodies who would want to be involved in the processions. It seemed like hours of work just to map out everything that had to be done.

At midday the bells were still ringing. There was a knock at the door. Vettor went to see what it was.

'Deputations for the festival?'

'No, actually,' Vettor said. He read the message aloud: an Imperial general had just made warp transit and landed that morning.

The cardinal pressed his hands together in a symbol of thanksgiving. 'Thanks be to the Holy Throne.' He made the sign of the aquila and when he opened his eyes Vettor was still holding the parchment.

'Is there more?'

'Yes. Shaliah, the Bringer of News, arrived this morning. He also sends his greetings. Actually, it appears he is waiting downstairs. He asks for a private meeting.'

Shaliah was the private emissary of the Richstars, an odd post, something like the family's private chaplain. And as their chaplain, Shaliah had access to the heads of each of the ruling families of the sector. Xereum had learnt in his few years on Potence that Shaliah probably wielded more power than he did, as the cardinal archbishop.

It was an important meeting.

Xereum adjusted his purple gowns, and reached for his stick. 'Show him up.'

There was theatre in any religious observance, and Cardinal Xereum was not unaware of this. He wore his purple gowns well, and always carried a short walking stick – not for any infirmity, but almost as a stage-prop that a mountebank might use to complete his costume.

It was a short cane, made of makila wood that had, over a number of seasons on his home world of Dimmamar, been carved, straightened, blessed and then shaped into an object worthy of a cardinal. It had a ferrule of intricately carved silver and a tiny silver-chased servo-skull for the handle.

The tap-tap of the staff upon the black marble floor of his private chambers focused him as he looked out of the library window, down into the cathedral gardens.

There was a faint scrape at the door. Vettor cleared his throat. 'Shaliah, the Bringer of News.'

Shaliah came through the doorway with a rush. He was barefoot, Xereum noted, and he envied him the simplicity of his life and appearance.

'Your eminence,' Shaliah said, and bowed. He took the cardinal's outstretched hand, and kissed the signet ring. 'How is the flying?'

Xereum blushed a little. 'Oh. My little hobby. Well, I have not been able to indulge for a while now. We are all on tenterhooks for the festival.'

Shaliah smiled indulgently. 'Well, perhaps afterwards you can indulge me too. But what a day to meet, when the Feast of Saint Ignatzio has been declared.'

'Indeed.'

There was much to talk about, and Vettor served them both sweet meats and recaf as they discussed news from across the sector.

'There is something else,' Shaliah said at the end. 'I took a liberty. We are both aware of how bare the defences of the Gallows Cluster are. Because of this, I was approached by many of the displaced people, and they asked my permission to gather. An armed band of the holy. A force of Frateris Militia who wish to use their faith to throw back the heretics and the unholy. I told them that I could bless them, but that I could not declare a crusade.'

'Why not? Of course. As long as the Patridzo does not mind.'

'Peculiar Law states that matters religious are not strictly his preserve. *You* are the cardinal. You govern religious matters. A crusade can only be declared by the representative of the Ecclesiarchy. It is only with *your* authority that the Frateris can be armed.'

Xereum paused. 'So it is in my power to contribute to the defence of the planet?'

'More than contribute. To multiply its defences many times over!'

'How many men do you have who are ready to bear arms?'

'At last count, there are over a hundred thousand souls,' Shaliah said.

'And do they have weapons?'

'I have accepted donations from ruling members of the Richstar family. I think we have enough lasrifles for each man.'

'This is good news!' Xereum smiled broadly. 'I have prayed to the Emperor for help, and I think this is His gift to us. You fill me with courage. Vettor, come here. Have the papers drawn up for a religious crusade and I will put my seal to them immediately!'

As they waited, Xereum stood and walked to the window.

The midday sun lit the long curving contrails of planetary landers with golden light. The sky was criss-crossed with the dissipating threads of cumulus, scattering before the high winds.

Xereum sighed. 'For months lighters have been ferrying unfortunates to the planet. Do you know what the locals call these people? Influxers. They are not permitted in the Evercity, by order of the Patridzo. Their number has tested the resources of Potence sorely. Vettor tells me that convoys of food go there each day.'

Vettor nodded in confirmation. Xereum sighed. 'It is a shame that we do not help them here, in the Evercity.'

He and Vettor were rehearsing a well-worn conversation. 'The Patridzo did not think it proper. Not with the festival coming,' the ordinand said.

'It seems a shame to banish them from the great feast.'

'There are many rituals. And you know how many undesirables have landed on the planet.'

'So I have heard.' The cardinal pressed his knuckles to the point at the top of his nose, where his brows came together in prayer. 'We are all being tested, Vettor. But think of the Emperor who has endured the torture of the Golden Throne for ten thousand years. What are these trials we are facing now compared to those that He has endured on our behalf?'

Vettor made the sign of the aquila. 'You are right, your holiness.'

'Should I intervene on their behalf?' the cardinal asked. 'Do you think the Patridzo would listen?'

'Yes, I am sure,' Shaliah said. 'If the urgency was made clear to him.'

'I shall come with you,' said Vettor.

Shaliah nodded and stood, his feet almost silent on the parquet floor of the library. 'Cardinal, your heart is good. I am sure that if you went to see the Patridzo and spoke to him of what is in your heart, of your concern for the people, then he could not fail to be moved.'

SEVEN

Xereum and his ordinand made their way down the sweeping ceremonial staircase of the Basilika, the cardinal's walking stick tap-tapping with each step. There were high ceilings and occasional landings with gilded furniture in opulent style set against the wall.

In the three years he had been posted to this system, Xereum had been impressed with his ordinand, but he had not managed to break the air of formality between them. Vettor kept one step behind the cardinal, hands held before him in a posture of reverence.

They passed a pair of choirboys who were running up the stairs. They stopped when they saw the cardinal, and stood to the side with stiff formality. Xereum put his hand on their heads. 'Benedictus. Go with the faith of the Holy Emperor.'

The boys ran off, and the two men continued down the long, wide spiral. 'I have been here three years and still I am finding much that is strange about the Gallows Cluster.'

'How so, cardinal?'

'Before, I was Primary Xereum on the shrine world of Grater Treen. It was within a week's warp jump of Holy Terra and every building, every field, every four-way junction had a shrine to a saint or the Emperor. It was a world of prayer and devotion.'

'And you think that Potence is not?'

'Not in the same way,' Xereum said, pausing on the third landing down.

'I do not understand.'

Xereum turned towards him. 'The Cathedral Ignatzio is the largest cathedral in the Gallows Cluster. A wonder. A supreme monument to the glory of the Emperor! And yet barely a soul comes to it. But the chapels and oratories of the Evercity are thronged day and night. Is it the climb up to the acropolis that tests their faith so much? If the Emperor could sacrifice His life and existence to our protection, do you not think the people of the Peculiar could climb up these steps, to pay homage?'

'You do not do them justice, your holiness. They hold the Saint's cathedral in too much awe. They *do* come.'

'When?'

'After the morning mass on the Feast of Ignatzio. There is a great procession from the chapel to St Ignatzio up to the cathedral.'

They reached the bottom of the stairs and crossed towards the gate of the Basilika. The gates were of reinforced steel. They opened silently as the two figures approached.

Outside the courtyard it was dark where the vast cathedral stretched up into the sky.

Before them, the cardinal's grav-palanquin waited, pennants hanging from its square platform, moving gently in the light air. It tilted slightly as he mounted the steps, lowered his weight upon the ornate seat, and started forward.

Before him went clerics and priests bearing torches, and a servitor choir set into a mikoshi shrine. The procession skirted the buttresses on the east side of the Cathedral Ignatzio and the wind caught the yellow torches and flattened the flames sideways as they processed past the members of the local Calibineer, who raised arms in salute. They fell under the shadow of the gatehouse, with its loopholes, portcullis and armoured gates, which was now home to thirty Sisters of the Order of the Ebon Chalice.

As they approached, a lone figure strode from the gatehouse doorway.

It was Celestian Simmona. She wore black power armour, inscribed with the skull-filled cup of her order, the oldest of all the daughters of the Emperor. She carried her helmet in the crook of her power-armoured elbow and made the sign of the aquila. Her white cloak, lined with red fur, flapped in the breeze as she addressed them. 'It is late to go out, your highness.'

'You are right,' he said. 'But I was moved by the spirit of the Holy Emperor. The plight of the unfortunates weighs on my soul.'

'You are going to see the Patridzo?'

'Yes.'

'Will he see you?'

'I do not see why not.'

'He never sees the head of our order.'

'He is often working,' Vettor put in. 'His devotional work is revered by many for the sublimity of his painting.'

'Is that so. We are your honorary guard, cardinal. If you go out then let us accompany you.'

From the arch of the gateway ten Sisters stepped forward at her command. They clutched their bolters to their chest as they pushed through the choir to stand beneath the grav-palanquin, and only then did the gates of the cathedral swing slowly open.

EIGHT

'Up, child,' the man said. He put out a hand and Carkal took it.

He did not know who the owner of the hand was. All he knew was that it was a friend. A comrade. A brother.

'Sit at the back. There's many more to come.'

Carkal sat at the back of the halftrack as the carriage quickly filled with others like him, with sheepish attitudes, growing confident with the promise of belonging and purpose.

He nodded to each of them as they pressed in about him.

'All set!' a brother shouted, and the back flap was hauled up on chains, and pinned into place. 'My name is Brother Zephan,' the man said. 'Welcome!'

He banged the side of the halftrack. The engine revved, and they moved forward.

They were driven through the tent city. The threat of the place had gone now that he was no longer alone.

'Where are we going?' one of the others called out.

'To be tested,' Brother Zephan said.

'What sort of test?'

Brother Zephan's face was impassive. 'It is one of faith.'

The convoy stopped at a checkpoint. Carkal heard the shouts of ganger-glot.

Zephan was speaking to one of them.

Carkal felt sure that the gangers would be asking for him. 'A murderer and a bread-thief,' they would be saying. 'Not worth taking. Not worth anyone's trouble. Put a las-bolt through his neck before he betrays your trust.'

He kept his head down.

But then Zephan waved, and the convoy was moving forward once more.

The gangers let them drive straight through the checkpoint and when they were out onto the plains, heading south, the convoy accelerated, until the men inside were thrown about.

Carkal did not try to speak. He concentrated on his faith. On the confessions he had made. At last they stopped. He prayed as he had been taught as a child.

'Up now!' Brother Zephan called.

Carkal's legs were stiff from being bent for so long. He pushed himself up and tried to get his bearings.

They had driven for what felt like an hour. The tent city was just a thin white line on the horizon, and behind it, hazy with distance and dust, rose the rock of the Evercity, and the golden domes of the Cathedral Ignatzio.

They had stopped at what looked like a disused agricultural warehouse. Weeds grew from the rockcrete foundation slabs. It looked derelict, with cracked glass in the windows and gaping holes in the mesh-wire fencing.

Carkal slid down to the ground. Six trucks had disgorged hundreds of young men out onto the entranceway. The press of bodies had a nervous scent to it. 'This way!' a loudhailer instructed. Carkal moved with the others, shuffling towards the nearest building.

The slide-doors were open wide. The loudhailers were stationed at each step of their progress. 'Over here!' one ordered and Carkal took a place in one of the many queues.

He could smell food.

At the front of the line was a man with a cauldron of slop. He handed Carkal a bowl.

Carkal looked down in wonder at the generosity. 'Move along now!' he was ordered, and he did what he was told.

They fed him until he could eat no more, and then he was taken to a room and stripped to his bare, shivering flesh. Carkal was one among fifty, standing, ashamed by their nakedness. He did not think. He followed, he obeyed, he felt gratitude.

They were herded forward into a low chamber with rock-crete walls and bare pipework. 'Shower,' Zephan ordered, as the water came on with a gurgle, spurting out of the pipes. It was pungent with sterilising chems. There was slab-soap and brushes. The water was lukewarm. Carkal did not care. He stood and let it wash over him, and then when it ran out, he followed the others through a new door, where each of them was treated with counterseptic powders.

'Sit and pray, my children. The test is coming,' they were told.

As they sat, their heads bowed, a servitor came around with a clipper, to shave their heads. Carkal felt the metal work its way over his head in strips, watched clots of his wet, matted hair fall to the ground at his feet. A hand brushed his scalp, which was alive to sensation in a new and extraordinary way. It skimmed the last of his hair away from his head. It was not the hand of a servitor.

He looked up.

'Come, brother,' Zephan said.

Carkal stood. He was dressed in a long kirtle of brown wool that hung in folds to his knees.

'It is time to see if you are pure.'

Carkal was led, bare-legged, into another room.

There was blood on the floor. A body was being dragged by the heels out to the left. A man in a black gown and mask stood in the middle of the room. His only other ornament was a steel aquila hanging from his neck.

He beckoned Carkal forward.

'Kneel,' a voice from behind him commanded.

Carkal knelt. He kept his head bowed. To the side, in a neighbouring room, a man was talking. There was a shout, and a scream, and then silence.

It seemed to take an age, then a door opened.

'Is he ready?' a voice said. The voice was deep and resonant.

'Yes, confessor.'

The footsteps moved forward.

Carkal saw Guard boots, scuffed and worn.

'I am Harkham Pitt,' the voice said. 'Look up, my child.'

Confessor Harkham Pitt wore military dress. From his belt hung a trio of grenades and pouches for power packs, and there was a sword-length bayonet in a sheath at his side. The strap of a lasgun was thrown over his shoulder, and marks of rank were upon his right arm: a triple skull. He had a

Richstar banner draped about his shoulders and a laspistol holstered at his hip. But it was his face that made Carkal start.

Confessor Pitt's eyelids had been stitched open. His eyeballs stared out, bloodshot and unblinking.

His voice was a gravelly rasp. 'What is your name, child?'

Carkal spoke, but his voice was not the frightened croak that it had been last time he had heard himself speak. It was a voice full of confidence and strength. It was a voice with conviction. 'Carkal.'

Carkal heard someone behind him and felt metal touch the back of his scalp. He flinched for a moment at the sudden cold, but kept looking into the mad, staring eyes.

'There is a gun pressed to the back of your head,' Confessor Pitt said. He smiled kindly. 'But do not fear, my child. The faithful have nothing to fear, not even from death itself.' He took Carkal's right hand and held it between his own. 'I shall ask you some questions. Answer them truthfully. If you lie I shall know, and the payment for lies is death. Do you understand, my child?'

Carkal nodded and the man before him smiled. 'Good. Now, close your eyes. Faith often comes to us in the darkness. Shut your eyes to the world and look into your heart for the one true way.'

Carkal did as he was instructed, and then the questions began. 'Do you believe in the future of humanity?'

'I do,' Carkal spoke solemnly.

The gun was still pressed into the base of his skull, but the metal had warmed now and he did not flinch at its touch.

'Do you believe in the one true Emperor, divine and exultant?'

'I do,' he said.

His hand had been sweating, his heart thunderous, but

now he felt calm. He did not fear the gunshot that would end his life. Did not fear the darkness or the light.

The questions went on. 'Do you believe in the Temple of the Sacred Emperor that once stood on this planet, and will stand here once more?'

Carkal pressed his eyes closed.

'Yes.'

In the darkness of his own mind he saw a golden light. Radiant, pure, divine. His hand was cool. The hands about it pressed tenderly on his own. Carkal spoke fervently now. Defiant. Believing. Absolved of all his previous heresy and failings.

'Do you want to cleanse those who befoul our world?'

'Yes.'

'Do you want to travel the stars to return the Imperium to the one true way?'

'I do, my father.'

'Will you kill and burn those who stand against us?'

'Just give me the word,' Carkal said. 'I have killed the unholy and will do so again. I shall drown them in slime. I will eat their flesh.'

'Thank you,' Confessor Pitt said. There was a long pause. 'Now, stand, my child, and step forward as a brother.'

Carkal opened his eyes, and realised that the gun muzzle no longer rested against the skin of his head.

Confessor Pitt lifted and embraced him. The ragged white beard was soft as he kissed Carkal on both cheeks. He held him tight, as a brother. 'You have been reborn. You are no longer a child, wandering lost through the world. You have been initiated. Henceforth you shall be known as Brother Carkal, with the rank of gallant, and taught the lesser pass-words. Remember these, for your life might depend on it.'

Carkal looked to his right arm, and saw a single skull badge stitched into the cloth.

The man embraced Carkal again.

'Welcome, Gallant Carkal, into the Brotherhood.'

'How can I serve you?'

'You will serve as the Emperor served mankind. With blood.'

'My blood is yours,' Carkal said.

'And body.'

'I will do whatever you ask.'

'Then come, my brother. The time for sacrifice is near.'

NINE

Rudgard Howe found the Patridzo having supper on the lower terrace of the Kalvert gardens.

'Rudgard, is that you?' the Patridzo called as Howe approached.

'You were expecting me?'

The Patridzo did not turn. 'No. But no one else walks as heavily as you.'

'You do not sound pleased.'

'You only come to see me when there is bad news. So, tell me. What disaster is about to befall us?'

Howe did not answer, but spoke with his accustomed brusqueness. 'Not painting today?'

'Not today,' the Patridzo replied. 'A ruler has both the realms of the soul and the hand to govern.'

'I can take care of the second,' Howe answered.

The Patridzo had a single honey cake on a gold-worked porcelain plate. The cake had been cut into four. One of the pieces was missing. The Patridzo took a sip of recaf. He appeared irritated by the man's interruption. 'I hope this is important.'

'Of course,' Howe said, and pulled a chair out for himself and sat down.

Rudgard Howe was the chief enforcer on Potence, an ugly, broad slab of a man, whose forebears had come to the planet with the Adeptus Arbites six generations earlier. He still wore the black Arbites carapace handed down through the family.

'Are you aware of what is going on out there?'

'What do you mean?'

'Out there. South of the starport. In the agro-defence facility. That idiot Shaliah has landed an army.'

The Patridzo remained unmoved. 'Not an army. They are Frateris Militia.'

'Same thing,' Howe stated.

'No, actually, it's not. But as an outlander, I doubt you'd understand. The Decree Passive declares no man can bear arms for the Ecclesiarchy. The men of the Brotherhood have landed under Peculiar Law. It's Ecclesiarchy business, not mine.'

'Well, they're my problem. I have six hundred enforcers and they're barely enough to control the Evercity. But with the influxers as well! Every time another lighter lands on this planet a thousand more criminals arrive. I've given up arresting them. We just shoot them now.'

'Then stay away from their camp. They will not cause any trouble.'

'I've been an enforcer for a long time, and one thing I know is that men and guns means trouble.'

'Chief Enforcer Howe. I do not employ you to ask me questions. *Everyone* is landing armies on Potence. These men are the army of a crusade. They are Frateris Militia. There is official sanction from the cardinal himself.'

Howe eyed the honey cake for a moment. 'I'm concerned about Lady Bianca.'

'She's sick. I have sent my own physician to care for her.'

'Her life-wards have been found dead.'

'Oh dear. I hope they did not catch anything from her.'

'They were shot.'

'How unfortunate.'

Howe read between the lines. 'So I can put the squad who were watching her on other duties?'

'Yes. I'll let you know when she's feeling better.'

'Where is she?'

'None of your business.'

Howe sat back. He did not judge. It was one way he kept his job. 'If any of the Richstars had a backbone, they'd be the only one.'

'Of course,' the Patridzo said, taking another quarter of the cake and putting it into his mouth in one piece. He chewed for a moment. 'But backbone or not, they're Richstars.'

'They're lesser sons of lesser sons,' said Howe. 'A family needs to weed out the weak. My brother, for example...'

'I remember your brother. Or what was left of him.'

'It was what our father wanted.' Howe grinned. It was not a pleasant sight. 'You are funny, Patridzo! It does not change the fact that it's a miracle some of those Richstars survived infancy. I'd have exposed them. They're useless. If they can't hang on to their planets why the Throne should we take them in here?'

The Patridzo said nothing. He took another sip of recaf. His face appeared to say that he agreed with his chief enforcer, even if he didn't agree with the manner in which the opinion was expressed. 'The Richstars have always held together. We're fed family loyalty with our mother's milk.'

'I wish you'd told me about the Frateris.'

'I think they're calling themselves the Brotherhood.'

'I don't care. They're a bunch of armed and crazed fanatics.'

'Of course they're armed.'

'No. I mean they have heavy weapons and armoured vehicles.'

'Good,' the Patridzo said. 'I hope so. We need all the help we can get.'

'I thought the Ecclesiarchy were not allowed to have men under arms.'

'They're not.'

Rudgard Howe lifted his eyebrows. 'So…?'

The Patridzo sighed. 'You're so slow, Rudgard. The cardinal has declared a crusade.'

'Is that why the cardinal is coming to see you?'

This time it was the Patridzo who looked surprised. 'He is?'

'Yes.'

'He's brought a guard of Sisters with him.'

'Send him away.'

'He will insist.'

'Who rules this planet, me or him?'

'You do,' Howe said.

'So,' the Patridzo said, 'send him away.'

Celestian Simmona went forward to announce herself at the gates of the Kalvert.

'Open your doors. His holiness Cardinal Archbishop Xereum has come. Do not bar his entry.'

The doors swung silently open. The Calibineer, in full dress uniform, bowed as the cardinal's grav-palanquin moved into the Kalvert courtyard.

A lone figure stepped out from the tall, glass doors, and moved quickly down the steps.

It was Shanttal, the Patridzo's equerry. 'Greetings, cardinal. I am afraid that the Patridzo is busy.' He tried to sidestep Celestian Simmona. She was too quick for him. He yelped as her power-armoured fist closed painfully on his shoulder.

'Cardinal Xereum is the manifestation of the Emperor in this system. The Patridzo cannot be too busy to see him.'

'I will deal with this,' Xereum declared. He stepped down from the palanquin, and put up his hand.

Simmona only reluctantly let the equerry go.

'The Patridzo has forbidden the Sisters to enter the Kalvert,' Shanttal insisted. 'They are the daughters of the Emperor. I do not think the Patridzo doubts their faith. It is just that there are many precious pieces within the palace and the contemplatorium. He has never liked men or women of war inside.'

Celestian Simmona looked to the cardinal and Xereum nodded. 'Thank you for your protection, Celestian. I will be safe now, I am sure, and perhaps the Patridzo could provide an escort for my return journey.'

'I will personally ensure that, your holiness. Let me go and break the news to the Patridzo.'

'I will come with you,' Xereum said, and stepped around the equerry.

Shanttal had to run back to attempt to get in front of the cardinal. 'Let me go and announce you, your eminence.'

But the old man set a quick pace and was deaf to Shanttal's entreaties. The cardinal's short black staff tap-tapped on the marble floors and the equerry did not dare lay hands upon this eminent guest. As the cardinal mounted the black marble steps that led to the lower terrace, a dark figure stepped out of the shadows and halted the cardinal in his tracks.

It was Chief Enforcer Howe. He graced the cardinal with his ugliest smile.

The cardinal stopped abruptly. 'Ah. You,' he said.

'Evening, cardinal. Are you ready for the festival?'

Cardinal Xereum forced a smile. 'I am always ready. How about you? I hear there have been explosions in the city.'

'Nothing more than we can handle.'

'You sound very relaxed about it all. All I hear from Vettor is of the horrors of the tent city.'

'Really? What does he tell you?'

'Starvation, violence, murder. Does he exaggerate?'

'I do not know. I have never been there.'

The cardinal blinked. 'You have not been?'

'No. The Evercity takes up all of my time.'

'But there are hundreds of thousands of people out there on the plains. If you do not bring law to their lives, you abandon them to criminals. You should be ashamed of yourself.'

Howe laughed. 'I don't do shame. And for the record, I'm the enforcer, not Saint frekking Arabella. I deal in law, not charity. That's your concern. Have *you* ever been to the tent city?'

'Why no,' Xereum said, 'but that is not the issue.'

Rudgard Howe laughed. 'Too mighty for the weak, I see.'

Xereum was still fuming when he found the Patridzo in the orangery at the west end of the Kalvert.

The building was a small confection of glass and plasteel set on the top terrace of the gardens. Inside it was hung with vines and climbers, with heavy, scented black lotus blooms hanging down, their large bright stamens thick with pollen. There was the faint buzz of insects, though he never saw any and had the strange impression that they were not real.

The Patridzo acted as if he had not expected a visitor. 'Ah. Your holiness,' he said. 'What a pleasant surprise.'

Xereum tap-tapped forward and Vettor entered behind him.

'Patridzo, I am concerned. This morning Vettor told me a dead family was found at the gates of the Evercity.'

'The fates are cruel.'

'Not just the fates. Vettor tells me that the guards on the gate would not let them into the Evercity. That none of the influxers are allowed in.'

The Patridzo put his hand out to one of his blossoms. 'I wish I could do more, but you are well aware that the feast day is almost upon us. The augurs have spoken.'

'I am aware of that,' Xereum said. 'But the Imperium has entrusted you with the care of this sector. If you gave food to the tent city, it would be like a gift for the Saint's feast day. What better way to uphold his memory?'

The Patridzo's gaze seemed to harden. 'What do you know of Saint Ignatzio?'

'What Vettor tells me.'

'And what is that?'

'I know Saint Ignatzio would welcome all his people to the Evercity.'

The Patridzo snorted at the idea. His face was cold as he said, 'We are being overrun by influxers. We have prayed to the Imperium to save us from the enemy, but it seems the soldiers of the Astra Militarum have lost the ability to fight.'

Xereum started to speak, but as he did so one of the Patridzo's praisebirds swooped down and settled on a branch above his head.

The praisebirds were mechanical creatures of cogs and wheels with blue enamelled feathers. They each had the Richstar emblem on their chests, and had lived in the Kalvert as far back as records began. Xereum found them strangely disconcerting, for within their beaks they had vox-units, and when they sang, their voices were oddly human.

This one had a brass beak and green eyes. It cocked its head and opened its beak. *Seek honour as you act and you shall know no fear.*

The Patridzo lifted a finger to it, and it ran its beak along his outstretched digit in an oddly cat-like gesture. The Patridzo smiled faintly. 'I wish I could do more.'

Xereum lost his train of thought for a moment. He was sure there was some hidden message in the songs of the metal avians.

Smite those who disbelieve, for they have fallen into darkness.

'Can you send that thing away?' the cardinal said. 'It's hard to concentrate.'

The Patridzo made a discreet gesture and the construct put back its long neck, let out a long screeching call, then spread its metal wings and took flight. The Patridzo put a hand on the cardinal's arm.

'I shall see what I can do. It will all happen as the Emperor wishes. The Richstars have always been devoted servants of the Golden Throne. The most devoted, I think.'

TEN

The day began to darken as the Brotherhood assembled on the plains beyond the tent city. The massed brown-clad ranks fell silent as Shaliah Starborn, the Bringer of News, climbed barefooted onto the back of the Leman Russ *Faith of our Fathers* and prepared to address the faithful.

He could feel their gaze upon him. Their mood was expectant. The wind caught his robes as he closed his eyes and felt the spirit of the Emperor settle upon him like an eagle on his shoulder. He inhaled deeply.

'Brethren! For four thousand years we have suffered. The Imperium has suffered. Humanity has suffered. At this moment the fate of our race is in doubt. We are weighed down by the criminals and apes that hang about our neck.'

The crowd began to fidget. His heartbeat quickened. His speeches always went like this, a little clumsy and hesitant at first, before finding their route, in the way that water will find a path down from the mountainside.

As he started to warm to his theme, his volume and tempo began to rise and quicken. Within minutes he was shouting and the crowd was responding with cheers.

'Darkness surrounds us, brothers! Shadows encroach upon our world. Dread stalks through Holy Terra. The foundations of the Imperial Palace tremble. The Gallows Cluster itself falls to darkness. It is at this moment that the God-Emperor calls out to us. He cries for help. Will you help Him?'

'Aye!' a hundred thousand voices chorused back.

'Will you fight for Him?'

'Aye!' The words rolled over him, louder and more passionate now. Some lifted lasrifles into the air.

'Will you return His Holy Church back to its rightful place? Will you throw down the unrighteous?'

The Brotherhood answered with resounding words. At the end there were flecks of foam at the sides of Shaliah's mouth and in his beard. 'Will you kill His enemies?'

'We shall!' his army answered as one.

In the distance, over the plain, he could see the acropolis of the Evercity. At the top of the rock stood the ancient cathedral. Its bronze roof gleamed gold with setting sunlight.

Shaliah pointed over his shoulder. 'They cannot hear you!' he roared.

A hundred thousand voices roared back, 'We shall! We shall! They shall die!'

The voices were like thunder. As he spoke, files of transports began to make their way among the bands of the Frateris.

The crowd's voices made the earth beneath their feet tremble and when all was ready, Shaliah Starborn lifted his arms wide and took their hatred into himself. He let them chant, and then, at last, he held up his hands for silence. 'The time for violence has come!' he announced. 'Brothers! Are you ready to die for the Emperor?'

They answered with another roar.

Squad by squad, the gallants of Pitt's company pulled themselves up into the vehicles. There was a struggle to be the first. Carkal elbowed the others aside, shoved to be in Confessor Pitt's own truck.

The confessor stood on a metal crate. His bloodshot eyeballs seemed to gleam with excitement. 'Brothers! The Emperor is calling you. Today we shall shed blood in His name.'

He was their leader in faith and in arms. He was their father. Their captain. Their confessor. As the vast convoy set off, he called out and the gallants answered.

'The Emperor is our lord! Our shield and our knife!'

'Cowards seek compromise! Abhor the night! Destroy the heretics!'

Carkal chanted in time with the others. His faith kept him warm as the wind whipped dust into their faces.

The gallant next to him was a short, older man, with care-worn cheeks and grey stubble. As the gang fell silent, he clutched at Carkal's arm. 'I've heard you. You're from Guardia Rex.'

'I was, before I was reborn.'

The other man nodded. 'I thought so, from your accent. Which hive?'

Carkal told him and the man nodded. 'I am Gallant Bashin. What is happening?'

'Greetings, Gallant Bashin. We are going to kill heretics.'

Bashin nodded. It was all new to them. 'I suppose we must have faith.'

'Yes,' Carkal hissed. 'The Emperor protects.'

Harkham Pitt shouted over his shoulder. 'Silence, brothers!'

Bashin tried to speak to Carkal again, but this time Carkal would not answer. The truck bounced along. Someone grunted as they hit a pothole and they were thrown about.

'Are you lacking in faith?' Harkham Pitt demanded as they hit the main arterial road towards the tent city.

'No!' Carkal shouted. All of them were shouting. 'Our faith is strong. We believe in the Holy Emperor and the teachings of Saint Vandire!'

There was another pothole and grunts of pain and alarm as one of the gallants at the very back was slammed against the tailgate. Confessor Pitt turned on them. 'Who does not believe?'

'We believe!' they shouted back.

Pitt's face glared down at them. 'If any do not believe then I will find them and root them out, like a cancer from a body.'

'We believe,' more voices intoned. Carkal was among them. He believed, and to prove it he returned Pitt's stare.

'Doubt is weakness!' Pitt shouted, and they repeated his words.

'Doubt is weakness! I shall not question the Will of the Emperor! I shall crush the enemies of the True Emperor! I shall grind my boot into the faces of our enemies. They have despoiled the Throneworld. They have betrayed His Will.'

Carkal punched his fist into the air, just like the others.

'Test yourselves!' Confessor Pitt commanded.

Each gallant found a partner next to them. Carkal avoided Bashin. You were not allowed to struggle with someone you knew.

Carkal's partner had black hair and thick eyebrows, and intense dark eyes. They each put a hand on the other's shoulder. 'Do you believe?' the other said.

Carkal had seen what failure to answer in these struggle sessions brought.

'I do,' he told him.

'What do you believe?'

'I believe in the one true Emperor. I believe in His Holy Church and the right of the Frateris Militia to be His strong right arm.'

'And what is life?'

'Life is the chance to kill our enemies.'

'And what is death?'

'Death is the punishment of the enemies of the Holy Emperor.'

'Do you fear death?'

'I fear not death, for with death I shall be one with the light of the Imperium.'

'What do you want in life?'

'Life holds no joy, except for the death of my foes.'

The gallant nodded. It was Carkal's turn now. He asked the questions and the gallant responded with the appropriate creed.

'In the truth, brother,' they said, affirming their union, and they held each other's hands. They wanted nothing but death.

There was autogun fire as the Brotherhood column approached the outskirts of the tent city. The lead trucks were already pulling over and firing into the camp. The hiss of hard rounds was in the air above their heads.

Confessor Pitt seemed oblivious. He showed no fear, but stepped down from the crate and called out, 'Here, gallants! Take your guns. Be glad, for today you shall kill in the Emperor's name.'

Crates were thrown open and lasrifles were handed from one to another.

At the bottom of the crate was a heavy stubber, still wrapped in its factorum oilcloths, with belts of hard rounds coiled neatly beside it.

'You!' Pitt shouted and pointed to the dark-haired man. 'Take this gun!'

The dark-haired man struggled to pull it up.

Carkal leapt up to help, clamping the tripod fitting onto the front of the truck.

'Fire it!' Pitt ordered, and Carkal pushed the other man aside.

'I fire in the name of the Emperor!' he shouted, and put his shoulder to the back of the weapon and pulled the firing mechanism back fully.

The force of the kickback surprised him. The butt cut his lip and the next time he braced himself and fired off a burst of tracer fire into the enemy positions.

He had fired a number of salvos before he even aimed. No one about him seemed to care. They were pulling other stubbers out, and passing around bandoliers of powercells and grenades.

Carkal could see the Brotherhood vehicles lined up to left and right, rapidly approaching within charging range of the gangers' positions. The night was turned to day by the amount of weaponry brought to bear. Everyone was firing. Lasrifles, stubbers, pistols, it did not matter as long as one had faith in the Emperor.

Carkal wanted to kill. As their halftrack edged forwards he looked for a target. Before him, at a checkpoint under a water tower, the gangers had a flakboard barricade. He could see their heads appearing briefly as they fired their weapons over the top, and then there was shooting from the water tower itself.

Carkal felt hard rounds whip through the air about him and sprayed the base with return fire. Tracers stabbed out as his gun added to the crescendo of hatred.

He had no idea if he had hit anything, but Confessor Pitt clapped him on the back. 'Well done, my son! Have faith in the Emperor!'

In the truck next to them someone had a missile launcher. The first shot went wide, but the second hit the flakboard barricade and detonated inside it, showering the enemy with searing fragments of shrapnel.

Carkal kept firing at anything he could see. The edge of the city was burning, fabric tearing away from the metal tent-struts, ropes giving way under the heat, and whole marquees collapsing in flames.

At last they moved into the city, their faces flushed with heat and joy.

In a little over ten minutes the Brotherhood had swarmed into the tent city.

Carkal kept hold of the heavy stubber as the gallants chanted religious slogans, tore down the gates to the food stores and let the crowds surge in. As they passed under the water tower Carkal saw the body of a dead ganger, lying as he'd fallen, one leg crossed over the other. Another had been cut in half by shrapnel, and lay in a pool of gore and guts. Another was slumped forward, over a chair, itself broken by his fall.

He felt powerful as he saw his enemies dead. Emboldened. Filled with faith.

Some gangers had changed into civilian clothes, while others tried to cover up their tattoos and piercings, but the crowd found them and beat them, and turned them over to the Brotherhood.

A line was kneeling by the roadside.

Confessor Pitt jumped down, and drew his pistol. He put it to one man's head and fired, then strode along the line and killed each one.

'Death to our enemies!' he shouted, as the line of gangers slammed face down in the dirt, then Carkal strung the dead bodies up from the struts of water towers and lamp posts at the crossroads.

Vengeance had come. And it was the mad, staring face of Confessor Harkham Pitt.

ELEVEN

Archmagos Marquex was a thin man with a mane of cables and a long robe that hid whatever contraption had replaced his legs. He moved too smoothly, as if he were on wheels, and as he crossed the room he extended a silver mechadendrite to touch Bendikt's face in the manner of a blind man. There was a low whine of machinery from his torso.

'Analysis of your genetic code confirms that you are who you say you are,' Marquex announced in staccato tones. The inset plug sockets moved independently of each other, gecko-like. One turned to Mere while the other examined Bendikt. 'You are deficient.' Data-processors whirred for a moment. 'Your state is unsatisfactory. A warrior should have four limbs. You have only three.'

'I lost my hand.'

'It can be replaced.'

'And it will be. In time.'

'Time is short, General Bendikt.'

'Indeed it is. Please. Let us waste no more time talking about limbs. You have, I see, more than enough for all of us.'

The archmagos' multiple mechadendrites lifted into the air, as if to emphasise the fact. 'I am generally short of digits.'

'Well. Tell me. What defences do we possess within the Evercity?'

'The Evercity is a sacred site. A place of human pilgrimage. Of mystic delving. Its function is not defence.'

'No. But we need to defend it.'

Data-cogs whirred for a moment as the eyes continued to move independently of each other. Bendikt had met many of Marquex's type. Data and the processing was never their problem, but understanding those who remained fully human was.

'There is a perimeter wall. You will have seen it. It is primarily ornamental. It will not keep out an assault.'

'What about the acropolis?'

'The Mechanicus is not allowed onto the acropolis without the permission of the cardinal.'

'You will have his permission.'

Both of the magos' eyes turned to Bendikt. 'Thank you. In the meantime I don't know if you are aware that Intake Barracks has its own void shields. So does the Kalvert and the Basilika. I inspected them all ten years ago and they were in full working order.'

'Let's get them checked,' Bendikt said. Mere nodded.

'Anything else?'

'Nothing I am aware of.'

'Thank you, archmagos. Please have maintenance teams prepared to inspect the void generators.'

* * *

Chief of the forces drawn from the Gallows Cluster was a Barolan general, a dark-skinned, heavyset man with a high-pitched voice, named Kamak. Bendikt saluted him.

'Your unit is in charge of key infrastructure.'

'Yes, sir. I have units at the starport and Nullem Apek, and then smaller units protecting the grain silos and major generatoria. The Calibineer are manning the polar defence silos.'

Bendikt was not interested in the grain silos. 'Of key importance to me is the security of the starport.'

Kamak nodded. 'I don't have enough men to encircle the whole compound, but we have thirty Leman Russes and a squadron of Hydras well dug in.'

'Do you think you could repel an orbital assault?'

'No. But are the Scourged capable of such?'

'It's possible. I'm afraid to say that intelligence reports heretic Guard units among their ranks.'

'Holy Throne!'

'Yes. I am afraid so. The Scourged are the most dangerous form of heretic we know. Within their insanity is a malevolent form of intelligence – they're like wild beasts that retain human cunning. We have to assume that even in their degenerate state they still retain the ability to launch a complex assault from orbit.'

Kamak made the sign of the aquila. Bendikt turned to the local defence commander. She was a tough-looking lady, with wide hips and a tight-fitting blue jacket. She had overheard the previous conversation and blanched. 'I was unaware that our position was so bad.'

'I am here to hold this planet. Complacency is a fatal flaw. I am expecting the very worst.'

She nodded, then collected herself. 'Sorry, sir. I have not

introduced myself. My name is General Dominka. I am commander of the Potence Mountain Infantry.'

'Good to meet you,' Bendikt said. 'I'm...'

'Cadian,' she said. There was a moment's hesitation as she looked to Kamak, then went on.

'You're the first Cadian general I've met.'

'And what do you think?'

'Well,' she said. 'Four years ago, I would have been impressed. But now... Perhaps I should be direct. I was born and bred on Potence. And, general, I don't want to lose my planet.'

Bendikt nodded. 'I understand. Trust me, we will do all that we can. But let us not waste more time talking.' Bendikt bristled a little as he pulled out the star charts. He addressed Kamak and Dominka. 'You have heard about Kypra?'

She puffed out her cheeks. 'Yes. But I'm not surprised.'

'Why not?'

'Kypra was ruled by Garrison Richstar. He was mad, by most accounts. Kept a bodyguard of female warriors about him. Named them the Sisterhood. Had a replica of the Imperial Palace built. Or at least he started it. Something stopped him.'

'The Inquisition?'

'If only they had, then Kypra might still be standing. Garrison also insisted on commanding the local defence.'

'Did he have any military training?'

'No.'

Bendikt nodded. 'Well, that is one advantage we have. The local defence is in my control. And Potence is the planet upon which we will break the Scourged. We have your units and one regiment of Cadians at full strength. That is right, Mere?'

Mere nodded quickly. 'Yes, sir. The 101st have been brought up to full strength with units from the–'

'No need to list them. They're Cadians. Enough said. On top of that we have fifty thousand troops inbound on the *St Matthew*. They are a mix of Elizabethgrad Hussars, Serennian Irregulars and troops from the Crinan, Phrygian and Bifrost Systems. They should have been here a week ago, but apparently their transport struck an asteroid passing through the circumstellar belt at Waxin Gate. No serious losses, but there was damage to the Geller field generator.'

'Any warships?'

'Yes.' Bendikt listed the ships. 'And Potence, I believe, has a fine array of orbital defences.'

'In theory. Yes. Though a grand-nephew of the Patridzo is in charge of them.'

'Is he also mad?'

Bendikt got a wry smile out of the local officer. 'No. But I cannot say how well prepared the crews are.'

'Well, I saw the complement of defence monitors. How many were there?'

'Twelve,' Mere said. 'I'll find out if they're all operational.'

'Good. And give me a full breakdown. Orbital defence platforms. Defence lasers.'

An hour later Bendikt issued another set of orders for relay from Nullem Apek. 'These are Code Red.'

There was a knock at the door. A vox-officer handed Mere a sheaf of vox communications. He flicked through it, and put the file down.

'Anything of import?'

Mere shook his head.

At last Bendikt said, 'Right. I'm going with my gut instincts.

I expect an attack on Potence imminently. A move like that would be characteristic of the Scourged. But if they reach this far then their supply lines will be dangerously thin. We can cut off their supply routes at the moon of Cinnabar's Folly. We will keep a nominal force here to hold the Evercity. Any idea how long it will take to patch up the *St Matthew*?'

'Last communications from their shipmaster stated that they expected to make the warp jump within three days. That was three days ago.'

'Well, contact them again. Confirm they are ready to make the jump, and when they will be here.'

When at last everything was set in order, Dominka and Kamak led their staff from the room. When they were alone, Bendikt drew up a seat and lowered himself into it.

'Done?' Mere said.

Bendikt nodded. He picked the vox sheaf up and flicked through the pages, looking for anything relevant to his plans. Mere walked across to the drinks cabinet. Through the cut-glass windows he could see a selection of local liquors. The door was a little stiff as he opened it, and the glass tinkled with the movement.

'What is there?' Bendikt said.

'Nothing I know,' Mere said. He took a bottle at random, unstoppered the cork and took a sniff.

He poured a little into a narrow glass, and took a sip. 'Not bad,' he said. 'Says it's called "Myrto".'

Bendikt took the glass and drained it, then held it out for another. He felt the liquor burn down his gullet and into his stomach. 'Ah!' he said. 'Thank the Throne we are in the field once more! May I never be promoted again.'

Mere poured him another glass. 'I think you've managed to guarantee that. Now, why don't we go up top? The troopers of the 101st have been hanging about the command bunker all day hoping to get a glimpse of you.'

Bendikt nodded. Military reunions were mixed affairs. Amongst the old friends there were the faces that were missing and gone, and the new faces that you did not know, and who did not know you.

Bendikt finished his drink, and steeled himself. 'Yes,' he said. 'That would be good.'

TWELVE

Confessor Pitt led the purge of the tent city with pistol and blade. He gloried in killing, and when a local magister was brought to him, Pitt tore the black top hat from the man's head, and pulled it down over his own, adding to the air of menace and horror.

'We must seek out the unclean and the unholy!' he told his gallants. 'Bring them to me and I shall judge their faith!'

The young men shouted their war cry, but Carkal put up his hand. 'How shall we know them?'

'Trust your heart,' Confessor Pitt told him as he pushed the crumpled top hat down onto his head. 'The Emperor will guide you!'

Carkal led his band from block to block, seeking out the unholy. They grabbed men with tattoos, old women, anyone that they thought looked suspect or frightened.

When they brought the prisoners to Confessor Pitt, he marched along the line with chainsword and laspistol, his black top hat at an angle on his head. 'Guilty!' he declared, and dispatched each one with either a swing of the sword or a shot to the head.

At the end of the line he spun around. 'Where are the others?'

The stitches that held the confessor's eyelids back were starting to tug and strain. The bulging eyeballs fixed on Carkal. 'Is that all? There are no more heretics?'

'Not that we could find,' Carkal told him.

Confessor Pitt strode towards him, revving his chainsword with fury. 'You haven't looked hard enough! There are heretics everywhere. Bring them to me and I will judge them guilty!'

They found more heretics. Two men with beards. A sickly youth in tattered silks. A woman and a crone that she said was her mother.

'Take them!' Carkal ordered.

As they moved on to the next block Carkal suddenly realised he recognised this place. It was where he had spent his first night on Potence. It felt like an age ago now. He had gone from a weak and frightened young man to this, a gallant in the Brotherhood, powerful, focused, fearless.

The sign was still there, though the House of Matteo was shut.

'Open up, in the name of the Emperor!' Carkal shouted.

There was no response. He drew his knife and cut a huge hole in the side of the tent.

The gallants burst inside. The faces were immediately familiar. The man with the gun stepped before him. 'Back!' he said, but the command his presence had once instilled was gone. He was alone now, and Carkal was many.

He stepped forward without fear and took the gun from the man's hands. 'The Emperor protects,' he said.

'What do you want?' Matteo asked. He still wore his apron, but now, instead of the weary look, his face was an image of terror.

'I want heretics!' Carkal spat.

'There are none here,' Matteo stammered. 'Just victuals and honest men trying to make a living.'

'Honest men! How dare you judge yourself. Who says you are honest? It is we who decide who is honest or not!' Carkal kicked Matteo to the floor. 'You lock your door to the Brotherhood and you call yourself honest! Do you lock your heart to His truth? Darkness lurks in the hearts of the dishonest.'

Matteo was shouting a response, but Carkal kicked him again. 'Lies!' he spat. 'A viper in our midst. Take him to the confessor.'

Matteo clutched at Carkal's legs. 'I can explain…!'

But Carkal kicked him away. 'Conversation costs extra.'

They went from tent to tent, dragging away whoever seemed unholy.

It was a time of screams, beating, shouting, judging.

When they found Confessor Pitt, hours later, he stood atop a heap of corpses, chainsword revving. His hands were red. His hat was splattered with gore and his face dripped blood.

'Guilty!' he hissed, stamping on the bodies as if he were trying to flatten an uneven carpet. He staggered over them as they tilted and turned underfoot. 'They are all guilty!'

He turned and looked back. There were hundreds of corpses heaped before them.

'You have done well, brothers.'

'More?' Carkal asked.

The confessor's eyes were mad and staring. 'No. We must leave some for the others to judge. The Emperor calls us for another sacred duty.'

A file of transports was waiting for them. Confessor Pitt's brigade climbed up into their vehicles.

'Up, brother!' he said to Carkal. 'Ride with me. You have a good nose for heresy, and we have a sacred mission!'

Carkal stood at Pitt's right hand as the convoy wound its way out of the tent city onto the plains. His top hat remained rammed down on his head.

'Where are we going, confessor?'

Pitt turned his wide-eyed gaze on him. 'Up there!' he pointed. 'To the mountains!'

'Why there, confessor, when there are so many heretics to purge?' He pointed towards the Evercity, but they were heading in the opposite direction.

Confessor Pitt grinned. 'Don't fear. We are part of a much bigger war, my child. A war that has been thousands of years in the planning.'

'I don't understand.'

Confessor Pitt laughed at him. 'Good, Gallant Carkal. Understanding is for the weak.'

Confessor Pitt's brigade crossed the flat plains, and began to climb up foothills of the Supramonte.

The gradient became steeper with each switchback and soon the rock face became so steep that the road had been drilled and blasted from the cliff face. The halftracks slowed almost to a walk as they went around each hairpin turn. Carkal held his lascarbine close to his chest as he was thrown from side to side, and prayed. As they climbed higher the land fell away.

Men too timid to address the confessor came to Carkal now.

'What is our mission?' one man asked.

'We are going to kill heretics,' Carkal told him.

'I do not like this road,' the other man said.

Carkal gripped his shoulder. 'Have faith. The Emperor protects.'

That was what they were all saying. But late in the afternoon, as clouds began to gather, the halftrack behind them took a corner too wide. There were shouts and screams as it skidded off the road. Stones tumbled into the drop and the halftrack held as the driver slammed the accelerator down.

The tracks whirred. Dust engulfed the open carriage. The truck slipped backwards. The others stood transfixed as one side tipped over the edge and dragged the whole thing with it.

There were screams as it fell. Men tumbled out as it plunged through the thin mountain air, bouncing on the slopes three times before hitting the road far below them.

Carkal pulled his eyes away. He looked to Confessor Pitt for a way to understand this dire omen.

Snow had started to fall. The confessor's bulging eyes were expressionless. 'They were weak,' he declared.

At the next turn, part of the road had crumbled away. The driver took this bend very slowly. Confessor Pitt remained standing at the front as part of the road gave way.

A voice cried out in fear. Confessor Pitt turned on them. 'Who lacks faith?'

He looked to Carkal first. Carkal's face was earnest. 'I believe,' he declared.

The confessor nodded.

He looked to each of them and the gallants returned his intent stare, each face defensive with faith and belief. The halftrack scraped and ground slowly about the corner. The confessor's gaze held them all. None of them dared show fear.

They climbed higher and higher, and the gallants began to hold themselves against the biting winds. But there was no protection here. The clouds grew darker with the fading day. The rain turned to ice. The wind began to howl through rocky hollows. It tugged at the halftrack with such force it seemed that they would be plucked from the mountainside like a rodent in a raptor's claws.

The tracks kicked up a cloud of ice crystals, and through the flapping canvas he saw faces like his own: ruddy, cold, resolute. Confessor Pitt gripped the front railings, glorying in the tumult. The wind whipped at the canvas roofing as the wind drove ice into them. Carkal had never seen snow before or felt such cold, but he did not dare show weakness, did not dare breathe a word of complaint as Confessor Pitt's sermons became increasingly wild.

It was as if the storm that darkened the sky above them fed his rage. 'We are the blade of the Emperor, the bludgeon to the faithless. Hear me, brothers, and lock your hearts against our foes. Woe, I tell you. Woe to the unworthy! Woe to the corrupt! Woe to him who pours oil upon the waters that the Emperor has whipped into a tumult! Woe to any who seek to please rather than to appal! Woe to any who are not the chosen!'

At last the road began to level out, the bare rock replaced by pine trees standing in silent, black ranks.

Carkal had never seen a forest. It seemed a strange, foreboding place that flickered past like a row of iron posts, black against the white of the snow, which kicked up from the whirling tracks. He felt hidden eyes in the shadows. Wild animals were watching.

Confessor Pitt seemed oblivious. He had not stopped his sermon. 'Give thyself up to fire. Recall the Emperor's wounds. His woe brings wisdom. He is our lord! Our shield and our knife! Only cowards seek compromise!'

Carkal chanted the confessor's words.

Other voices joined in, teeth rattling against the cold.

He clutched his lasrifle, fingers frozen on the wooden butt.

'Doubt is a sign of weakness!' Carkal repeated, echoing back each chant. 'I shall not question the will of the lord! I shall crush the enemies of the Emperor! I shall grind my boot into the faces of our enemies. They have despoiled the Throneworld. They have betrayed His will.'

'Struggle now, gallants!' Confessor Pitt commanded. 'Seek out the weak!'

They were half frozen, but each of them hurried to obey.

'What do you believe?' they demanded, through cold-numb mouths.

'I believe in the one True Emperor. I believe in His Holy Church and the right of the Frateris Militia to be His strong right arm.'

'In the truth, brother.'

'In the truth.'

THIRTEEN

To celebrate the return of General Isaia Bendikt, the quarter-master of the 101st Hell's Last released three days' worth of liquor ration. The troopers cheered their general as he came into the mess. Minka stayed at the back, as the crowd engulfed Bendikt.

She looked about. Despite the enthusiasm, the new Cadians were notable by their absence.

She found Viktor. 'Any idea where the others are?'

He shrugged. 'The barracks?'

'I'm going to go and find them. They're my squad.'

Minka grabbed a bottle.

She found most of her squad sitting outside the barracks, playing cards. The air was still. It was hot and stifling. A mosquito droned in her ear.

Donson had a grin on his face as he scooped up the metal tokens they were using as money. The rest of them had a weary look. The sound of cheering from the mess resonated across the yard. It only added to the air of despondency and isolation.

She tried to lift the atmosphere. 'Celebration time,' she said. 'Where are your mugs!'

They found enough enamelled cups, and she passed the bottle around.

'Thank you, sarge,' Jaromir said. He blinked at the taste. 'Oh, that's good. That's just like home. Know what I mean?'

'Yes,' she said and slapped the big guy's arm.

Jason winked at her. Lasmonn drained his in one go. Dreno took the bottle without looking at her, passed it on to Emerson. Rustem took it from him. 'This is very kind of you, sarge.' She had stripped down to her undervest. There was a sweat stain between her flat breasts. Her biceps bulged as she took the bottle and poured a shot for Minka and herself, and then tapped mugs.

'Thank you for including us, sarge,' she said, and drained her cup.

Minka did likewise. At the end she said, 'Anyone seen Laptev?'

They shook their heads.

'I'd better find him.'

'I'd leave him be, if I were you.' It was Rustem.

Minka felt guilty now. It was her responsibility to reach out. 'We should include him.'

'I wouldn't bother.'

'I'll talk to him. It'll be fine. Trust me.'

FOURTEEN

Confessor Pitt called a halt an hour after sunset.

The halftracks slewed off into knee-deep snow. The gallants stamped it down as the vehicles lined up. Carkal heard howling in the forest. He had no idea what kind of animal made that noise. He had never been so glad of military boots and thick camo trousers.

'Food!' Confessor Pitt shouted. The last truck carried barrels of slop. The gallants queued as the cooks handed out stamped metal bowls of hot, thick broth. Carkal stood in a circle with some of his brothers in the lee of a halftrack. They shovelled the food in before it went cold, then handed the bowls back for others.

'Gather round!' Confessor Pitt called out.

The stitches that held his eyelids open were pulling. Drips of blood marked his cheeks, and icicles hung from his nose into his beard. The wind whipped under the chassis, tugging at their legs. He stared at each of them.

'The Imperium of Man has languished for too long in the hands of the unholy. The bell tolls for its myriad sins. Even now, the enemies of mankind knock at the door of our home worlds. Those without faith turn to heresy. The open mind is easily corrupted. Our minds are shut. Our faith is strong. We deny their false proofs for we are the few. We are the holy. We are the spark that starts the conflagration.'

Confessor Pitt's breath steamed in the air before him. 'We, of the Temple of the Holy Emperor, are the Emperor's Truth. You are the foot-soldiers who shall restore His power to the Imperium of Man. We shall cast down the unholy who despoil His Throneworld. We shall burn the unrighteous and the unbelievers. You!' he said suddenly.

Carkal realised he was being singled out.

'What do you believe?'

Carkal felt both terror and elation. He shouted out his creed. 'I believe in the one true Emperor. I believe in His Holy Church and the right of His Brotherhood to be His strong right arm.'

The confessor's staring eyes fixed on the next man. 'Brother, what do you believe?'

The man repeated the same lines. The third was stiff with cold. 'I,' he started, teeth chattering. 'I... I...'

Confessor Pitt shoved the gallants aside. 'Tell me what you believe!'

The other man's back teeth were rattling so hard he could barely speak.

'Do you have faith?' the confessor demanded. 'Speak through your courage. Speak through your faith.'

The other man tried, but as the confessor came forward the man dropped his lasrifle.

Confessor Pitt looked down on him with sudden disgust. 'Do you refuse to fight?'

'N-n-no!' the man said and fell onto his knees, claw hands desperately trying to pick up his gun.

The confessor stood over him, staring down, eyes twitching as his lids strained against the stitches. He turned to the rest of the company. 'Brothers. We have one among us whose faith is weak.'

Carkal looked down at the man on the floor. It was the other man from Marquis. Bashin.

Bashin reached out for him, and Carkal stepped backwards as Confessor Pitt drew his laspistol. 'There is no place for the weak among us. We are the chosen. We are the future. We are the spark that will ignite the Imperium. You! Punish him!'

One of the other brothers, a burly man with a stubbled scalp and a scraggly, black beard that jutted out from his chin, stepped forward. He lifted his lasrifle with both hands and brought the butt down onto Bashin's back. Pitt called on each of them to strike a blow. A second stamped on a frozen claw of a hand. A third brought the heel of his boot down onto the man's forearm. There was a distinct crack as the bone sheared in two and the man groaned.

'I believe,' Bashin started, as if the pain had shocked his frozen mind back into function. 'I believe in the one true Emperor.' There was a grunt of pain. The man fell onto his face. 'I… I… I believe in His Holy Church.' Another blow fell. When the man spoke again, his voice was barely a whisper. '…And the right of the Frateris Militia to be His strong right arm…'

Carkal was about to say that he had spoken the words, but the brothers were not listening any more. Confessor Pitt's blood was up. He had found a traitor among their number. Blows rained down on him. Rifle butts. Fists. Feet. Knees.

A hand took his shoulder. He turned to see the confessor's bloodshot eyes streaming tears of blood. 'You alone have yet to strike. Do you fear to kill in the name of the truth?'

Carkal remembered throttling the life from others in the darkness of the transport. He shook his head. He shouted again. 'I believe in the one true Emperor. I believe in His Holy Church and the right of the Frateris Militia to be His strong right arm.'

Confessor Pitt's eyes were disbelieving. 'Why do you not strike?'

Carkal stammered. 'I was recalling my sins! Before I joined the Brotherhood, I was not a bad man, but I did things that I am ashamed of. I sinned.'

The confessor put a hand to Carkal's face. His eyes were understanding now. 'Who has not sinned? Look about you. Brothers, are any of us sinless?'

'No,' they said.

Confessor Pitt put a hand to his own chest. 'Am I sinless?'

'No,' came the reply, even stronger than before.

'No. We all sin,' the confessor said, 'because we are human. We fail the Holy Emperor every day. But there is one way we can make up for our transgressions. Do you want to know how?'

Carkal nodded. His teeth were starting to rattle and he suddenly feared that he would be next. All he wanted was to live and feed and be warm once more.

'The way to salvation is through the blood of unbelievers.'

Carkal nodded. He understood this.

'Here!' the confessor said, pointing down at the man on the floor. 'This is unbelief. One who wanders in darkness. One who is not within the truth.'

'But he said the words–' Carkal started, but the confessor shook his head.

'You *think* he said the words. But you are wrong. He has learnt the words but he does not believe. Faith would make him strong. Faith would make him resolute. But look at him. He is weak and bloodied. He is close to death, and his soul will wander the void, lost and alone, spurned by the light of the Holy Emperor. Is that what you want for yourself?'

'No,' Carkal declared.

'You don't sound sure.'

'I am sure,' Carkal announced.

Confessor Pitt's left eye started to twitch. 'Then show me. This heretic is guilty. Kill him with a single blow. You can do it. You must do it, for if you don't then the Emperor spurns your service and you too are unworthy.'

Carkal looked up at the others. They were like wolves standing about a dying beast, and looking to see if the guard dog will fight them or not. He turned his gaze down. Bashin was pushing himself up to his knees. He held one limp arm to his body. His nose was broken. One eye was swollen shut. Blood streamed from both nostrils and from a cut in his hairline. The ice beneath him was freckled with red. His blood had frozen. 'Forgive me,' Bashin begged. 'I believe. I believe… in the right of the Frateris Militia to be His strong right arm. I walk in truth.'

Confessor Pitt's voice was close to Carkal's ear now. 'Kill him,' it hissed.

Carkal lifted his lasrifle. 'You are a heretic!' he shouted. 'And I cast you into the darkness of the void, away from the light of the Holy Emperor.'

He closed his eyes, drove the rifle butt down and heard the sound of a human skull breaking.

FIFTEEN

The barracks were quiet and empty, rooms unlit.

Minka called out Laptev's name. Her voice echoed back as she pushed through the rows of empty bunks. She called his name out again.

The men's barracks had a distinct smell, sweat mixed in with the scent of leather boots, damp socks, wax-cloth webbing, mouldy wet mops. She got to the end of the wing, and turned back. Laptev was nowhere. She could hear her own footsteps, could hear her own breath. There was a distant gurgle of pipes from the floor above.

Something was odd. She waited until the distant gurgling stopped, and listened.

There were twenty bunks. Backpacks. Boots. Dress uniforms laid out on cots. A faded picture of the Caducades. An icon of Ursarkar E. Creed pinned high up on the wall. A beret full of old Redskulls cap badges, the threads showing where they had been cut away. It struck her how the other regiments must feel, to be broken up like this. They were like war-orphans, taken away from their siblings and assigned to new families.

She rested her head on the cool metal of the bunk.

She heard a stifled sob and looked about. She could see no one.

'Hello?' she called out. The note of the silence changed, as if someone was in there, holding their breath.

Minka's skin shivered. She had a terrible feeling that she was back in the dark pits of Markgraaf Hive.

There was a sound. She moved silently towards the door of the closet. The unknown was always the most terrifying, her mother had told her. Minka had learnt that her mother was wrong, because Minka had seen the most bone-chilling sights that the galaxy could offer with her own two eyes.

But even so, it took all of her courage to reach out and take hold of the round brass doorknob and pull the door open. Something fell towards her and she leapt back.

It was a broom handle.

She cursed herself, and was about to shut the door again, when she saw boots, legs, bent knees.

The sweet smell was overpowering. She pushed the stack of mops and brooms aside.

'Laptev, is that you?'

There was a slurred response.

It was Laptev. He was limp as a dead man, eyes rolled back to the white, snot and drool hanging from his face.

She knelt down and slapped his face. 'Laptev! What have you done, you stupid bastard?'

He gurgled.

She slapped him again. She'd known lots of Cadians who'd ended their own lives in the last two years. She'd been tempted too, in her darker moments. She pulled him forward, took his head and lifted it.

'Laptev!' she hissed. She knelt down and slapped his cheek again. 'What the frekk have you done?'

She checked his wrists. No blood. Checked his pulse. Checked his neck. His mouth was clear. His hands were sweaty. She had a sudden fear. What happened if he died? She'd be the sergeant who cursed her squad.

Clutched in his left palm was a glass phial. There was a residue of blue syrup inside. She sniffed it. 'Oh, frekk,' she cursed, and punched him in frustration.

She knew what she was supposed to do. Report him to the bats.

But she knew how that would end. His body being dumped in a black bag over the side of the cliff. She cursed him again, put the phial back into his hand, stood up.

He spoke.

She bent down. 'Laptev? Say that again.'

He tried to speak. She shook him. 'If I can't hear you I can't help you.'

Laptev's eyes blinked open for a moment, and she thought he was coming back.

'Don't shoot me,' he mumbled.

She slapped his cheeks. He took her hands in his, and held them tight.

'Is that you?' he asked.

His eyes rolled back. The pupils were gaping wide and dark. He blinked.

'Sergeant. Is that you?'

'What do you mean?'

'Is that you?'

'Yes. It's me. Sergeant Lesk. What did you take?'

There was a long pause and she thought she would lose him again. At last he rasped, 'Medicine.'

'Laptev. What have you taken?'

His fingers were like vices on her arms as he hissed, 'The red giant. The bloody warrior!' Minka felt a wave of horror pass through her. She remembered her own moment of abject terror and it clutched at her throat. She could not speak. 'Don't let them shoot me,' he said. 'Not because of the red giant. We could not fight it. We could do nothing.'

Minka squeezed her eyes shut. She could not go back there. It was too terrifying. She pushed his hands off. 'Listen, Laptev. This cannot happen again. Understand? You are a corporal in the 101st Cadian Shock Troops. That has got to mean something to you.'

His eyes lost focus.

'Listen. I've been where you are now. I've been there, and there is a way out. The Emperor forgives. But He needs you to step up. I need it. I want all that you have. Understand. No more nonsense. Understand?'

A shudder went through him, and he lifted a hand in what was probably a salute.

When she came back into the mess, the exuberance was reaching a crescendo. Troopers were sitting and standing in groups. She bumped into a figure.

'Lesk,' Commissar Shand said. 'In a hurry?'

'Yes,' she said quickly. 'Weak bladder.'

'Where are your squad?'

'They're in the yard. They didn't want to intrude on a family occasion,' she said, nodding towards where Bendikt sat, laughing with the oldest members of the unit. 'I went out to drink with them.'

'How's Laptev?'

'Don't know,' she said.

Shand's face was side-lit by the mess lights. It threw his features into hard and dark relief. 'No?'

'No, sir.'

'Sure?'

'Yes.'

'I need you to watch him closely, Lesk. All the Redskulls. Do you understand?'

Minka nodded solemnly.

'Anything strange, you let me know.'

She saluted. 'Yes, sir.'

SIXTEEN

As the Cadian 101st were enjoying the last round of drinks in the Evercity barracks, Captain Ashtari was making an impromptu inspection of the Guard compound that surrounded the astropathic tower of Nullem Apek.

The base was a doughnut shape of barracks, habs, tower blocks, sentry towers, gun emplacements and perimeter fencing, hung inside and out with a triple row of concertina wire. Inside the girdle, the astropathic tower rose up, dark and foreboding. Ashtari had had no contact with the denizens inside, and that suited him fine.

The Barolan Mechanised had been on Potence for six months now, and this was Ashtari's second posting up to the Supramonte. The cold was not the worst thing. There were warm barrack halls, half sunken into the frozen earth, a good supply of victuals and good hunting too, in the forest, when the weather was clear. Last trip he'd bagged three mountain tigers and an aurox. Hunting was not allowed, of course. The whole Supramonte was the preserve of the Richstars, who had stocked it with big game felines. But, so Ashtari had been told, the current Patridzo had no interest in hunting, and the tigers of the Supramonte had become abundant.

He'd go hunting again, Ashtari told himself, just as soon as this snow passed.

No, he thought as he stamped through the half-cleared path to the pillbox in the north circuit. The worst thing was the tower itself.

He gave it a glance. The Nullem Apek was a tall pinnacle of windowless black basalt, stabbing up into the clouds or, perhaps, raised like a finger in warning. It had the stink of xenos to it, like something brought forth without human hands, riven from the bedrock in an unholy manner. And this was the worst time of all, as pale, corposant witchfire began to play across the pinnacle of the tower and a thunder-head of psychic power built about its summit.

Two men patrolled each quadrant, their greatcoats fastened tight, their fur-lined shakos pulled low onto their heads. He waved to them as he approached the nearest pillbox. The metalled steps had been scattered with grit and chlorides. He was careful nonetheless. Last thing he needed was a fall. They hurt twice as much when you were this cold. He put a thickly gloved hand to the iron door clamp. The lock had frozen. He thrust it down with a grunt and bent low to step inside.

The rockcrete bunker had a ruddy glow from the brazier. The squad inside had made themselves as comfortable as possible, building on the modifications made by each Guard unit unlucky enough to spend the winters up here. They sat playing cards on a camp table while one of them kept watch at the firing slot. They had strung Munitorum-issue blankets around the walls, and across the firing slot a simple curtain of padded cotton had been hung to keep out the draughts. It was like stepping into a nomad tupik.

They stood as he entered.

'At ease.' He stamped to get the snow from his shoes. 'So, who's winning?'

'Bijan!' they all said.

Bijan was a short trooper who was still growing his distinctive Barolan moustaches.

'Well done, lad. Keep it up!' Ashtari told him.

They passed the time with small talk, until there was the crackle of an electronic discharge in the air above them.

'It's starting again, is it?' Bijan asked. 'How long did it go on for the last time?'

'A whole watch. At least.'

The lightning flared again.

The sergeant, Abbas, rubbed his hands together. 'How long till we're back at the starport?'

'Good news there. Our stay has been shortened. Apparently there's a new general planetside. He's expecting invasion. Wants the garrison at the starport reinforced.'

The news of invasion didn't cheer any of them.

'At least something is going to happen,' Abbas said.

'Well, carry on,' Ashtari said and made for the door. As he did there was a crackle of static. Abbas lifted the vox-receiver.

'Is the captain there?' a voice said. It was unmistakably Karvan. *'Yeah. Great. Can you ask him to come to the gate. We've got guests. Just need his clearance.'*

Ashtari frowned. 'Guests?' he repeated, but Karvan had closed the vox-link.

There was another crackle of electrostatic power above his head. It was bright enough to throw sudden shadows through the pillbox doorway. Ashtari ducked outside and closed the door behind him, calling out, 'Bijan, keep beating those bastards!'

There was a light in the darkness that crackled and spat, like an angry snake.

Carkal's head began to throb. It was like a low drone inside his skull. He put his hands to his ears but the noise did not go away.

Confessor Pitt did not seem to notice. He stood at the front of the carriage and stared ahead. More lightning flashed above their heads. No one dared cry out.

The mist cleared as they came closer. Carkal saw a high fence brightly lit with lumen-globes, a rockcrete pillbox and a stablight pointing straight towards them.

A Guardsman with a lasrifle beckoned them to slow down. The engines idled as an officer in trench coat and fur hat strode out from the command post. He went to the driver's door of the lead vehicle, his breath steaming in the high plateau air, but clearly the driver had pointed him behind, to where Confessor Pitt stood erect in the halftrack.

'We are here in the name of the God-Emperor. By appointment of the Patridzo and the cardinal archbishop of the Gallows Cluster,' Confessor Pitt shouted. He reached inside his chest and took out a sheaf of papers.

The officer had long moustaches, eyebrows pale with ice, and an ornate sabre slung over his back. He took the papers in a gloved hand, and looked at them without speaking.

He walked back inside as promethium fumes thickened about the waiting convoy.

Ashtari reached the front gate a few minutes after leaving the north pillbox.

The guards were up, looking smart. Sergeant Karvan had a roll of parchment on the desk in front of him. 'There's a bunch of nutheads outside,' he said. 'Says they have official sanction to relieve us.'

'Good luck to them,' Ashtari said. He took the papers. They had the official seal of the Patridzo. 'Looks good to me. Let's get clearance first.'

As they waited in the halftrack, Carkal could feel his heartbeat quicken. After a minute or two, another officer came forward. He held a piece of paper in his hand. 'Who is the commander here?'

Confessor Pitt spoke with all the gravitas of a prophet. 'I am.'

'I'm Captain Ashtari, Barolan Guard. Can you come down, please?'

Carkal felt a stab of anger. How could anyone question his confessor?

The gallants in the back of the halftrack stepped aside to let their commander through. As he passed Carkal, the confessor lifted a finger and touched him on the chest. 'Come with me,' he said.

He picked out ten guards as he moved through the crush.

They jumped down behind him onto the rockcrete road and walked to stand before the officer.

The officer looked pained. 'Sorry,' he said. 'Just you, confessor.'

'What is the problem?' Pitt demanded.

'I need to check your credentials.'

Confessor Pitt's staring eyeballs were full of intent. 'Why?'

'It's my job,' the officer said.

'The papers are correct. The seals are authentic. We are warriors of the faith. We have Imperial sanction.'

Carkal gripped his lasrifle. He could not bear his leader to suffer questioning. Others clearly felt the same. The sense of menace was palpable.

'Trust me. I'll be happy to leave this place to you.'

'Perhaps we could come inside, while we wait,' Confessor Pitt suggested, but there was nothing conciliatory in his manner.

Ashtari sighed. 'Sorry, confessor. That would not be proper. I just need to contact my commanding officers.'

Confessor Pitt braced his legs and spoke with authority. 'Captain. You are impeding the will of the Patridzo of Potence, and the cardinal archbishop.'

There was a sudden clap of thunder above. The waves of psychic energy washed over them. It seemed to reinforce the confessor's voice. Ashtari's temper was beginning to fray. 'Listen. Just wait here.'

'I'm afraid we cannot do that.' In a single movement Confessor Pitt drew his laspistol and fired. There was a flash of red light and a puff of bloody mist, and Captain Ashtari slammed back into the snow.

The halftracks surged forward. They slammed the roadblocks aside as the two Guardsmen standing close by dropped to their knees and fired.

The man next to Carkal was felled instantly. Confessor Pitt was hit in the chest. Carkal screamed with fury, but Pitt did not seem to notice, and put his chainsword through the nearest Guardsman's torso.

Carkal ran to the pillbox door. The Guardsmen had shut the door but not locked it. He kicked it open and sprayed the inside.

Las-bolts lit the chamber up. The men inside had dragged

the curtain aside and were swinging the autocannon round but he kept firing until the room was filled with acrid smoke and everyone was dead.

The storm muffled the shouting. The gallants stormed the pillboxes and killed all inside.

Confessor Pitt marched to the barrack hall. It was standard Munitorum issue, set halfway into the ground. A heavy load of snow sagged from its eaves. The windows had been covered over with padded cotton insulation. Three stairs led down to the double doorway.

Confessor Pitt threw one doorway open and stepped inside. To the left was a barrack hall, to the right the mess. The evening meal had finished an hour or so before. A trooper was moving round, wiping tables. From the kitchens came the sound of washing-up, plates being stacked, men calling out to each other as they looked forward to the end of their shift.

An officer stepped out of the latrine. 'Who the hell are you?' He was still buttoning up his greatcoat as he strode out of the headquarters.

'I am your judge and I declare you guilty,' Confessor Pitt pronounced. He fired three shots.

The gallants swarmed inside, firing and stabbing. The Barolan Guardsmen put up a desperate defence. They barricaded doorways, fired furiously, took a heavy toll on the forces that came against them.

Confessor Pitt ordered the inner gates of the girdle fort broken down, so a halftrack rammed the wire gateway, and left it in shreds. He turned his back on the dying and the screaming and strode towards the base of the tower. He was like a magnet, drawing his gallants after him. A crowd of men followed in his wake.

The astropathic tower rose dark and silent before them. He marched up the steps. The door was locked. He reached for the melta bomb that hung at his waist. He holstered his pistol to set the gauge, then slammed it onto the doorway.

It was not in Confessor Pitt's nature to take a step backwards, but he stood back now, as the charge went off with a hiss of smoke and then a sudden blinding flash.

The tower wardens of Nullem Apek wore ceremonial uniforms embroidered with religious iconography and wards and seals of purity. They were pure in faith, fearless in the face of heresy and corruption. But their role was to enforce purity throughout the astropathic facility, and to guard against warp taint or corruption. They wielded ornate bolt pistols, thrice blessed, and silver-etched with religious texts, the blunt tips of the stub-nosed bolts each engraved with pentagrams and the aquila.

They responded to the unauthorised intrusion, dashing from the higher chambers down along the corkscrew corridors, calling on each other for information and to put a plan of defence in place.

They came across the first intruders on the third level and fired. The wardens were expert warriors, killing two gallants each. But for each gallant they killed, four more took their place. And they were armoured for execution, not a vicious firefight against so many armed intruders.

Carkal charged with his finger on full-auto. The fusillade of incandescent las-bolts strobed the room. They were unaimed, but that did not matter. With him came twenty other brothers, each one firing as wildly as he.

Two wardens were hit by stray rounds. A third threw himself down on the ground and fired off three kill-shots before Carkal drove his bayonet into the gap between his collarbone and his neck. He felt the grate of the blade on bone, and snapped it in his fury as he yanked it free.

'For the Emperor!' he roared, and drove the broken blade into the groin of the next. The man swung at him with his ceremonial knife, and caught him across the face. Carkal felt the sudden splash of hot blood down his neck as he swung the butt of his rifle up and smashed the man's jaw with a satisfying crunch.

'The Emperor protects,' he spat into the face of the dying man.

The warden did not understand. Confusion clouded his eyes as his last rattling breaths left his body.

The Brotherhood swept the defenders aside.

Confessor Pitt was fearless as he strode ever upwards, raging and calling on the Emperor's Protection. As they entered the astropathic antechamber the climbers paused for a moment before the armoured metal doors.

The chamber was vaulted, hung with banners and tapestries of ancient texts. Vox-servitors hung from the ceiling in brass songbird cages, nutrient cables plugging each eye socket, vox-grille mouths open in everlasting psalmistry.

The astropathic tower's irregular staff had been herded before them, but now they were trapped and had no choice but to fight. Some had armed themselves with clubs and knives. They threw themselves at the intruders. Others hid behind tapestries and porphyry statues of the God-Emperor and Saint Ignatzio.

A number of wardens put up stiff resistance at the doors

of the astropathic chamber, but they were hopelessly out-numbered. All they could do was sell their lives.

In less than five minutes they were all dead.

The gallants dragged the bodies aside, and threw themselves at the warded portals. They hammered at them, fired las-bolts into the locking mechanism, and finally brought charges up from the Barolans' barracks.

Confessor Pitt's cheeks twitched as he ordered the gallants back.

The charges exploded and as the smoke cleared they saw the brass doors hanging on broken hinges. From the darkness came the sound of repeated mantras and the disconnected murmur of confused voices. Confessor Pitt wiped his knife on his robe. 'Stay back!' he ordered. He waved his blade at them. 'I will go alone!'

He stepped over the engraved threshold of the astropathic chamber.

They pressed behind him but they did not dare pass over the threshold.

As soon as Carkal's eyes became accustomed to the murk, he was struck speechless. The astropathic choir rose up in serried tiers of ornate balustrades. The shadows were lit with flickering candles, revealing mouldy pennants, emaciated servitors hanging in brass cages and rolls of tumbling script. It took a moment for him to appreciate the quiet bustle within the room, which continued despite Confessor Pitt's intrusion. There were data-servitors, bondservants, scribes shuttling back and forth between the choir and the scriptorium, crackling encryptors wreathed in corposant light, and psychic wardens with psi-prods and stun pistols. They all seemed oblivious, but as Confessor Pitt paced into the room, one of the wardens strode forward, his hand raised in warning. 'You cannot come here,' he said.

Confessor Pitt drove the knife into the man's gut and held him as he kept pushing the blade deeper into his innards, only letting go when the warden's legs gave way, and he slipped to the floor.

Pitt's hand and blade were stained red. He stopped in the middle of a brass hexagram and took in the opulence, the arcane witchery, the appalling nature of this place, and he pulled a vellum parchment from inside his robes.

He held it in one hand, and let it unravel from his raised arm. The parchment was marked with the Patridzo's official seal. Confessor Pitt pointed his bloody knife towards the other wardens. 'I am Harkham Pitt, representative of the cardinal of the Gallows Cluster in this facility. This is my warrant of authority. Failure to obey my commands will result in death.'

From high up in the darkness, an astropath screamed.

PART FOUR

'The Emperor will fetch the outcasts from the ends
of the world

He will lift you up and make you into a Holy
Army

He will deliver unto you the land that was your
fathers'.

And the children of the Emperor will be made
more prosperous

and more numerous than all the xenos of the
galaxy.'

– From the *Song of Hildeborg of Marquis*

ONE

It was the quiet hour after sunset, the night before the festival of Saint Ignatzio.

In the high chambers of the Basilika, Xereum looked out through the gothic windows. Three eunuchs were playing with a ball on a flat roof below him. Rising behind them into the sky were distant columns of black smoke. Throughout the day the fires had drawn steadily closer like a besieging army. The tent city was aflame.

The fact saddened Cardinal Xereum. He drew in a deep breath, and asked, 'Is all ready for tomorrow?'

Vettor nodded. 'Yes. I think so.'

Cardinal Xereum nodded. 'You have worked tirelessly.'

'I am only doing my duty,' Vettor said. He sat down on one of the stools in the corner of the room. He looked exhausted and after a moment he yawned loudly. 'Sorry, your holiness.'

'No. It is time we rested. Go. Sleep. I am going to pray for a while, and ask the Emperor for His guidance.'

Two hours before dawn Vettor made his way down through the inhabited parts of the Basilika, a hooded lumen in his outstretched hand.

He knew many of the hidden paths through the ancient palace, and his footsteps led him past old guard chambers, barracks, mess halls and armouries, through the old serving levels, where dust lay thick on old cauldrons, cold hearths and forgotten brew houses.

His footsteps were quiet as he descended the ancient steps, so worn by long-dead feet that in some places the stairs were more like a bumpy slide.

It took him an hour to reach the place he was looking for, the Cistern of Antonio. Vettor's lumen cast enough light to hint at the space before him: a large, square chamber, the massive weight of the palace above them held up by brick archways, and rows of heavy marble columns. The darkness was cool and wet. From the distance came the sound of dripping.

The water before him was still, a dark mirror that reflected Vettor as he found the coracle that was hidden in a niche.

It took a moment for the ordinand to settle himself in the unsteady craft. He rowed himself across the cistern, finding the opening in the opposite wall. He stowed the coracle, and lifted himself up into the rough-hewn tunnel.

The ground was less even now. It seemed like an age of endless steps going down. He paused a couple of times to check his direction, and at last he found the place he was seeking.

Before him was an arched doorway of well-dressed stone. It was armoured. There was no handle or means of opening it.

Vettor put his ear to the door, then he scratched on it. There was a moment's pause.

Then came a brief flicker as a spyhole was opened. Vettor held his breath and then the door was opened from the inside.

It was the Patridzo. He wore a painting apron and showed no signs of weariness despite the early hour. 'Ordinand,' he said simply, wiping his fingers clean with a cloth.

'Greetings, my lord,' Vettor said. 'I trust I have not pulled you from your bed.'

'No. Indeed not. How can I sleep on a night like this! Even when I was a child my father would have me stay up all night, in readiness for the Saint.'

Vettor made a non-committal gesture. 'We have been very assiduous in our preparations. The cardinal has been praying. I think he fears that he will make some blunder.'

'I trust not,' the Patridzo said.

'I will intervene if necessary.'

'Good,' the Patridzo said. 'That makes me feel better. Shouldn't you be with him now?'

Vettor nodded. 'I am sure that you have seen the flames.'

'We did not have enough enforcers to govern the tent city as well. Shaliah is cleaning out the gangs.'

Vettor nodded. 'Do you trust him?'

'Of course. He is a Richstar as well, you know. Not legitimate, of course. But the Bringer of the News has always been a position that is held by a minor line.'

'You mean a bastard?'

'A crude term, but yes. A bastard. But he is a useful bastard, nonetheless.'

'A tool?'

'Aren't we all tools of the God-Emperor?'

Vettor paused to consider the question and all its implications. 'Yes,' he said at last. 'I think we are.'

At last the Patridzo said, 'I am fearful.'

'Would you like me to hear your confession?'

'No, not now.'

They sat together for a long time, as the Patridzo recounted all the events from the Kalvert.

'It seems that all is in order,' Vettor said at last.

'I trust so. I am fearful, yes. But excited too. This is a new dawn about to shine out over our Imperium. And to think it shall start here, on Potence.'

Vettor drew in a deep breath. 'It is a great moment. I should return to the cardinal. Steel yourself, Patridzo. Much will be demanded of us all. These are days of great import. We are returning our planet to the faith of our forefathers.'

TWO

It was the morning of the Feast of Saint Ignatzio. While the Evercity had a refined, holy air, from the tent city rose the stink of war and fear and desperation.

Rudgard Howe had doubled the guards on the city gateways, and had issued strict orders that no influxers should be allowed to enter. But the truth was he did not have enough enforcers to keep influxers out as well as deal with all the malcontents that he had locked up in the reformatory.

There was only so much he could do.

All this Chief Enforcer Rudgard Howe understood intuitively as his bike wound up from the enforcer compound, nicknamed 'the Mousehole', in the lower reaches of the Evercity. He passed the neighbourhood bakeries, morning recaf carts, slop bars and street statues, which had been garlanded with flowers and laurels for the Saint's feast day.

Desperation drove good people to do evil. And evil was something that Rudgard Howe knew all about. The depravities that humans descended to were his trade. The only thing, he'd found, that kept desperate people honest was hope. And hope was what the Feast of St Ignatzio supplied.

If Rudgard Howe had his way, the Feast of Saint Ignatzio would never come, but would always be tomorrow. Hope would never be disappointed. The fact the festival was today filled him with trepidation. It made him ride faster than normal, dangerous with the crowds who were gathering in prayer and to prepare their local saints for the procession to the service.

The people stood back to let him pass. They knew the Patridzo's chief enforcer by the approaching roar of his bike's engine, his black-visored helmet and double-wide reinforced tyres, and he liked the looks of fear they gave him. He swung round the switchbacks, accelerating fast up the straights and kicking the throttle back once he was in the upper reaches of the Evercity. Enforcer checkpoints waved him through.

The city was already starting to move as he approached the gates of the Kalvert. He slowed, swung through the gateway and gave the Calibineer a brief nod.

Shanttal looked as though he had not slept. He hurried forward as Rudgard pivoted the bike to a halt, kicked the stand down and swung a leg over the back.

'Where is he?' Rudgard said.

He didn't bother with pleasantries.

'The Patridzo?'

'Yes, the frekking Patridzo. Who do you think?'

Shanttal shot him a poisonous look, but led the chief enforcer into the palace.

The Patridzo was in the contemplatorium. An icon of Saint Ignatzio stood on a stand in the centre. A palate of oil paints lay on the floor next to it. It looked as though he hadn't painted for a day at least. The paints were starting to scab and crack as they dried out.

'What do you want?' the Patridzo snapped.

Rudgard picked a sugared crab apple from a bowl on the Patridzo's table. He threw it into his mouth, and crunched through the crisp coating, then reached for another. He said, 'I want to know what the hell Shaliah is up to.'

'He is restoring order.'

'I don't trust him.' Howe took another sugared crab apple. The Patridzo watched him eat with displeasure. Rudgard lifted the silver lid of the red wine carafe and sniffed the wine. 'You should have let me raise an army. I would have sorted the gangers out long ago.' Rudgard popped another crab apple into his open maw. His teeth had long since been replaced with sharpened steel caps. They made swift work of the delicacies on the Patridzo's table. He gave the Patridzo a long, hard look. 'Don't think I'm blind to what you Rich-stars get up to.'

'I'm afraid I have no idea what you're talking about.'

'No? Well, I'm sure it would be interesting to those Astra Militarum officers who've just landed.'

'Is that a threat?'

Howe smiled. It was not a pleasant sight. 'I don't threaten.'

The Patridzo nodded. Howe was unbearable at times, but he was merciless and effective. Just the kind of man you wanted keeping the masses down.

The contemplatorium's ornate ironwood shutters had been thrown back and dawn sunlight streamed into the bust gallery.

The Patridzo turned to the Dawn Gallery that led off to the side. Busts of his forebears stood on pedestals on either side of the mosaic flooring. He stopped, and looked out towards the brick wall. A black smoke plume – dissipating in the high atmosphere – stained the sky. 'My father never came here much. He was not one for contemplation. It was shut up when I was a child. I remember sneaking inside when all these were covered with sheets. The treasures that mouldered here. There were icons, ancient robes, suits of archaic armour, and these, the collected faces of my ancestors.' He stopped before a severe-looking face. 'This is Festuca. He was ineffective and effete.' Of a bearded and heavy-browed bust he said, 'Elija was a warrior without a war to fight. His son, Racenia, waited for two hundred years to take the high seat. He only lasted fifty years, his reign notable only for the depths of his depravity.

'This is my father, Buthona. My mother, Benaza, was never happy here. She liked the bustle of her home world. My father despaired of me. He did not think I would make a good leader. He thought I was too bookish. I do not think I make a good leader, to be honest. But I have the right men serving me. You. Shanttal. Shaliah. You are all good men. Good at your jobs, I mean.'

The Patridzo turned his back on the marble images of his forebears. 'I never wanted to be like any of them. I wanted to be a holy man who led by example, who showed the people what it meant to be devout. Sometimes I fear that I have thought too much. I have spent too long worshipping the God-Emperor through my art. Who knew what unhappy times would come in my days! The Imperium of Man, trembling to its very foundations. The Gallows Cluster thrown into the forefront of the heretic attack. If I had known that such would come to pass, I would have spent my life in training. In fighting. In building up armies that could throw the enemy back. In turning our planets into fortresses, into bastions upon which the Archenemy would break like waves upon the headland.

'But I did not. I failed us all. I spent my time in painting and contemplation. I am unable to lead the armies as I should have done. Shaliah has shown us the way. It is little, and late. But at least he has shown us what the Richstars can do.'

THREE

The Saint's feast was celebrated in the Grotto Chapel of Saint Ignatzio, an arcane structure dug into the stone of the acropolis.

One legend had it that the cave was where the Saint sheltered from xenos ambush. Another said it was where he had been carried when he was dying. Either way, the cave had been smoothed out, widened and deepened, and a nave of stone had been built out from the cliff face to enclose the whole space into a chapel.

The structure had a classical façade, with narrow leaded windows of stained glass. Religious attendants were already at work, sweeping the street, setting chairs in neat rows, lighting consecrated tapers. Among them General Dominka's Mountain Infantry stood guard. They looked nervous as they set up barricades to keep the people back.

They were expecting trouble from the gangers. They had strict orders to keep anyone with ganger tattoos out. 'Facial tattoos. Arms. The lot,' their officers told them. The troopers nodded.

Before them it seemed that the square had never looked so clean. The hab-blocks that made up the borders had been washed and painted, and hung with religious pennants. Throughout the city the people prepared saintcakes with meat and raisins and off-world spices. There would be great feasts once the church service was over.

In the Intake Barracks, Minka woke early. She felt groggy after the previous night's indulgences, threw herself out of bed and found an empty sink and splashed water on her face. The barracks had a slightly subdued air, typical after a rough night.

As she moved out into the drill yard, Dido's squad were standing in number one dress, putting the finishing touches to their uniform.

'We're going to the chapel,' Dido said, as she gave her right boot a final buff. 'We're honour guard for General Bendikt at the festival. Women are not allowed inside the chapel, so Sparker picked me. I think it's his idea of a joke.'

Minka forced a smile. 'Say a prayer for me.'

Dido's squad were standing smartly to attention when General Bendikt came out and stepped up into the idling Salamander.

If he noticed Dido's squad then he did not say anything immediately, but after a moment he took a second look. 'Is that you, sergeant...' He paused for a moment, searching for the name. 'Dido?'

She saluted. 'Yes, sir.'

'Good to see you.'

'Likewise, sir. We thought you were going on and up to better things.'

Bendikt forced a laugh. 'High command is not all it's cracked up to be.'

'I see you lost your hand, sir.'

'Yes,' Bendikt said. He held his stump up ruefully.

'Forgive me, sir. I heard you were protecting our honour. The Cadians, I mean. I just want to let you know that we appreciate your courage.'

Bendikt nodded as Mere signalled the driver to move forward. 'Thank you, sergeant. It means a lot.'

Cardinal Xereum tried to calm himself as he looked at the items that Rovas had laid out for him. There was a robe, some boots, an ivory staff and the golden death mask of Saint Ignatzio. He paced up and down and the dark hollow eyes of the mask seemed to follow him across the room.

In his time within the Ecclesiarchy he'd been asked to pass judgement on the blasphemous nature of many festivals and practices peculiar to their own particular planet, and compared to cannibalism and child sacrifice, the donning of a death mask seemed rather mundane. But there was something unsettling about assuming the face of a long-dead warrior.

He rang the bell for Rovas, but his valet did not come.

Xereum cursed. He could not wait any longer. He put the ceremonial boots on. The robe was the kind of costume that buttoned up the back and required staff to dress him in, but Vettor had not been seen all morning, and Xereum was beginning to become concerned. Potence was a city ill at ease with itself, and the influxers had strained the peace to its limits. It would be typical for his ordinand to go missing on this, the very morning when Xereum needed his guidance the most.

The noises of the festival – cheers, chanting, singing, the ringing of many bells – filled him not so much with a religious thrill, but a growing sense that something ominous was going to happen.

Cardinal Xereum pulled the robe over his head and settled the shoulders into place.

There was a brief scratch on the door. 'Ah! Rovas. At last. I was beginning to worry. Where have you been?'

But it was not Rovas; it was Vettor. The young man walked calmly to the windowsill. 'Are you ready, cardinal?'

'No,' Xereum snapped, 'I am not! And I am not ready for guests...' But as he spoke, he saw Vettor draw something from under his robes. 'What are you doing?'

Vettor's narrow face was intent. 'This is a pistol, cardinal. And I declare you heretic. In fact, you are the worst kind of heretic – a man who thinks he does good while all along he serves the forces of the enemy.'

Xereum stared in astonishment. 'What are you talking about?'

'You know what I am talking about,' Vettor said, stepping forward, pistol still held in his fist.

Xereum stepped behind an ornate chair. He rested his hands on its velvet back. 'I do not,' he said. Then shouted, 'Rovas! Help!'

There was no sound.

Nothing.

'Rovas is dead.' Vettor stepped sideways to get a good angle for a shot. 'I killed him. He was also a heretic. All who do not believe are heretics and they shall burn.'

Xereum held out both hands, as if he wanted to pacify a

crowd. 'I am Cardinal Xereum of the Ecclesiarchy, Vettor. I fear for your sanity.'

Vettor fired. The poison dart quivered in the back of the chair. 'Oh, I am sane,' he said, and flipped a fresh needle into his gun. The sharp end dripped toxins. 'This is the moment we have all waited for, when the Gallows Cluster will rise up and overthrow the corrupt and the unholy.'

Cardinal Xereum put up a hand. 'Ordinand Vettor, I command you to put down your gun. Killing a member of the Ecclesiarchy is a grave sin. The Emperor will not forgive such a transgression. Your soul will burn in the plasma flames of infamy.'

Vettor smiled. 'I am a member of the Temple Church. The Keepers of the Faith. An unbroken line back to the earliest days of the Imperium of Man.'

'You cannot believe that heretical nonsense!'

Vettor smiled broadly now. 'Oh, but I do. And I think you will find that most people on this planet do as well.'

The sounds of feet and shouting were coming up from below. Xereum knew if he could just delay Vettor, he might hold him off until help came. 'I know the blasphemous creed of the Templars. But think! The Emperor showed His displeasure in the Storm of the Emperor's Wrath. What could be a clearer manifestation of the Divine Will?'

Vettor did not put the gun down. But he seemed caught. 'How many warp craft disappear each year?'

'Hundreds. Thousands...'

'Yes, and do we see the will of the Emperor within their loss? The Storm of the Emperor's Wrath was an accident, nothing more,' Vettor said. 'A chance for the Emperor to test our faith. In the Gallows Cluster, we remained loyal and true. We have not forgotten.'

Xereum stopped behind his high, winged chair. 'Vettor. This is heresy. What about Goge Vandire and his sins!'

'There were no sins.'

'What about the murders. The heresy. The despoiling of Holy Terra?'

'Lies,' Vettor said. It was a simple fact. He stepped forward. 'Falsehoods. Heresy.'

'But…' Xereum said.

Vettor fired once more. This time the dart went over Xereum's shoulder and embedded itself in the plaster.

Vettor seemed to be enjoying himself. 'Look about you, Cardinal Xereum. Your Imperium hangs by a thread. We know what they do not. You are right. The Emperor's Will is clear. In His wisdom He has allowed the Cadian Gate to fall, He has allowed the Cicatrix Maledictum to divide the damned from those who might yet be saved. Your Imperium is a heresy! From the Gallows Cluster a new Imperium of Mankind shall arise. Stronger in faith. Fearless in endeavour. Defiant of our enemies.'

Footsteps were running along the corridor. Xereum fell to the floor as Vettor fired once more. The dart went straight over his head, and he crawled behind the desk as the door flew open. Shaliah Starborn burst in.

The cardinal put his hand to his heart in gratitude. 'Shaliah! I am glad to see you. He's trying to kill me!' The cardinal pointed at Vettor.

No one moved.

'He's gone mad,' Xereum insisted, but Shaliah still did not move. Xereum looked to the men who were with him. They were not Cadian, or Calibineer, or any other force known to Xereum. They were bearded warriors in black gowns and black body armour marked with the symbol of the Golden Throne.

'I am sorry,' Shaliah said. 'But we will not take orders from the Ecclesiarchy any more.' He spoke the word 'Ecclesiarchy' with hatred and contempt.

Xereum did not understand.

It was Vettor who smiled. 'Meet your crusaders. The new army of the Imperium.'

'The Frateris Militia?'

'No. The Frateris Templars.'

'Vettor!' the cardinal begged. 'I do not deserve this. I am a good man.'

Vettor paused for a moment. 'Yes, you are. But goodness is no protection, cardinal. This is not a test of merit or virtue. This is a matter of doctrinal belief and divine truth. And I condemn you, Xereum, as a heretic.' Vettor spoke matter-of-factly. Then nodded towards the men of the Brotherhood. 'Kill him.'

The warriors smelt of sweat as they surrounded the cardinal. He pushed himself to his feet but they knocked him back down. 'Oh, Lord Emperor, I am your servant,' he called out as he lay on the floor.

Then one by one the rifle butts fell.

FOUR

Mere and Bendikt stood in the Salamander as it drove through the barrack gates and onto the winding road down. There were clear views out over the tent city, towards the distant mountains.

After a long silence, Mere said, 'Should be easy to defend.'

Bendikt was distracted. He nodded. 'Yes. As long as Archmagos Marquex sorts out the void shields.'

'Any word from him?'

Bendikt shook his head. His manner stopped Mere asking any more questions.

Crowds packed the arterial streets leading to the bottom of the acropolis. Local troops forced them back. Between them was a narrow access corridor that seethed like a snake as the crowd bulged on either side. From side streets it seemed that the Evercity was emptying. Men, women, children, all dressed in their holiday best, pushing forward in family groups, street parties, parish congregations. They brought with them their family icons and shrines, the likenesses of Imperial saints, the ancient images of the Golden Throne that hung all year in the local chapels. Women pinned money to the carved images as they were carried by on ornate silken palanquins. Some sang psalms. The note of their music was joyous, fearful, devout.

One of the Calibineer waved their vehicles to a halt. Dido went forward.

The man had to raise his voice above the din. 'We can't keep the way open for the tanks. You'll have to go forward on foot!'

Dido summoned her squad.

Corporal Welt was a big man. 'Are you sure it's safe?' he asked.

'No,' she told him. 'But that's why we're here.'

General Bendikt was moved by the fervour of the crowd. 'This is eleven years' worth of faith.' He stopped and looked about. 'The last time this festival took place, Cadia still stood.'

That fact made them all take note. Each of them looked back to where they were eleven years before. So much had changed, for the worse. And each Cadian felt personally responsible.

Dido's squad surrounded Bendikt and Mere as they stepped down onto the cobblestones. The crowd barely noticed the Cadians as they advanced the last few hundred yards towards the back of the chapel, where it abutted the acropolis. They pushed through the crush, and mounted the rear steps of the grotto chapel.

Ecclesiarchy attendants in long black gowns and hoods stood guard, shock-pikes ready.

'General Bendikt,' Dido announced. 'He is expected.'

'Pass.'

Dido handed over the data-slate. The protocols lit up as the acolyte ran a hand over the screen.

'Bless you,' the man said, as he handed the slate back. The acolytes stood back to let the Cadians through. Dido went last. She paused at the top of the stairs and looked back. The corridor that they had passed through had been sealed up by the compression of the crowds. Far off she could see their tanks pushing slowly forward. Their turret weapons stood out among the sea of heads, the statues bobbing above them, like flotsam carried on a flood.

She turned and found the shock-pikes closed before her face.

One of the men stated, 'Women are not allowed.'

Dido's temper was up in a moment. 'I am bodyguard to the general.' She pushed at the pikes but the acolytes would not let her pass. Dido shoved forward and there was a brief scuffle before General Bendikt intervened.

He put his hand on the shoulder of the attendants. 'Let her through. She is part of my bodyguard.'

The acolytes looked to their leader. 'I am sorry, my lord,' he said. 'It is the custom. Common women are not allowed within the precincts.'

Bendikt leant in close. 'I am the representative of the Imperium of Man upon this planet. She is the commander of my bodyguard. You will allow my sergeant inside.'

Dido took advantage of the moment of indecision and thrust the pikes apart. 'Don't worry,' she said. 'I'm not a common woman. I'm Cadian.'

Battle Sisters Raye and Yoss were on duty at the cathedral gates. They could hear the faint echo of music and drums drifting up with the breeze. And then, over the sound of the wind came engines straining against the gradient. The sound grew in volume.

'I thought the pilgrims come after the mass,' Novice Yoss said. She was a thin, red-headed Sister, with a solid, square jaw.

Raye's face was stern. 'They do,' she stated. 'But there are always some who are keener than others.'

The Sisters watched as a file of pilgrim halftracks approached. Their faces were hard and expressionless as the trucks, full of young men visible behind heavy tarpaulins, drew up the last switchbacks to the cathedral gatehouse.

The men inside were chanting the Emperor's name. The volume of their shouts grew louder. It sounded almost defiant. Angry. Sister Raye stepped forward and put her power-armoured glove up to signal a halt. The lead truck slewed to a stop twenty yards off.

'The cathedral is closed until after the Saint has spoken,' she declared.

The driver waved at her to get out of the way. 'The cathedral is…' she repeated as the back hatches slammed down and the tarpaulin covers were dragged away and heavy stubbers were revealed. Gleaming, freshly oiled, weapons of war.

Then they fired.

The Battle Sisters reacted instantly. Yoss started to shout an alarm. Raye reached for her bolter as the pilgrims pulled laspistols from under their robes and began firing.

Las-bolts stabbed out. They were a thicket of searing light.

Raye was fearless. She ducked forward, engaging her vox-link.

'The cathedral is under attack,' she reported calmly as she aimed and fired, her boltgun bucking with each shot.

Yoss was beside her, the two black-clad sisters standing shoulder to shoulder.

The attackers were thrown back for a moment. But as each halftrack swung up, the odds began to lengthen sharply as more men joined the attack, and their vehicle-mounted weapons sprayed the Sisters with hard rounds.

'I will cover you. Fall back!' Raye ordered.

But as she turned she saw that there were warriors inside the cathedral gardens, running towards them from the direction of the Basilika.

'Throne!' she hissed. 'We're trapped!'

Bendikt and Mere were led through antechambers, robing rooms and sacristy, all bustling with nervous servers, and chalice and incense-bearers, their heavy ball thuribles waiting to be lit. At the doors to the chapel General Dominka's Mountain Infantry stood guard. They stiffened when they saw Bendikt, and saluted smartly. Dido stepped back to let Bendikt enter first.

He bent a little to pass under the low stone arch, removed his peaked cap and tucked it under his arm. Dido entered the hallowed space last. To the right was the carved archway of the rock grotto; to the left was the portico: a temple of marble and gold and precious stonework.

After the narrow corridors the sudden extravagance and the sense of light and air was staggering. The wide chapel nave was already filling. Although no one spoke in more than a whisper, the resounding hubbub echoed back, and through that noise came the sound of the servitor choirs as they hung above the congregation in cages of ornate filigree and sang psalms.

The Cadians moved forward to the carved wooden seats of the choir.

Another detail of Calibineer were checking everyone who went in. Their officer spoke in a low voice.

'Sorry, sir. Only invited guests allowed.'

Bendikt started to argue but the officer gestured forward. 'I understand, sir. But every seat is already taken. Look!' He gestured to the seats of the choir. 'Your bodyguard will have to stay here. I'm sorry, but everyone wants to bring a few extra. Each Richstar has their own life-wards and this is a holy place. It was not built for soldiers.'

'But we are protecting the general,' Dido put in quickly.

'I suggest you stand here. With me. You will be just yards away from the general. Should anything happen you can be there in an instant.'

Dido started to argue, but Bendikt put his hand on her arm. 'It's alright, sergeant. Adjutant Mere has kept me safe for a long time now, on and off the battlefield. And even one-handed I'm not entirely useless. I'm sure we'll be safe in there.'

Dido didn't like it at all, but she reluctantly consented. 'Alright, sir. But just signal and I'll be with you in a moment.'

'Thank you,' Bendikt said. 'I will.'

Battle Sister Raye threw herself at her attackers. She slammed fresh ammunition into her gun, wielding it one-handed.

As she fought, a hard round hit Yoss in the back of her head. She barely remained standing. Her training and discipline kicked in as she fired a furious salvo into the enemy streaming towards them.

'Fall back!' Raye ordered Yoss, slamming her gun into the face of a young man.

Blood was pouring from the wound in her scalp. 'No, Sister. I will fight and die with you!' Yoss fired furiously into her attackers. Another round struck her in the neck. She struggled to retain her feet but someone slammed into her, her boot slipped and she tumbled sideways.

Yoss fought for a moment as knives and boots rained down on her. There was a flurry of stabbing blades. The assailants were so numerous that they were already rushing towards the open gateway.

A confessor led Bendikt and Mere to their seats, right behind the altar. Each one was set into an arched niche, with a pattern of aquilas carved into the stonework.

At the back of the niches were carved the titles of Richstar family members. Bendikt was in the niche labelled 'Marquis'. Mere was in the alcove reserved for the Emir of Kyns. On the other side of the choir sat two members of the Adepta Sororitas. One wore a suit of power amour, chased with gold filigree. The other had a severe mono-brow and a spiked leather gag wrapped about her mouth. The two Sisters nodded towards the Cadians.

'So it's not just Dido who forced her way in,' Bendikt noted.

Mere nodded. 'They're the Order of the Ebon Chalice. Fighting strength is thirty Sisters Militant. Twenty other Sisters.'

'I should go and pay my respects.' Bendikt walked across the choir. 'Greetings, lady. I am General Bendikt of the Cadian 101st.'

The Sister in the ornate power armour regarded him with a look of cold disdain. 'Greetings in the name of the God-Emperor, General Bendikt. My name is Canoness

Maddelena. This is Sister Mennel.' The gagged Sister Militant tilted her head forward. The canoness went on, 'I hear you have come to bolster the physical defence of our system. We wish you the best, but you know the true defence is spiritual. No number of guns or tanks can make up for those with pure hearts.'

'I agree,' Bendikt said.

The canoness lifted an eyebrow. 'If the Cadians had paid more attention to their prayers then perhaps Cadia would not have fallen.'

Bendikt's face flushed at the insult. 'We are soldiers. If anyone's prayers let us down it was not ours.'

Canoness Maddelena's eyebrow lifted even higher. 'We have a saying that the bad shooter blames the gun.'

'I do not trade in blame. It is wasted breath, canoness. I deal with what lies before me, and the strength I have to throw the enemy back.'

'Well. The failure of the Cadians has meant our system is also in danger.'

'Thank the Throne that is something I can rectify, then,' Bendikt said.

His cheeks were still flushed as he returned to his seat.

'What is she like?' Mere asked.

Bendikt spoke through the side of his mouth. 'A right bastard.'

Celestian Simmona turned her vox-bead off for the duration of the morning's confessions.

When she had heard the last proclamation of wrongdoing, she made the sign of the aquila and pushed herself to stand. She had an old wound in her back that ached after so long kneeling. She relished the pain. Suffering was a gift from the

Emperor, and it left the patient wiser and purer. Celestian Simmona was admired for her purity.

The Sisters of the Ebon Chalice held the cathedral gatehouse as their nunnery. It had all they needed: barrack halls, chapels, places for religious observance. Through the heavy stonework and rockcrete she could hear the sounds of the Sisters going about their daily rituals: prayer, absolution, purification, target practice, swordplay, exercise. She closed the confessionary door behind her. Through the loophole she felt the chill of the morning air, and the sound of shouting.

The people's faith was weak, she thought. Celestian Simmona had found the people of this planet churlish and subject to wild superstitions and passions. As she passed another loophole she could hear sounds of gunfire. She paused for a moment and looked through. She saw the flash of steel. She engaged her vox-bead and immediately a wash of voices flowed in. Urgent. Calm. Focused.

'Who is attacking?' she demanded.

But Sisters Raye and Yoss were beyond the ability to talk, and as Simmona leapt down the stairs she drew her bolt pistol. The sound of fighting below her struck her with alarm – the enemy were within the gates.

In the Chapel of St. Ignatzio, the two Cadians watched as the nave filled, then the great bronze gates were thrown open, and beyond, in the bright square of daylight, they could see the massed crowd of heads and bobbing statues.

At last there was a roll of drums, and Bendikt saw one palanquin that was moving forward, over the heads of the crowd. Then another, and another.

It took a moment before he realised that it was the procession of Richstars on their ornate gilt-worked grav-barges.

There were seven in total. About them swooped a flock of blue enamel praisebirds. All the prominent members of the Richstar clan processed over the crowds, into the chapel and up the nave.

Beneath them the people seethed like the legs of an upturned caterpillar. Each man reached out in wonder as the barges passed overhead, trailing long silk pennants, before, one by one, the Richstars dismounted and took up their appointed positions in the choirs, their life-wards standing with Dido and the Cadians in the chapels behind.

Last of all came the Patridzo, in a golden barge. There were ten praisebirds swooping round his carriage, their songs reverberating from the vast ceilings, the round arches, the distant gleam of the painted vaulting.

When he too had taken his seat, all was ready for the cardinal.

He came last, at the end of a long procession of priests and confessors, acolytes and deacons, wearing the death mask of Saint Ignatzio and a golden robe. The pace of proceedings was starting to concern Bendikt. His mind kept rolling through all the work that needed to be done to defend this planet, and the larger system as well. 'Remind me. What's supposed to happen?' Bendikt hissed to Mere.

'The Saint appears...'

'Literally?'

Mere had done the research. 'It varies each time, apparently. From what I gather the cardinal might speak in voices. The sick might be healed. Sometimes a holy fire hangs in the air.'

Bendikt paused. He was holy enough, in his own way, but he was busy and was eager to get to his work: planning the war. 'How soon can we go?'

Mere checked his chronograph. 'Let's wait until the appearance happens.'

'Right. Come on, Ignatzio,' Bendikt urged. 'Time to rattle your bones.'

Celestian Simmona reached the entranceway. One of the bastion's doors was open, and a Sister lay in the doorway, a man bent over her. A hostile. 'This is holy land!' she shouted. 'Sacred to the God-Emperor!'

The warrior looked up. Any words he might have spoken were cut short as the mass-reactive shell hit him square in the forehead and threw him backwards. The effect was a balletic backflip. Then he crashed dead against the blood-splattered wall, and slid to a crumpled heap.

Celestian Simmona leapt down the remaining stairs in three great strides. Two more men appeared. She strode down to meet them. 'This is territory sacred to the Sisters of the Ebon Chalice. Unbelievers are not allowed upon these stones.' She slammed the first man back against the wall. The second doubled over as the bolt-round tore through the soft flesh of his belly. There were screams outside. She stood in the doorway and swung her torso around to fire on more intruders, each shot knocking one back.

She punched the polished iron alarm-stud with her left hand as she heel-kicked an attacker back down the steps. Klaxons began to ring above her. Hundreds of furious men were rushing through the open cathedral gateway. A band turned towards her, mounting the steps up to her position. She held her ground, firing constantly, and ducked back as cannon shells shredded the doorway about her.

At last she could hold no more. She kicked the dead out

of the way and dragged the doorway closed, slamming the lock-stud with the heel of her palm.

Steel wall-latches engaged, locking the portals closed, and an instant later there was a sound like the thunder of hail on a flakboard roof. The solid metal door shivered as it took a full round of cannon shells and las-bolts. It began to glow white-hot.

Major Kastelek was sitting in his office in Intake Barracks, dealing with the neglected day-to-day priorities of a regiment, when the klaxon sounded.

He leapt up and threw open his office door, and demanded to know what was happening.

'False alarm?' a young aide suggested, but the alarm kept ringing and Kastelek had a sixth sense that told him this was trouble.

He ran down the marble-tiled entrance hall in search of answers. No one seemed to know what was going on. In the drill yard, everyone was running about, and confusion reigned. A vox-officer appeared at the doorway on the adjacent wing. He hurried out into the yard, and suddenly the ground about him exploded with autocannon shells. Kastelek threw himself back. Years of experience told him in an instant that the shots had come from above... which could only mean the top of the acropolis. And there was nothing there but the cathedral and the Basilika.

'General alarm!' the vox-officer shouted across the yard. 'The Sisters of the Ebon Chalice have come under attack.'

Kastelek looked around but everyone was looking to him. In a moment he realised he was now in charge. Bendikt and the whole military leadership of the system was at that damned festival.

He slammed his open palm onto the alarm bell. Somehow he had to get down there and save them.

FIVE

The crowd inside the Chapel of St Ignatzio had been waiting for nearly an hour before a figure wearing Ignatzio Richstar's death mask appeared. A reverent silence fell.

The people strained to see as the robed figure strode forward and took his place behind the altar. They were full of eager anticipation and expectation, but none more so than the masked figure himself. Of course, it should have been Cardinal Xereum, but he lay beaten to death at the summit of the acropolis.

In his place stood Shaliah Starborn.

Shaliah had waited all his life for this moment, when he would channel the spirit of Saint Ignatzio. For this day, he was the manifestation of the Saint within the materium. He could barely believe he was standing here. His body was light, despite the weight of the robes upon his shoulders.

He went through the many small rituals, as he had in private for the Richstars themselves.

The crowd was breathless as he performed them all, faultlessly, and they answered his prayers with formulaic words and eager voices. With each minute the sense of expectation rose.

It would not be long now before the Saint would speak, and the link with their ancient forebear would be cemented once more.

At last there was nothing left but the moment of revelation.

Shaliah bowed to the altar then turned and moved back towards the golden shrine. In their cages the servitors lifted their voices in sublime worship. A pair of attendants stepped forward, a cushion held between them, and on it the key to the shrine.

Shaliah felt his hands shaking as he took the heavy golden key.

He set it into the hole, and pressed forward. The lock opened with a dull *click*. He returned the key, and opened the door.

Within, the air was cool and musty. It smelt of past ages. There was nothing inside except a faceted glass phial. He held it in his hands, lifted it out and knelt.

A hush spread from the nave, and seemingly out across the entire city. Shaliah could hear a distant dog bark. A door slamming shut. A woman's voice raised briefly.

He breathed deep and settled his nerves, then lifted the phial of the Saint's blood from its sacred shrine. Above him, the chapel ceiling was lit with glorious murals that depicted the might of the Golden Throne. The words of the servitor choir washed over Shaliah like a wave of hope and expectation.

The phial held the blood of Saint Ignatzio. At the bottom the liquid had thickened to a dark sludge. Shaliah lifted it in both hands and turned the glass one full circle. Then another. And again, the facets throwing the light up onto his face.

People started to shout. Single voices at first, then masses. 'Ignatzio! Show yourself! Heal the sick! Bring us your blessing!'

Shaliah's hands were clammy as he rotated the phial. The blood of the Saint remained dry and solid in the corner. His shoulders began to ache. Shouts from the crowd coalesced into chanting voices, calling the Saint's name over and over.

Shaliah had seen many festivals in his time. He had seen the blind healed, green fire play over the heads of the most worthy, and grown men weep. How would the Saint reveal himself?

His hands tingled for a moment, as if a warm shower ran over him, then he felt his feet lifting from the ground.

Shaliah started to rise from the floor. He did not resist. He came to a halt ten feet above the altar, hanging in the air, the phial of St Ignatzio held in his outstretched hands. The speed of the manifestation startled Shaliah. Stillness spread through the chapel. A hush fell over the chanting people. Shaliah Starborn laughed for joy. Relief spread through him.

Next to him an acolyte rose into the air. And another.

The young men started to weep for joy. 'Ignatzio!' the crowd chanted, the sound growing in strength and passion as all the assembled people began to call out as one.

'The blessed are being raised!' someone shouted.

Shaliah started to cry with joy.

The phial went cold. Frost crazed the glass. It was so cold it burned his hands. Stabbing agony lanced up his arms. He called on the Saint for his aid. He tried to pull his hands away, but they had frozen to the glass, and then the frost began to move up his arms.

The figure of the cardinal hung, hands upraised, the phial starting to pulse with light.

Then he started to scream. The masked face was thrown back as his feet kicked out against the air.

'What the hell is happening?' Bendikt cursed as the temperature dropped.

His hackles rose. The air smelt of witchcraft.

He looked about. The faces of the attendants and acolytes were turning from wonder to horror. 'Get him down!' Bendikt shouted.

Frost began to rime the alcoves where statues looked on with impassive faces. He barged forward as the priests panicked. He had to shove them aside. He could feel the frost in his lungs. His breath steamed before his face.

'Get him down!' Bendikt shouted.

Someone jumped on his back. 'Stop! It is the will of the Saint!' a voice hissed. Bendikt threw the man off.

He knew warp taint. He'd felt it on Cadia, when the boundaries of the immaterium had begun to fray and tear.

'Get him down!' he said again as more priests threw themselves at him. He heard Mere behind him, and punched and kicked. There was still someone on his back. He twisted and punched them with his stump. He followed up with his left hand.

Then someone screamed.

The cardinal hung, a living torch, kicking and writhing in agony. The screams spread, as one by one each of the hanging figures erupted in flames.

'Get him down,' Bendikt roared as drops of burning fat rained down on them all.

The Patridzo ran towards the back of the grotto, his life-wards ploughing a swathe through the crowd, cutting down any who might get in their way.

Dido's squad passed them going in the other direction. A life-ward swung at her. She ducked the powerblade and shoved forward, her squad with her. They shoved the priests and panicking dignitaries aside, and leapt over the ornate wooden altar rail. The place was turning to panic. Calibineer officers lining the front of the nave shouted conflicting orders, but they were few against the crowd. The thousands of terrified penitents in the chapel were like a muscle that twitches and thrashes under the touch of the electro-prod. Statues and icons were dropped. Some went mad, tearing the servitor choristers out of their cages, and smashing their skulls. They ripped tapestries from the wall, tore down statues, burned icons and murdered any ecclesiarchs that they could get their hands on. And over them, suspended figures kicked and writhed as they lifted into the air and then, with a *whoosh* of sudden flames, started to burn. The screams were terrible.

One Calibineer officer shouted at his men. 'Shoot them!' The Calibineer fired over the heads of the crowd. Each human beacon they killed stilled its screaming.

Canoness Maddelena was a powerful figure as she pushed bodies aside, bellowing prayers in a strident voice. Hand raised, she directed her faith at the body of Shaliah.

'*Nunc laudare debemus auctorem regni caelestis!*' she shouted. Her faith was like a balm to stormy waters. She stepped closer and the cardinal's corpse quivered in the air and then crashed onto the altar, the blackened cadaver scattering candelabras and chalices. One by one, the human torches fell.

At that moment the crowd's hysteria might have been calmed, but as the canoness strode forward a man hosed her with a laspistol at point-blank range. Her power armour took most of the damage but as the bolts scored a hole, the sting made her grunt in pain.

She spun and fired. The bolt hit the man in the middle of the forehead. It slammed him back with a brief spatter of gore. Another appeared. And another. And a fourth. She erased each of them with a single shot, and kept moving forward. For an instant the Calibineer stood transfixed, then their officers directed them to fire at the plain-clothed attackers, and there was a stampede as they shot wildly back into the crowd, hitting pilgrims at random.

The festival of Saint Ignatzio had descended into bloody mayhem.

SIX

The chief enforcer was exhausted. He'd barely slept that night. Throughout the morning, demands had kept coming in from the Richstar dignitaries about what each of them wanted in terms of escorts and entourages, until Rudgard had turned the vox-links off.

'Frekk them,' he'd said, and left the management of the ceremony to his second-in-command, Rastan. He'd spent the morning organising roadblocks and settling petty territorial disputes and the usual rounds of gangster activity both within and without the Evercity.

And as he mounted his bike and started back to the enforcer command centre, Officer Palek called him in. *'Got a pair of gangers,'* Palek voxed. *'Trading stimms. Got a sack of the stuff. Want to come down and take a look?'*

'No,' Rudgard told him. 'I'm done. Revoke them and bring the stimms to the Mousehole.'

Palek left his vox-bead open by accident. A moment later there was the sound of muffled shouts.

'Hell. Turn it off, Palek,' Rudgard shouted into his helmet vox. But Palek couldn't hear him. There was a swishing sound, another shout, and the roar of a bolter shot.

Rudgard cursed, and flicked his own vox off. He accelerated along the roads that wound down to the lower reaches. He didn't need to listen to that.

Chief Enforcer Rudgard Howe's vox was still off by the time he got to the long, straight road that led to the Mousehole. The vox-silence was like cool water on a hot head, with the roar of his engines the only noise as he powered along the road.

The armoured gates rose to let him inside and he swung his bike round the rockcrete perimeter and down the ramp that led to the underground depot. He screeched to a halt and tore off his helmet, striding towards the conveyor, slamming the door closed behind him, and punching the top floor with a stab of his gloved finger.

The conveyor rose steadily through the garrison levels, armoury, parking lots, training zones and the intelligence bureaux to the command bunker at the top. He was expecting to find all the work done, the ceremony ended and the people moving up to the cathedral for their pilgrimage. Tired and irritable, he walked into a shambles of shouting and fear and dismay. In a dozen vigilance pict screens he saw scenes of war. Armed men. Burning buildings. Las-battles raging.

Stunned, he looked from one rolling screen to another. In half an hour the city that he had spent a lifetime taming and controlling had ignited into a conflagration.

'Tell me this is a joke,' he hissed.

No one laughed.

Howe moved with purpose. He put out a general alarm. 'All units report to the grotto chapel immediately! Fire at will. Hear me? Fire at will.'

Within minutes he had all available guns assembled in the enforcer precinct. He had a hundred and fifty-seven hands. Each man carried an assault shotgun, loaded with man-stopping rounds. They wore standard-issue riot armour – flak jackets and thigh and elbow pads, their heads enclosed in dark-visored carapace helmets.

'You've all heard by now,' he said. 'I fear that Potence is facing an insurrection. I expect you to put it down.'

The enforcers piled into their Repressor-pattern tanks, each one painted in matt black with the four-pointed star embla-zoned on the sides. Chief Enforcer Howe took the lead tank, slamming his photo-visor down as he took up position on the benches inside.

His men's faces were pale and drawn, their jaws clamped tight.

'This is going to be a mess,' he warned them. He tried to think of a bigger fiasco, but he couldn't. Not in the six gen-erations of his family's service.

Reams of vox-chatter were streaming into his ear. His men were dying out there. He listened with growing tension as the tanks went as fast as was safe.

'Frekking cardinal,' Howe cursed. 'All he had to do was perform the ritual. It can't have been that hard. Get me the Patridzo.'

'No answer,' his comms officer responded.

'Then get me Rastan.'

'He's not answering.'

'What about Intake Barracks? The Calibineer. Get me some-one! We need guns down here. And as soon as there's any word of the Patridzo then let me know.'

'Roger that, sir.'

After a moment the lead tank slowed.

'What the hell is wrong?' Howe demanded.

'Rioters,' the tank commander said.

Howe dragged the man out of his cupola seat. He threw the top hatch open and wriggled into position. He liked to see the world through the clear-plas screen of his helmet. It blocked out the periphery, gave him a view straight ahead. No deviations. No messing. He pulled the heavy flamer round, and pulled the ignition bolt back. It let off a gout of smoky black flame as he settled into position.

'I'll clear the crowd,' he said, and fired. Promethium fuel arced across the gap and the scum scattered or died; he didn't much care which.

He spoke in a low voice, full of command and menace. 'Forward!'

The convoy accelerated again. The lead tank juddered as it went over an impromptu barricade, but whether the bumps were bodies or beds or sacks of food, they did not wait to find out. They slewed into a square. More gangers fell back into the side streets. 'Wheel left,' Howe ordered and fired another spurt of flaming promethium at them.

They returned with hard rounds. He didn't bother with them anymore.

'*Approaching the grotto chapel*,' his driver informed him.

Crowds of terrified locals ducked out of the way at the sight of the enforcers. The higher they climbed, the more tense the Evercity became and the thicker the press.

Howe's photo-visor picked out individual faces with reams of criminal records and surveillance data. But most of them were plain, law-abiding citizenry: scared, angry and many of them in pain.

He could see the loathing in their eyes, and he did not care. He was the law on Potence. From the left a shot rang out, hissing overhead. Howe barked a short order, and his Repressor slewed to a crawl. 'Take the flamer,' he ordered the commander as he threw himself back to the rear turret and slid into the underslung seat.

He casually engaged the storm bolter. 'Anyone see where that shot came from?'

'*Eight o'clock, I think,*' the driver said.

Rudgard hosed the crowd with mass-reactive bolts. They spun bodies round, left gaping holes, punched grown men to the ground. Another shot. Closer this time. It pinged off the Repressor tank's upper armour. He saw a shape, a darting body jumping to the side behind a building with a built-in water tank.

'Keep moving!' he shouted as he returned fire. The convoy pushed forward behind him. They were in the middle of the main street. At the end he could see the cliff face of the acropolis, and at its feet the golden domes of the grotto chapel.

Howe let off a stream of full-auto rounds. They thundered into the stone walls, letting off a storm of sparks. By the time he had finished, the stone had dissolved into dust.

He banged the top of the Repressor with his gloved fist as he felt hard rounds thrum the air about him. The tank jerked forward, metal tracks kicking up dirt and dust in its wake. The tanks behind added to his firepower. Empty casings tumbled in their wake as Rudgard kept firing. They massacred their way through the crowd.

As they chased the rioters they turned into Magdelena Street, and found it blocked by a roaring conflagration of oil drums, rockcrete slabs and metal girders.

The driver panicked. 'Straight!' Rudgard shouted. 'You frekking idiot. Straight! Drive through it! Full speed!'

The driver shouted as he slammed his foot down. The engine roared and the flaming barrier buckled under the impact. Rudgard was thrown forward. They slewed to the side, and for a moment the heat alarms sounded, before they were through.

The second tank slammed through the hole that they had made. The next tank rumbled forward.

As the third approached the barricade there was a monumental explosion. Rudgard spun around.

The Repressor tank was lifted ten feet into the air, before the buildings to either side collapsed and the whole street was lost in smoke and debris.

'I've just heard from the Patridzo,' his vox-bead reported. *'He escaped via tunnels. He's back at the Kalvert. He wants you to know that he is safe.'*

'Great. And now we're not.' Rudgard gritted the words out as the aftermath of the explosion rocked them.

SEVEN

The Cadians of the 101st responded to the growing emergency in minutes. The alarm klaxon was still sounding as they streamed out of the barracks in their armoured transports. Minka's squad were third from the front in a convoy of twenty. As the Chimera jerked forward she slammed the door-locks in place and took her place on the benches.

'Weapons check,' she ordered, and joined the rest of her squad as they went through the routine, checking power packs were fully charged, safeties were on, bayonets were ready and armour straps were all buttoned down.

She couldn't look in Laptev's direction. He kept blinking. 'Check his gear,' she told Belus.

'I can do it,' Laptev hissed, and shoved the other man off.

Belus gave Minka a questioning look.

They left Laptev to it.

'Right,' she said to the rest. 'Bendikt is down there. We're going to get him out alive and head back here. I want no crap. You shoot on my orders? Understand?'

The Chimera accelerated and the soldiers slid backwards along the bench, then readjusted their backsides as the armoured transport swung out of the main gates of the barracks and into the street.

'Picking up anything?' Minka asked the driver Breve.

'Nothing unusual,' he said.

There was a thud, and a jolt ran through the vehicle.

'Contact?' Minka said.

There was a long pause. *'Pothole,'* Breve reported.

The descent to town was a sickening switchback as the Chimeras went at combat speed. The squad went through their routines, then fell into silence as they prepared themselves.

Out of the corner of her eyes Minka could see Laptev's booted feet. He had one ankle crossed across the other, like he was relaxing in the mess.

'A whole company,' he said.

'Bendikt is one of the best there is,' Minka snapped.

'Then how the hell did he get himself into all this trouble?'

There were beads of sweat on Minka's upper lip. She felt anger rise up her neck. Outside, they could hear the shouts of angry voices and through the vents they could all smell burning.

As they levelled out, an autocannon started to bark.

The roar of the engine rose in pitch as the Chimeras accelerated to full speed. No one spoke. They were thrown about violently. *'Getting warm now,'* Breve said.

Minka flicked her vox-bead onto the open channel. The exchanges were short and curt. Reports of enemy sightings and strength. Fires burning. Ammo loadouts. A machine-spirit needing the Ritual of Pacification.

She closed her eyes for a moment and took in a deep breath.

If the road is easy, her father had liked to say, *then the destination is worthless.*

Hard rounds ricocheted off the Repressor. Chief Enforcer Howe ducked. Only his helmet was showing. He scanned the square for the best means of escape. 'Bear left!' he shouted.

'I'm trying! There's another barricade!' his driver shouted and put his foot to the floor.

They hit the barricade with a screech of tortured girders and rockcrete. Rudgard was thrown forward. He wanted to shout orders but the blow had winded him. *'We're stuck!'* the driver shouted as the engines whined.

The tank was still inching forwards.

'Put your frekking foot down!'

'We're stuck!' The driver tried to slam into reverse and the tracks turned frantically. Within seconds the ceramite box became a red-hot oven. Rudgard's step became sticky as the rubber of his soles started melting.

'Do something!' Rudgard shouted, and suddenly, the Repressor lurched forward.

The driver was blind. All he could see was flames and smoke. They hit a wall and kept moving through it. Rudgard was thrown to the floor.

'I can't see!' the driver shouted. Rudgard cursed. He had to punch the hatch open again. He dragged himself up. For a moment his vision was obscured by dust and smoke. The impact had torn the storm bolter from its mounting. He shouted down to his driver, but the glass of the driver's vision slot had shattered in the heat, the glass crazed white with fractures. He batted broken window frame wood from the

top of the tank, and then they were in one of the cobbled squares. The tables that lined the square were overturned, the recaf stalls smashed.

A missile streaked overhead. The tank slowed for a moment, its engine screaming as debris entangled its tracks.

Suddenly he saw a warrior with a demo-charge running at them in a crouch.

'Right!'

The tank swerved. Rudgard was thrown about the turret so hard it bruised his ribs. He saw the flash of las-bolts out of the corner of his eye. He ducked down; somehow his helmet had been torn from his head. 'They're closing in!' he shouted. He saw another demo-charge out of the corner of his eye and scrambled for the bolt pistol at his hip. He tore at the holster, and threw himself up.

The smoke launchers fired and the air was full of sulphurous white smoke that burned Rudgard's throat. He put a hand to his mouth. His eyes were streaming. He wiped away the tears on the back of his arm, drew his pistol and fired at the darting ganger.

'Just you try,' he hissed as another ganger ran out. The man had a cloth tied over his face. He managed three steps before Rudgard caught him with a barrel full of man-stoppers. They did what they claimed.

The next attacker was a tall, rangy youth. Rudgard did not miss.

The barrel smoked angrily. Rudgard was starting to enjoy this. He sniffed as he paused, and dropped back down into the compartment. The air was thick with propellant smoke.

'What the hell is going on?'

There was a crunch of gears. His enforcers were praying quietly. He knew the prayer. 'Lord Emperor, we shall not deviate from the course that You laid out for us. We are armed with righteousness and armoured with faith…'

'Listen. It's not faith that's going to get us out of here. Get your guns and shoot them!' Howe shouted.

The driver slammed the Repressor forward. Another explosion ripped the ground. There was smoke and grit in Rudgard's mouth. He shouted into his vox-bead and the driver shouted back at him. The Repressor spun about in a tight circle, its gears whining as the tracks slewed off, and the tank came to an abrupt halt.

Now they were completely frekked.

'Get out!' Rudgard ordered, but he did not wait for the others. It was each man for himself now, and he was damned if he was dying today. He was halfway out when the Repressor's magazine suddenly exploded and flames ripped through the inside. The explosion fired him out of the top of the tank like a cork from a bottle.

He landed with a bruising thump in the middle of the inferno, and screamed as the flames began to bite through his armour.

In the Grotto Chapel of Saint Ignatzio, armed men threw themselves at the Sisters of the Ebon Chalice. They were fearless and furious, and died in their droves as Canoness Maddelena stabbed and fired into them.

'The Patridzo went this way!' she told her gagged companion, Sister Mennel. 'There must be a way out.'

They fell back into the rear of the chapel.

Acolytes were huddled in the shadows. 'Where is the Patridzo?' Maddelena demanded.

They pointed to a low doorway, set into the stone. She put her hand to it, but the portal did not budge. She kicked it, but still the armoured portal did not move. She fired a couple of bolt-rounds, and even they did not dent it.

Mennel tugged her arm.

The attackers were swarming through the choir. They were trapped. Whichever way the Patridzo had gone, it was not open to them.

Dido's squad surrounded Bendikt and Mere as they cut their way through the choir towards the back of the chapel. Bendikt fired his pistol left-handed. His aim was almost as good as with his right hand, but changing the powercell was difficult. Bendikt handed the gun to his adjutant.

Mere returned the reloaded weapon.

Dido kicked a low wooden door open.

In the sacristy, two choir boys were hiding under the table. There was an explosion in the choir just behind them. They pushed through a corridor, past rooms strewn with abandoned robes and books and incense burners.

They stopped at the door they had entered the chapel by. There was no sign of the transports. The crowd filled the square, and men were firing.

Dido cursed inwardly, but she remained calm. 'Don't worry, sir. We'll get you out of here.'

Canoness Maddelena fought her way out of the grotto chapel, leaving a swathe of dead behind her. As las-bolts speared towards her she smashed through a glassaic window and leapt down into the cobbled courtyard.

Mennel clambered after her.

Their power-armoured boots thudded as they sought a way to escape. The canoness kicked a wooden gate down. There was a crowd on the other side. Maddelena strode out, pushing the bodies aside. The crowd reacted with fury. They threw anything that came to hand, stones, shoes, litter.

'Traitors!' one woman shouted at the Sisters, and the crowd about her took up the call. 'Killers of Vandire!'

Numbers gave them courage. Numbers fired their hatred. Maddelena tried to shield Sister Mennel but the crowd surrounded them. The bravest began to run forward, aiming kicks and punches.

Canoness Maddelena swung her bolt pistol round. She fired, killing with each shot. A bearded man charged, knife in hand. Maddelena's bolt hit him in the middle of the forehead. The blood enflamed the crowd. The two Sisters were trapped, but they were fearless and deadly, more so because they were hopelessly outnumbered. And the crowd *hated* them, chanting as one, 'Traitors! Traitors!'

Minka's transport rattled into the upper reaches of the Evercity.

Breve's voice came from the front. *'Engaging.'*

The gears of their Chimera ground as the tracks swung them round. The multi-laser whined as the barrels spun and the power pack ignited bolts of bright energy that stabbed out from the turret.

'Positions!' Minka ordered and in an instant her squad were up. A cord hung above each of their seats, with heavy-duty carabiners. She clipped her webbing to the one above her head, and thrust her lasrifle through the firing slot. There was a low whizz as a grenade screamed over her head. Minka had a moment to steady herself and then she felt a blast of heat on her exposed skin and cursed. 'Chimera down! Fire at will. Breve!' she shouted. 'Are those Calibineer?'

'No idea,' Breve voxed back. Something impacted their tank. Breve cursed. *'If they are, they're not friendly.'*

361

Minka shot the nearest enemy. Something hit the front amour. It rang the Chimera like a bell.

'We're good,' Breve reported, still calm. 'Almost there.'

There was a *boom!* of ordnance. '*Throne!*' Breve cursed. '*They've got tanks!*'

There was another *boom!*, closer this time. '*We're backing up. Get out, guys!*'

Minka yanked open the door-locks and slammed her open palm against the ramp release. The ramp slammed down and the stink of ozone, camp-filth and burning rushed in as they rushed out.

Another squad's Chimera was on fire. Someone was screaming. A medic, Streck, was kneeling at a wounded Cadian's side. The scene before them looked like a civil war. Buildings were burning, there were tanks on the streets, fighters and civilians were mixed up. It was hard to see who was who.

Lasrifle fire stabbed from the higher buildings to the left, and also from the chapel bell tower. They were thirty feet from the chapel walls. The hab-blocks facing onto the chapel square were aflame. The whole square was awash with enemy warriors. They had a tank as well. It fired once more, and the shot went high, slamming into the third floor of a baroque hab to her left.

'Forward!' Minka shouted, crouching low, aiming and firing. Her squad followed behind her. She ducked into doorways, through smashed windows, under the overhang. City-fights were where she'd earnt her spurs. This felt natural. Thrilling. Terrifying. Normal.

A ganger suddenly appeared round the corner. He levelled his pole arm and charged. She hit him twice but he took three more steps before his legs gave way and he slewed to the side. A fat, sweating man, with full beard and a rudimentary augmetic arm, burst from the ruins of the hab to her right. His teeth were very white. The serrated edges of his claws were dark with blood. He moved as wildly as a beast, knocking tables and chairs aside as he came forward in a hunched run. She put five shots into him before he fell and sprawled out.

Minka suddenly realised her squad were out, alone. The grotto chapel was thirty feet away. The square was filled with the dead and dying.

'Sergeant Lesk!' a voice said in her vox-piece. It was Colonel Sparker. She looked back and saw him in the smoke, waving one hand in front of his face while the other held his bolt pistol. He looked veteran, practised, calm. 'Keep pushing forward! I'm sending reinforcements.'

There was a wall of dead about the two Sisters of the Ebon Chalice. The mob hurled missiles and abuse, a storm of stones and sticks, chunks of rock, and then a home-made firebomb that shattered about their feet, and sent a *whoosh* of flames up about them.

Canoness Maddelena knocked the missiles aside. Power armour protected them against all but the largest. But they could not last unsupported.

'Keep moving!' she ordered, and the two of them started to cut a way towards the cliffs of the acropolis. They got halfway there when the dropped head of a statue hit Mennel on the back of the head. She fell like a block, blood running from a dozen cuts.

Maddelena scooped her up. The cliff was thirty yards away. It could have been a hundred miles.

A shot rang out.

Maddelena felt the round hiss past her ear. She ducked as

a second shot followed. It grazed her temple. She staggered as a curtain of blood streamed down her face.

She spun around, blade out for any attackers. The third round struck her cheek. She spat clots from the ruin of her mouth, wiped the blood from her eyes, held the enemy back with wide sweeps of her combat blade.

More hard rounds chipped her power armour. Someone dragged Sister Mennel from her arms.

A las-bolt hit her full in the face. Her power armour kept her upright for a few moments.

'Traitor!' The roar of the mob was a wave that pounded against her.

She was a bride of the Emperor. She was pure. She was devout. She was fearless as the mob fell on her.

Minka paused as her squad caught up. Laptev was last. He came at a run, and behind him was the dark shape of Commissar Shand. His greatcoat flapped as he strode forward.

The commissar crossed the last few yards. His face was grim. She looked at the bolt pistol in his hand and her mouth went dry. 'Lesk!' he shouted. 'Move forward!'

The squad split into two fire-teams.

'Laptev, cover us! I'll take point. Your lot bring the krak charges up.'

Laptev nodded. He wasn't going to refuse her now.

'*Heavy weapons teams in place,*' Colonel Sparker's voice reported into her vox-link.

'Going in four!'

She held up a hand with four fingers raised. Counted down. On one, the heavy bolters started to fire. Their heavy *put-put* roared out as she hit zero. They hosed the open space with mass-reactive shells. The enemy threw themselves into cover and in that moment of opportunity Minka was up, boots scuffing on the cobblestones, sprinting into the open. She zigzagged forward, firing full-auto, las-bolts spearing the swirling dust and smoke, setting off eddies and whirls in the dust clouds.

She ducked into a doorway.

Emersan was down, blood puddling about him.

Behind her Commissar Shand appeared. He was like a shade clinging to Minka's back. He had his bolt pistol drawn. His face was severe.

'Keep moving, sergeant!'

Rudgard did not know how he was still alive, but somehow he had thrown himself out of the fire, and it lay between him and his attackers.

Luck was fickle. He was not going to question her, but cut his way through anyone standing in his way, desperately slapping out any flames that still burned.

But his right arm was a charred mess. The agony was something he could bear, because stopping meant he would die.

A ganger ran towards him through the smoke and Howe fired at point-blank range. The attacker fell. Another appeared behind him. Howe downed that one too, staggering for a moment, but the enforcer did not fall.

Rudgard's pistol clip was empty. The skin was falling off his right hand in strips. Beneath, the flesh was red and raw. There was grit and ash in the wound. He fumbled with his ammo belt as he tried to reload, but the pain was too much.

He fell back into the corner of an overturned cargo 6. It had been firebombed. The metal was still warm, and the paintwork had been scorched away. His right vambrace was still smouldering. He slapped at the last flames. The carapace armour was shredded.

He jammed his pistol between his legs and used his good hand to trip the spring.

The ammo clip came free. It took a maddening moment to load the last one.

He pushed himself up. Ten rounds to go. He started counting now. He'd save the last one for himself because if there was one thing Chief Enforcer Howe knew, it was that he was not going to be taken alive.

The enemy were closing in from all directions.

'Tank!' Welt hissed and Dido threw Bendikt back against the wall.

They felt the vibrations as the machine rumbled past.

'Can't go that way,' Dido said, and pulled them in the opposite direction.

Welt led them out of the back of the chapel.

'Sorry, sir,' Dido said as she put an arm about the general's waist. 'Just want to keep you safe.'

They hurried across a gap. Welt rounded the corner and ran straight into an armed mob. He knelt as another trooper, Gakn, fired the flamer. There were screams as the enemy fell backwards. Gakn sprayed the chapel wall. He gave the doorway a few extra seconds. The flames licked up, through roiling black smoke.

Dido kept Bendikt moving. There were narrow stone stairs running up the back of the retaining wall. There was no handrail or means of support, but the Cadians ran up as Gakn and Welt covered them.

Mere did not like it. 'This leads to the cliff. We need to get away from here.'

'I've no idea, sir. But I don't see any escape for us that way.' She pointed back the way they had come.

Mere relented. Dido took Bendikt's arm. 'This way, sir.'

They hurried up the steps and ran thirty feet up the retaining wall. They were halfway up when someone started firing at them. Fragments of stone were thrown out into the long drop.

'Keep moving!' Dido said.

Welt hung back, sighted the shooter in a second-floor window and fired.

'Keep moving!' she repeated, pushing them up.

Dido went first. At the top an iron gate blocked the way. It did not give way. 'Stand back,' she said. She put her carbine's barrel to the lock, held the trigger down on semi-auto. The las-bolts glared red, and within moments sparks of molten metal rained out.

She kicked the gate open, and then they were scrabbling up among the thorny bushes on a near-vertical slope.

'Where is this heading?' Bendikt said.

'I don't know,' she said, helping him catch his balance. 'But it's safer than down there.'

They zigzagged along precipitous tracks, between spiky shrubs and overhanging outcrops. There was a narrow ledge with a sharp drop. Dido put her foot on the rocks to make sure. The rock crumbled. Scree skidded down the rock face.

'Are you alright, sir?' she asked the general.

'Yes,' Bendikt said, but it was difficult going one-handed. He was halfway across the ledge when he slid, and set off tumbling clouds of rock dust and scree that gave their position away. Las-bolts flared about him as the enemy pointed his shape out among the mountainside. There was little cover.

Dido made her way back to him. She took his elbow and

helped him slide along the rock face. She was cool, determined, fearless, even as the las-bolts started to hiss past them. Dido kept her head down.

There was a sharp retort of ordnance.

The ground before them exploded suddenly, and Dido was thrown backwards.

She heard the scream as the blast threw Eyon off the edge.

Dido scrabbled for purchase as she slid down the steep slope. She grabbed at whatever was to hand. A bush snapped. A clump of dry grass came away at the roots. She dug her fingers into the gravel, and the stones fell towards her.

Dido cursed as she felt her feet go over the edge.

All her movements felt awkward, as if she were wearing an extreme environment suit as she slid into cover. It was like being in the military scholam again, Minka thought. The seconds were like heartbeats.

'Laptev!' she roared.

The pause was painful, then Viktor appeared, crouching low, and one by one the rest of the squad came forward. Laptev was last.

She lobbed a frag grenade round the corner then dashed forward, but one of the dead suddenly leapt up. His blade caught the top of her helmet. She grunted as she buried her bayonet into his guts and twisted – a simple trick she'd learnt in the early days, when they had practised by stabbing inanimate dummies lashed to a stake in the ground.

The gush of hot blood on her bare knuckles brought her back to the moment. The body slumped towards her. She sidestepped it and kept moving. Through the smoke she could see the burning remains of a cargo 6. Bodies were slumped over the rear ramp, and flames licked up the side.

Shand was still behind her, bolt pistol smoking in his hand.

'Laptev!' she shouted. Her voice was getting hoarse now. 'What the frekk is wrong with him?'

Shand had his bolt pistol ready. 'Sergeant Lesk, failure sits at the door of the commanding officer.'

Minka lost Donson before they reached the far side of the square.

If only they'd shoot Shand, she thought, as she threw herself into the porch and heel-kicked the doorway open. It opened into a kitchen, or storeroom.

She took the room in at a glance: a flight of stairs, antechambers to either side, loaded with sacks of rice and flour, each one stencilled with Munitorum letters.

Shapes were moving through the room above. She shot one through the broken floorboards, and fired at another as he hurtled down the steps. His words were cut short as her las-bolts punched him back against the wall. He slid and fell, his legs crumpling beneath him as she took the broad steps two at a time.

The remains of her squad were with her. They reached the top of the stairs. She engaged her vox-bead.

'Laptev!' she shouted. There was a pause.

There was no answer.

Minka risked a look behind her. For the moment she had to keep her fury restrained. 'Laptev! Get the frekk up here!'

Hard rounds shattered the brickwork on the other side of the street. Minka leapt up. There was the dull rattle of heavy weapons on the floors above. She smashed a loop-hole, and ordered her fire-teams to form up.

Someone was firing at them. The shots were wild and

sporadic. The Cadians hugged the walls. Minka ducked into the window and fired, then ducked back again as the enemy returned fire. Plaster fell from the ceiling above her.

'Keep moving,' Shand hissed.

Viktor and Rustem had kicked a hole through the wall to the next building. She ducked into a family's dining room, shoving the chairs and table out of the way. Shand was right behind her. She had no idea where Laptev was.

Dreno followed up first, then Thaddeus, Silas and Viktor, his grenade launcher primed with frag. Viktor knelt for a moment and braced himself, then fired a grenade up the hallway. The charge exploded from the barrel of his gun with a bang and the hiss of compressed air. It was as ungainly as a flying fist. It glanced off the wall at the top of the stairs. There was a moment's pause, then the frag charge exploded. The sound rolled down the stairwell towards them, smoke clouds following in its wake.

Minka ran to the top of the corridor. Two of the enemy were lying where the blast had killed them. A third had been hit in the face. He was sitting with his back to the wall, hands held to his eyes as if he were crying, but it was blood – not tears – that poured between his fingers. She let Thaddeus kill him as she secured the intersection.

The corridor split left and right. There were oil paintings hanging on the walls. One of them was shredded, the broken frame only held together by scraps of the landscape. Behind it the gilt wallpaper was freckled black with shrapnel. She looked back. She only had half her squad. 'Where the hell is Laptev?' Minka asked them. 'Is he hit?'

'He's coming,' Dreno said.

Minka cursed. 'Laptev! Get your frekking backside up here!' she hollered down the hallway, then she engaged her vox and spoke in a different voice entirely. 'Colonel Sparker. Building taken. Pushing forward.' She flicked the vox-bead off. Tyson didn't have to hear the rest. 'Dreno, I'm relying on you. I'll take the others forward. Cover us, and then assault. Understand?'

She caught Dreno's eye. He nodded.

Viktor took another frag grenade from his belt pouch. He fitted the heavy black charge into the launcher's muzzle and looked for Minka, as if to ask which way she wanted it firing.

They were a hundred feet up on a narrow goat track when Dido slipped.

Bendikt was right behind her and threw himself forward. He caught hold of a low shrub and swung his foot down. 'Catch it!' he ordered.

Dido grabbed the general's boot. Her feet were hanging over the edge. She felt them both slide and knew this was going to be the death of both of them.

'Hold on!' Bendikt ordered her.

'Sorry, sir. You're too important. I can't drag you with me!'

Bendikt cursed. 'Hold on, Dido. That's a damned order.'

Mere edged along the narrow ledge. He grabbed Bendikt's stump and took some of the weight.

Dido had started to slip again. 'Hold on, damn you,' Bendikt hissed as his whole body tensed. 'Or I will hunt you down and shoot you.'

Dido felt her fingers slip. She cursed. Falling off a rock wall was not how she had thought she was going to end her service to the Golden Throne.

EIGHT

As chaos engulfed the grotto chapel, the Patridzo had fled.

Meroë was not with him, but Wyryn was more than enough protection. One arm was about the Patridzo's shoulders, while the other held her Carthae force sword out before her, batting any attack away.

She was a hand taller than the Patridzo. He had never quite got used to the fact that she could be both so slender and beautiful, yet also so deadly and threatening.

It was a scramble through the rear of the grotto chapel, past the clerics and choirboys, to a private doorway set between the black marble tomb of one of the Patridzo's consorts, and a kneeler monument to a general named Wilburt Richstar of the Western Ranges.

The bio-lock responded to his touch. Wyryn covered the doorway before slipping in after him, then the door closed behind them both, leaving the others to their fate.

* * *

The Patridzo was trembling as Wyryn led him along the ancient catacombs.

Generations ago, the Richstars had indulged in all kinds of nocturnal assignations, and the catacombs had gone from being a place of rest to a way of moving unseen. Most of these passages had long been sealed up and abandoned. But there were still enough to allow for swift passage between the Kalvert, the Basilika and other shrines and barracks of the acropolis.

And there was only one place to which the Patridzo wanted to go at this moment of crisis.

It took a little more than half an hour before they reached the designated chamber. The Patridzo made the sign of the aquila as he put his hand to the bio-lock. When the doors parted he stepped inside and moved into the dull glow of the stasis field, which up-lit his face. Wyryn stayed outside the door.

Inside the vast dome, the Saint's body lay still, the expression unchanged. Only moments before, that face had been on the figure in the chapel as it writhed in agony.

He mumbled a prayer. 'What happened?' he whispered, but if the Saint's soul heard anything there was no sign.

'Was he supposed to die?'

There was no answer and the Patridzo did not know what else to do, so he knelt to pray. He imagined the days before the treachery of Sebastian Thor. The pure faith that had been founded in the earliest days of the Imperium of Man. Here, at Saint Ignatzio's tomb, the old faith, with its art and icons, had remained unchanged. Unpurified. Heretical to the minds of the present ecclesiarchs.

Generations of Richstars had lived in that pure faith. They had worshipped in the cathedral when the fortress was manned by Frateris Templars, and his family had ruled from the massive bastion of the Basilika. All he wanted was to bring that back. That glory. That closeness to the God-Emperor. 'Speak to me, forefather. Send me a sign. Have I done wrong? All I have ever wanted is to return our people to the faith of their ancestors...'

The door opened and a dark-robed figure entered. The stranger put two hands to his hood and slid it back.

It was Ordinand Vettor.

The Patridzo leapt up. 'What happened?' he demanded.

Ordinand Vettor was calm. He smiled. 'What was supposed to happen.'

The Patridzo shook him. 'But he *died*.' He looked shaken. 'Shaliah *died*.'

'Of course. That was what was foretold for him.'

The Patridzo didn't understand. He shoved Vettor away. 'What are you talking about? He was supposed to lead the Brotherhood in a great crusade to Holy Terra. What is going to happen now?'

'The Great Crusade *has* begun. They have already taken half the system.'

'I don't know what you're talking about! The Fall of the Cadian Gate confirmed all the prophesies. It is the sign that we have all been waiting for. A sign that our enemies' rule is over. A sign that our time is ripe.'

The Patridzo stepped back. It had been a long time since he had been called on to defend himself, but no Richstar reached adulthood without a rudimentary knowledge of self-defence. A needle pistol appeared in his hand. He lifted the pistol but found Vettor's grip about his wrist.

'Who *are* you?' he spluttered.

'Stop,' Vettor said. His voice was low. There was a strange command in the syllable.

The Patridzo lifted the needle pistol and fired.

Except he didn't.

He tried to move his arm but it would not move.

'Put that down.'

The Patridzo looked down in horror as his fingers opened and the needler fell from his grasp.

'*What* are you?'

'I am the Ordinand. The One Who is Ordained. The Bringer of News was destined to go before me. To make the way clear.'

The Patridzo was trying to make all this fit the secret signs and prophecies that he had grown up with. 'So *you* are the One who was prophesised to liberate us?'

Vettor put his fingers to his lips. 'Shh. No one is going to listen to you anymore. The blood of the Richstars has run thin. You are weak, corrupt, immoral. The Saint has no more faith in you. Your time, Patridzo, is over.' The Ordinand lifted the needler from the floor. He turned the gun in his hands. It was a fine weapon. He put the needler to the Patridzo's neck.

'Wyryn!' the Patridzo shouted, but Vettor shook his head.

'She's dead.'

The Patridzo struggled but he could not move.

Vettor fired.

Blood bubbled from the Patridzo's mouth as haemorrhagic venom began to liquefy his insides. The Patridzo's dissolving physique began to run to the floor. Within seconds his remains fell like a wet sack, and burst.

PART FIVE

'Shout to the Emperor, the rock of our salvation,
In whose hand are the depths of the earth
And the peaks of the mountains

For He is the Emperor, and we are the pure,
and the holders of the Truth,
the sword in His hand.'

– Psalm 666

ONE

Saint Ignatzio had spoken. The cardinal was unworthy. The portents for the future were dire.

From the grotto chapel, a tsunami of fear and anger rippled outwards. Mobs sated their despair by smashing and burning and stealing, hunting down symbols of law and order, and indulging in violent murder. Chief among their targets were symbols of authority and oppression. And the physical manifestation of that were the city's enforcers – who were being hunted down and beaten to death.

Chief Enforcer Rudgard Howe knew he was alive because he hurt so badly.

He'd barely escaped with his life, and his black carapace armour was blistered and charred. He did not dare look under the plates to see the damage to his body beneath.

Rudgard limped down the narrow steps towards the lower city quarters. There was debris everywhere, smashed windows, broken furniture, torn-up cobbles. At the end of Holy Street the local enforcer depot was ablaze, the dead crew lying in the street where they had fallen.

Chief Enforcer Howe had no choice. He had to go this way. He approached the crossroads warily. If only he could reach the Mousehole…

He had a number of faults that he was well aware of. Chief among them was his stubbornness. If he stripped off his suit of black carapace armour he might just make it to the Mousehole without being marked. But he refused to do that. It was against his nature. He'd inherited it from his great-grandsire, and it had kept him alive more times than he liked to remember.

He was still approaching when a pair of boys spotted him. 'There's one!' the cry went up.

More shouts followed. Rudgard pulled his pistol and the gang backed off for a moment, gathering strength. They shoved and egged each other on, working themselves up to a pitch of courage necessary to charge him.

Any moment now… There was no point in running. Rudgard Howe stopped in the middle of the crossroads and lifted his pistol to firing position.

'First one dies,' he said. His low voice carried enough threat and warning to hold them back. They hesitated. No one wanted to be the first. He backed off slowly, got to the corner of Redemption Avenue, and edged into a doorway. He felt behind himself, found the handle and pushed the door open.

'Right,' he said. 'I'm going through here. And if anyone follows me, I'm putting a round through their stupid skull. And then I'll find out who you are and come down on your family and take you all to the Mousehole, and then you'll wish to the God-Emperor that you forgot all about me. Understand?'

They did not respond. They were young, and hungry, and they sensed a wounded beast. He could see in their eyes that they were losing their fear of him. He slid through the doorway, and pulled it shut behind him, slamming the top bolt-lock into place. He tried to close the bottom one but it was rusted shut.

He cursed as he ran along a dark corridor, looking for the back of the tenement. He reckoned the door would give him ten seconds' reprieve.

From the sound of splintering wood, he realised he'd only been given half that time. He ran through a communal kitchen, still littered with rolls of breakfast bread, platters of beans, pots of oil. The rear door had a simple fly screen of knotted string and cheap plastic beads. He tore through it into a kitchen garden, neat rows of garlic sprouts, a lean-to shed against the side wall, and a square wooden water butt against the rear wall.

He flung himself up. His arm gave way with the pain, and he snarled as he heard the gang behind him drawing closer.

From the top of the butt, the top of the brick wall was within reach. He scrambled up, and cursed as he pulled his hand away.

There were glass shards set into the mortar. He had no choice and jumped again, but his carapace gloves saved him this time as he swung a leg up, caught the lip of the wall, and then dragged himself over.

It would slow his pursuers down, he thought, as he dropped down to the other side.

He was in a narrow street, dark in shade, and overhung with balconies, strings of hanging chillies and sacks of meal, kept out of the way of rats.

He didn't recognise it, but it looked like one of the old

lanes that wound along the contours of the acropolis. He ran to a doorway opposite, kicked the door open and dashed inside. The air was cool, and smelt of fried onions. He pushed along the narrow corridor, past an old man in underwear and stained vest coming out of the toilet, through a simple kitchen. 'Oi!' the man shouted.

Rudgard clambered up the roof of the outside toilet and dropped into another garden, this one set ten feet lower.

He didn't know this part of town so well, but he had a sense of where he was heading and swung round corners, past piles of rubbish, up weed-strewn alleys. A cat yowled. He almost ran over a child. A mother was carrying a basket of clothes. She shouted at him, a string of curses chasing him up the street.

By the time he reached the next main street, he was sure he'd lost his pursuers. He stood in a dark room, heavy with worn velvet curtains and a smell of mildew. An old, infirm lady hissed at him from her wooden chair.

'Where am I?' he demanded.

'I know who you are,' she spat.

'So do I. Now tell me, what street is this?'

She cursed him and he laughed. 'Save your curses, grandma. My mother said worse to me many times.'

She was still spitting his name as he opened the door onto a high porch, with old coats and a low stack of firewood set against the wall. A tall, narrow staircase of dressed stone led down to the road. He was three steps down when a halftrack swept past, throwing him backwards.

It was full of rioters chanting the Emperor's name. Two more halftracks followed immediately after, throwing up dust from the street. The third had a heavy stubber on the back of the vehicle.

Rudgard crouched back into the shadows. He gave them long enough to pass along the road, then slid out of the doorway. This was Atonement Avenue. He took the shady side, and limped along Martyrs Avenue, gun ready.

The long, straight artery of Martyrs Avenue gave him a clear view down. It was a mile or more to the enforcers' compound. The air was hazy with heat and dust. The street was full of rioters. He could see fires, crowds and, over the top, the low rockcrete buildings of the enforcer's base.

But there was no way of getting there from where he was. Not dressed in black carapace.

Howe limped back up the hill to take the winding, narrow streets, and drop down to the Mousehole from the north. The streets were quiet. People here were hiding, their doors shut and locked.

A few shouted at the chief enforcer. They called him 'that frekking *bofia*' – street slang for the enforcers.

He kept on, hurrying across each side street, where he had brief images of the violence below on Martyrs Avenue.

Each time he expected to see the violence decreasing, to see a wall of enforcers driving the enemy back. But instead he saw gangers wielding enforcer shotguns.

The closer he got, the more uneasy he felt. He risked a quick look down the street. The gates of the compound were open. Crowds milled in and out. Archives were being broken open, records being thrown into an improvised incinerator. Data-servitors were being dragged out of their data sockets, the brain-numbed savants mewling incoherently as they were beaten to death with clubs and wood. But most chilling of all he could see bodies hanging from the gateway. The black-clad bodies of enforcers.

Chief Enforcer Rudgard Howe had grown up in the enforcer

command depot, when his father held the position he would go on to inherit. He'd spent his entire life within the enforcers. He knew each commander, had known many of their fathers as well. Now, as mobs rampaged through the city, he did not know if any of the men he'd known were left alive. He didn't, in truth, know if he'd be alive by the end of the day, either.

The sickening realisation hit him. The Mousehole had fallen.

He was now a fugitive in his own city. A marked, unmistakable face. He laughed at the irony of it all. Now *he* was on the run.

He threw himself back into the doorway and tried to think. Where next?

He had to get to the Kalvert. He'd be safe there.

Rudgard limped back up the street. He heard the roar of a bike, and had a bare moment to react, slamming his bolt pistol into its holster, and pulling his stub-pistol out.

The biker was a blur as he passed along the bottom of the steep street.

Rudgard fired instinctively.

The report was loud and sharp in the narrow canyon of tenements.

The bike kept going. But a second later there was a screech of metal and the tone of the engine changed. He limped towards it as fast as he could. The shot had knocked bike and rider sideways. Both of them skidded along the road. The rider was a ganger. He lay ten feet away and did not move. The bike was rammed up against a rockcrete barricade. The wheels were still spinning.

Rudgard limped out. He could hear the alarm being raised, but they were too far away.

'Shout, you frekkers,' he hissed as he pulled the bike upright and kicked the engine back on. He got a feel for the pedals. It was standard Munitorum issue. Stolen, no doubt. The front headlight was cracked, the mudguards scratched and dented.

He swung his boot over and the machine bucked forward. He held on for dear life as shots rang out, slaloming through the crowd. Some of them cheered him – thinking he was dressed in stolen armour.

There was a roadblock ahead.

A leader, bearded and armed, held his hand up and directed Howe to stop.

'Who are you?' he demanded.

'Rudgard Howe, Chief Enforcer,' Howe said, and shot the other man through the head, then gunned his bike forward with a screech of rubber.

The Evercity was burning by the time Howe reached the Kalvert. The entrance was barred. He shouted up at the guards, who trained their weapons on him as he swung in through the ornamental gateway, set his bike against the wall, and limped through the palace gates.

Two witless Calibineer were on duty on the palace doors.

He waved them away as he pushed his way past them.

The Kalvert had a strangely deserted feel. He was suddenly aware of how he looked and smelt. The stink of smoke and cordite hung about him.

'Where is he?' Rudgard demanded.

The servants scattered before him.

'Where is that half-brained idiot?'

No one dared stop him. He entered the Patridzo's private chambers, and found the door locked and two life-wards with bronze body armour and helmets standing outside the door. They were not Meroë or Wyryn.

'Access is denied,' one of the life-wards announced.

Rudgard paused. 'I'm Chief Enforcer Howe,' he said.

'I do not care who you are.'

The other life-ward lowered his power lance and engaged the activation stud.

Rudgard cursed. He held up his hand in a sign of peace. 'Where is Meroë? Where is the Patridzo?'

'None of your business.'

'I'm supposed to be running this place. I need to talk to him. Do you understand that?'

The other life-ward spoke. 'The Patridzo has gone to see the forefather. The Ordinand will pass on the message.'

'Great.'

'You're wounded.'

Rudgard forced a smile. 'Right.'

'I will see that the physician attends you.'

'You're too kind.'

TWO

Dido let go of Bendikt's boot.

But she did not fall.

His hand shot out and gripped her wrist tight.

'Up you come!' he gasped as he dragged her back over the long drop.

'Let me go!' she shouted.

He ground out the words. 'Don't tell me what to do, sergeant. I am a general in the Imperial Guard.'

She cursed silently, and held her tongue.

The Cadians all worked together. A human chain with a one-handed man pulling Dido back from the brink. Her chainsword snagged on the edge. It almost tore free.

It was a struggle bringing them all to safety. But they were a team.

She struggled up the last few feet and dusted herself down.

'You shouldn't have, sir,' she told him. 'I mean, putting yourself at risk.'

'You're a Cadian,' he told her. 'That means more to me than anything else. One day there'll be none of us left. So let's put that time off for as long as we can. Now, before we do that, let's get around this hummock of rock, and get out of the sight of those people below.'

Rudgard waited in the Yellow Room, a small, intimate boudoir on the middle floors of the Kalvert, with yellow satin ottomans and embroidered chaise longue, and a series of landscape paintings giving the place a light and airy feel.

It had been used by the previous Patridzo for private entertaining. It was snug, comfortable and only a little musty from lack of use. The rumours said that the last Patridzo had entertained his many mistresses here, and maybe this was why the current incumbent had not favoured the space. Rudgard had only been here once before.

He felt awkward. He was too dirty to sit on the yellow satin and had no interest in the art that hung on the wall. He was in pain.

There was a knock on the gleamwood door.

'Who is it?'

'Scanio Primus.'

The door opened and Scanio let himself in.

He was a small, thin man with a monocle augmetic that stood an inch out from his nose, a set of medicae servo-limbs that arched over his back, and a fussy, over-protective air. 'Chief enforcer,' he said, stepping forward and taking in Rudgard's appearance. 'I heard that you were injured today.'

'I'm burnt,' Rudgard said.

'Yes, I see that. Any other wounds?'

'Yes. I cut my fingers.'

Rudgard slid off his right glove to show the cut. It was on a joint and it stung with sweat.

The physician swept forward. 'The Ordinand and the Patridzo are praying together. They asked me to come and tend to you.'

Rudgard nodded. 'That's very kind.'

'Shall we sit there?' Scanio said. He pointed to a small table by the only window. The surface was inlaid with hexagonal pieces of wood that created the impression of a three-dimensional pattern. Rudgard did as he was told but he didn't warm to the medic.

Scanio sat opposite. His fussiness seemed an act to disguise the automated method. 'Now. Please. I would like to see the arm.'

Rudgard took his pistol out of its holster and laid it on the table.

'No injections,' Rudgard said. He stared into the medic's human eye then the augmetic one. The red-lens monocle dilated as it focused. There was no perceptible reaction in either eye.

Scanio simply nodded and said, 'Show me your arm.'

Rudgard eased his elbow armour off. Next he had to remove his carapace armour.

'I can assist,' Scanio said.

Rudgard spoke quickly. 'No. It's a point of pride.'

It took him five minutes to undo the latches on his groin armour. The plates hung loose. The medic watched him intently as Rudgard unlatched the rib-buckles one-handed. His shoulder guard came away first, and then the carapace, which he had to slide over his burnt arm, being careful not to touch the wound. Beneath the armour was his black body suit with his tactical belt, which held his knife and concealed sidearm. He paused for a moment and then unclasped the seal and let the belt drop to the floor.

'That is some sidearm,' Scanio said.

'Hecutor .10,' Rudgard said. 'I got it from a Naval officer. It's for ship combat. Works just as well in the city. It fires these.'

One-handed, he fished a round-nosed slug as large as a child's fist from a pouch on his left thigh, and tossed it onto the mat. 'Hand-grip magazine. Holds ten man-stoppers.'

The medic lifted the heavy blunt round up in a human hand. 'Explosive?'

'Soft tip,' Rudgard said, taking the slug and slipping it back into his pouch. 'Expands on impact.'

'I know,' Scanio said. 'In fact. I have seen the wounds weapons like these make. Usually when performing an autopsy. Very effective indeed against any kind of soft tissue.'

'I suppose that's your job, medic. And mine is keeping men like you busy.'

Scanio didn't get the joke – or if he did, he didn't smile. His red augmetic eye blinked slowly as Rudgard opened up the seals of his bodysuit and lifted the cloth from his shoulder. He slowly peeled it down his arm.

'I can help,' the medic said, stepping forward.

Rudgard held out a hand. 'I said I'd do it.' His tone was sharp.

'As you wish,' Scanio said.

When Rudgard had stripped to the waist he sat across the table and laid his burnt arm down between them. He winced. It was worse than he thought. His arm had been flayed by the fire. The skin had fallen away in sheets and now the pink flesh oozed blood and clear fluids. He moved his fingers and stared with curiosity as he saw the fibres of the muscles contract.

'You have been burned.'

'I can see that.'

One of the medic's augmetic arms appeared from over his shoulder. It was a syringe arm.

'No,' Rudgard said. 'No syringes. Humour me. I had a bad childhood experience.'

'I will need to clean it.'

Rudgard nodded. 'Then clean it.'

'It will hurt.'

'I know.' Rudgard clenched his fist. He could see his muscles move in response. It made him feel queasy. He ground his teeth. He would not show pain.

The syringe arm folded back into place as the medic rattled in a tray and finally picked out a pair of sharp metal tweezers. They were needle-pointed. Rudgard swallowed. He grimaced as Scanio carefully picked away scraps of burnt cloth and laid them in a small metal tray. Some of them were threadbare, all were charred. They mounted up, one on top of another, all wet with blood and clear serum.

'Ah,' the medic said at one point, holding up a wet drape in the tweezers. 'That looks like skin!'

Rudgard felt nausea rise with the pain.

'I'm afraid that there is a lot of dirt.' The syringe appeared over the medic's shoulder. 'I recommend that I take away the pain.'

Rudgard took his left hand out from under the table. The medic's augmetic eye clicked as it focused. 'Another weapon?'

'Yes.'

'That is a needler.'

'Yes, it is,' Rudgard said.

'Why are you pointing it at me?'

'Because I do not trust you,' Rudgard said. 'If that syringe comes near me I fire. It is loaded with toxins that will stop your heart in seconds.'

'This is not appropriate. I do not perform under threats of violence.'

'I don't care. Just do what you have to do. Clean the wound and strap me up.'

The medic's human eye looked shaken. 'The Patridzo sent me.'

'I am aware of that,' the chief enforcer said.

'I am the best.'

'At what?'

'At healing the sick. Repairing the wounded.'

'Then shut up and start cleaning,' Rudgard said.

The chief enforcer watched as the ends of the tweezers worked into his flesh. The pain was intense. Blood started to well up from the holes. It poured, warm and wet, over the side of his arm. Rudgard gritted his teeth. He started to sweat. He felt sick. He kept his eyes open as Scanio wiggled the fragment from his arm. When the piece finally came out, the medic held it up. The augmetic eye clicked and whirred. 'Shrapnel. Krak grenade markings here and here.' He dropped it into a metal tray. It rang out, and lay in its own pool of gore. Scanio hunched forward.

A siren wailed. And another. Scanio pulled another sliver of steel from Rudgard's arm, and then looked up. 'I hear there is unrest in the Evercity.' Scanio spoke as if this were a distant, almost passing concern.

'I think it's a revolution,' Rudgard said.

'What would people have to revolt against?'

'Their fate,' Rudgard said, and laughed at his own joke. The pain in his arm was throbbing. But he could not waste time here.

'All foreign objects have been extracted,' the medic said at last. 'I will now clean it.' He looked up. 'This *will* hurt.'

'Pain is a sign of life,' Rudgard said.

Scanio paused, assessing this piece of information. 'Yes,' he nodded. 'Or imminent death. You have served the Rich-stars well. But I am afraid that now your service is at an end.'

Something in the medic's tone gave Rudgard a moment's warning. As he spoke, Rudgard dropped down and to the right and heard the thud as the syringe embedded itself into the backrest where he had been sitting.

Rudgard threw the table up and himself backwards as Scanio came at him again. Rudgard's arm was agony, but he held on long enough to fire three needle darts.

There were enough toxins there to stop a grox herd. But Scanio didn't seem affected at all.

'If you think your poison will work on me, chief enforcer, then I regret to tell you that you are mistaken.'

Rudgard emptied the magazine into the medic's chest as he backed into the corner.

'Nerve toxin,' Scanio said, as if sampling the poisons that ran within his body. 'Yes. If I were a street-ganger or a Cal-ibineer, I would be dead now. But medicine has been my life. The art of living, and the art of death.'

Rudgard looked to see where his pistol lay. He knew many tricks, but he did not have any to get himself out of this par-ticular mess. He let the medic come almost within range, then threw the needle pistol into his face. It was a cheap, ganger trick. Throw sand. Throw anything.

Howe kicked out with his booted foot, slamming into the medic's chest. Scanio fell backwards, but as he did so the med-ic's needle stabbed out and embedded itself into the two-inch rubberised soles of his combat boots. Rudgard twisted his foot, punched the medic and then threw himself back, hitting the floor. The pain from his wounded arm almost blinded him. He cried out in agony as he slid over the carpet.

The medic had grabbed the needle gun and aimed it at him.

'Nerve toxins,' he smiled and stepped forward. 'I am sure you know the effect that these will have upon your system.'

Rudgard said nothing. He knew perfectly well how the nerve toxins worked. One dart induced uncontrollable spasms that wracked the body within seconds. The last man he'd killed with it had spasmed so hard his muscles had broken almost every bone in his own body.

'Goodbye, Chief Enforcer Howe,' Scanio said, and pulled the trigger.

THREE

Bendikt led Dido's squad up the rocky path. It was dangerous going at times, but they had quickly climbed out of earshot of the Evercity, the smoke and gunfire growing distant, replaced by the breath of mountain air and the buzz of crickets in the thorny grass.

Bendikt kept a fast pace. He knew that the enemy had a march on him, and that the forces of the Imperium were on the back foot. This was the moment of crisis that could end his career – and probably his life. Or not.

Throne be damned, he was not going to end his – or any other Cadian – life on Potence, not without a fight.

Half an hour later General Bendikt, Mere and Dido's squad were lying in hiding in the deep flood gutter at the side of the road, listening to the gathering noise of a vehicle coming towards them.

Welt hissed to Dido, 'If I'd known I'd was going to end

up in a ditch, I wouldn't have worked so hard on my creases.'

She looked at the dark dress trousers of his number one uniform. Then at her own. Her trousers were torn and dusty. 'I'll be glad to get a dressing down at the next parade,' she told him.

'I'll remember you said that,' he told her.

The Cadians crouched low as the first cargo 6 came around the corner. From the rockcrete storm drain at the side of the road they watched it approach. It was passing them by when suddenly a grenade exploded and the vehicle jumped from the ground. The report was a loud, high *crack!* as it echoed off the rock face. The cargo 6 hit a metal road barrier and skidded before flipping over. There were screams as the passengers were flung out over the side of the mountain.

The second cargo 6 came to a halt with a hiss of burning tyres. The driver was trying furiously to keep control of the vehicle as he slammed the brakes on.

Dido was first up. She lobbed a grenade. It hit the bonnet and bounced left. The explosion tore the tyres to ribbons, and hid the side of the vehicle in a cloud of coloured smoke.

Hard rounds started to fizz through the air about her. She did not have to look back. She knew the other Cadians were with her. Time seemed to slow as she ducked forwards, throwing her pistol into her right hand. She had left her chainsword behind and, regretting it now, she pulled her knife out in a reverse grip.

One of the enemy leapt out. He was a young man with a thin ginger beard. She fired. Two shots, straight down into his gut. She was over him in a second, running into the smoke as a figure loomed before her. She could not slow down, and shot the second in the face, bending low to shoulder-barge him out of the way.

Welt shouted, 'Another cargo!'

The odds swung wildly against them once more. She felt the deep thud-thud of a heavy weapon go through her bones. She did not have a moment to look round and see what the hell was happening.

Bendikt unleashed a furious salvo of incandescent red bolts and felt the rumble of a vehicle coming up the road behind them.

Mere pushed him back and stood before him. 'Run!' he shouted at his commanding officer. 'Go!'

It was too late. Down the slope came the rumble of a tank and the sound of psalms being chanted. 'Throne,' Bendikt cursed. They were trapped with the enemy coming up and down the hill, and them in the middle.

The sound of singing grew louder, and the new arrival swung around the corner. It was a black tank, with fluttering pennants and a series of golden tubes rising behind it.

At the front was an armoured cockpit, with storm bolter, and behind it the pale face of the woman taking aim.

Bendikt felt as though the weapon were pointing straight at him, then flames and smoke flared from the dark barrel openings and he fell to the ground.

A fuel tank exploded. The noise was deafening.

But Bendikt had not been hit.

As the hail of fire came to an end he lifted his head. The torrent of shots had torn through the enemy. A red mist rose from a charnel slop of heaped and confused body parts where men had stood.

One of the warriors still lived. He crawled towards them

on hooked fingers, dragging the ruin of his lower half. He was hissing 'Faith in the Emperor, faith in the Emperor' over and over.

Dido put a las-bolt into him.

The tank that had come down the hill came to a halt with a hiss of brakes. Its heraldry was a black cup filled with flames.

A black-power-armoured woman stepped down. Her boots rang out on the rockcrete roadway. The bulk of her armour exaggerated her petite frame. She had close-cropped dark hair, a tattooed face and a steel aquila etched onto her armour.

There was nothing frail or weak about her. She exuded confidence and strength as she strode forward and put out her hand. 'Greetings. My name is Celestian Simmona. You are men of Cadia?'

'We are. I am General Bendikt.'

'What are you doing here? Why are you not with your warriors?'

'I was at the service this morning…' Bendikt started.

'I am looking for our canoness. The Holy Maddelena.'

'Then I am afraid your search is over. She died this morning. With the cardinal.'

Bendikt briefly described the scene earlier that day.

Celestian Simmona watched him closely. At the end she said, 'I do not know who you saw die this morning but I can assure you it was not Cardinal Xereum.'

'What do you mean?'

'When we drove off the attackers we sealed the acropolis so that none may enter. I went to the Basilika and searched it. We found Cardinal Xereum's body in his chambers. He had been beaten to death. But tell me. You saw our canoness fall?'

'She died fighting those who call themselves the Brother-hood. We were too far away to help.'

Simmona looked at him with compassion. 'Forgive me, general. You are a one-handed man. How could you help our canoness, who I have seen fight on a hundred battlefields?' A shadow fell over Simmona's face. She made the sign of the aquila, and when she spoke there was emotion in her voice. 'But tell me. Did our canoness die well?'

'She was a lioness. The dead were heaped about her. I heard her die with the name of the Emperor on her lips.'

Simmona nodded. She swallowed back her emotion and set her jaw. 'Your words bring me comfort. She died in grace. Her martyrdom will fortify us all.'

A tear began to bulge on her lower eyelid. It surprised Bendikt. He had not had much to do with the Adepta Sororitas, but he had never imagined them to be subject to human emotion. But there was no weakness in her display. Even as the tear dripped down her left cheek, she set her jaw in a hard and merciless expression. 'The holy acropolis has been defiled by heretics. The authority of the Imperium upon this planet has been betrayed. We have a great battle before us.'

'Indeed we do,' Bendikt said. 'If you can take me back to my barracks, I will drive back our enemies.'

Celestian Simmona nodded. 'We will do our best.' She pointed to Dido. 'She may come inside our tank, but the rest of you must ride on top.'

FOUR

Minka's squad were in a narrow three-storey hab-block, holding off a gang of young men, when the message came over the vox, loud and clear on all channels.

'We have General Bendikt.'

Chief Commissar Shand stood to the side of the window and fired his bolt pistol. Three rapid shots that brought dust filtering down from the cracked plaster ceiling.

There was an explosion.

Minka needed to hear the message again. 'Are you sure?' she demanded.

There was a long pause as she risked a quick look over the windowsill. She fired off a quick burst. *'Lesk!'* It was Sparker this time. *'Affirmative. Bendikt is safe. He is on the way to the barracks.'*

Shand had clearly heard the news as well. He fired another salvo. 'Order your squad, sergeant. It is time to pull back.'

Minka slammed another powercell into her carbine. 'Sir!'

she shouted to the commissar. 'Laptev! Back! Laptev?' There was no answer.

The enemy were breaking in downstairs. They could hear shattering windows. Hard rounds impacted the floor where she had been standing. The floorboards disintegrated under the weight of fire and clouds of plaster fell from the ceiling.

Shand's voice was calm, but urgent. 'Command your squad, sergeant. Maintain good order.'

Minka dropped a grenade through the hole in the floor. She evacuated to the next building before the blast went off. She shouted down the stairs. 'They're in the building. Viktor. Get Laptev's team to withdraw.'

A young man charged through the doorway where she had just been. She swung round and hit him in the chest.

'Go!' Minka shouted. She put her gun around the corner and fired off a wild salvo, then threw herself through the hole in the wall, and down the steps. Hard rounds shattered the wall behind her.

The Cadians retreated through the holes they had broken in the interior walls. At the end of the row she fired off a quick burst through a first-floor window. The enemy responded from a number of vantage points. They were zeroing in on her. She fell back as brick dust swirled about her. A grenade bounced off the wall above the window. She swung round the door frame, and threw herself down the wooden stairs. A grenade exploded behind her, in the room she'd just been in.

Shand was waiting for her at the bottom. He caught her arm as she skidded down the stairs. 'Are you ready, sergeant?'

'Yes, sir!'

She felt less threatened now, and was almost reassured by his presence. She risked a quick look out of the doorway. They'd come a long way. It was going to be a long run back.

Donson's body was lying exactly where she'd last seen him – but she saw that the Cadians were still holding on to the other side of the square.

'We're going to cover you,' Sparker voxed. He counted down from five.

On two Shand pushed her out and Minka started running. As she and the commissar broke cover, the Cadians who were dug in on the other side of the square opened fire with everything they had.

Minka had a brief impression of searing blue light. She could smell the ozone as the bolts flared past her face. She had a panic that she'd be hit by her own side. She bent low, running hard, conscious of Shand's tall shape just behind her. He ate up the ground in long, loping strides.

She passed Donson's dead body and kept going. With twenty yards to go she thought she might just make it.

Something had changed, she realised, as she reached the far side of the square and skidded into cover. She caught her breath, counted her squad, and then spun about and saw Shand.

'Are you alright?' he said.

'Yes, sir.'

He held her gaze for a moment too long.

'Good,' he said.

Minka waited till Shand was out of sight, and then threw herself at Laptev, slamming him with her open palms. 'Where the frekk were you?' she raged. 'What the hell were you doing out there?'

He fought back but she was powerful in her rage, and she knocked him down and stood over him. It was a long time since she'd felt such primal rage at a fellow Cadian. 'I lost two men out there. Both of them were better than you. We're a unit. You need to step up. Do you understand?'

She felt her squad gather round. They were shielding her from anyone else's view. It was a silent show of support. She grabbed him by the collar and shook an answer from him.

'Yes,' he said at last and she threw him back to the ground and cursed.

M Company fought their way back up to the barracks as sleeper cells of the enemy threw bombs or barricades across the roads. But the Cadians were tough veterans, with Chimeras, able to hold their own.

They pulled back to Intake Barracks as columns of the Brotherhood armour rolled into the lower reaches of the Evercity. Leman Russ tanks, Chimeras, halftracks and cargo 8s all wound along the streets, with black-robed warriors sitting on the backs, waving Richstar banners, and the yellow banners of Vandire. The Brotherhood cheered wildly as they passed the burning enforcer block and moved into the old city, with its narrow streets and overhanging houses. By lunchtime, yellow flags hung from all the main towers of the city, proclaiming a return to a world and a faith that had remained hidden for thousands of years.

The Brotherhood took each quarter of the Evercity, then set to work destroying what they considered idolatrous iconography. Pictures of Sebastian Thor were torn down or defaced, while his statue in Faith Plaza was toppled, and his marble head tossed, chipped and cracked, onto the cobblestones. Saints, holy men and women were defaced and broken. The tombs of Sisters of Battle were treated to special bouts of rage. Their mausoleums were shattered, and the musty, browned bones were scattered in the streets.

By mid-afternoon, the Brotherhood had pushed their way to the upper terraces of the Evercity, where the Leman Russ columns slowed to a crawl as they funnelled towards the narrow roads that led up to the Kalvert, the Intake Barracks and the massive fortress-cathedral at the summit. The Brotherhood were already rejoicing. They believed that the God-Emperor was on their side and that He had already granted them victory. All they had to do was take the fortress and the planet would be theirs.

In the command bunker of Intake Barracks, Bendikt and Celestian Simmona threw a plan together to hold the acropolis against their enemies.

'If they try to take the cathedral, my Sisters and I will throw them back,' Celestian Simmona assured him.

'Will you be able to hold against tanks?' Bendikt asked.

She looked at him with a mixture of contempt and pity. 'General. The walls of the faithful are impenetrable to the unworthy.'

Bendikt smarted. 'Are you accusing the Cadians of being unworthy?'

'I am not accusing you of anything. But the Emperor's Will is clear. Can you say that you and your troopers are all pure?'

'Pure. What is pure?'

Celestian Simmona gave him a compassionate look. 'The Sisters of the Ebon Chalice are pure.'

Bendikt cursed inwardly. 'Well. Good luck to you, Celestian. I am sure your purity will keep you all safe.'

Celestian Simmona made the sign of the aquila before she left.

Mere had new reports for the general to read. Bendikt absorbed the information quickly. By the time the lead tanks of the enemy were pushing up through the final switch-back streets, the Imperium's fist was already preparing for the counter-blow.

'Get General Dominka,' he told Mere. When the contact was made, Mere handed the handset to Bendikt. 'Hold at all costs. Understand?'

'*Yes, sir,*' the Calibineer commander answered. There was a pause. '*Yes, sir. I understand. We will hold to the last.*'

That morning Dominka's Mountain Infantry had worn their finest dress uniforms: blue woollen zhuba with broad red silk sashes wound about their waists. That morning on parade they had looked magnificent.

Now, they looked incongruous as they took up positions in front rooms, balconies, at crossroads and behind make-shift stockades of cargo-trucks, hand carts, barrels, sacks of meal and rice.

She was proud of their discipline. But they were a skir-mishing infantry force, specialising in mountain warfare. They had almost none of their heavy weaponry and only a smattering of specialist weapons.

When the lead tanks of the Brotherhood appeared at the end of Via St Sabine, she lifted her scopes. The lead tank was a Thunderer, low profile, wide-barrelled and menacing. On the back she could make out the faces of young men, clap-ping and singing as if they were on a victory parade.

'Time to spoil the party,' she said when the Thunderer was two-thirds of the way along the road. 'All squads. Open fire!'

The roar of missiles in the confined street was deafen-ing. One missile skewed off the angled armour, decapitating a singing warrior and ricocheting into the top floor of a hab-block, which exploded in a cloud of rubble dust.

The others impacted head-on and detonated, filling the street with a billowing cloud of fyceline. 'Hit!' Dominka grinned, but as the smoke cleared, the low profile of the Thunderer nosed aggressively forward, now shorn of passengers, like a bull-shark coming through murky waters.

The Demolisher cannon panned for targets. It shook as it fired into one of the buildings flanking the street. There was a dull roar as the massive shell thrummed the air. It impacted an ornate hab-block halfway along the street. The building shuddered under the impact, and then the chemical core erupted and the building seemed to lift into the air before falling back to ground and collapsing in a heap of dust and rubble. Dominka cursed as the lead tank rumbled forward.

Unless her troops could do something, the way to the cathedral lay open.

Reports of the fighting reached Bendikt as he set up his command post in the mountain bunker of Intake Barracks.

He started to work out who the enemy were.

'The Frateris Militia call themselves the "Brotherhood",' Mere said.

'And who is leading them?'

'Their nominal commander is the cardinal.'

'He's dead. Who's their military commander? Find out who and get them on the vox.'

Mere saluted. 'Yes, sir.'

There was a pause as Major Kastelek hurried in. 'I have the 101st ready, sir. Just let me know where you need us.'

'Thank you,' Bendikt said. 'I am still unsure exactly what is happening here, and which of the local troops are loyal. At best the Frateris Militia are rioting. At worst they are infected. I suspect the taint of heresy here. Have your troops on standby. As soon as we know what is happening we will move.'

Kastelek nodded. Bendikt paced up and down as reports came in. The Patridzo was not answering, but at least the majority of Calibineer commanders reported themselves ready.

'Any action?' he demanded from Major Kamak, whose troops has secured the starport.

'Scattered contacts. I've set up an exclusion zone. A lot of armour heading your way. Tanks. Armoured conveyors.'

Bendikt went very still. 'Thank you for the warning.'

The link dropped. Bendikt was outwardly calm, but the air was strained. 'When are the reinforcements due in-system?'

Mere looked through the day's vox traffic. 'There's no word from them yet.'

'Nothing?'

Mere paused. 'No.'

'Get me a link.'

Vox-officer Hesk nodded. 'I've been trying to get through to them for three hours now. I presumed that because of the festival...'

Bendikt did not have time for this. 'Well get them now.'

'Yes, sir.'

Hesk stabbed at the call button. There was a long pause. 'Nothing, sir.'

Bendikt cursed. 'I have a hundred thousand Imperial Guardsmen out there and I cannot get in touch with them! What the hell is happening?'

No one answered. They had only been on the planet for a few days and everything was going wrong. Hesk kept trying to contact the astropathic tower but there was only the crackle of static.

Bendikt paced up and down, his expression hardening as the silence continued.

At last Hesk stopped. 'Nothing, sir.'

Dominka's troops took cover in doorways and front rooms as Destroyer-pattern tanks panned around to fire more shots. Another building crashed to the ground with a thunderous explosion. The squads fell back.

'They're coming up Via Pietist,' one of her captains reported. Soon the enemy were approaching along side streets, threatening to turn their flanks.

'All squads, hold your ground,' Dominka ordered.

As she sent reinforcements to Via Pietist, the tank rumbled forward once more. She ordered her melta squads to meet it, but as they got into range there was a sudden explosion from within and raging gouts of flame burst from the tank's open hatches, incinerating those inside.

They held for an hour before the enemy managed to encircle them. Dominka felt the morale of her troops begin to wobble. She looked at her command team as the sound of fighting drew ever closer.

'It has been a pleasure serving with you all.'

They shook hands briefly, then she drew her sidearm. 'Tell General Bendikt we have not abandoned our position.'

The vox-officer nodded, then Major Dominka led her troops outside.

The fighting was fierce, close-quarters stuff. The enemy were fearless, and worst of all they came in such numbers that the Calibineer started to find themselves overwhelmed.

Dominka shouted to her soldiers to hold but they were in full retreat, running back along the burning corridor of

Via St Sabine. As they broke cover, a Leman Russ belonging to the Brotherhood rumbled through the side of a burning building, chunks of flakboard and fiery debris spilling from its armoured panels. Its engine whined as it became stuck, and the driver struggled to get it into reverse. 'Bomb it!' Dominka shouted, but no one was listening any more, and with ominous slowness the immobilised tank's Punisher cannon turret panned round.

There was a whine as the gun started firing. The barrels spun, smoke hissing from the weapon's vents, and a hail of deadly hard rounds ripped through flesh and flakboards and brickwork alike.

Dominka saw her troops cut down. Panic spread among those not hit. She felt their morale waver and stepped forward, drawing her sabre. 'For the Emperor!'

She fought her way forward, cutting down any who stood in her path. But then the Punisher cannon fired again, and she disappeared in a pink mist.

Bendikt received the news from the Evercity with stoic calm. Dominka's forces had been swept aside. The enemy had taken the whole city, and only the Sisters of the Ebon Chalice held out. But they were surrounded and cut off, with no word from the rest of the Imperium.

He would not fail, he told himself. This would not be a story that ended with Bendikt's death.

He remembered his father, who never forgave himself for not making it off the planet. He remembered all the Whiteshields he had been enlisted with, and all of their deaths in the service of the God-Emperor. He remembered Creed before the fall of Cadia. How the two men had stood and talked on the bridge of the *Fidelitas Vector*.

He took in a deep breath. 'So, all we have left at our disposal is a regiment of Cadians.' His words fell on silence. Bendikt nodded to himself for a moment. 'Well, planets have been won with less.'

There was a knock on the door, and Mere went to answer it.

After a moment he let the visitor inside. It was not a Cadian, or even a soldier, but an ugly-looking man, dressed in black carapace. He looked in a bad way – burnt, wounded and with scraps of his armour missing.

'General Bendikt,' he said. 'I am Chief Enforcer Rudgard Howe.'

There was something in the man's manner that Bendikt did not like. 'Do you know where the Patridzo is? Did he escape from the chapel this morning... He is not responding to our vox hails.'

'He won't.'

'Why not? Is he dead?'

'I cannot say. But if he is alive then he is on the same side as the forces who have taken over the Evercity.'

'You mean he would wish this on his own planet?'

'For a greater good, yes.'

'What is that good? Heresy?'

Rudgard shook his head. 'Well. Yes, in a manner of speaking. But not that of the arch-deceiver.'

'Stop speaking in riddles, man. Speak plain.'

Rudgard nodded. 'Have you heard of the Temple Tendency?'

Bendikt laughed. 'The followers of Goge Vandire... They're just swivel-eyed lunatics. Are you saying–'

'Yes,' Rudgard said. 'I am. On this planet, the prophecies of Vandire are considered the most sacred texts, and ever since the fall of your home planet, the lunatics have been growing in confidence and conviction. They need no more omens now. This is their moment to seize back control of the Imperium of Man.'

'You cannot be serious.'

Rudgard drew in a deep breath. 'I am afraid that I am completely serious.'

'So why would you tell me this now?'

Rudgard held up his arm. 'Because I have just found that my services, and the service of six generations of my family, are considered disposable.'

'Explain.'

'The Patridzo has just tried to have me killed. But he didn't have the guts to come himself. He sent his physician. And he came very close to succeeding. Would have done if he could count.' Rudgard laughed. 'He knew his toxins, but he didn't know when a magazine was empty. I used his own saw to cut off his head. It was the one thing that stopped him. So, I have no other place to go to but here, with the blood still warm on my hands.'

He opened his fists and showed them the evidence, then caught the cloth that was thrown to him, and wiped the clotting gore from his hands. He had to rub harder to get it from between his fingers.

Bendikt watched him with ill-disguised dislike. 'Is that so? Then explain this to me. How did you get here? The roads are blocked...'

Rudgard nodded. 'Yes. But when you have lived on Potence as long as I, you start to learn what lies beneath the façade. This whole acropolis is a honeycomb of catacombs and passageways and hidden doors. Without me, your position here would be a deathtrap. The enemy have taken the city and they have the Sisters holed up in the cathedral gatehouse. They think they have won. They believe that your regiment is trapped here, in Intake Barracks. When they have taken the rest of the acropolis they will come for you. When they are ready. At a moment of their own choosing. They will starve you out. Or pound you from the top of the rock. But with my knowledge you can strike the enemy without them knowing where you have come from. In short, general, you need my help as much as I need yours.'

'Prove you are who you say you are.'

Rudgard paused. 'I am privy to the secret communications of the Imperium. I know you lost your hand in a duel, against a Praetorian named Ser Reginald de Barka and were sent here in disgrace after the 101st were threatened with disbanding by Warmaster Warmund.'

There was a long pause as some of these details sank in. Bendikt was convinced. 'I don't like you. And I don't trust you. But I believe you are telling the truth.'

Rudgard's smile was as ugly as the rest of him. 'Good. Because I have important news for you. You might have noticed that there have been no astropathic communications from outside the planet.'

'We have.'

Rudgard seemed incredibly pleased with himself. 'The Brotherhood captured the astropathic tower yesterday morning. It's an inhospitable place. Snowbound at this time of year. Local troops shun it. The guards were half-staffed and surprised.'

Bendikt bristled. 'You *knew* the attack was going to happen?'

'No. If I had I would have come to you.'

Bendikt paused. 'So none of my messages have got out?'

'We cannot say. We must fear not.'

'The forces of heresy have made us look like amateurs. Drakul-zar could be days away. We will need to retake it as a priority.' Bendikt turned to the map on the wall and pointed. 'The astropathic relay is here, yes?'

Rudgard nodded. 'The Supramonte Plateau, at Nullem Apek. But if I were you I would take the cathedral first.'

Bendikt's reply was withering. 'Do not tell me my job. *I* am the commander here, Enforcer Howe.'

Mere stepped forward quickly. He turned to Howe. 'It would take us weeks to fight through the entire city... Is there a hidden way there?'

'No.'

'Nothing?'

'No. It's a hundred miles distant, up steep mountain roads. It's twelve hours without opposition. But even if you could get out of the Evercity, twenty men could hold the mountain roads against you.'

Bendikt cursed. 'Kastelek. Enforcer Howe is going to lead your troops in an assault on the fortress-cathedral. Leave a company here to hold the barracks, and have the rest ready to move out in twenty minutes. If there is any doubt about Howe's loyalty, execute him. Understand?'

Kastelek saluted.

Bendikt turned to Rudgard. 'There are hidden ways up to the cathedral. You will lead my warriors there. They are Cadians, the finest troops of the Imperial Guard. You will lead them faithfully, or you will die. Do I make myself clear?'

Rudgard knew he had no choice. 'Perfectly clear.'

The Cadians started to prepare for the assault on the cathedral. In the command bunker orders were given and received. Mere checked the charge on his pistol's powercell. The others loosened their bayonets. Bendikt practised loading his bolt pistol, checked his spare clips. Should he take the sword, he wondered? He could shoot left-handed, but he was never much of a swordsman, and left-handed he thought he would be a danger to himself and his troops.

'Here,' he said to Mere, unbuckling his sword belt. 'Take this.'

'It has just occurred to me how to get to Nullem Apek,' Rudgard said suddenly.

They all turned to him.

'I know how to do it. It'll only be a hundred men. But I think it will be enough.'

'Are you sure?'

'Yes! I've worked it out! Let me show you.'

FIVE

The Sisters of the Ebon Chalice responded with furious right-eousness to the attack on their priory.

The Sisters Militant closed the gates of the fortress-cathedral, manned the great immolator canons that were mounted on the gatehouse turrets, and prepared to hold unto the last. The dead of the Brotherhood were flung off the acropolis, while the bodies of the dead Sisters were carried with care and reverence into the sacred cloisters and laid out in the Alicia Chapel, at the foot of the statue of Saint Dominica, the founder of their order.

The attack came an hour after noon, with siege tanks rumbling slowly up the switchbacks and then lining up at the summit, the crews shouting to one another to get into position.

It had been a long time since Celestian Simmona had flown with the Seraphims, but the weight of the jump pack felt like an old friend as she watched the enemy approach.

'They think they are beyond the reach of our weapons,' Superior Bequith said.

'There is no limit to the fury of the holy,' Celestian Simmona told her.

There was a rumble as the tanks moved forward. Gouts of melta spewed out from the immolator cannons, and then the tanks responded with a roar as the squadrons of Demolishers fired, and the gatehouse shook as the siege shells ripped great holes in the rockcrete bastions.

Smoke and rubble dust rose like a cloud, and as the warriors of the Brotherhood waited for the dust to clear to see if they had broken a hole through the defences, they saw dark figures rise from the smoke, like phoenixes, and then tilt towards them.

Celestian Simmona and the Seraphim swooped down on the enemy like angels of death. She hovered above the lead tank and fired. Highly pressurised pyrum-promethium gases ignited, and shot a superheated melta beam through the upper armour plates. The backwash was hot on her face as molten slag bubbled and toxic gases filled the inside of the tank. She tasted the smoke that billowed up about her as she moved on to the next. It had the sweet, smoky flavour of vengeance.

The battle was two hours old when the first Cadians finished the long climb through the tunnels of the acropolis, and came out in the basement of the Basilika.

Rudgard led them through the labyrinth of storerooms and chambers. The fighting at the gatehouse was a dull vibration through the rock. The higher they rose, the louder it grew, and the more the earth trembled.

Bendikt was among the first to reach the acropolis' top.

Cadian teams were already taking up positions as smoke plumed up from the gatehouse, and the air was thick with gunfire and explosions. The cathedral complex was the focus of a sustained assault, the bare handful of Adepta Sororitas spread dangerously thinly across the palisades.

He stood with Kastelek and was ordering the warriors into position when Celestian Simmona suddenly landed in front of him.

There was ash on her cheeks, her hair was singed, her crackling blade was stained dark with blood, and even two yards away, Bendikt could feel the radiant heat of her melta gun. She smelt of fire and war. She exuded threat and fury. 'General. You have come,' she said simply.

'We are here to help you hold the cathedral against our foes.'

She pointed her gun to the bastions to either side. 'You may not enter the gatehouse. But your warriors may fight from there.'

Rudgard Howe strode towards Bendikt as the Cadians took up positions on the low rockcrete ramparts on either side of the gatehouse. 'Trust me now?' he said.

'We shall see. Are you sure you can get us to the Supramonte?'

'Yes. The cardinal had a fondness for ornithopters. Only six of them are large enough to carry passengers. But I think we can get enough inside.'

Heavy weapon teams were already finding their ranges when the Brotherhood's bands charged with a great roar. They fired en masse.

'I hope so,' Bendikt said, drawing his pistol, and hurrying up to the firing parapet.

The Cadians let the enemy come almost up to the wall

before they opened fire. The Brotherhood's front rank was mown down by las-bolts and heavy weapons fire. The warriors behind surged over the tumbling bodies, and were engulfed in panning bursts of wall-mounted flamers. Wind blew as the flames roared upwards, and within the inferno there were small explosions as grenades and powercells overheated.

It was like a great wave rolling right up to the cliff and then falling back, leaving the high beach strewn with the ruin from the sea. But this flotsam was not sticks or bottles or lumps of plastek, but the dead and the dying, as thick as a carpet.

Bendikt and Major Kastelek strode up and down, encouraging their troops. They were righteous, disciplined and deadly.

Colonel Sparker stood on one of the level roofs on the western end of the Basilika, looking down on the platform where the woven plastek tarpaulins were being dragged off the ornithopters and the 101st's enginseers were going to work, waking the machine-spirits, checking fuel, starting the craft for a long and punishing flight. The mass of the cathedral rose up behind him. To the right, the gatehouse was swathed in smoke, and before him, the flat roofs of the Basilika's many apartments fell sharply down the acropolis' flanks.

From the top they could take in the opulence of the Evercity, the scale of the tent city, and the glittering, cold peaks of the Supramonte on the horizon.

Sergeant Tyson stepped back from the troops, and turned to the colonel. 'So that's where we're heading...'

'Yes,' Sparker said.

'And what are our orders?'

'To retake the astropathic facility.'

It was clear that Tyson did not approve. 'Do you know what we're going up against?'

'The same. This crusade. The Frateris Militia.'

'Call themselves "the Brotherhood".'

'That's right, sergeant.'

M Company were passing out musty hostile environment overcoats, ration packs, powercells, medical supplies. Tyson nodded towards the ornithopters. 'And we're going in those?'

Sparker sucked in a deep breath. 'They don't look very reliable, do they?'

Tyson paused. 'Forgive the language, sir. They look like a frekking deathtrap.'

Sparker nodded. 'Yes. They do. I think your description is quite apt... Think the Brotherhood have a Thunderbolt?'

'If they do, we're dead.'

'Tyson, we were dead the day we joined the Guard.'

'You're grim today, sir.'

Sparker paused. 'Yes. I am. I think it's the prospect of flying to battle in those contraptions.'

At that moment a sudden alertness passed through the soldiers. They turned quickly. Walking towards them was Chief Commissar Shand. The tall man's eyes were narrowed. 'Colonel. I hope your troops know the importance of this mission.'

'Yes, sir. I have made it very clear.'

Shand's face was stern. 'Good. Considering its importance, General Bendikt has asked me to assume command. I trust that is acceptable to you, colonel?'

'Well, sir...' Sparker started.

Shand fixed his gaze on the officer. Sparker's voice trailed off. Shand went on. 'There is no insult to you or your men. But I want you to know that the fate of every Cadian on this planet depends on this mission.'

'Right, sir. Thank you.'

Shand nodded. 'Well, gentlemen. Let's get aboard.'

Minka passed on the news that she had been given. All the time she could see Laptev's eyelids growing heavier and heavier. As she sketched out the plans of the Nullem Apek, she saw his eyelids finally close.

'Laptev,' she snapped. He jerked awake. 'This is important.'

Laptev nodded and forced himself to stand upright.

Minka finished describing the operation. When she was done, Jaromir frowned. 'We are flying in those?'

'Yes.'

'How many of us can get in them?'

'I can't tell you,' Minka said.

The mood of her squad was unhappy. Dreno rolled his eyes. Belus grinned. 'Good luck, sarge,' he said and winked. 'Looks like they can't get those things flying.'

Minka turned. The enginseers had four of the ornithopter engines running. They appeared to be giving up on the last two.

Daal strode over to them and raised his voice. 'Right. There's only four ornithopters for all of us. That means we're leaving all unnecessary equipment behind. Coats, guns, grenades and powercells only.'

Dreno shouted, 'No packs?'

'What did I just say? Guns, grenades, powercells.'

'No water? Rations?'

Daal turned towards Dreno. 'What is going to get this into your thick skull, trooper? Coats. Guns. Grenades. Powercells. Only. No water. No rations.'

Dreno turned to Belus and rolled his eyes. 'You heard him,' Minka said. She already had her pack off, and was pulling out her spare cells. The eight remaining troopers in her squad moved slowly. Even Viktor.

'Frekking mess,' Dreno muttered, loud enough for Minka to hear.

Laptev hadn't moved. He was sweating. When she was done she threw her pack against the parapet wall and went to him. She'd not spoken to him since their fight, but now she felt a mix of pity and irritation.

'If you're sick, corporal…' she started.

She'd hoped he'd say yes, but he shook his head. 'No. I'm fine.'

'You'd better be,' she said. 'You've heard the job they've given us. There's no room for frekk-ups.'

'I'm fine. Honest.'

'Empty your pockets!'

He swallowed and then turned out his pockets. There was string. A well-worn compass. Bandages. Flashlight. A metal pick. A bent pict-slate and a short stub of a black marker.

'Keep going,' she said.

He reached inside his jacket and pulled out a scrap of wax paper. It lay in his trembling hand. She didn't want to touch it and only reluctantly took it from him. Inside were the dried shells of some kind of flying pollinator, the soft maggot bodies now dry and flat, while the insectoid legs were long and hairy.

They smelt like musk-rats. Her face was full of disgust. 'Is that what you're taking? What the frekk is that?'

Laptev had a hungry look in his eye even as he held them out to her. He had to cough to clear his throat. 'It's Union,' he said. 'The priests on Frael take it.'

It looked foul. 'It's bugs. You're a Cadian, man!' She screwed her hand up. 'I'm throwing this stuff away. And you have got to stop taking whatever you're on.'

Laptev nodded. 'I have. Honest.' He puffed out his cheeks. 'I'm getting myself straight.'

'I need you. I need a great corporal. This lot need you. I don't want to lose any more of this squad. Not another Cadian life for this planet. Understand?'

There was sweat on his forehead. He wiped it away and put his hand to his chest. 'I'm going to be fine. I swear. Cadian honour.'

Minka did not know if she could believe him. 'Right. But hear me. This is your last chance. Any more of this and I'm turning you in. Understand?'

Laptev nodded. 'I swear it.'

The command staff had rustled up men with flying experience. They conferred together, working out how to pilot the craft. The sight didn't inspire anyone with confidence.

The ornithopters had narrow, dragonfly bodies perched on triangulated struts, and large wings, now folded back and resting on the ground. The enginseers rolled each one to the take-off point, and loaded up.

The first machine-spirit woke with a splutter of promethium fumes. From the engine puffed clouds of dark smoke. Pistons began to drive up and down, and then they started to flap with long, elegant strokes. The craft didn't lift an inch.

'Out!' Daal shouted. He bundled half of C squad through the side-hatch. The ornithopter lifted from the floor with each down blow. It was like watching a bird learn to fly. It bumped against the ground a couple of times then it began to gradually lift, flapping slowly upwards and then forward as the wing angle shifted.

'Right. The rest of you leave your coats!' Daal ordered.

The Cadians didn't argue, but Viktor said, 'How cold is it going to be?'

'It's freezing,' Minka said.

Viktor nodded. They'd trained as Whiteshields in arctic temperatures. He repeated what his drill master had told him. 'We'll just have to keep moving, then.'

'Sounds like a plan,' Minka said.

She turned and found Prassan standing next to her. He put out his hand. 'Good luck, Lesk,' he said.

She smiled and took his hand and returned the shake. 'Thanks. You too.'

Prassan blushed at that, and as Minka turned to her squad she felt eyes watching her, and turned to catch Commissar Shand's gaze as he climbed into the second ornithopter.

Minka was last. She took her place in the narrow fuselage as the hatch was thrown closed and the craft began to lurch up from the rooftop.

She looked to Laptev. His face was pale. Beads of sweat were running down his forehead. She reached out and took his hand in hers, and squeezed it.

He gave her a quick sideways glance.

She mouthed to him, 'Cadian honour.'

He swallowed and nodded and repeated the words.

'Cadian honour.'

SIX

Storming Nullem Apek had been straightforward, Carkal thought.

All it had involved was the massacre of the defenders. Managing the astropathic tower was much more complicated. They were not allowed to kill anyone without Confessor Pitt's express permission, and the strain was beginning to show in the gallants. They had become used to simply killing those they didn't like the look of. It was simple: they were faithless, and the faithless must be shot.

But now Confessor Pitt forbade them from executions. 'Any sinners must be brought to me,' he commanded. Veins in his stitched-open eyes were starting to burst, and dark haemorrhages were turning the whites red. 'I will judge them!'

The staff and scribes of the astropathic choir found that the gallants were easily offended. They were seized for superficial failures such as not making the sign of the aquila with enough speed. Not bowing when Confessor Pitt passed by.

Not moving quickly enough when a gallant summoned them.

Confessor Pitt heard each accusation with his unblinking gaze, as blood began to drip from his tear ducts.

He had not lost his appetite for violence, but some of those brought for judgement were deemed necessary for the smooth running of the choir.

For those, he held back from ordering their execution, and instead let the gallants beat them till blood flowed.

'Stop now, brothers,' he ordered. And stood over the accused. 'Next time we shall not be merciful. Next time I shall turn you over to the Emperor's Will.'

Carkal and the others made their home in the barracks that they had recently cleared. The dead Calibineer were dragged outside and stacked in piles. Their blood was left where it had fallen. They quoted Confessor Pitt. 'The blood of the unworthy will flow in rivers. Their heads will rise up like hills.'

These gallants were the armed, elite fanatics of the faithful. Duty rotas were nailed to the doors. Struggle sessions weeded out impure thoughts. Slogans were daubed on the walls, and the gallants took to their new responsibilities with enthusiasm, sitting together in study meetings, chanting the sayings of their confessor.

Blood is the ink of history.

Dare to think. Dare to act.

Seek truth through bloodshed.

Where there is oppression there is opportunity.

It was late in the day when Carkal's sentry duty came up.

He had helped pile the cadavers outside. Now the corpse-piles were frozen into one vast heap, the faces frosted over, the eyes frozen shut.

The dead must beseech the Emperor for mercy. Their bodies are meat. They will fertilise the Emperor's soil.

Carkal was one of fifty guards. They wore the coats of the Calibineer. His coat was too big for him, hanging down to his ankles. He had pulled it tight about him and had his hands shoved deep into his pockets.

He clenched his fists as the wind howled about him. The pockets were full of a dead man's knick-knacks. He wished he'd stripped the boots and socks off as well. He'd long since stopped feeling his feet.

As the sun rose, a bell rang inside. One by one the sentries were summoned for their struggle session.

Doubts are weeds that must be uprooted and burned.

When he got inside, the other members of his struggle group were drawn up in a circle. Their faces were pinched and nervous.

Confessor Pitt stood in the middle. His red eyes bulged. 'Good news, my gallants. The Evercity has fallen. The heretics have been driven to their holes. They still resist us. They refuse to see the light. They are shameless in their deviance. Their days are numbered. The Emperor has turned His face away from them.'

Carkal cheered. The Emperor loved him. He loved the Brotherhood. He hated all others.

'But still our job is not yet done. The world is in a state of struggle. Heresy is all around us. The worst are those who claim to love the Emperor. They are snakes who cling close to our breast. Those that have the sweetest tongues have poisonous bites! We must never relax our vigilance against their heretical thoughts. Doubts are weeds. They must be stamped out.'

Carkal wanted to trample on their enemies. He stomped his feet as Confessor Pitt took a set of cards from his breast pocket. They were wrapped in a dirty cloth. He untied the knot and shuffled them all, walked around the circle and handed each gallant a card. Carkal took his own and put it against his chest.

'I smell treachery,' Confessor Pitt declared. 'I sense those who wish to betray us. The seeds of doubt, settling among us.'

'No!' they shouted.

Confessor Pitt roared for silence. 'Do not deny the truth, gallants. Do not deny that there are traitors amongst our fellows. Traitors are like cockroaches! They crawl into the rockcrete. They sneak under floorboards. I smell them. I smell heresy!'

'Find them!' some shouted. Others pressed their hands together in prayer and shouted out, 'Seek the unholy! Put their faces under our boots that we might stamp them out!'

Confessor Pitt paced up and down like a caged beast, sniffing and snorting, his black top hat now crumpled and bent. 'My nose has never betrayed me and I smell heresy... One of you is a traitor. One of you seeks to betray our cause. Which one is it?!'

The gallants looked about the circle, as if trying to see who it was.

Confessor Pitt moved up and down, pounding the plastek flooring. 'Lord Emperor. We are the sons who have remained loyal to you through the centuries. Our enemies seek to destroy us. They send armies against us, infiltrate our ranks with liars and the devious. Help us, lord. Show us who is the heretic among us. Through darkness let us seek light!'

Carkal pressed his eyes closed. 'Lord Emperor. I am your devoted servant. Save me and I will paint murals to glorify you. I will go penniless. I will go barefoot. My soul is pure. I am sorry for all my sins. I am your chosen instrument of punishment and war.'

The room was full of prostrate gallants. Each one of them looked within themselves, looking for heresy, looking for the seed that would grow into doubt.

'I can see your shape,' Confessor Pitt called out. He held up one hand, as if reaching forward to grasp something from the shadows. 'Come to me, trickster! Come into the light so I might see the face of the one who betrays us. Lord Emperor, push our enemy forward. Show me the card that he holds in his hand.'

Carkal fell to his knees, and pressed his hands to his face, squeezing his eyes shut as if his devotion might be revealed in this gesture.

Confessor Pitt sucked in a shocked breath. It was like the hiss of a snake. 'I see you!' he whispered. 'Trickster. Traitor. Come forward. Reveal yourself.'

The pause was terrifying.

Pitt laughed. 'The one who hates us with a smiling face holds the Shattered World. Show me your cards, gallants. Let the guilty one reveal his shame.'

Carkal opened his eyes. Confessor Pitt walked around the circle, standing over each gallant as they turned their cards over.

The first man held the card of the Jackal. The next, the Great Eye. Round they went, turning their cards over.

The Sword, the Squat, the Star, the High Priest.

Then Confessor Pitt was standing over Carkal. The black top hat blocked out the light. He was a black silhouette.

Carkal felt warmth spread through him and he knew the Emperor protected him.

He closed his eyes and turned the card. He looked down.

It showed a wounded lion lying prostrate, and a warrior in bronze armour, standing over it with a gun, delivering the Coup de Grace. He held it up and showed it to Confessor Pitt, whose staring eyes saw it and nodded.

'You are marked for greatness, my child. Our enemies are prostrate and dying! You are one of those who will put them out of their misery.'

Carkal put his hands together in prayer. He was blessed. He was loved. He was the executioner of the dying.

It took nearly an hour for the ornithopters to cross the flat farmsteads of Potence.

The planet seemed peaceful from their height. Through the round viewports they could see rotary fields that dwarfed the tiny square farm-habs at their core. They saw straight roads disappearing out of sight, where no traffic moved. And then they saw the foothills where the roads began to zigzag up the slopes.

It was then that the journey became rough. The sky darkened and suddenly there were clouds ripping past, dark with storms, ominous skirts of rain and hail lashing the light craft.

The ornithopters lurched and bounced as they struggled against the mountain winds. They were buffeted violently as they circled slowly up, the laborious climb marked with each flap of the wings.

The temperature dropped dangerously. Minka put her hands into her armpits and drew her knees up to her chin. 'Alright?' she asked Viktor.

He nodded, but to be honest, all of them were cold and miserable.

No one spoke. They were all too cold. They were trying to stay focused, trying to rest themselves before the action happened. The sheer rock slopes appeared at times, dangerously close.

At one point there was a violent lurch and Dreno shouted and pointed.

'Frekk!' Dreno said. 'They've crashed.'

Minka strained to look, as scraps of ornithopter plunged earthwards, slowing only as it hit ledges and promontories, each contact shattering the fragile craft, and throwing bodies out, which tumbled and bounced until she could watch no more.

She swallowed back her feelings. There was no time for emotion in war. That time would come later, alone, when the death-tally had been settled.

'Which one was that?' Belus asked.

Minka shook her head. She did not know and she had no words of comfort.

There was nothing they could do but pray and hope that the pilots and storm would see them through this.

Confessor Pitt moved on round the circle. The drama took on its own terrible air, as one by one, the other members of his squad turned their cards over.

The Hulk, the Harlequin, the Magus, the Throne, the Host.

The last in the circle, a man named Adum.

Confessor Pitt stood over him, snorting and sniffling. 'I smell you, traitor!'

Adum shook his head. 'I am pure!' he said.

They all stared at him.

Adum's face was pale. His cheeks pinched. 'No,' he said and half stood, and tried to back away.

Confessor Pitt forced him back to the ground. 'Show me your card.'

Adum's hands trembled as he turned the card over. His eyes were intent. Every gaze was fixed on the image in the terrified man's fingers.

It was the Shattered World.

'You!' Pitt hissed.

Adum fell to his knees. 'No,' he said. 'The cards have lied. The enemy have betrayed you. They have shown you the wrong image. It is not me. I am not a traitor. I love the Emperor!'

But no one listened. If he was guilty then they were innocent.

'Come, brothers! Help him understand his guilt.'

They obeyed Confessor Pitt. The heretic must be helped to accept his shame. He must be converted before he was killed. He must be beaten until he submitted.

'Fetch the instruments of persuasion!' Pitt shouted. In the corner of the room was a pile of hammers and wrenches. 'Easy confessions are false. Only through pain can the heretic be saved.'

'But I'm innocent!' Adum proclaimed.

Confessor Pitt stepped forward. The first blow fell, and Adum let out a groan of pain.

'None of us are innocent,' the confessor said. 'To claim purity is the vilest form of heresy.'

The porthole was white with driving clouds.

As the temperature dropped there were shapes within the pearly glow. Angular, feathered lines of ice crazed the panes.

'We've levelled off,' Viktor said.

Minka nodded. When the clouds cleared she could see a white plateau, punctuated only by the tall tufts of winter grasses sticking up through the snow. It looked like a hell of a place.

Minka looked up as Commissar Shand made his way forward to the pilot's cabin.

There was a brief glimpse through the open doorway, then he came back and stood bent over, one arm braced against the curved roof. He was alert and tense.

'Ten minutes,' he said.

They nodded, and started to get themselves ready.

The gallants continued long after Adum stopped moving.

Each one of them had to strike blows and afterwards Confessor Pitt blessed the weapons that they had anointed with the traitor's blood.

Carkal felt powerful and enthused with the Emperor's fierce will. 'Should we throw his remains out?'

Confessor Pitt turned his red eyes to Carkal's face. 'His soul must beseech the Emperor for mercy. Now his body is meat. Take it to the kitchens. It will nourish the hungry. It will fortify the righteous.'

They dragged the body along the corridor to the kitchens.

Gallants were there, stirring large square tanks of slop.

'Get that out!' one of them shouted, meaning the bloodied corpse.

'Confessor Pitt's orders. His body is meat. Let it nourish the hungry. Let it fortify the righteous.'

'I'm not that hungry!' the cook spat. 'Throw it out.'

Carkal felt a shiver of fear run through him. It was heresy to contradict the confessor. If he did not report this comment, then he too would be fertile ground for the seeds of unbelief.

They dumped the body out into the snow and Carkal went straight to the confessor's door and knocked.

'Enter!'

Inside, Confessor Pitt was kneeling on the floor, his top hat on his head, his chainsword laid out before him.

'I heard a traitor speak,' Carkal whispered. 'The cook did not want to use the flesh that we sent.'

Confessor Pitt took the handle of his chainsword. 'Tell me the words that he spoke.'

Carkal repeated them.

There were scabs of semi-congealed blood at Confessor Pitt's tear ducts. His mad staring eyes looked to Carkal's face. 'He is not righteous. Take hammers. Take knives. Help him to understand that he is tainted. And when he is done, bring his head to me.'

They killed the cook and brought the head to Confessor Pitt.

It was misshapen with the beatings, and one eye had been gouged out.

'Did he confess?' Pitt demanded.

'Yes,' Carkal said. 'And then we tore out his tongue so that he could not take back his confession.'

Pitt put his hands on Carkal's shoulders. 'You did well, brother.'

That night Carkal was on duty again.

He felt buoyed up by the day's activities. He had revealed three more heretics to Pitt, and each of them had been forced to confess before being sent to the Emperor.

He felt worthy. Powerful. Successful. When he gave commands now he was listened to and he took it upon himself to go around the guard posts, making sure that each squad of gallants was doing their duty.

When he reached the front gate he could see a speck low, against the horizon.

'See that?' he said to the guards. The closest was Marchant, a pot-bellied, yellow-toothed man, with his chewed fingertips stained lho-stick yellow. Marchant squinted into the white distance.

'I don't,' he said.

'Something's coming.'

Marchant looked at him. 'We must tell the confessor...'

No one wanted to go. Carkal drew in a deep breath. The others were contemptible and weak. 'I will tell him.'

The tower had been dark and silent, but now there was a brooding watchfulness as Carkal approached. Confessor Pitt was working inside. He hurried forwards. He'd not been inside since they had taken it. Two of the Brotherhood were standing guard at the wire fence gates that opened to the steps inside.

'I have a message for the confessor,' Carkal said. 'Tell him that there is a vehicle approaching.'

'Who is it?'

'I don't know.'

The guards nodded Carkal inside. Green light flickered in the air. 'You go tell him. The password is "Hope is eternal".'

Carkal took a deep breath and hurried past them. As he put his foot onto the steps there was a metallic clang high above him that might have been a bell striking, and corposant light began to crackle above him. He mounted the steps and paused for a moment before the dark carved doorway. He took a deep breath and plunged inside.

'Who walks here?'

Carkal paused for a moment. He spun round and standing at his left was one of the tower guards, the man's face obscured behind a visored helmet.

'I am Carkal,' he announced. 'I am here to see the confessor.' He repeated the words he had been given and the guard motioned for Carkal to move inside.

Carkal started up the steps. There was a heavy sense of vigilance. He had the strange feeling that Confessor Pitt was watching each step he took, but his faith kept him strong, the conviction that the Emperor loved him, and hated his enemies.

By the time Carkal had reached the first floor he could hear voices in the darkness. Whispering, rambling, incoherent, immaterial, incessant. By the time he reached the second floor he was trembling. He reached the floor where the astropathic choir was situated and mounted the last step slowly, reluctantly, and saw with relief the figure of Confessor Pitt standing in the broken doors of the vaulted choir chamber.

Carkal hurried forward and fell to his knees, clutching the confessor's robes. Pitt turned and looked down on him. His eyes were bleeding freely and the skin of his cheeks was tugged upwards. His eyeballs bulged. It was hard to read his expression.

'Lord. There is a vehicle approaching.'

Pitt grasped Carkal with both hands and Carkal shuddered at the touch.

Pitt's face was intent. '*He* has come?'

Carkal jittered. 'I don't know.'

The confessor grasped Carkal by the shoulders. '*He* is here! I feel it. It is time. Are you ready, my child?'

'Yes,' Carkal whispered, though he did not understand what

he should be ready for. But whatever it was, he would be faithful and ready.

PART SIX

'Death and destruction are never satisfied.
Their hungers are insatiable.
To the Unworthy I say this,
I shall bring ruin upon the heads of the faithless.'

                 – Song of the Shining Saint.

part six

ONE

The three remaining ornithopters came in from the north, low to the ground.

The storm threw them about. Minka felt the craft lurch and slow as the gale howled.

Shand seemed unaffected. He stood at the front, a hand on the fuselage, staring over their heads, as if daring any of them to show fear or timidity. The cabin door was open. Through the narrow opening Minka could see the pilot's back, and a small section of the narrow front screen, which was white with the storm. The pilot looked back and shouted something over his shoulder. Shand relayed the information to them all. 'We're bringing it down. Hold on.'

Minka and Viktor exchanged looks. There was nothing to hang on to.

'We're landing,' Minka announced. Laptev's eyes snapped open. He was pale and shaking. 'You alright?' she asked him.

He nodded, but he looked like he was going to be sick.

'Not long now,' she said. She could see they were close to the ground. The landscape was flat and white, broken only by frozen tussocks of winter grass.

They skimmed so close to the snow she felt she could reach out and touch it. Chief Commissar Shand put a hand to the curved roof. The pilot shouted, 'On three!'

There was a pause before he started counting.

'Three,' Minka heard and then suddenly there was a roar as they crashed down. There were shouts of alarm and pain. The craft bounced and skidded. The tumult lasted seconds and when at last it was done, Minka found herself upside down with snow down her collar and sleeves, and ice covering her face. There were groans of pain about her.

Minka kicked at the weight on top of her. The ornithopter was on its side, but she was still inside. The fuselage was full of debris. There was a gaping hole where Dreno had been sitting. She pulled herself towards it and felt the sting of the cold on her face. The opening was full of snow. She found Dreno and helped drag him out. There was blood running from his nose. The red was very vivid against the white.

'Troopers disembark!' a voice shouted. It was Commissar Shand. He was wading through the snow as if it were knee-deep water. He threw the hatch open. He grabbed Belus and pushed him through. 'Up!' he shouted. 'Out!'

Minka struggled to pull Dreno up. 'I'm fine,' he kept saying. She pushed him towards the hatch.

Commissar Shand was pulling the survivors out.

'Are you injured?' he demanded.

'I'm fine,' she said, though it wasn't true. The shock was passing and she felt as though she'd been beaten with truncheons. But she was good enough to fight. 'Just bruised.'

'Good. I'll get everyone out. Call the troops to order!'

Minka hauled herself up through the hatch as Commissar Shand dragged all the Cadians out who could still fight. She looked about, but she couldn't see the other craft. She clambered towards the front. She wanted to speak to the pilot to find out where they were, but as she got to the front of the ornithopter she saw through the cracked glass that he was slumped over the controls, neck bent at an unnatural angle.

A wing had broken, and the landing gear had torn away from the fuselage. A figure stumbled out. It was Prassan. He was carrying the vox-unit. He blinked and shook himself. 'Throne,' he said. 'What happened?'

'We crashed,' she told him.

'Where are the others?'

She spun about, and couldn't see anyone. 'I've no idea.'

Prassan blinked. He put his hand to his forehead and saw the blood on his fingers. 'Frekk. Which way are we supposed to go?'

'We'll work that out. See if you can raise the other ornithopters.'

Confessor Pitt stood on the steps of the astropathic tower as the vehicles approached. He stood alone, his face blood-stained, like a groom expecting his bride – but the newcomers, as they approached in a convoy of three vehicles, appeared to be more of the Brotherhood.

First came a halftrack, full of cold-looking warriors. Another halftrack came last. In the middle was a Richstar sedan, now draped with the banners of the Brotherhood.

An expectant hush fell across the crowd as the gilt-edged sedan came to a halt and the door opened, and after a long pause a figure stepped out. He was a thin cleric, with hooked nose and piercing blue eyes. He looked about, blinking away the cold, his face grave and authoritative. As he approached the top, Confessor Pitt fell to his knees. The gallants watched with awe as the newcomer lifted their cleric up, and spoke quiet words to him that none of them could hear.

Confessor Pitt's demeanour was submissive. They could barely imagine such a thing.

It took a few moments before the confessor stood. The two men embraced formally.

After another long moment, Confessor Pitt took the other man's hand and lifted it up.

'For four thousand years the Imperium has suffered under the rule of infidels and traitors! Today we have thrown off that brood of vipers. We have thrown off their oppression and raised the standard of redemption. Repent, brothers. The Imperium of Vandire is near! This is the true cardinal of the Gallows Cluster, the one who has kept the light of faith alive. The great mover. The one who was predicted. The Wielder of the Axe. The one who shall cut down the unfruitful trees. Brothers, I present the holiest, Cardinal Vettor.'

Gallants began to fall to their knees.

Carkal joined in, all of them shouting thanks and praise. He felt the eyes of the cardinal pass over him. They were cold and hard and hungry.

It was like a predator looking over a flock, seeking out the weak – and it left Carkal feeling guilty and exposed and vulnerable.

Cardinal Vettor accepted the adulation of the crowd.

He looked down on the Brotherhood with a mixture of pride and contempt. The Brotherhood were a weapon that had been many years in the making; the work of many of the faithful, who had brought centuries of dissent to a moment of action, through speeches, talks and covert conversations within the cells of the followers – with men like Shaliah, who, in his igno-rance, had thought they were returning the Gallows Cluster to the faith of their forefathers. And here they were, united like a band of the blind, each one led forward by the man in front.

He paused in the doorway to speak to Confessor Pitt. He kept his voice low. 'The astropathic choir has been kept pure?'

'No one has entered,' Pitt responded quietly. 'I have done all that you asked.'

Vettor lifted his hand in benediction, and spoke loudly enough for them all to hear. 'Bless you, my child. Let us go.'

The Cadians were under-equipped and exposed. In the cold and snow it took fifteen minutes to locate the other two ornithopters.

One of them had hit the ground nose first, killing many of the troopers inside. Colonel Sparker was amongst those who clambered out. He had broken his arm. He worked one-handed to help dig the other survivors and weapons out. Seven had died, including Sergeants Rosan and Var-druna, and eight more were too badly wounded to fight. In total there were ten squads of troopers.

Medic Hassan reset the colonel's arm. Sparker gritted his teeth as Hassan bandaged the splint in place. When Sergeant Tyson suggested that he should stay behind, he waved his hand in irritation. 'I'm coming with you,' he insisted.

The hand-held auspex showed that the site they were head-ing to was a mile to the north-west.

'Sir. We're about half an hour away,' Minka told Sparker.

Shand took the auspex from her. He and Sparker consulted together. They exchanged brief words.

'Right,' Sparker called. 'Move out!'

* * *

Confessor Pitt led Cardinal Vettor into the astropathic tower. The gallants followed behind – nervous, excited and apprehensive. They mounted the steps slowly, passing the dead who lay where they had fallen. When at last they reached the choir room, the darkness was quiet and watchful, and as Cardinal Vettor stepped over the doorway, it seemed as though a hundred voices started speaking at once in urgent and concerned tones. The words came from high above them, in the arching darkness of the astropathic chamber.

Cardinal Vettor stood and lifted his eyes to the hanging cages, the banks of servo-scribes, swaying banners and mouldering texts.

He put his hands together in benediction. 'You have not damaged anything?'

Confessor Pitt's eyes were bleeding again, the drops running down his cheeks and disappearing into his beard, like tears. 'No, sire.'

The warden lay where Pitt had killed him. The pool of blood had spread about him, and started to dry. 'But you killed this one.'

Confessor Pitt turned his head down to see. 'Yes, lord. He resisted.'

'Did he? Or were you just enjoying the killing?'

'He resisted, lord. Killing brings me no joy. The only happiness I have is in serving the Truth.'

Another warden shuffled forward. Pitt addressed him. 'Show respect. This is the true cardinal of the Gallows Cluster, the holiest man upon this planet.'

The warden bowed. 'Welcome, lord. Forgive us our poor welcome. We are but wardens of the astropathic choir. We serve the Emperor and we obey.'

'*Obey*. Good,' Cardinal Vettor said, savouring the words. He moved forward. He let his fingers trace the brass pipes that ran about the base of the chamber. At the end were the docking ports of the maintenance servitors. They were dressed in the green of the Astra Telepathica, the sign of the aquila branded into the skin of their chests. They had neither eyes or tongues, only ridged pipes that filled their sutured mouths, and wound bundles of wires attached to their eye sockets.

As Vettor moved closer to them they started to shake. The pipes twitched rhythmically and the three bodies rocked back and forth, a low moan sounding deep in their throats.

'Sorry, lord,' the warden said. 'The boundary between our world and the immaterium is thin here. There are minds here that are tuned to things that common men cannot see.'

Cardinal Vettor looked up. From the shadows above there was a scream or shout and then a babble of many voices.

'They feel the coming,' Vettor said. His eyes were wide.

Above them the screaming grew louder. It was wild and incoherent. The cages started to shake and rattle. From the shadows came the sound of wardens' voices shouting in alarm and anger. Even the servitors rocked back and forth. A low keening came from their plugged throats.

There was the sound of a shot, and then blood dripped down. It puddled on the marble floor. The screaming continued. More voices now. Another shot, and a third.

The servitors rocked back and forth, like the delirious inmates of an asylum. Confessor Pitt hit one of them. The moaning did not stop. He hit them again.

'Stop,' the cardinal said. There was such command in his voice that Confessor Pitt reacted immediately. The low keening continued as the servitors rocked faster. Carkal tried not to hear it but the lobotomised movements were strangely sickening.

The voices from high above were incoherent babbling. They rose in pitch and volume.

'What is happening?' Confessor Pitt demanded from the warden.

'There is a storm in the immaterium,' the warden hissed. He looked up as a fourth shot rang out. 'Please. You must leave. It is not safe!'

A fifth shot rang out. And a sixth.

'My lord, I am so sorry!' the warden stammered. 'Please. This way.'

Blood now drizzled from the hanging cages in half a dozen torrents. It splattered down, splashing their legs. Cardinal Vettor was unaffected. 'Confessor Pitt. Give me your weapon.'

Confessor Pitt passed the pistol, handle first, to the cardinal. Vettor looked down on it as a gobbet of hot blood splashed his neck.

Vettor put his head back and let the blood fall into his open mouth.

The warden started to back away. 'Lord...' he said.

Vettor lifted the gun and fired into the nearest servitor. The body slumped forward.

The warden gasped in horror. 'Please, sir. No! They are part of the dampening system! They keep us...'

Vettor swung the gun round and fired it point-blank into the warden's face. There was a stink of burnt flesh as the man fell backwards, dead.

TWO

Waves of infantry swarmed against the gatehouse of the cathedral as the ornithopters disappeared from view.

Celestian Simmona looked to where the chief enforcer was standing at the base of the parapet. He was a lonely figure, rejected by the people of his adopted planet and betrayed by his master.

'Can you trust him?' she asked Bendikt.

The general narrowed his eyes. 'I do not know. But he has no other friends on this world. And so far he has done all he promised.'

The Cadians and Sisters of the Ebon Chalice put up a determined defence as the Brotherhood brought up their ordnance, mounted on the back of tracked carriages. Gaping dark Medusa barrels pointed directly at the walls of the gatehouse, while Earthshakers aimed skyward.

Dido was among the troopers of the Cadian 101st who

manned the ramparts. Her squad were still in their formal dress uniform.

'Didn't you hear the news?' Captain Firwuud snapped as he paced up and down with the command squad of Second Platoon.

'I thought we'd go down looking good,' Dido told him.

Firwuud laughed. 'You mean we don't look good?'

'Captain, I'm sorry, but it's time someone told you.'

Firwuud laughed again. But he was soon calling for reinforcements as the Brotherhood spread around the perimeter walls and the Cadian defenders on the left-hand ramparts were spread dangerously thin.

Dido took her place with the others, firing down into the massed ranks of the enemy. They used cargo 8s and scaling ladders to scramble up the walls. By sheer weight of numbers the enemy were starting to get close to assaulting the top of the ramparts. Cadian supplies of ammunition began to run thin. As the first few enemy reached the top of the parapet, reserves were thrown in. Storms of las-bolts flickered and rose like an electric storm reaching a crescendo of destruction, and then the Brotherhood's heavy weaponry added to the assault.

General Bendikt and his staff had made an impromptu command post in the sheltered lee of the gatehouse. His vox-officer was in constant communication with General Kamak, whose 66th Barolan Mechanised were fighting their own battle around the starport.

'Can you hold them?' Bendikt demanded.

Kamak's voice was deep and determined. *They have left thousands dead. It was as if they did not think that we would fire on them.*

'They imagined your loyalty to the Richstars was greater than that to the Emperor.'

Kamak's laugh was humourless. *'Well, we have shown that they were wrong.'*

After half an hour the Cadians tried to raise a vox-link to the ornithopters to check on their progress, but there was no response. 'Atmospherics,' the vox-officer said.

At that point an Earthshaker shell roared overhead.

'Someone's clearly taught them how to fire,' Adjutant Mere stated, as the shells impacted against the low sloped walls of the gatehouse and landed in the cathedral courtyard behind them. They hit the flat roofs of the Basilika and the derelict wings crumbled under the high explosive, while the cathedral gardens were full of hissing shrapnel.

One shell tore just over the heads of the command staff. Even Colour Sergeant Daal ducked. The shell impacted on the dome of the cathedral, and chunks of masonry tumbled down the side of the building and crashed into the cobbled yard with an explosion of dust and rockcrete. The Cadians moved closer to the wall as more rounds rained down. Shrapnel whistled as it ricocheted off the rockcrete walls. Then another round fell, and a third.

The only person who did not flinch was Celestian Simmona. 'General, you have a sacred duty here. You cannot let this unholy rabble take control of the cathedral. It's symbolic importance within the sector is immeasurable.'

Bendikt spoke through gritted teeth. 'Thank you, Celestian. I am well aware of that. But until the astropathic tower is retaken we are deaf and dumb. The Imperium has no idea of the heresy happening here, and we cannot call in the aid that we need.'

Another shell drowned out his words.

Celestian Simmona had to shout to be heard. 'How long until your troops take the tower?'

More shells impacted. Bendikt could not tell her that he had not heard from the troops he'd sent since they had departed. He felt powerless and impotent, one-handed and without the military strength he needed. 'I cannot tell you. What I do know is that the conditions they are facing are brutal.'

Celestian Simmona started to speak, but as she did so the man standing beside her slumped against her, blood running from his mouth. She spun round, thinking that he had been hit by shrapnel. But as she did so she saw the Brotherhood's warriors inside the cathedral.

There were hundreds of them, swarming from the derelict wings of the Basilika.

'General, they have come up through the catacombs!' she called.

Mere stepped in front of the general as the members of his command squad closed protectively about him. Pistol raised, he fired off a salvo at the enemy, but there were too many of them, and too few Cadians. 'Cadia stands!' a voice roared, and Mere was shoved aside as General Bendikt swept towards the enemy, fighting one-handed.

It was all the adjutant could do to keep up.

The snow was deep and soft enough to make the going slow.

It took an hour for the Cadians to get within eye-sight of Nullem Apek.

A road that ran from what Minka guessed was the Evercity cut a straight line across the plateau. The end was lost in sheets of driving mist and snow, while before her rose the dark mass of the astropathic tower, its upper floors wreathed in blue light. Half buried in the snow were signs that read 'Restricted Area. Deadly force authorised'.

Shand led the force round to the back of the fortifications. Soon the Cadians were within a hundred yards of the rear fence. Rather than sending someone else, Minka took the job of cutting the wire herself. She'd done this many times in her days on Kasr Myrak. She took the wire cutters and crawled forward, cut through the hoops of razor wire, and then made a long, low flap through the fence, wide enough for four troopers to crawl through at a time.

She slipped through and kept moving forward, then took up a position with her carbine.

The others came forward as fast as possible. They followed Minka, slipping through the flap, and crawling through the snow towards the rearmost rockcrete pillbox.

The Cadians moved silently. They used hand signals now. Silent. Quick. Efficient. Outside the rear door of the pillbox was a low hump. As she crawled closer Minka realised what it was: a handful of bodies, now half buried with driven snow.

She used it as cover as she led her squad forward. She paused as the Brotherhood sentries made their way across from the nearest pillbox. They were keeping to the same patterns, the same routines, following the same paths trodden in the snow. Their patterns were too easy and predictable.

Rabble, she thought, keeping her head down as the sentries made their way to the back door of the pillbox, stamped their feet to get the snow off, and went inside.

They pulled the door closed behind them, but she lay listening, and did not hear the clunk of the lock being engaged. In a moment she was up, Dreno and Belus right behind her, knives drawn. Minka put her hand to the locking bar. It moved a fraction. She closed her eyes for a moment to remove the ice glare and then burst inside.

The dead brothers were still warm, their blood still dripping, as Minka and her squad wiped their knives clean and moved out of the rockcrete bunker.

'Good work,' the chief commissar said, as he joined her. Other squads were already moving forward.

Minka didn't think she'd ever heard the commissar speak kindly. Her cheeks coloured. 'Thank you, sir.'

'Take Rosan and Vardruna's squads counter-clockwise. We attack in one minute.'

Minka checked her chronometer, and saluted.

The defensive camp was a doughnut shape about the astropathic tower, with razor wire fences on the inner and outer circuits. In the middle the tower rose up, sheer and vertical, with crackling witchlight flickering high above. The air fizzed with electric charge. They hurried towards it, and then cut their way through the inner circuit. In the no-man's-land, the snow was deeper, and untouched. They waded towards the base of the tower, and then crept round it.

Shand led them. As he worked his way round to within sight of the entranceway, he paused. There were twenty men on guard. Their attention was directed towards the main gateway, but they were heavily armed and armoured, and Shand knew enough about fighting to know that warriors with faith punched hard.

He checked his chronometer.

There were five seconds left.

He knew that the other half of his force had moved around

the other side. They would be waiting, just like he was, ready. He signed to the others, with five fingers held up.

Five, four…

On two, Shand was out, leading the charge. He saw the enemy turn towards him, and lift their guns. Their backs were turned to the Cadians coming up behind them. They were dead men, Shand knew, as he lifted his bolt pistol and fired.

Minka came at the Brotherhood at a sprint. She fired her carbine from her waist, leapt over a fallen brother, killed and kept moving, over and again.

Commissar Shand was already inside the opening to the tower.

Minka leapt up the stairs and her squad blasted their way into the entrance hall. Brothers slammed against walls, were punched back by a furious fusillade of las-fire. As more came from a side-corridor Minka threw a grenade in low, sent it skidding through their feet.

She rolled, fired from the floor, a double tap into the gut of a terrified brother. This was slaughter, she thought, as she rolled up to her feet and killed three more who came bumbling through the doorway, fingers scrabbling for their triggers.

She started forward, and there was a hail of las-fire as Shand led them upwards. His pistol was smoking.

'Keep moving!' he ordered.

Bendikt's clip was empty. The next man was thin and wiry. His fingers clawed at the general's face. Bendikt pistol-whipped him. The man fell back in an explosion of teeth and bloody spittle, and the general was onto the next, ramming his stump into a face.

The blow jarred Bendikt's arm, but it threw the other man off balance. In a moment Mere was next to him, grunting with exertion as he drove the butt of his rifle into the face of another enemy.

It was brutal, close-quarters action. Bendikt was dimly aware of shouts of alarm spreading through the Cadians on the parapets. This was a moment of ultimate danger for a fighting force, when they suddenly found themselves surrounded, cut off and assaulted from a new and unforeseen direction.

He felt a surge of fury rise through him as if – by superhuman exertion – he could save them all from this moment of crisis by his own monumental exertion. And for a moment he thought he might do it. He hoped that he could kill all these enemies, could destroy the lot while his warriors held the enemy off on the parapets.

Of course, it was too much to hope for. He heard the curses as the Cadians about him were wounded and cut down. He sensed the thinning of the officers about him, heard even Mere go down with a grunt of pain.

And then he realised that he was standing alone. Onehanded, with an empty bolt pistol clip, desperately fighting off the hands that were grasping for him. Something clubbed him on the back of the head. He swung and punched, shouted 'Cadia stands!' to rally his own courage.

Except he didn't. The words barely fell from his bloody lips. He was on his knees, with booted feet all about him, and he feared that he was about to breathe his last.

Janka's squad held the doorway of the astropathic tower as newly alerted warriors swarmed out of the barrack blocks and charged.

Rodin and Streck were kneeling on the opposite side of the

doorway, with Grogar lying between them. The three veterans put out a punishing amount of firepower. It was deliberate and targeted, and downed each of the Brotherhood who got as far as the doorway.

Prassan was crouched low, with his back to the stairs, covering the northern arc of the tower. The Brotherhood were coming at them from all directions. The trooper next to him was Sartak. He shivered, but not from the cold. 'What the hell is happening up there?' he hissed.

Prassan could feel the static as well, and as las-bolts streaked towards him he threw himself forwards. The snow was now crusted hard with ice.

'It's getting colder,' Prassan said.

He slammed a fresh powercell into his lasrifle, but within ten shots it was already starting to flag.

'Bad batch,' Sartak hissed and shouted up to where Grogar lay. 'Got more powercells?'

There was a pause as Grogar tried to push himself up, but he could not move. He realised with sudden horror that his jacket had frozen to the ground, and that the slush of the stairs was now slick, black ice.

Lightning struck the tower in rapid succession, and blue witchfire started to play along their weapons.

'What the hell is happening?' Grogar hissed.

'I don't want to know,' Prassan said.

Sartak turned to him. 'I've never heard you say that before.'

'Well…' Prassan started, but he didn't know what to say. His powercell was starting to flag and this was the last one he had left. 'I'm too busy trying to stay alive.'

The screams from the astropathic choir chilled Carkal's soul. He was one of fifteen brothers standing outside the choir room.

'Do not look!' Confessor Pitt ordered. He stood in the broken doorway, the unhinged doors slumped to each side, facing outwards.

There were panicked shouts coming up the staircase. The sound of firing. There were intruders inside the building. Somehow the warriors of the Temple had been betrayed. As a movement it was something that they had become used to, over the centuries. The might of the authorities were stacked against them – the armies, the civil enforcers and the militant arms of the Inquisition. But all these powers were directed by a corrupt faith, a rotten Ecclesiarchy, and venal opportunism that had nothing to do with faith, fealty and certitude.

'Stand firm,' Confessor Pitt ordered. 'Our enemies seek to stifle the True Faith! They are the forces of heresy. Defy them with the God-Emperor's Holy Will.'

Carkal gripped his lasrifle hard. He knew he was going to die. But he believed in the Emperor. He had only ever killed in the Emperor's name. When he died he would be united with the God-Emperor, and would sit with Him by the Golden Throne.

Behind him the howls of the surviving astropaths were like the screams of demented souls. But whereas before they had been speaking with different voices, now they started to howl together. The sounds made his ears bleed.

'Have faith!' Confessor Pitt was shouting. He began to chant psalms and the warriors with him joined in, their voices drowned out by the howls from within the chamber.

As the screams became one it was like a single voice projecting out into the immaterium. A beam of focused light cutting to the heart of the maelstrom.

A clarion call. A psychic wail of anguish that was a beacon for those who were waiting for it.

And for them it was a summons.

Three systems away, on the war-plains of Nepata, the coven of Drakul-zar's Augurs heard the hail and the chainmailed war-chief gave the sign for the conjuration to begin. At the drop of Drakul-zar's hand, the throats of a thousand apostates were cut, the minds of a hundred psykers were burned out. Dust whipped up as a vortex grew in the air above their heads.

The fabric of the material world began to spin. It sucked dirt and tumbleweed towards it. The spinning accelerated. Sky and earth mixed in a whirlpool, and then the centre of the maelstrom began to glow with a putrid red light. Waiting in close order were the armies of the Scourged. At Drakul-zar's signal, the front ranks began to march forward, their footsteps heavy with steel-shod boots.

The beacon had been sent. The armies were ready.

The capital of the Gallows Cluster was about to fall to the armies of heresy.

THREE

Chief Commissar Shand led the Cadians up the broad spiralling staircase through the astropathic tower. They were one floor below the choir chamber, and they could hear the screams from above as balls of green witchlight crackled through the air.

The Brotherhood mounted a desperate defence as Commissar Shand charged forwards and roared his war cry.

Minka felt the same rage and fury she had first experienced in her home town of Kasr Myrak. It was like a storm behind her, pushing her forward. She had a moment's view of a wall of lasrifles, all aimed at her, and then the blinding flare as they fired.

Sparks burst from the walls as the two bands closed. Corposant played along the stone as the tower groaned and pulsed. There was a sound like tearing steel, and green witchfire began to hang in sheets in the air as shouts reverberated from above.

The Brotherhood did not seem to know which way to turn. There were panicked shouts as the Cadians charged. Minka dropped and rolled, and fired from the floor. The Brotherhood scattered. Shand cut down any who stood, and then the others fell back in panic and the Cadians were after them. Minka kept close to Shand as he took the steps three at a time.

He was merciless as he cut down the stragglers. The Cadians had to hack their way through them, but as they mounted the steps at the top of the stairs, the Brotherhood had nowhere left to run to. They were making a stand, forming a living wall across the broken doors of the astropathic tower. And at their back stood a single warrior in a black top hat, eyes wide and bloody, chainsword in one hand, pistol in the other.

The wild warrior stepped forward with a roar of fury. He met Shand in the middle, chainsword sparking as it struck the commissar's blade. Shand's momentum slowed and then paused as the other warrior threw himself at the Cadian with berserk strength and fury, and then – in a terrible moment – Shand was forced backwards one step and then another, and then the Brotherhood took heart and courage and they dashed forward.

Shand was driven back to the brink of the staircase. He teetered there with his feet scrabbling on the stair's edge and fought to retain his position. He had seen enough of the galaxy to know that this was a moment when the fate of worlds could be decided.

Minka knew it too. As the mad-eyed warrior swung wildly at Commissar Shand, the light within the astropathic chamber grew wild and incoherent. The temperature began to drop and Minka felt the sudden chill in the air about her. From the choir room came voices screaming in many tongues.

The shouts grew in volume, their unwords incoherent and sickening.

A ball of light began to form in the darkness of the chamber. It was a roiling sphere of knotted light, spiralling in on itself in an impossible fashion. She had seen such light before, in the dying hours of her planet.

Any Cadians who had been on their home world in those fateful hours understood that something terrible was about to happen as spears of green light stabbed out from within the astropathic chamber, and low moans and wild laughter could be heard. Shand parried desperately and sparks flew off the chainsword's razor teeth.

'Warp portal!' Shand shouted. 'We have to destroy it!'

This was a moment when a commander had to lead. Laptev was just behind her.

'With me!' Minka hissed and leapt forward with a snarl of ferocity, carving her way like a wedge into the squad of the Brotherhood. She cut down one, two, three men, but with each step she could feel her momentum slowing. She spun around but she was alone and isolated as the wail of insane voices poured out of the astropathic choir. She fought her way to the doorway, where the brass doors hung precariously, and had a brief glimpse of a blinding red-and-purple hole in the fabric of reality, through which armed figures were streaming.

They had plain metal helms with nose slits and punched round vision slots. From their carapace breastplates hung links of mail and crude brigandine, scraps of Guard uniform now covered with tightly wound prayer strips. They stank of death.

Minka knew in an instant that something terrible was going on here. These were not the shaven-headed hotheads of the Brotherhood. They were the shock troopers of the Archenemy. And they were streaming towards her.

Celestian Simmona led the charge to save General Bendikt. The Sisters made a tight wedge as they drove into the Brotherhood. Disciplined bolter fire cut the trespassers down in their droves, and then they closed to assault range and felled the Frateris Militia like wheat.

Rudgard Howe fell in with them, found Bendikt and stepped over the general's body to protect him. He blasted a Frateris militiaman. The man-stopper threw the other man back off his feet.

Another Frateris was crawling towards the general's body. The shaven-headed militiaman lifted his hand. 'Save me,' he whispered.

'What from?' Celestian Simmona demanded.

'Save me from the witches,' the man hissed. He reached for Howe and the chief enforcer stepped away and fired. The shot lifted the body a hand's breadth off the floor.

Bendikt pushed himself up. He was bleeding from a cut in his chest, and there was blood running from his nose. 'Throne!' he gasped.

'They came up through the Basilika,' Rudgard Howe told him.

Bendikt found Mere. He had taken a las-shot to his chest, and there was a pool of blood leaking from his carapace. Medic Banting was already crouched over him with a syringe of sealant in his hand.

'He's alive,' Banting reported.

'Good,' Bendikt said. 'Keep him that way.'

Bendikt looked up. The Cadians were still holding the parapets. Kastelek had gathered a counter-assault squad.

He came rushing up. 'General, are you well?'

'No,' Bendikt said. 'But I am alive, thank the Throne. But clearly we need to plug that hole they crept through. Chief enforcer, you know the tunnels. Kastelek, you and I will hold the parapet. Colour Sergeant Daal, take your best squads. Go with the chief enforcer and seal whatever cavity they crawled through.'

The Scourged poured through the rent in reality. They came forward silently, landing on the marble floor and charging, cutting down servitors, attendants, brothers and Cadians alike. They were heavily armed and armoured and shrugged off small-calibre rounds and las-bolts alike, hacked and shot, and kept moving forwards.

It took a moment for the Brotherhood to understand what was happening, and they fell back to protect themselves as the Scourged cut them down.

Carkal spun about. He had been struggling with a Guardsman, but now he threw him off.

The sound of las-bolts hitting flesh was distinctive. It was an unmistakable sound, wet and sizzling, that was accompanied by the scent of scorched flesh. 'Confessor Pitt!' he roared as a hail of las-bolts cut down the figures next to him. 'We have been betrayed!'

Confessor Pitt paused briefly, his eyes wide to the freakish green light. He saw the warriors of the Scourged cutting their way out of the choir chamber. 'Cardinal?' he roared, but the only sound was the howl of tortured astropaths, the war chant of the Scourged and the cries of betrayal.

Dido was with the counter-attack squad. She liked tunnels even less than she liked heights, but she was damned if she was going to turn down any special mission. She bit the inside of her cheek as Daal handed out pistols, close combat weapons, bandoliers of grenades and melta charges, and gave each trooper a fresh set of powercells.

'Get yourself a helmet,' Daal told her.

There was a pile of helmets and flak armour outside the medic's tent. Dido took a helmet, adjusted the straps and as she strode over to the others she took a bill hook from among the dead and hung it from her belt. She checked herself. She had a pistol and a bandolier and she wanted to get back into the fray.

'Right, move out,' Daal ordered, and he led them along the tracks that the Frateris had made. When the Sisters had come they had fled back towards their entryways. They lay sprawled as they had fallen, blood pillowing about their lifeless bodies. The trail led them through a storeroom, along an unused corridor, and then down a flight of steps, where two Sisters of Battle stood guard.

They gave Chief Enforcer Howe a cold look, but Dido came at the end of the file of warriors and the blonde Sister caught her eye.

'May the Emperor protect you,' the Adepta Sororitas said.

Dido put her finger to her forehead in a brief salute. 'He's watching me,' Dido said, 'and I'm not going to disappoint Him.'

And then they were moving down the worn, ancient stairs, only dimly lit with stray beams of light filtering through broken doorways and roofs.

Daal led, Howe behind him, offering advice on which way to go.

They kept descending, pausing at each level and listening. The deeper they went the quieter the battle on the surface, the more threatening the silence, until at last they were feeling their way along excavated corridors in the pitch-dark, the only illumination coming from the stablight underslung from Daal's carbine.

Dido stayed at the back. She had a strange sense that they were being hunted, and turned, expecting to see figures behind her. But each time she swung round there was darkness, and silence, and the oppressive weight of the mountain above her.

Minka knelt and fired. She hit the foremost warrior, but he shrugged it off, kept moving forward, shooting off deadly salvos.

She switched aim. You had to hit warriors like this in the softer areas where the carapace interlocked. Throats. Armpits. Visors. But it was hard nailing an armpit in the dark.

It took her six shots before the lead man fell. Three more Scourged surged from behind him.

Carkal ducked as a Guardsman fired at him. He slammed the stock of his rifle into the torso of a Scourged, felt it scrape off panelled armour, and cursed as his las-bolts impacted on the armoured warrior making barely more than a dent.

A shot hit him in the small of the back, and his legs gave way.

He crawled backwards, his left leg useless. He left a smear of blood on the ground. The pain was excruciating. One of the Scourged had a serrated hatchet. He came at Carkal with a snarl. Carkal used his gunstock to turn the blow aside, then reversed the weapon and fired.

The shot hit the Scourged under the chin. There was a hiss of burning flesh and then the warrior fell forward. Two more Scourged appeared above him. They were hunting for wounded. He tried to fire but he couldn't hold them both off. He knew he had bare moments left. He scrambled onto his hands and remaining knee, desperately trying to retreat. The warrior stepped over him. He felt a boot on his back. It crushed the breath from his body, and then fire stabbed into his back. He couldn't tell if he'd been knifed or shot. It did not matter much. There was blood in his mouth and nose. Boots stepped on and over him. There were grunts and shouts and snarls in the room about him.

A Cadian was above him. She ducked a blow, body slammed the man about to kill him, and then shot two bolts in the man's gut, beneath his body plate.

She kept moving forward. Carkal covered her back, firing one-handed.

Dido felt the breath on the back of her neck as the blade descended.

She spun about and twisted, and heard the grunt of surprise as the blade slammed into Fryd, who was standing in front of her.

She rolled to the side as a second knife swung down and shouted a warning. Daal's stablight swung about, and Dido had a brief image of a four-armed warrior, coming at her.

A knife caught her arm and she dropped the pistol as blood poured down her hand.

She struggled to pull the billhook from her belt, kicked upwards as a knife stabbed down and went straight into the flesh of her foot.

She snarled with pain and kicked sideways, throwing the enemy off balance, and then swung her billhook forward and felt it impact with the dull weight of chopping flesh.

* * *

Confessor Pitt charged the Scourged, wielding his chainsword double-handed.

The first blow caught one low in the gut. The man doubled over as the razor-sharp teeth gnawed through carapace armour, flesh, bones and then came back out the other side with a roar. The next was a downward blow that cut a man through the shoulder, cleaving his chest in half. The head of the third flew off with a spray of viscera. By the time he reached the doorway of the astropathic chamber he was just warming up.

Faith kept him moving. Conviction was his armour. Fidelity his shield.

At his side Chief Commissar Shand moved with poise and efficiency, his blade dark with the blood of the Scourged. The two of them battled the Scourged backwards.

The Cadians opened fire over Dido's head.

The catacomb was incandescent as the shots tore into the assailant.

The hiss of burning flesh filled the narrow corridor. 'Hold fire!' Daal shouted at last.

He pushed his way along the corridor and stared down at the body. It was not a warrior of the Brotherhood.

'That's Meroë,' Rudgard said. 'Life-ward to the Patridzo.'

'What is he doing here?'

'I have no idea,' Rudgard said. He looked to Daal.

'What about the other one?'

They looked around now, suddenly expecting another attacker, but the tunnels were empty and still and silent. They turned back to the four-armed warrior.

Daal lifted his stablight. There was an armoured doorway before him, bolts drawn shut. He stepped forward and put his hand to the first bolt. 'Well, let's see what this is hiding.'

Confessor Pitt and Commissar Shand stood together, fighting desperately as the surviving Cadians and Brotherhood ran to help them.

'Destroy the portal!' Shand roared as he struggled to force a way forward. The Cadians responded with disciplined rigour, Minka among them. She had to duck the confessor's chainsword as it roared through the air.

She held back at a safe distance and picked her shots, aiming for visors. The Scourged fell, but not fast enough. There was no way they could hold them all back. The heretic shock troopers were coming at a jog. They were more heavily armed than the troopers of the 101st. They had supplemented their carapace with skirts of chainmail and crude brigandine. The armour told. They were winning the firefight as the two bands of warriors stood bare feet apart and fired into one another. And they had reinforcements coming at pace.

Minka killed three of them before a las-bolt hit her in the hip. The shot spun her round and she fell to the floor, landing with a grunt of pain. Anyone on the floor was easy game. She struggled to find her attacker. She had not seen the shooter. She pushed herself up as a shape paused over her. She waited for the blow to fall, but instead hands caught at her.

'How do we stop this thing?' a voice hissed. It was Viktor.

Minka had no idea. 'Say a prayer,' she suggested. 'Or throw a grenade.'

'Give me your grenade.' He tore it from her webbing. 'Cover me,' he said, and darted forward. 'You say the prayers.'

'I believe in the one true Emperor,' Minka prayed. 'I believe in his Holy Church and the right of Cadia to be His strong right arm.' She clutched for her carbine as another shape loomed over her. She could smell this one. He had the stink of old blood and metallic dust about him. But what concerned her most was the hatchet, dripping gore, that he swung at her.

She managed – just – to roll to the side.

He swung again, and the blow fell closer this time. She knew she wouldn't get away a third time. Across the room she heard Viktor shout in anger as he was cut down. She looked about. The room felt suddenly empty of Cadians now. It was filling up with Scourged warriors, their blank metal helmets giving them a sinister appearance. The first was standing at the top of the stairs, firing down.

Minka cursed that she did not have her grenade left. She grabbed her carbine, opened the side panel, pulled out a connector and shoved the muzzle forward.

It was an old Cadian trick she'd learnt in Kasr Myrak. The explosion ripped through the chamber, throwing the Scourged back.

Viktor had fallen in the lee of the broken brass doors. He crawled forward, the grenade in one hand, but he was too weak to throw.

'For the Emperor!' he hissed, but he was too far to affect the infernal warp gate.

'Traitor!' Confessor Pitt roared as he came face to face with the man he had known as Cardinal Vettor.

'I am no traitor. I have remained true to the facts. The Imperium of Man is doomed. It cannot survive. Only a fool would stay loyal to a dying cause.'

'Where is your faith?' Confessor Pitt demanded.

'I do not believe in faith. I believe in facts.'

Confessor Pitt spat at facts. They were traps for the weak-willed and unsteady. Facts divided people, faith united them. He rebelled against Vettor's facts with all his being, the skin of his cheeks tugging in fury as he threw himself at the other man. The chainsword raged as it thrummed through the air. Vettor jumped back as it passed through the place where he had been standing.

Scourged warriors threw themselves before Vettor, and Confessor Pitt ripped them apart. But within moments they had surrounded him, and it was all he could do to hold them back.

In the catacombs beneath the acropolis, Daal had his las-pistol ready as he pulled the doorway open.

The hinges were old and stiff. They creaked as he pulled.

Inside there was darkness.

But it was a gloom that was alive, watchful, poised.

It had the musty, dry smell of a crypt. Daal's stablight panned about the room. There were niches dug into the walls, filled with the mouldering remains of ancient bodies, mummified by the centuries, ancient uniforms and clothes and grave-goods brown and frayed with age.

Something moved. His stablight jerked to track it and illuminated a young girl, standing before him. Her skin looked strangely artificial, with plump rouged cheeks and full lips and neon-yellow eyes. She spoke.

'I am Lady Bianca Richstar. Gerent of Tokai. Who are you?'

'I am Colour Sergeant Daal, of the Cadian 101st.'

'Does that mean they have failed?'

'Who?'

'My cousin, the Patridzo.'

'Yes.'

'Good,' she said.

'But I cannot say that we have won. We are fighting desperately to hold back the Brotherhood. They have rebelled against the Imperium.'

'Where is the cardinal?'

'Dead.'

'Throne. It seems as though this crypt has been the safest place. Maybe I should stay here.'

She paused as Daal tried to understand what this all meant.

'We are here to stop the enemy from infiltrating the Basilika,' he said finally.

'Stop shining that light in my eyes!' Bianca said, sweeping imperiously forward. 'If what you tell me is true then I think you need my help.'

Chief Commissar Shand tugged the grenade from Viktor's grasp and body-barged a Scourged trooper aside. He rammed the pommel of his sword into the face of the next fighter, shielded his eyes from the sickening warp light and struggled towards it.

The hole pulsed like a living thing. It was like wading through bow waves of unholy energy. He felt blood in his throat. It was streaming from his nose and eyes. He was ten feet off when he could go no further and with a desperate call to the Holy Emperor, he slung the grenade through the open maw.

It disappeared with a crackle of energy. There was a pause, while everyone expected a blast.

But there was none. At least, there was no explosion *here*. For a long moment nothing happened, and then with a sudden groan of unearthly voices, the warp rift began to spiral backwards. Vettor threw himself at the portal and the priest with bleeding eyes threw himself after, chainsword whining as he shouted, 'For the Emperor!'

As they disappeared into the swirling light, three final Scourged shock troopers leapt out in the opposite direction.

The third one was halfway through when, with a sudden gulp of swallowed air, the warp gate closed and his dissected torso fell to the ground and landed with a wet slap.

The warp gate had been closed. The shock troopers of the Scourged had nothing left now but to sell their lives as dearly as they could.

On the parapets of the cathedral, Bendikt stood, encouraging the Cadians as they weathered another assault from the Brotherhood.

Hesk found him as he fumbled to reload his pistol. He had a scrap of vellum in his hand. 'Sir!' he shouted.

Bendikt looked up and saw a girl approaching. There were Cadian warriors on either side of her. Daal. Dido. But there was something about them that showed that it was the girl who was giving orders.

He looked back at her. He knew he recognised her, but so much had happened in the last few days that it was a struggle for him to place her. He tried to recall her name, but she supplied it before he could do so. 'I am Gerent Bianca. I have been told by the chief enforcer that the Patridzo is dead.'

'We fear so,' Bendikt said. 'The Evercity has been lost to the forces of the Brotherhood.'

He signalled to the parapet, where the warriors of the Brotherhood were still throwing themselves against the ramparts. Bianca stepped forward to the parapet, and Bendikt put out a hand. 'Careful!' he said, but she looked at him with contempt, and looked out.

'They have died bravely. They are courageous warriors.'

'They are fanatics,' Bendikt said.

Bianca nodded. 'They make the finest warriors. Just think, if they could be persuaded to fight for us, we could put their fanaticism to use.'

'Yes,' Bendikt said. 'But how?'

'I think I have a solution,' Gerent Bianca said. She tilted her head down to where Daal's company stood over a grav-bier, upon which a body lay in ornate armour.

'What is that?' Bendikt said.

'It is the body of my forebear Ignatzio Richstar. If you allow me to present him to the Frateris, I have both the rank and the right to command them.'

FOUR

It was an hour since the warp portal had been sealed up.

The wind had dropped on the Supramonte Plateau and a gentle snow was falling around Nullem Apek. It only served to exaggerate the stillness and quiet. The Cadians were piling up their dead into the back of a truck. The wounded had been carried inside, where the medicae were stabilising the most serious, and patching up those who could walk.

Minka's hip had been filled with a gelatinous mixture of sealant and stapled closed. Opiates were just starting to kick in as she picked her way up the broad staircase towards the astropathic choir. It was slick with blood. Her hip ached and she used the butt of her lasrifle to keep herself steady. It was a charnel pit.

The Scourged wore plundered Guard uniforms, the symbols ripped off and replaced with the marks of the heretic. They'd be dragged out and burned, just as soon as someone sent some help up from the Evercity. She found men that she had killed. They looked smaller now.

Belus and Dreno were helping out in the medicae unit. Viktor had been stabilised. Jaromir had made it through, somehow, which surprised her the most. 'That was tough,' he'd said, slowly, when she'd shaken his hand.

'Tell me about it.' She slapped his arm. She'd seen him fighting furiously in the opening moments, but since then she had no idea what he had been doing. 'Well done.'

'Thank you, sarge.'

She found Jason slumped against the wall, a single shot wound to his chest. Lasmonn had bled out from a leg wound. Rustem was lying under two of the Brotherhood, a bayonet still embedded in her chest.

The only one left unaccounted for was Laptev.

Guards were on duty on either side of the ruined choir chamber. One of them stepped forward to stop her, but she waved him off.

'I'm not going in,' she said to them. 'I'm looking for Laptev.'

'Not seen him,' the guard said.

'Nor me.' Minka left the rest of her sentence unspoken. She'd seen the living and she'd been in the medicae chamber and seen who was dying, stabilised or recovering, which meant that Laptev had either fled, or was dead.

She hoped for the latter.

She found his body in the doorway of the antechamber, buried under three of the Scourged. She curled her lip in disgust as she dragged the heretic bodies off him. He'd gone down well.

Laptev's eyes were open, but there was no breath left in him. He'd been disembowelled, and his throat had been cut. 'Well fought, warrior,' she said, as she knelt down next to his body, put her hand to his face and closed his eyelids.

It hurt to see another dead Cadian. One fewer of the Imperium's finest Guardsmen. But her overwhelming feeling was relief. She kept her hand there to hold them closed. It was for the best, she thought.

There was movement further along, near the ruined doors of the astropathic choir. She pushed herself up, and limped towards it. She'd hoped it would be one of her own, but as she came closer she saw it was one of the Brotherhood, a young man with shaven head, thick eyebrows and long, dark lashes. They would have made him look almost pretty, if he hadn't been dying.

He'd been shot in the back, and there was blood at his mouth and nose and ears. His breath was coming in rattling breaths. He smiled when he saw her. The sight was chilling.

'For the Emperor,' he coughed through bloody lips.

Minka stared down at him without responding. Heretics appalled her, and worse. These fanatics were responsible for every dead Cadian that lay about.

'For the Emperor!' the boy hissed through bloody teeth.

Minka paused to lift her carbine. She put the barrel to his forehead. 'I do not know what Emperor you serve,' she said and fired.

EPILOGUE

It was a flight of Valkyries that landed at Nullem Apek. They brought enginseers to oversee the repair of the defences, and fresh troops to take over the garrison as the interior was cleaned of the dead and hosed down.

The numbers of the astropathic choir had been reduced by violence and insanity to a paltry handful of survivors, and support staff worked desperately to purge the place of the taint of Chaos and to get the apparatus working again.

It took them hours of prayer and sacred unctions to bring the choir back to some degree of functionality. Chief Commissar Shand had his right arm in a sling as he oversaw the repairs, and then made his way down the pockmarked staircases, out into the chill.

The first two Valkyries were full, the flight team closing the ramps.

Sergeant Lesk was waiting at the back of the last craft. She watched as the commissar crossed the snow towards her. She had fought well, he thought.

'All correct, sir?' she said.

'Yes, sergeant. And how are your squad?'

'Viktor went yesterday. Banting came up to bring them all back. Gave me one of his looks.'

'What look is that?'

'Like I'm a butcher.'

Shand laughed. It was rare for him to do so. 'It's your job to lead, his job to put soldiers back into battle. That is all the Emperor expects.'

They took their places on the benches as the ramp closed. The engines whined as the Valkyrie lifted off, and then they were skimming over the Supramonte.

'I hear our reinforcements have arrived,' Lesk said.

'Thank the Throne, yes.'

'So what next?'

Shand paused, considering how much to tell the sergeant. She was looking up at him in that way she had. Her indomitable spirit impressed him. 'Well. I think we have discovered how it is that the Scourged have managed to spread so quickly through the Gallows Cluster. Preying on the weak through an old heresy, and using portals like these. And now General Bendikt is in charge I think we can say that the opening moves have been played out. Think of this as the opening sequence. Now each of the commanders have a sense of each other, the real fight is yet to come.'

Sergeant Lesk nodded, and looked away.

'How old are you?' Shand asked after a long pause.

'Eighteen,' she said.

He puffed out his cheeks. 'You fight well for an eighteen-year-old.'

Minka made no obvious response, but he thought he saw a softening in her face. A slight colouring of her cheeks. She looked down for a moment. 'Thank you, sir.'

Once the reinforcements landed, the fight for the Evercity had begun in earnest with General Kamak's armoured columns spearheading the assault against the bands of gangers and Brotherhood who had not surrendered.

The fighting was fierce, but Bendikt marshalled the blunt might of the Imperium with ruthless efficiency. Gerent Bianca had protested vehemently, but she was the scion of a suspect house and he had a much greater war to conduct. The Evercity was a hindrance he had to clear away to allow him a clean slate.

In a week the battle for the Evercity was done. Survivors picked their way through it with stunned faces, feet wrapped in rags and trousers belted with knotted cord. Smoke rose from the ruins as indentured work-gangs cleared the collapsed houses from the narrow streets. The air stank of charred wood and dust and decay as the crushed bodies began to putrefy and black clouds of flies steamed out of cracks in the broken hab-blocks like smoke.

The ruin of the Evercity was both majestic and terrible. Even the Patridzo's palace lay broken, the once opulent sweeping staircase now open to the sky, high ceilings fallen into the gilded rooms, the opulent furniture lying about in splinters, and broken icons of the Emperor Pantokrator, worked with gold leaf, lying shattered. And over it all squatted the pockmarked ruins of the fortress-cathedral, its golden dome now cracked open, like a shattered egg.

In the plain, the tent city was a burnt ruin. Where the Brotherhood had camped, the land had been reformed by the ferocity of the orbital bombardment. Smoke still gouted up from the tectonic rifts. It rose into the eastern sky like a colossal pulsating brain.

Only the starport was left almost untouched. And it was there that the Cadian 101st, Hell's Last, waited for re-embarkation.

Mere was on crutches as he accompanied Bendikt to the lander's exclusive ingress.

He turned to take one last look back at the ruins of the Evercity. 'We have saved them from themselves,' he said.

'We have,' Bendikt said.

For a moment neither of them spoke. Their minds were full of unspoken thoughts. The devastation was almost complete. 'Did you hear?' Mere said.

'What?' Bendikt spoke with irritation.

'There is a regiment of Praetorian Guard aboard the transport.'

'Yes,' Bendikt said.

'Their commander is named Gurtuud de Barka.'

Bendikt's face gave no hint as to his feelings. 'I heard.'

'Perhaps we should do something to make amends.'

'Yes,' Bendikt said. 'Or we send them into the meat grinder.' There was a pause. If Bendikt was joking, he did not smile. 'You might be interested to know that while you were in the medicae unit, I requested an augmetic limb.'

'Good,' Mere said. 'It will save me having to reload your pistols.'

'Yes. I'm sorry. That was impractical. I didn't expect to be back in the front line quite so soon. I found out what kind of hand Lord Militant Warmund had, and where it came from. I've requested one of the same.'

'He had a particularly firm handshake.'

'He did,' Bendikt said.

They waited as the lander's engines began to warm up, and then as the noise grew in volume they made their way towards the ramps. Bendikt started forward and the two men paused at the bottom. 'Do you regret it?' Mere said.

'What?'

'Refusing to appoint Gerent Bianca to the rank of Patridzo?'

Bendikt feigned offence. 'I didn't refuse. I said I would think about it, when the time came. Which is not now.'

'So, you're bringing her with you?'

'Of course,' Bendikt said. 'What could be a better symbol than for the body of Saint Ignatzio to be carried into battle by our troops? And who else would be better than Gerent Bianca, herself, to accompany us all?'

Mere smiled. 'Do you think Rudgard Howe will make a good regent?'

'He's one of the most odious men I have ever come across, and yes, I think he will rule Potence with the kind of ruthless rigour that this planet needs.'

Mere had spent a lot of time in Hassan's care. He quoted the medicae. 'Only by severe surgery can the patient be saved.'

'Exactly,' Bendikt said, and turned his back on the smoke and the flies and the acres of destruction and made his way inside the lander.

Inside the chamber Colonel Baytov was sitting with a plasteel box on his lap.

'What is that?' Bendikt said.

'Ah.' Mere paused, and made a sign that Baytov should open the casket.

Inside was a red velvet cushion. Set into it was a glassy decanter, ashy and soot-stained.

'What is that?' Bendikt demanded.

Mere took the object in his hand. 'Inside this, apparently, is the blood of Saint Ignatzio.'

'Where did you find it?'

'General Kamak found it among the ruins of the Brotherhood's camp.'

Bendikt remembered the sight of the cardinal, hanging in the air of the grotto chapel, burning. He forced the memory from his mind. 'Does Bianca know we have this?'

'No.'

'Good,' he said, and motioned for Mere to put it back into the casket. 'Let's keep it that way.'

Bendikt took his place in the lighter, as Mere went to close the chipped metal door.

He paused on the lip of the portal for one last look at Potence. The rebellion had been crushed, the Scourged had been thrown back and most importantly, Cadian honour had been restored.

Some might call Potence a wasteland. But to the military minds of the Astra Militarum, this was peace.

ABOUT THE AUTHOR

Justin D Hill is the author of the Necromunda novel *Terminal Overkill*, the Warhammer 40,000 novels *Cadia Stands* and *Cadian Honour*, the Space Marine Battles novel *Storm of Damocles* and the short stories 'Last Step Backwards', 'Lost Hope' and 'The Battle of Tyrok Fields', following the adventures of Lord Castellan Ursarkar E. Creed. He has also written 'Truth Is My Weapon', and the Warhammer tales 'Golgfag's Revenge' and 'The Battle of Whitestone'. His novels have won a number of prizes, as well as being *Washington Post* and *Sunday Times* Books of the Year. He lives ten miles uphill from York, where he is indoctrinating his four children in the 40K lore.

YOUR NEXT READ

ON WINGS OF BLOOD
by various authors

Take the battle to the skies with stories of death-defying pilots and devastating far-future aircraft! Brutal Space Marine gunships, graceful alien fighters and hellforged Chaos war engines fight for air supremacy in a collection of aeronautical short fiction.

An extract from
'Acceptable Losses'
by Gav Thorpe
Taken from *On Wings of Blood*

Jaeger grinned as he gazed out of the cockpit's canopy and saw the rest of the squadron flying alongside the ship's hull, each pushed forward on quadruple tails of plasma. Beyond them, he saw the firing ports of the *Divine Justice*'s gun decks opening slowly, revealing battery upon battery of massive laser cannons, mass drivers and plasma projectors. Immense firepower, enough to destroy a city.

The comm-link in Jaeger's helmet crackled into life.

'Thunderbolt fighter squadrons Arrow and Storm ready for rendezvous.' The familiar voice of Flight Commander Dextra, given a metallic grate over the long-range communicator.

Jaeger flicked the brass transmit rune on the comm-link panel to his left. 'Good to hear you, Jaze. Take up a diamond-ten on the aft quarters.'

'Affirm, Raptor Leader.'

As the smaller fighters took up their escorting position around the bomber squadron, Jaeger increased the throttle, taking his plane to the front to form a flying-V formation, with his Marauder as the arrowhead. The craft swept over the prow of the cruiser, looking like tiny flares of light against the backdrop of the immense torpedo tubes.

'Bridge, this is Raptor Leader. Formed up and ready to attack. Awaiting target data, by the Emperor,' Jaeger reported.

Berhandt gave a thumbs-up signal as the target information was transmitted from the *Divine Justice*. The bombardier's gruff voice gave Jaeger the details over the internal communicator. 'It's a point at the rear of the 'ulk, in the engines somewhere. Can't tell what it is exactly, this far out.'

'What do you mean?' Jaeger asked.

'Just what I said, sir. It's just some coordinates – no details of target type and a notation that says the attack trajectory is at your discretion.'

'Very well. Inform me as soon as we get further details,' Jaeger replied, before addressing the rest of the squadron. 'Listen up, Raptors, this is the real thing. No bickering, no whining and no stalling. I am not going to let you get me and your flight comrades killed. We're here to blow things up in the name of the Emperor, and that's what we're damned well going to do!'

Jaeger smiled as he heard the laughter of the other crew members come over his headset. Sitting back in the pilot's seat, he began to relax. It would be a while before they were anywhere near within range of the hulk's considerable defences, and being tense for two hours was sure to do his reactions no good, not to mention the nerves of his crew. To occupy his mind, Jaeger went through the pre-battle checks once again. He ran his eye over the cockpit's interior to check everything visually. There were no chinks or scratches on the tinted armoured shielding of the Marauder's cockpit. The snaking wrist-thick pipes that twisted from the control panel in all directions seemed to be intact, with no insulation breaks or kinks. The pressure gauges for the engines had their needles pointing comfortably in their green quadrants, and numerous other dials, meters and counters indicated that nothing was amiss. Jaeger tested the flight controls, worried by the stiffness he was feeling in the movement of the control column. A few gentle turns and rolls later and everything seemed fine, easing Jaeger's suspicions.

Berhandt had told him that this Marauder had been almost cut in half by an eldar laser during its last mission. It had been then that his predecessor, Glade, had been sucked out into the void, never to be seen again. Jaeger cursed himself for such morbid thoughts and to calm himself he began to think of his home world. Unfastening a couple of catches, Jaeger pushed his helmet onto the back of his head and closed his eyes. With a thin-lipped smile, he began whistling a hunting chant from back home.

Veniston paced back and forth across the command deck of the bridge, watching the various screens that gave updates of the progressing battle. As the *Divine Justice* slowly moved in closer to the hulk, the smaller ork ships in its escort were trying to break through the cordon of frigates to attack the cruiser. They were having little success, and the one or two that managed to get within range were soon obliterated by the overwhelming firepower of the *Divine Justice*'s gun decks. The floor shook with regular throbs as the immense plasma drives pushed the ship towards the distant foe, bringing all on board ever closer to death or glory. One of the communications officers was muttering sharply to Captain Kaurl, while he glanced over his subordinate's shoulder at a flickering screen, directing the efforts of the escorts and fighters.

'Is there a problem, Mister Kaurl?' Veniston enquired as

he stepped up to the captain, trying to keep the tension from his voice.

'Not really, sir,' Kaurl answered, standing up straight to look the admiral in the eye. Veniston raised an eyebrow in query. 'There's a wave of ork fighter-bombers which has made it through the blockade. They'll be intercepting the Marauders of Raptor Squadron shortly. But the fighter screen should be able to protect our bombers,' Kaurl assured the admiral, rubbing the tiredness from his eyes and running a thick-fingered hand through his dark hair.

'Send the Thunderbolts on an intercept course,' Veniston decided, looking past Kaurl at the display screen. 'If the orks get too close, the bombers will have to slow down, and timing is all-important. If the Raptors don't attack in time, the whole plan will be off course and the hulk will still be fully mobile when we get within range. We can't let that happen, Jacob.' The admiral's eyes narrowed and his jaw clenched tightly for a moment as he considered the prospect of the *Divine Justice* suffering the same fate as the *Imperial Retribution*.

'What if a second wave of fighters comes up? They'll be unprotected…' the captain protested, his voice suddenly hoarse at the thought.

'If that happens,' Veniston stated coldly, 'then we shall pray that the Emperor is watching over us.'

The admiral turned towards the main display again, indicating that the conversation was ended. Kaurl suppressed a grimace and looked to the waiting comms officer.

'New orders for Arrow and Storm Squadrons,' the captain began.

Their Thunderbolt escort had peeled away regretfully a few minutes ago, and now the Marauders were on their own. As

Raptor Squadron thundered towards the hulk, more details of the battle ahead could be seen. A swarm of ork attack ships duelled with the frigates escorting the *Divine Justice*. Manoeuvring just outside range of the orks' crude weapons, the Imperial ships were taking a heavy toll; the wreckage of at least five ork vessels was drifting lifelessly across the battle-zone. Much closer now, the hulk seemed truly immense. Around it orbited a cluster of defence asteroids, floating bases crewed by the orks and bristling with rockets and gun batteries. Some were simply pieces of the hulk that had broken off but hadn't escaped the pull of the hulk's gravity. Others, Jaeger had been taught in command training, were deliberately captured by the orks, who used bizarre field technology to grasp on to asteroids and debris, purposefully creating a swirl of obstacles to protect themselves against attack. Whatever the cause of their orbit, and whether they were just floating chunks of stone and metal, or had been fitted out with rocket pods or gun turrets, throughout the Navy they were known simply as Rocks.

As Jaeger considered this glorious example of understatement, there was a sudden hiss of escaping gas and the control stick in his left hand started juddering uncontrollably.

'Ferix!' Jaeger snapped over the internal comm-link. 'These damned controls are playing up. I need stability right now, if you don't mind.'

The small tech-adept crawled into the cockpit and took the tool belt from his waist. Pulling a glowing, gold-etched device from one pocket, he set about the fastenings on a panel under Jaeger's legs. As Ferix unscrewed the compartment beneath the control column he began a low-voiced chant: 'To see the spirit of the machine, that is to be Mechanicus. To find the malaise of malfunction, that is to be Mechanicus. To administer the Rite of Repair, that is to be Mechanicus.'

Jaeger let the man drift from his attention as he looked through the armoured glass of the cockpit. The frigates had done a good job punching a hole through the ork attack ships, leaving the way clear for the Marauders. However, something wasn't quite right. Jaeger's spine tingled with some inner sense of foreboding. Looking at the approaching hulk, a sinister suspicion began to rise at the back of his mind.

'Berhandt, can you get a fix on that Rock, five o'clock, about twelve by thirty-five?' Jaeger asked the bombardier, his unease rising.

'Got it,' the bombardier replied, a question in his voice.

'Plot a trajectory prediction, impose over our course.'

'Okay, Commander Jaeger. Metriculator processing right now. Coming through... Damn! You were right to ask, sir. We're heading straight for the damn thing!' Berhandt exclaimed.

'Avoidance course?' Jaeger knew that there wouldn't be one even as he asked.

'No, sir. Not with the time we've been given. Emperor's mercy, we're gonna have to deal with the bloody thing ourselves...' The bombardier's voice was barely a whisper.

Jaeger pressed the long-range communicator. 'Bridge, this is Raptor Leader.' he announced. 'We have a problem.'